JAY LAKE

This special signed edition is limited to 1,000 numbered copies.

This is copy **203**.

THE SKY THAT WRAPS
Collected Short Fiction

THE SKY THAT WRAPS
Collected Short Fiction

JAY LAKE

Subterranean Press 2010

First Edition

ISBN
978-1-59606-266-5

Subterranean Press
PO Box 190106
Burton, MI 48519

www.subterraneanpress.com

TABLE OF CONTENTS

ANYTHING COULD BE TRUE *An Introduction by Ken Scholes*......................................11

THE SKY THAT WRAPS THE WORLD ROUND,
PAST THE BLUE AND INTO THE BLACK 15

JOURNAL OF AN INMATE...27

ACHILLES, SULKING IN HIS BUICK...51

CROSSING THE SEVEN..57

THE LEOPARD'S PAW...89

COMING FOR GREEN...97

PROMISES 119

WITNESS TO THE FALL...129

NUMBER OF THE BUS..139

A DIFFERENT WAY INTO THE LIFE...153

GREEN GRASS BLUES..169

FAT MAN...193

DOGS IN THE MOONLIGHT..225

LITTLE PIG, BERRY BROWN AND THE HARD MOON 239

ON THE HUMAN PLAN...247

LEHR, REX..257

THE MAN WITH ONE BRIGHT EYE..277

TO RAISE A MUTINY BETWIXT YOURSELVES..287

SKINHORSE GOES TO MARS...319

A VERY OLD MAN WITH NO WINGS AT ALL...335

PEOPLE OF LEAF AND BRANCH..339

A WATER MATTER..353

TO THIS THEIR LATE ESCAPE..373

CHAIN OF FOOLS...385

THE AMERICAN DEAD...399

Introduction and Acknowledgements

I haven't had a new collection in several years, so when Bill Schafer asked me to assemble one for Subterranean Press, I was thrilled to do so. This book in your hand represents some of my favorite stories among my recent short fiction. I have no particular theme here, just work that is fun, interesting and thought provoking.

In order for this book to exist at all, it was quite necessary for Bill to reach out and invite me. First and foremost, I'd like to thank him for his support of me and my fiction. I'd also like to thank all the rest of the fine people at Subterranean Press, with whom I've shared drinks, meals and bad jokes aplenty. I want to extend my especial gratitude to artist Aurélien Police for the lovely cover.

Likewise all the editors and publishers who've featured my work over the years. Also my agent Jennifer Jackson, of Donald Maass Literary Agency, as well as my daughter, the rest of my family and most importantly, Shannon Page. She is my partner, my collaborator, my sweetheart, and most importantly, my dearest friend. The sky that wraps the world round wraps her first and foremost.

Preface

When Bill Schafer asked me to put together a collection for Subterranean Press, I jumped at the chance. I've long admired Bill's work in featuring authors such as Elizabeth Bear, Cherie Priest and many others, with astonishing production values. A writer is always a sucker for a beautiful book.

The challenge, of course, was selecting what fiction to include in *The Sky that Wraps*. I've had over 250 short stories in print, so a truly comprehensive collection would require several volumes the size of telephone books. However, it's been several years since my last collection was assembled, and my work has continued to grow and strengthen as my writing career progresses.

Bill and I decided to feature the best of my newer work, leavened with a handful of older favorites to show my range. Our desire was to find stories which we both felt represented my best work. The result is this collected short fiction, which, while neither comprehensive nor complete, is some of my most beloved work of my own.

I trust you will enjoy reading these stories as much as I enjoyed writing, and later, selecting them.

Anything Could Be True

An Introduction by Ken Scholes

Oh. There you are. Come in, come in.

Take a seat and watch the stage.

See that curtain moving ever so slightly? That's where he's waiting for the lights to dim, for the page the turn, for you to meet his level gaze and miss exactly what he's doing with his hands until he wants you to see it.

Take a seat and watch the stage. You will enjoy this show.

To some, he is Esarov the Magician. To others, he is the Great Lake. I am fortunate to call him friend, this top-hatted, word-wielding menace to our comfort, and fortunate to have watched him build his repertoire over the years that I've known him.

I think the first piece I read from Jay was his Writers of the Future award-winning story "Into the Gardens of Sweet Night." Or maybe it was "Hitching to Aurora," read aloud at a con. No wait. It had to be the "The Goat Cutter." I guess I'm not all that clear on the matter but whatever rabbit he first pulled from his hat in my presence, I know it delighted and dazzled.

Over the years, we've followed each other's work pretty closely. And when it was time, in 2006, for my first stand alone project—a limited edition hardcover novelette *Last Flight of the Goddess*, published by Fairwood Press—Jay was kind enough to write my introduction. Now three years later I'm returning the compliment.

And what a three years it's been! Largely due to Jay (and my wife Jen's) crowbar tactics, I've found myself writing a five volume series. It's taken me largely away from this stage we sit before now. I hear stories about the stories and sometimes I catch glimpses of his latest rabbit or rose pulled straight from thin air, the current Poor Soul voluntarily sawn in half, and I offer up my distracted applause. Still, I've not had the opportunity to keep up with what the Portland Boy Wizard's been up to.

Until now.

This book you're holding? It's the magic you've been needing. I have everything Jay's written on my shelf, especially his many short story collections. What you have here, my friend, is his best show yet in the short form.

He strides onto the stage with "The Sky That Wraps the World Round, Past the Blue and Into the Black" followed up by "Journal of an Inmate," two sober pieces that explore redemption in worlds we can see and taste, snow and sun that we can feel on our skin. And then he moves us into that old familiar voice in "Achilles Sulking in his Buick" to retell a bit of the Trojan War with its street-racing gods and heroes. That familiar voice shows up again in "Fat Man" and "Dogs in the Moonlight" among others—a voice I recognize from his earlier tales, honed and sharpened now.

Lake's magic show specializes here in breadth and scope, offering us a variety of entertainments. I'll name a few.

In "Crossing the Seven" we hear echoes of the City Imperishable and the world of his character (and novel) *Green* in a rich, dark tale about an accidental messenger of heaven who brings hope and gains wisdom to seven cities that each amaze with the originality of culture portrayed. Still, hands waving,

And fans of *Green* and *Trial of Flowers* will be delighted to find a few extra rabbits in Jay's hat—stories like "Coming For Green," "People of Leaf and Branch," and "Promises; a Tale of the City Imperishable," all set in the lush worlds of those novels while *Mainspring* fans can return to the Wall in "Chain of Fools."

Mix in with that the wildly original Portland wizard stories , "Number of the Bus," "A Different Way into the Life," and "Green Grass Blues," that I hope will someday transmogrify themselves into a Jay Lake urban fantasy novel.

Add next, then with a flourish, stories that evoke the Ghost of Writers past, each with Jay's unique voice carrying the melody while echoes of their inspiration add harmony. Robert E. Howard croons back-up on "The Leopard's Paw" while Cordwainer Smith hits the high notes in "On the Human Plan" and "The Man with One Bright Eye." In "Lehr, Rex"—the piece from which I shamelessly lift the title of this introduction—Lake blends his own voice with those of Philip K. Dick, William Shakespeare and a choir of Golden Age SF writers into a tale that, for me, captures the theme of the entire collection.

Anything could be true, Lake whispers to us through one of the characters of that tribute to classic film Forbidden Planet. *That,* he tells us, *is what it means to be human.*

He moves easily across the stage, each part of his act coming off without a hitch whether it's fantasy, space opera or that mash-up of urban and rural fantasy with mythology and folklore and through it all, his stories each point to that phrase.

Anything could be true.

Magician that he is, he makes us believe it.

Then, at the end of it all, he closes out the collection with a piece of Post-Apocalyptic literary fiction that gives Cormac McCarthy's *The Road* a run for its money in far fewer words. I'll admit, this one made me uncomfortable the first time I read it. It made me uncomfortable this time, as well, but there is truth layered into all of Jay's fiction and the raw power of his closer stays with you and punctuates the end of a great collection of stories. There's a reason that "The American Dead" has been reprinted so many times.

Even there, anything could be true.

So take a seat and watch the stage.

Keep your eye on that curtain and the man behind it.

Are you ready for the show to start?

Okay. Take one deep breath and hold it.

Now, turn the page.

The Sky That Wraps the World Round, Past the Blue and Into the Black

This story was originally written on a whim for an anthology call where the theme was the color blue. It draws from some of my own thinking about Deep Time as seen in the "Guests" stories of mine, as well as the years of my childhood spent living in Asia. The anthology folded before it ever neared print, and the manuscript was released back to me. I couldn't figure out if it would have general interest or not, so I shipped it off to Clarkesworld, *where they ran with it. The story later was picked up by Gardner Dozois for the 26th edition of* Year's Best Science Fiction, *my first solo appearance there. All of which goes to show how much I know about my own work. This story has a prequel, "Human Error," which appeared in* Interzone.

I believe that all things eventually come to rest. Even light, though that's not what they tell you in school. How do scientists know? A billion billion years from now, even General Relativity might have been demoted to a mere Captain. Photons will sit around in little clusters of massless charge, bumping against one another like boats in the harbor at Kowloon.

The universe will be blue then, everything from one cosmic event horizon to the other the color of a summer sky.

This is what I tell myself as I paint the tiny shards spread before me. Huang's men bring them to me to work with. We are creating value, that gangster and I. I make him even more immensely wealthy. Every morning that I wake up still alive is his gratuity to me in return.

It is a fair trade.

My life is comfortable in the old house along the alley with its central court crowded with bayberry trees. A narrow gutter trickles down the center of the narrow roadway, slimed a greenish black with waste slopped out morning and evening from the porch steps alongside. The roofs are traditional, with sloping ridges and ornamented tile caps. I have studied the ones in my own courtyard. They are worn by the years, but I believe I can see a chicken stamped into each one. "Cock," my cook says with his thick Cantonese accent, never seeing the vulgar humor.

Even these tired old houses are topped with broadband antennae and tracking dishes which follow entertainment, intelligence or high finance beamed down from orbit and beyond. Sometimes the three are indistinguishable. Private data lines slung on pirated staples and cable ties from the doddering concrete utility poles. The poles themselves are festooned with faded prayer flags, charred firecracker strings, and remnants of at least half a dozen generations of technology dedicated to transmission of *something*.

Tesla was right. Power is nothing more than another form of signal, after all. If the lights come on at a touch of your hand, civilization's carrier wave is intact.

Despite the technology dangling overhead in rotting layers, the pavement itself holds life as old as China. Toddlers wearing only faded shirts toss stones in the shadows. A mangy chow dog lives beneath a vine-grown cart trapped against someone's garden wall. Amahs air their families' bedding over wooden railings worn shiny with generations of elbows. Tiny, wrinkled men on bicycles with huge trays balanced behind their seats bring vegetables, newspapers, meat and memory sticks to the back doors of houses. Everything smells of ginger and night soil and the ubiquitous mold.

I wake each day with the dawn. Once I overcome my surprise at remaining alive through another sunrise, I tug on a cheaply printed yukata and go hunting for coffee. My cook, as tiny and wrinkled as the vendors outside but decorated with *tong* tattoos that recall another era long since lost save for a few choppy-sockie movies, does not believe in the beverage. Instead he is unfailing in politely pressing a bitter-smelling black tea on me at every opportunity. I am equally unfailing in politely refusing it. The pot is a delicate work of porcelain which owes a great deal to a China before electricity and satellite warfare. It is painted a blue almost the shade of cornflowers, with a design of a round-walled temple rising in a stepped series of roofs over some Oriental pleasaunce.

I've seen that building on postage stamps, so it must be real somewhere. Or had once been real, at least.

After the quiet combat of caffeine has concluded its initial skirmish, I shuffle to my workroom where my brushes await me. Huang has that strange combination of stony patience and sudden violence which I have observed among the powerful in China. When my employer decides I have failed in my bargain, I am certain it is the cook who will kill me. I like to imagine his last act as the light fades from my eyes will be to pour tea down my throat as a libation to see my spirit into the next world.

There is a very special color that most people will never see. You have to be out in the Deep Dark, wrapped in a skinsuit amid the hard vacuum where the solar wind sleets in an invisible radioactive rain. You can close your eyes there and let yourself float in a sensory deprivation tank the size of the universe. After a while, the little mosaics that swirl behind your eyelids are interrupted by tiny, random streaks of the palest, softest, sharpest electric blue.

I've been told the specks of light are the excitation trails of neutrinos passing through the aqueous humor of the human eye. They used to bury water tanks in Antarctic caves to see those things, back before orbit got cheap enough to push astronomy and physics into space where those sciences belong. These days, all you have to do is go for a walk outside the planet's magnetosphere and be patient.

That blue is what I capture for Huang. That blue is what I paint on the tiny shards he sends me wrapped in day-old copies of the high orbital edition of *Asahi Shimbun*. That blue is what I see in my dreams.

That blue is the color of the end of the universe, when even the light is dying.

▲▼▲

Out in the Deep Dark we called them caltrops. They resemble jacks, that old children's toy, except with four equally-spaced arms instead of six, and slightly larger, a bit less than six centimeters tip to tip. Many are found broken, some aren't, but even the broken ones fit the pattern. They're distributed in a number of places around the belt, almost entirely in rocks derived from crustal material. The consensus had long been that they were mineral crystals endemic to Marduk's surface, back before the planet popped its cork 250 megayears ago. Certainly their microscopic structure supported the theory—carbon lattices with various impurities woven throughout.

I couldn't say how many of the caltrops were discarded, damaged, or simply destroyed by being slagged in the guts of some ore processor along with their enclosing rock. Millions, maybe.

One day someone discovered that the caltrops had been manufactured. They were technology remnants so old that our ancestors hadn't even gotten around to falling out of trees when the damned things were fabricated. The human race was genetic potential lurking in the germline of some cynodont therapsid when those caltrops had been made.

It had not occurred to anyone before that discovery to consider this hypothesis. The fact that the question came up at all was a result of a serious misunderstanding of which I was the root cause. In my greed and misjudgment I forced the loss of a device one of my crewmates discovered, an ancient piece of tech that could have allowed us to do *something* with those caltrops. My contribution to history, in truth, aside from some miniscule role in creating a portion of Huang's ever-growing millions. That the discovery of the caltrops' nature arose from human error is a mildly humorous grace note to the confirmation that we are indeed not alone in the universe.

Or at least weren't at one point.

The artificial origin of the caltrops has been generally accepted. *What* these things are remains a question that may never be answered, thanks to me. Most people prefer not to discuss the millions of caltrops lost to Belt mining operations over the decades that Ceres Mineral Resources has been in business.

Despite their carbon content, caltrops viewed under Earth-normal lighting conditions are actually a dull grayish-blue. This fact is not widely known on Earth. Not for the sake of being a secret—it's not—but because of *Deep Dark Blues*, the Academy Award-winning virteo about Lappet Ugarte. She's the woman who figured so prominently in the discovery of the artificial origin of the caltrops. The woman I tried to kill, and steal from. In their wisdom, the producers of that epic Bollywood docudrama saw fit to render the caltrops about twice as large as they are in real life, glowing an eerie Cherenkov blue. I suppose the real thing didn't look like much on camera.

So most of the citizens of planet Earth don't believe that they're seeing actual outer space caltrops unless they're seeing end-of-the-universe blue.

Huang sends me paint in very small jars. They're each cladded with lead foil, which makes them strangely heavy. When I take the little lead-lined caps off, the paint within is a sullen, radioactive copy of the color I used to see behind my eyelids out there in the Deep Dark.

Every time I dip my brush, I'm drawing out another little spray of radiation. Every time I lick the bristles, I'm swallowing down a few drops of cosmic sleet. I'm the last of the latter day Radium Girls.

Huang doesn't have to order the old cook to kill me. I'm doing it myself, every day.

I don't spend much time thinking about where my little radioactive shards go when they leave my house off the alleyway here in Heung Kong Tsai. People buy them for hope, for love, to have a piece of the unspeakably ancient past. There's a quiet revolution in human society as we come to terms with that history. For some, like a St. Christopher medal, touching it is important. Cancer will be important as well, if they touch them too often.

The truly odd thing is that the shards I sit here and paint with the electric blue of a dying heaven are actual caltrop shards. We're making fakes out of the real thing, Huang and I.

A truth as old as time, and I'm dressing it in special effects.

I swear, sometimes I kill myself.

▲▼▲

This day for lunch the cook brings me a stir fry of bok choi and those strange, slimy mushrooms. He is as secretive as one of the Japanese soldiers of the last century who spent decades defending a lava tube on some Pacific island. There is tea, of course, which I of course ignore. We could play that ritual with an empty pot just as easily, but the cook executes his culinary warfare properly.

The vegetables are oddly ragged for having recently spent time in a searing hot wok. They are adorned with a pungent tan sauce the likes of which I had never tasted before entering this place. The whole mess sits atop a wad of sticky rice straight from the little mauve Panasonic cooker in the kitchen.

Food is the barometer of this household. When the cook is happy, I eat like a potentate on a diplomatic mission. When the cook is vexed by life or miffed about some slight on my part, I eat wretchedly.

I wonder what I have done this day to anger him. Our morning ritual was nothing more than ritual, after all.

When I meet the cook's eyes, I see something else there. A new distress lurks in the lines drawn tight across his forehead. I know what I gave up when I came here. It was no more than what I'd given up long ago, really, when the fates of people and planets were playing out somewhere in the Deep Dark and I went chasing the fortune of a dozen lifetimes. Still, I am not prepared for this new tension on the part of my daily adversary.

"Have you to come to kill me?" I ask him in English. I have no Cantonese, and only the usual fractured, toneless pidgin Mandarin spoken by non-Chinese in the rock ports of the asteroid belt. I've never been certain he understands me, but surely the intent of my question is clear enough.

"Huang." There is a creaky whine in his voice. This man and I can go a week at a time without exchanging a single word. I don't think he speaks more than that to anyone else.

"He is coming here?"

The cook nods. His unhappiness is quite clear.

I poke the bok choi around in my bowl and breathe in the burnt ginger-and-fish oil scent of the sauce. That Huang is coming is a surprise. I have sat quietly with my incipient tumors and withering soul and made the caltrop shards ready for market. They are being handled by a True Hero of the Belt, just as his advertising claims. Our bargain remains intact.

What can he want of me? He already holds the chitty on my life. All my labors are his. I have no reputation left, not under my real name. I bear only the memory of the heavens, and a tiny speck of certain knowledge about what once was.

It should be enough.

After a while, by way of apology, the cook removes my cooling lunch bowl and replaces it with a delicate porcelain plate bearing a honey-laden moon cake. I suspect him of humor, though the timing is hideously inappropriate.

"*Xie xie*," I tell him in my Mandarin pidgin. He does not smile, but the lines around his eyes relax.

Still, I will not stoop to the tea.

▲▼▲

Huang arrives to the sound of barking dogs. I stand behind a latticed window in my garden wall and look out into the alley. The gangster's hydrogen-powered Mercedes is a familiar shade of Cherenkov blue. I doubt the aircraft paint his customizers use is hot, though.

There is a small pack of curs trailing his automobile. The driver steps out in a whirr of door motors which is as much noise as that car ever makes. He is a large man for a Chinese, tall and rugged, wearing the ubiquitous leather jacket and track pants of big money thugs from Berlin to Djakarta. His mirror shades have oddly thick frames, betraying a wealth of sensor data and computing power. I wonder if he ever removes them, or if they are implants. Life in this century has become a cheap 1980s science fiction novel.

The driver gives the dogs a long look which quiets them, then opens Huang's door. The man himself steps out without any ceremony or further security. If there is air cover, or rooftop snipers, they are invisible to me.

Huang is small, with the compact strength of a wrestler. His face is a collapsed mass of wrinkles that makes his age impossible to guess. There are enough environmental poisons which can do that to a man without the help of time's relentless decay. Today he wears a sharkskin jacket over a pale blue cheongsam. His eyes when he glances up to my lattice are the watery shade of light in rain.

I walk slowly through the courtyard. That is where Huang will meet me, beneath a bayberry tree on a stone bench with legs carved like lions.

▲▼▲

He is not there when I take my seat. Giving instructions to the cook, no doubt. The pond occupies my attention while I wait. It is small, not more than two meters across at its longest axis. The rim is walled with rugged rocks that might have just been ejected from the Earth moments before the mason laid them. Nothing is that sharp-edged out in the Belt, not after a quarter billion years of collision, of dust, of rubbing against each other. The water is scummed over with a brilliant shade of green that strikes fear in the heart of anyone who ever has had responsibility for a biotic air recycling plant.

They say water is blue, but water is really nothing at all but light trapped before the eyes. It's like glass, taking the color of whatever it is laced with, whatever stands behind it, whatever shade is bent through its substance. Most people out in the Deep Dark have a mystical relationship with water. The very idea of oceans seems a divine improbability to them. As for me, my parents came from Samoa. I was born in Tacoma, and grew up on Puget Sound before finding my way Up. To me, it's just water.

Still, this little pond choked with the wrong kind of life seems to say so much about everything that is wrong with Earth, with the Deep Dark, with the little damp sparks of colonies on Ceres and Mars and elsewhere. I wonder what would happen to the pond if I poured my blue paint out of its lead-lined bottles into the water.

"Your work holds fair," says Huang. I did not hear him approach. Glancing down, I see his crepe-soled boat shoes, that could have come straight off some streetcorner vendor's rack to cover his million-dollar feet.

I meet his water-blue eyes. Pale, so pale, reflecting the color of his golf shirt. "Thank you, sir."

He looks at me a while. It is precisely the look an amah gives a slab of fish in the market. Finally he speaks again: "There have been inquiries."

I reply without thinking. "About the radioactives?"

One eyebrow inches up. "Mmm?"

I am quiet now. I have abandoned our shared fiction for a moment, that pretense that I do not know he is poisoning thousands of homes worldwide through his artifact trade. Mistakes such as that can be fatal. That the entire present course of my life is fatal is not sufficient excuse for thoughtless stupidity.

Huang takes my silence as an answer. "Certain persons have come to me seeking a man of your description."

With a shrug, I tell him, "I was famous once, for a little while." One of history's villains, in fact, in my moment of media glory.

"What you paid me to keep you…they have made an offer far more generous."

I'd sold him my life, that strange, cold morning in a reeking teahouse in Sendai the previous year. Paid him a substantial amount of cash, my labor and the last bare threads of my reputation in exchange for a quiet, peaceful penance and the release of obligation. Unfortunately, I could imagine why someone else would trouble to buy Huang out.

He was waiting for me to ask. I would not do that. What I would do was give him a reason not to send me away. "My handiwork meets your requirements, yes?" Reminding him of the hot paint, and the trail of liability which could eventually follow that blue glow back to its source.

Even gangsters who'd left any fear of law enforcement far behind could be sued in civil court.

"You might wish me to take this offer," he says slowly.

"When has the dog ever had its choice of chains?"

A smile flits across Huang's face before losing itself in the nest of wrinkles. "You have no desires in the matter?"

"Only to remain quietly in this house until our bargain is complete."

Huang is silent a long, thoughtful moment. Then: "Money completes everything, spaceman." He nods once before walking away.

It is difficult to threaten a man such as myself with no family, no friends, and no future. That must be a strange lesson for Huang.

I drift back to the latticed window. He is in the alley speaking to the empty air—an otic cell bead. A man like Huang wouldn't have an implant. The dogs are quiet until he steps back into the blue Mercedes. They begin barking and wailing as the car slides away silent as dustfall.

It is then that I realize that the dog pack are holograms, an extension of the car itself.

▲▼▲

Until humans went into the Deep Dark, we never knew how kindly Earth truly was. A man standing on earthquake-raddled ground in the midst of the most violent hurricane is as safe as a babe-in-arms compared to any moment of life in hard vacuum. The smallest five-jiǎo pressure seal, procured low bid and installed by a bored maintech with a hangover, could fail and bring with it rapid, painful death.

The risk changes people, in ways most of them never realize. Friendships and hatreds are held equally close. Total strangers will share their last half-liter of air to keep one another alive just a little longer, in case rescue should show. Premeditated murder is almost unknown in the Deep Dark, though manslaughter is sadly common. Any fight can kill, even if just by diverting someone's attention away from the environmentals at a critical moment.

So people find value in one another that was never foreseen back on Earth. Only the managers and executives who work in the rock ports and colonies have kept the old, human habits of us-and-them, scheming, assassination of both character and body.

The question on my mind was whether it was an old enemy come for me, or someone from the Ceres Minerals Resources corporate hierarchy. Even setting aside the incalculable damage to our understanding of history, in ensuring the loss of the first verifiable nonhuman artifact, I'd also been the proximate cause of what many people chose to view as the loss of a billion tai kong yuan. Certain managers who would have preferred to exchange their white collars for bank accounts deeper than generations had taken my actions very badly.

Another Belt miner might have yanked my oxygen valve out of sheer, maddened frustration, but it took an angry salaryman to truly plot my ruin in a spreadsheet while smiling slowly. Here in Huang's steel embrace I thought I'd managed my own ruin quite nicely. Yet someone was offering good money for me.

Oddly, Huang had made it all but my choice. Or seemed to, at any rate. Which implied he saw this inquiry as a matter of honor. Huang, like all his kind, was quite elastic in his reasoning about money, at least so long as it kept flowing, but implacable when it came to his notions of honor.

Even my honor, it would seem.

All of this was a very thin thread of logic from which to dangle. I could just keep painting shards until any one of several things killed me— radiation sickness, cancer, the old cook. Or I could tell Huang to break the deal he and I had made, and pass me back out of this house alive.

Given how much trouble I'd taken in order to surrender all control, there was something strangely alluring about being offered back the chitty on my life.

▲▼▲

That night when the cook brings me the tea, I pour some into the tiny cup with no handles. He gives me a long, slow stare. "You go out?"

"With Mr. Huang, yes," I tell him.

The cook grunts, then withdraws to the kitchen.

The tea is so bitter that for a moment I wonder if he'd brewed it with rat poison. Even as this thought fades, the cook comes back with a second cup and pours it out for himself. He sits down opposite me, something else he'd never done. Then he draws a small mesh bag on a chain out from inside his grubby white t-shirt.

"See this, ah." He tugs open the top of the bag. Out tumbles one of my little blue caltrop fragments. I can almost see it spark in his hand.

"You shouldn't be holding that."

The cook hefts the mesh bag. "Lead. No sick."

I reach out and take the caltrop arm. It is just that, a single arm broken off below the body. I fancy it is warm to my touch. It is certainly very, very blue.

"Why?" I ask him.

He looks up at the ceiling and spreads one hand in a slow wave, as if to indicate the limitless stars in the Deep Dark far above our heads. "We too small. World too big. This—" he shakes his bag "—this time price."

I try to unravel the fractured English. "Time price?"

The cook nods vigorously. "You buy time for everyone, everything."

I sip my tea and think about what he's told me. I'd *been* out in the Deep Dark. I'd touched the sky that wraps the world round, past the blue and into the black.

"Blue," he says, interrupting my chain of thought. "We come from sea, we go to sky. Blue to blue, ah?"

Blue to blue. Life had crawled from the ocean's blue waters to eventually climb past the wide blue sky. With luck, we'd carry forward to the dying blue at the end of time.

"Time," I say, trying the word in my mouth. "Do you mean the future?"

The cook nodded vigorously. "Future, ah."

Once I've finished eating the magnificent duck he'd prepared, I trudg back to my workroom. I'd already bargained away almost all of my time, but I could create time for others, in glowing blue fragments.

It doesn't matter who is looking for me. Huang would do as he pleased. My sins are so great they can never be washed away, not even in a radio-active rain.

I can spend what time is left to me bringing people like the old cook a little closer to heaven, one shard after another.

Journal of an Inmate

This piece holds a special place in my heart. It's something I wrote many years ago, well before I'd reached a professional level of craft. The idea stayed with me long after the manuscript had died a messy and well-deserved death, and so I tackled it again from scratch. (I've only done this a few times, but it's always worked out well when I have.) I workshopped "Journal of an Inmate" with the Wordos, the writers' group which meets in Eugene, OR. The post-story discussion was one of the funniest I've ever been involved in, because of the moment near the end of the story (very minor spoiler alert here) where the protagonist burns a letter with the envelope unopened. The Wordos looked at me, nearly in unison, and demanded to know what the letter had said. They were fine with the manuscript being ambiguous on this point, but so long as they had me, the writer, in the room, they wanted to know. I pointed out that since the character hadn't opened the envelope in-story, I had no idea what was in it, either, only the same fruitless speculations everyone else had already shared. I'm not sure what this says about either them, or me, but years later I still treasure the memory of the frustration on Jerry Oltion's face.

March 9th, Year of 89.

I despair. The trial was a farce of the highest order. No one's loyalty could be stronger than mine! Why, I am a twice-decorated veteran of the recent war against our neighbors to the west, commended by the Premier himself for taking an enemy artillery battery at bayonet's point with only the few survivors of my shattered company.

My attorney says not to fear, that the appeals process takes time and I will surely be freed once the charges and testimony have been reviewed by higher authority immune to the bribes and blandishments of my petty rivals in the Capital. In the meantime, I must not discuss them, even here within these pages, for my attorney advises that any words I write here may be read by my jailors, and sent to the courts for review.

Surely justice will prevail, for our State is the perfection of social evolution, and no one is ever made victim without it being his just dessert.

I shall write nothing herein that might be prejudicial to my case.

▲▼▲

May 17th, Year of 89.

It has been a journey of some weeks to my prison, traveling with the first supply caravan of the spring. The pass at V____ does not open before the lindens take leaf in the Capital, and so I was held a while at the great hussar's camp on the banks of our noble river. There I dined with the officers and was permitted to ride, and even hunt a time or two. In their company I sought hints as to my situation, and tried to play upon a soldier's natural sympathy for a veteran, but to no avail. They would chatter like birds on every other topic, but fall silent as bones when I mentioned myself. Still, the life was comfortable for that short while.

How terrible the contrast, then, when I was chained to a mule and forced to walk so many miles into the mountains, mud and excrement churning beneath my feet at every step. I had no notion that our little country had borders that extended so high and far.

The prison, which I shall not name in an effort not to undermine my appeal, lies beyond the V____ Pass in the high Vale of V____ filled mostly with swamps and pines. Bears may be heard to growl at night, and the air is bitterly cold even after the end of the winter season. The mule caravan descended from the saddle of the pass late in the day, the sun at our backs staining the snow banks a lambent rose, the valley below us already cloaked in shadow. Watery fens glowed silver within the darkness. The prison was little more than a flickering spark in the distance, perhaps another half day's march by the measure of a mule's tread, but those were the first lights we had seen aside from our own fire in better than a week, and I rejoiced in a feeling of deliverance.

As we made camp that night, the detestable Sergeant F____ who led the mule train began to laugh at me, the sole prisoner in the supply train. Soon his entire band of men chuckled and guffawed, boisterous expressions of crude humor, though none would let me in on the joke.

▲▼▲

May 21st, Year of 89.

I am praying for my appeal to advance with alacrity. This place is a den of gentlemen lunatics. There are no other words to describe what I have seen thus far. It is to be expected that so far from the Capital, perched on a border made hostile by both Nature and Man, such a place as this prison should loosen some of the strictures of civilized society. The State even in its august perfection does have some limits, though I shudder at my disrespect in even voicing such opinions.

Regardless of the State's omnipotence, there are boundaries within every cultured man, limits that go deeper than the question of tails or tuxedo at dinner and which age of cognac to serve over raisin trifle. I fear I shall never taste of my ample cellar again. The most basic of needs will not be met here. My attorney is far from this place, and there are no mails.

I must therefore begin my efforts at appeal with the Warden. He is a distinguished gentleman, to be sure, who served for a time in the Constituent Assembly at the Capital whilst pursuing a career in the imports business. His is a name that would surely be known to you were I to mention it here, even by his initials only, so suffice to call him the Warden. There was some scandal, when I was still a boy, and he entered service to the State in a civil capacity to avoid the unpleasantness of investigation or trial. The Warden, then, has sat in this place like a toad in a stone for more than two decades. I would say that prison life has not treated him well.

The Warden's carriage is good enough, and he maintains the great walrus-moustache that was popular among gentlemen of our fathers' youth. He is slim yet, despite advancing age and silver hair, and would doubtless fill out his Assembly robes with dignity even now. But when I stumbled in amongst the jackanapes of the dreadful Sergeant F___'s mule train, did the Warden greet me as a gentleman should? Not in the slightest. Rather, he ran to Sergeant F___, hugged that worm of a man as if they were brothers, and demanded of the Sergeant whether the mule train had brought any ink to the prison.

Ink, I say. Once a tradesman, always a tradesman. This despicable concern with commerce that so overruns the Capital is obviously an older and deeper infection than most of us had realized, for it to have roots decades old here on the frontiers.

The Warden did not deign to greet me until after he had read through a thick portfolio of orders and dispatches, while I toiled under the curses and kicking boots of Sergeant F____'s two Caporals, men even lower and less couth than he. Finally the old gentleman walked over to me, looked me up and down, then grabbed my hand. He studied my fingers and palm for a moment with no more dignity or purpose than a traveling fortune-teller before peering into my eyes.

"Tell me, Citizen J____," he said. "You have soft hands. Can you do sums?"

I told him that I was a gentleman, not a clerk, but that my education had in fact extended to the mathematical arts, including arithmetic, algebra, geometry, trigonometry and even rudiments of the calculus. I began to explain the error of my assignment to this desolate place, but he interrupted me.

"Yes, yes," the Warden said. His gaze was steady, burning as if with fever. "But can you do sums?"

I admitted I could, whereupon he spun on his heel and began calling for the commissary, paying me no further mind than he did one of the mules. It pains me now to write this account of how low I have already fallen, and they are shouting for me in the main office, so I must go.

▲▼▲

May 23rd, Year of 89.

This place perhaps bears some careful description before my eyes grow so accustomed to the view that I can no longer see what lies before me. The high Vale of V____ is an ancient frontier, contested by one and another tribe and kingdom long before Rome's noble banners unfurled over all the lands of our portion of the Continent. I have already been told in leering confidence—by a one-eyed man with scarred lips and ropy burns where his scalp should be, no less—that many of the pine-topped hummocks of the vale are in fact graves of kings, and that a man with wit, a steel shovel and a good lantern may dig fortunes out of the bog any night of the year.

One cannot eat the red gold of the ancients, and jeweled diadems will not enlarge my cell, and besides I already hate the tiny red midges that swarm over the water everywhere here, so this is not an item of great interest to me. Once my appeal succeeds, I might imagine coming back here at the head of an army of porters and laborers, but for now, this rumor shall rest safely in the bosom of the vale.

I recount it here in my journal only to give some perspective to the nature of the prison. I, who have fought in the recent war, and traveled extensively as far even as Kiel and Marseilles to the west and Tbilisi to the east, can clearly recognize the structure as a defensive fortification. The foundations are broad, built up out of the swamps and extending back into the rise of a hill the inmates call Hangbranch. These retaining walls are sturdy enough for mighty towers of stone, though they now support only vegetable gardens tended by the more menial of the prisoners. There are rubble-filled depressions among the gardens that are clearly the remnants of stairways leading down to magazines, barracks or dungeons beneath what had been the old castle.

The prison itself is a substantial structure, even though it is only a portion of what clearly had once stood here. It has grim, gray walls of close-set stone that does not match the exposed rock on the slopes of Hangbranch Hill, though it is of a kind with the foundation courses. Someone once quarried and hauled a great deal of stone up into this vale.

The architecture of the prison has some ceremonial vestiges of Medieval siege architecture, though I would estimate the main portion of it as being no older than the end of the past century. It is built, like a castle, in a rectangle, and the southern wall rises with the hill, essentially part of a carved-away cliff. That south wall is much older than the balance of the structure, being composed of shaped cliff face and cyclopean stones, and riddled with bricked-up doors and passages that once led back into the bones of the hill. The four corners feature square towers rising perhaps fifty feet above the ramparts, which themselves have a waist-high battlement, though not crenellated. The other three walls have rows of cells built against them, so that the gatehouse is a sort of tunnel between the cells on the north wall, leading into the court surrounded on three sides by cells and on the fourth by the ancient structures of the south wall.

The whole effect is that of a dungeon, or a particularly grim military prison, brought to scale.

We are divided into three wards, with the Warden over us all. The first ward inhabits the western cells, which are deemed the least desirable as they face the prevailing easterly winds during the winter. They are primarily the violent criminals, career incorrigibles, men of the gypsy, the Turk, or other foreign races—in general, those with no hope of rehabilitation.

The second ward calls the northern cells home, which also contain the offices and apartments of the keepers of the prison. These are the trustees, for the most part, as there are very few staff assigned to this place other than the Warden and the commissary. The trustees are men promoted to supervise the gardens and fields around the prison, or run the orchards higher up on Hangbranch Hill, as well as guard the walls and gates. The prison contends with little in the way of escape attempts, for there is nowhere to go, and this high country is inhabited by Hostile tribes who have never accepted the suzerainty of the Capital. Also kept here are those convicted of moral or social deviancy, and those unspeakable crimes that are normally met with a swift execution but were for some purposes spared by the kindness of Lady Justice.

The third ward lives in the eastern cells. Here I have been placed, in a high cell on the fourth level as befits my lowly status as a newcomer. We are the politicals, those convicted of crimes against the State, defrocked priests and disbarred attorneys, as well as the merely unclassifiable, such as Petit Cochin, a man whom I am told arrived some years ago alone, without papers, who seemed to possess only those two words of vocabulary that gave him his name. Petit works in the orchards in the summer, and otherwise labors in the laundries beneath the second ward, and was held up to me as an example of uncomplaining obedience.

▲▼▲

June 10th, Year of 89.

The despicable Sergeant F____ is gone with his mules and his men. I am given to hope that his return with the autumn caravan will bring me word of the success of my appeal. I briefly considered sending a letter home to my attorney, but that seems moot. First of all, he certainly knows where I am. Second of all, the likelihood that Sergeant F____ and his merry hooligans would actually manage to bring the letter all the way to the Capital intact and in confidence seems a foolish hope.

In accordance with the orders of the Warden I have been set to work with the commissary. That worthy manages the logistical affairs of the prison. His old clerk died of some unspecified illness last winter that seems to still have people whispering behind their hands, though none will tell me of it. The clerk's office has been shut up ever since, and I was given a torch, a long knife, and a stout stick and told to clean it out and bring the accounts up to date.

These people are crazed, whether by time, isolation, or inner nature I cannot tell.

▲▼▲

August 7th, Year of 89.

I should note, I suppose with some shame, that I have taken up smoking of the yellowleaf. This is an herb which grows here in our high vale, and many of the inmates and prison staff alike use it in lieu of the far more civilized but unattainable vices of tobacco or hashish. Yellowleaf tastes like nothing so much as burning horsehair, and overconsumption will induce bloody visions and a sense of hysterical strength, which is by luck for all of us quite false, but it remains something to while away hours in this place where there is so little to occupy a thinking man's time.

I found myself outside the main gates one day, smoking a yellowleaf "troc," as the inmates call the little hand-rolled cigarette, allegedly from a word from the language of one of the Hostile tribes of this benighted region. The trusty on duty was one Teodor Borogov, a heavy-lipped man with cow eyes who is a convicted panderer and launderer of funds. Borogov claims to have been sent here because one of the women in his string was in fact the daughter of a judge. Her father had brought his case to the bench after meeting the little chit in his already rampant state in a silk-curtained room Borogov maintained for that purpose. I keep meaning to look into his file, for this seems an unlikely abuse of power in our noble State, but have not found the occasion, even though one of the few privileges of my position as clerk is access to such normally forbidden material.

Borogov and I were passing the troc when I noticed a party of men digging along the edge of the marshlands some small distance below the edge of the artificial plateau on which the prison rests. Thinking back on the rumors of ancient treasure, I asked him what they were about.

"Graves," Borogov said, and spat across his shoulder as is the superstitious wont of those crude Bulgars who are a substantial minority of our country's peasantry.

I was fairly certain no one had died since my arrival, and stated the same.

He laughed, took a very long drag on the troc, then stared at me with a countryman's shrewd eye. "You'll see, my friend. Just try to strike shovel into the earth up here when winter's got us in 'er cast iron grip."

I asked how many died in the winter, but he just laughed again.

▲▼▲

September 21st, Year of 89.

One of the trustees, that same scarred, one-eyed man that I now know as Moseley Iamandu, reported today that the autumn caravan has been spotted in the V____ Pass. We are preparing for it tomorrow, myself torn between the expectation of news of the success of my appeal, and the desire for some decent writing materials in this wretched place.

I have come to appreciate the Warden's obsession with ink. The account books are difficult to keep without it, and I have already been forced to introduce strict economies, taking my notes with handmade charcoal pencils provided me by Petit Cochin, a man of unexpected talents. The Warden fears, perhaps as a result of his experiences in the Capital, to ever break the chain of official forms and record keeping which is the due of every enterprise of the State.

Yet it would help if the Capital ever sent us those supplies we requested, instead of what is apparently in each season the detritus of some warehouse or other. According to the records kept by the old clerk, in the Year of 87 the prison received as part of its autumn caravan one gross of reciprocating rods as replacement parts for steam-driven looms of British manufacture. As there is neither steam engine nor loom within many leagues of this vale, I am at a loss as to understand the logic of hauling such items at great expense and trouble all the way here from the Capital. Every season since, the clerk has returned a form counter-signed by the commissary and the Warden requesting permission to reject the shipment, but these have gone unanswered so far.

As for my appeal, surely the State's machinery of justice has already seen to the rectification of my blamelessness in the matters in which I stood accused. Upon my return to the Capital, I shall lay down the finest meal in town to be shared between myself, my attorney, and some young ladies of Borogov's recommendation.

▲▼▲

September 23rd, Year of 89.
Despair! Again I despair! There has been a failure, of the courts, of the mails, of the despicable and vile Sergeant F____ I cannot determine, but there is no letter at all from my attorney. The miscreant sergeant, of course, denies all knowledge of me and my case, and is full only of talk of new unpleasantness between the Russians and the Ottoman Turks. As the State has military alliances with neither power, I fail to see the fascination with such matters in the face of the far more important question of my freedom.

I did receive four barrels of ink and a case of dispatches. I set the dispatch case aside and drafted a letter of query to my attorney. I have yet to imagine a method by which I might reliably convince Sergeant F____ to deliver the letter. My former wealth in the Capital is lost to me, held in trust by my attorney if it has not been attached by the courts. I have nothing here with which to bribe him, and no power to intimidate.

It has occurred to me to conceal my letter among the outbound dispatches, but that would be an abuse of the privileges so generously extended to me by the State.

This is something upon which I shall have to think.

▲▼▲

September 26th, Year of 89.

Sergeant F____ has departed today, disappearing with his men, breath steaming about their heads and mules braying amid the first flurries of snow. I tucked my letter within a selection of memoranda variously destined for the Ministry of Resources and the Bureau of Penal Statistics, artfully arranging the papers so that my letter's inclusion appeared to be an innocent mistake in order to further its chances of being sent on to my attorney.

The arrival of snow has set the prison to a furious stir of activity. Safe in my little office in the second ward, I have ignored the footfalls and the shouting, but it seems that the Warden and the trustees have turned virtually everyone out to finish harvesting the orchards and the root vegetables, and to bring in all the deadfall and cut wood which remains within a day's walk of the walls.

How cold does it get up here?

Also, I should note that the Warden has pulled me aside to inform me that he expects no more prisoners to come for some time. "You were a surprise, in fact, Citizen J____," he said, "and must have incurred the considerable wrath of someone of stature in the Capital, for we have had no other inmates sent to us for more than two years. This last round of dispatches included the advisory that our institution is being formally removed from the sentencing lists, though we are charged with continuing our work of incarceration and reform with the inmates we have to hand."

I thanked him, though I was not sure for what, and went back to checking the accounts of the old clerk, who seemed to have possessed either an astonishing incompetence or a talent for corruption unrivalled since the departure of the Ottomans from our region.

▲▼▲

December 1st, Year of 89.

It is cold here. The troc has already run out. Two men of the first ward have died of the weather. And today the Hostiles attacked. I almost welcomed the bloodshed as an alternative to the painful crackling of the air within my lungs.

They came from the pine breaks to the east, and must have been leading their horses with muffled hooves until they were close to our walls. Even in this cold we would have noted their mounted approach. I was on the walls with Iamandu, carrying hot water steeped with dried sage to the trustees on watch, when the Hostiles erupted from the woods. For one brief moment I rejoiced in the thought that the dire Sergeant F____ had come back for me. Then I realized that the oncomers moved too fast for the State's supply mules.

Iamandu took a bullet in his neck even as he screamed at me to get down below the parapet. He fell then, his tray spinning away from him as the mugs of hot water took flight of their own. I watched the steaming streams arc in different directions like Iamandu's soul seeking the next life as he gargled out the last red streaks of this one. His harsh, ragged breath was the only sound I could hear save for hoofbeats, which seemed more like the farewell measure of Iamandu's heart.

Then there was a great clashing of gongs from the northeast tower. The trustees tipped boulders over and screamed insults at the Hostiles, who screamed back in their Heathen tongue. Though the prison has some few firearms, we are under strict orders from the Warden not to expend ammunition except in the gravest of need. Forty feet of wall below us would seem to remove the gravity of this need, save for Iamandu.

He needed little now, though I held his hand until his heels stopped drumming. After a while the gunfire from below stopped, too, and the Hostiles vanished into the snow as surely as if they had never come. I could see no purpose to their attack at all.

Three of the winter graves are already filled and it is not yet even the solstice. I never thought I would long for my time in the war, but this place is more terrible than the western front in the late war, for all that death comes more slowly here.

▲▼▲

February 11th, Year of 90.
The prison has a library. It is of moderate size, crowded with towering shelves, tucked high in the north wall just above the tannery. The library is no warmer than any other place in this icy stone shell of a building, but it does contain books. Judging by the flat sheets of ash clinging to the ancient iron stove, some appear to have been burned for warmth in winters past. There is nothing left of zoology and paleontology

except a flame-damaged example of Lambshead's long-discredited treatise on disease theory. Little is left also of law, drama, or the apparently once-vast section concerning medical curiosities.

Still, the shelves of political science, ethics, and citizenship virtually bulge with books, most of them editions from the end of the last century if not, in a few cases, somewhat earlier. With some gentle hints from the Warden I have come to the conclusion that my general attitude toward the State and our inherently perfected system of justice is of less than optimal quality. Perhaps this is what the court saw in me when they sentenced me to this frozen exile. At any rate, it is clear that the Warden can exert influence over my case through letters back to the Capital, and so I have taken his hint and retired to the library for a course of re-education in the fundamentals of our glorious society.

It is my hope that by re-establishing my best, right loyalties, I may be able to communicate to my attorney the changed nature of my outlook, and that further in my position as the commissary's clerk, I might influence the Warden in the preparation of his dispatches so that he in turn could commend me to the courts.

Also, I should record the total number perished of cold has risen to eleven, plus Iamandu felled by Hostiles. We will soon be out of graves. Borogov tells me that in the bad winters the bodies are stacked frozen in the wood ricks, as the numbers of dead increase in direct proportion to the diminishment of our combustibles.

▲▼▲

May 10th, Year of 90.
The anniversary of my incarceration approaches. There has not yet been a sign of the dreadful Sergeant F____ and his caravan, but everyone tells me they will soon come. Spring certainly has, with a suddenness of which only mountain weather is capable. There was snow across the entire vale two weeks ago, then a day dawned rose-pink and not much warmer than before, but it was enough to set the snow to slush, then water, in the course of a few hours. After that the snow on the mountains melted as well, flowing downward to transform the Vale of V____ from a maze of fens to a broad, shallow lake.

Some of the trustees went rafting on the broad water using a little boat made of lashed-together coffins. There they cast nets for a tiny silver fish that shoals among the trunks of the pine trees. The commissary went with them, and was attacked by a fish-eagle for his troubles.

I stayed upon the wall, marking the hours and watching the V____ Pass for signs of our spring caravan. There would be a letter from my attorney, a fresh wind of justice blown up from the low lands of the Capital. By way of a form of spiritual insurance, I have also written letters to my attorney and the judge of my court, seeking to demonstrate my own advancement as an ideal citizen of the State.

I go now to the wall again, having borrowed the commissary's spyglass to watch for the caravan which will bear my salvation.

▲▼▲

May 28th, Year of 90.

There is a letter here upon my desk. The envelope is simple and plain, unmarked brown paper of a crude make, the grain grossly visible within. Handwritten on the face is a name, an address, in an ink not much better than lampblack. The writer must have been shaking when he made out the envelope, with nerves, or fear, or desperation.

Though Sergeant F____ arrived two days ago, late even by his usual imprecise standards, I have not yet opened the letter. I do not need to. It is my own, sent in the dispatches of last autumn, returned to me by some prickle of fate to this place where no legitimate correspondence ever seems to reach. I could try to send it again, by means fair or foul.

But to what end? All my hopes are false.

I believe I shall open my veins, instead.

▲▼▲

August 1st, Year of 90.

Worked in the orchards today. Meditated on citizenship and loyalty. Left wrist still very stiff. Petit Cochin fell off a ladder, had to be carried down to the prison. Alone on the hill a while, I saw a Hostile. Bared my chest for the bullet. He took his aim and stared down the barrel a while. Welcomed him to finish what I could not do. Seeing my smile he spat and walked away.

▲▼▲

September 20th, Year of 90.

They have been watching me. All of them. I had trained the sights of my misappropriated carbine on Sergeant F____ as he approached the prison, when Borogov attacked me. They will not let a man be!

"You can be hanged, even here," he warned me after he took the weapon from me.

I hid from the Sergeant and the commissary alike, taking refuge in a close and musty shelf low in the library, of just barely enough size to accommodate my substantial frame. Perhaps my absence will spur my messages onward.

▲▼▲

September 28th, Year of 90.

There were no new prisoners, again, and no new dispatches either. Along with various mundane supplies, Sergeant F____ brought bullets, lamp oil, a hundredweight of Arabica coffee, and three hundred telegraph keys. Perhaps we could throw them at the Hostiles.

The Warden asked me today if I wished to be a trusty scout. I inquired what need a prison had of scouts. "The movements of the Hostiles are of interest to us," he said. "They shoot most of us on sight, when found alone. Only you seem to be immune to their bellicose nature."

So they have been reading my journal. The State cares for all its children in different ways, but I do not like this kind of surrogacy. I told him I would take on the role, if that meant privacy and peace of mind.

"Privacy I can guarantee you," the Warden told me, "once you are well away from these walls. Peace of mind..." Then he shrugged, seeming to forget the intent of his words.

I do not know how far I will go, but to leave the gates without being under the guns of trustees will seem a fine, private escape from this hellish place.

▲▼▲

October 11th, Year of 90.

These mountains are a glory as great as any work of the State. I know we are alleged to be within the borders of my country, but surely only a creator deity could lay claim to such a land as this. No wonder the Hostiles worry at us, drawing blood and taking lives where they can. We pale, squamous lowlanders are like a canker on their pure land.

From where I sit now I can see a great herd of elk picking its way across a stream. The watercourse foams over tumbled rocks, drops in little falls, loses itself among tiny fens, forms larger pools where beaver live. There are stands of divers pines and firs around me, that creak in the wind like a ship under sail. Eagles scream in the cold air, and the stars above glitter like diamond knives that have cut the fabric of night.

I am a poor outdoorsman, but it is not yet cold enough to kill me here if I wear my woolens always and make a small fire of moss and twigs each night to keep my fingers unfrozen. I shall have to go back soon to that great square tomb of men, for simple shelter if nothing else, but out here I have discovered a freedom no one within the shelter of the State could ever imagine.

No longer do I need to go home. I am home.

I must thank the Warden.

October 13th, Year of 90.

Attempted to cross the vale in blizzard conditions. The slopes were too harsh. Prison is somewhere south of my position. No hope of finding it now as visibility has become perhaps an armspan. Made a shelter of folded reeds which has become walled with snow.

Another Hostile came to me here. He wore furs and white wool, with a red woolen sash. More daggers than I can count, and more bullets than daggers. His skin is dark, cannot tell if he is well-oiled against cold or that color from birth.

I prepared for death, praying that perdition would at least be warm, but the Hostile smiled. He settled into my shelter, and we shared our heat side by side as he passed a leather flask of something that tasted of steel and brought sparks to my vision.

Later there were ice devils and blue-furred monkeys, though I am fairly certain they were citizens of the leather flask rather than inhabitants of this desolate country of our glorious State.

October 14th, Year of 90.

Woke alone. Sky the color of ice. Snow deep as my neck. A path has been broken for me, heading south. I will follow.

April 7th, Year of 91.

This spring I have a weapon of my own.

I suppose that means I am a permanent trusty now. There has been no ceremony. I have come to see that the Warden made me a scout to turn me out. Some of the men, even from among the hard cases in the first ward, step away from me and mutter when we chance to meet in the corridors or courtyard. The Warden has made it clear that I am to be well away from the prison when Sergeant F____ arrives.

I shall scout east this spring, mapping the vale to its farther reaches and looking into whatever countries lie there beyond the borders of our glorious State. There is a weighty treatise on the obligations of citizens I am to take with me, reading it before I use the pages to wipe my bum and light my cook fires.

▲▼▲

June 21st, Year of 91.

Herein I make my report to the Warden:

I have seen walls of blue-veined marble like giant slabs of goat cheese in the mountains to the east. I have walked a broken road that spiraled up a peak so tall the air thinned to a pained emptiness in my lungs, as if the builders could evacuate their lungs and still travel smiling onward. Three golden statues stand watch over a plunging waterfall, that I finally named Justice, Loyalty, and Citizenship after their solemn clothes and dour countenances. I hiked days through a valley of pale roses, where the smell cloyed so deep in me that it dyed my passwater pink and made even my shit sweet scented.

Nowhere did I see railroads, telegraph lines, border posts, men with guns, men without guns, animal herds, crops, or any other sign of military or political significance. I know the Black Sea lies to the south and east, and the great wheatfields of the Ukraine almost due east, but some inimical angel has removed them all and replaced them with mountains the likes of which have never been chronicled by the State's geographers.

There were no Hostiles to report, either, though once when I shot a tiny white deer it spoke to me, prophesying good fortune for my family and a larger house on Wilhelmstrasse in the Capital. I hesitated with it in my sights, as that Hostile in the orchard had once hesitated with me in his sights. But I am civilized, so I shot it again and ate it, and had no more visions. I have kept with me one of its delicate bones, on a thong beneath my shirt.

I can see the prison from my camp now at the east end of the Vale. Some of the men are having sport outside the walls, dancing and playing in the thin heat of the mountain summer. Or perhaps they are Hostiles assaulting us. I cannot tell from this distance, though upon reflection I realize that the white puffs I have taken for the smoke of troc cigarettes are more likely from the firing of guns.

▲▼▲

June 23rd, Year of 91.

Upon arriving at the prison, I found thirty were dead, mostly lawyers. It seems some of the trustees took advantage of the confusion of the recent battle to eliminate the worst of our troublemakers. The commissary is dead as well, of an honest Hostile bullet, but as Sergeant F____ seems not to have come this spring, that late worthy's role is less than it might otherwise have been.

"Citizen J____," the Warden said to me. His voice was immensely sad, as my father's had been at pronouncing punishments upon me when I was a child. "I have a mind to appoint you to the duties of the commissary."

I demurred, insisting instead on presenting my report of my journey east. One of the men lounging about shovel in hand loudly declared that they had all seen the smoke of my campfire the entire time of my alleged travels toward an airless Heaven, but the Warden shushed him.

"It is an important job," he told me. "And will grant you much privacy in the taking of inventories and balancing of the books."

Though I longed for that privacy, I resented the Warden's assumption that he understood my requirements. Still, such work was a steady improvement on shoveling graves or tending apple orchards, and I could scarcely spend my life voyaging among the glittering wonders of the State's corner of Europe.

I told him I would take on the labors he asked of me.

▲▼▲

September 5th, Year of 91.

A caravan was spotted in the V____ Pass today. I have examined my feelings concerning the devious Sergeant F____ and determined that perhaps I should remain busy somewhere within the warren of corridors and rooms that form the second ward and prison offices. I see no need for further violence. The voice of the white deer haunts me yet, and there are graves aplenty outside.

I do wonder a bit about the contents of his dispatch case. Perhaps I should write another letter. Surely my interests in the Capital have been too long neglected already. At the least I will send my attorney a lovely pine cone I found in my journey east, that the winds twisted into the face of a screaming man.

▲▼▲

September 12th, Year of 91.

The Warden has informed me that due to reasons of economy of State, the deleterious Sergeant F____ will be making only one trip per annum to our prison, in the fall. There were no dispatches pertaining to my case, he has said, nor indeed dispatches pertaining to much of any use to us. The primary communication was a revision to the standing orders from the Ministry of Justice requiring the prison to maintain at least one electric lamp for every ten yards of corridors, and mandating a new style of lock for our cell block doors.

As we have no electricity here in the Vale of V____ save what nature provides during our summer thunderstorms, and no one is sure where the keys to cell blocks may be found since the death of the commissary—there is speculation that he was inadvertently buried with them upon his person, and the Warden has grown forgetful in his latter years—the standing orders were sent to the kitchen to be used as tinder for the stoves.

Otherwise there were a few memoranda concerning naval operations, which seems odd as the State lacks a coastline upon any of Europe's seas, and some inventory lists bound for the consulate in Alexandria, Egypt, which had been misdelivered to us.

It is clear that the State intends me to serve out my life here in obscurity. I can do no less as a citizen than to make that effort with the purest heart and clearest head I can bring to the task.

Besides, the mountains *are* beautiful.

▲▼▲

October 7th, Year of 91.

The Hostiles attacked at dawn. It is difficult for me to say, given my own unique experiences with them, what their goals might be, other than the sheer joy of harassment, but they killed one Anton Boordmann, a trusty charged with manning the southeast tower. Their assault put a fright into a number of others, including Petit Cochin, who screamed like a woman.

I sickened finally of the crackle of gunfire and the screams from the battlements, and showed myself upon the walls, clutching the white deer's bone close in my hand. As soon as the Hostiles caught sight of me, they left off firing their weapons and drove their horses in a tight circle for some few minutes before racing off into the swamps of vale, water splashing around them in brilliant curtains.

Most of the prisoners will no longer speak to me, save Borogov who remains my friend, and the Warden, who is like a father unto me. In our little circle of three, we are a mirror of society—the Warden the wise power of the State, Borogov the impulsive but essentially obedient citizen, and I the august machinery of law and government that mediates between the State and its people.

▲▼▲

January 1st, Year of 92.

I have built a sculpture from the telegraph keys left to us by the droll Sergeant F___. I will not say it is a thing of beauty, for a law machine like myself is no judge of such, but it is a thing of awe. I believe that were we to face it into the fires of the sun, we might send a pulsed signal of bright focused light all the way to the Capital, and show the people there what constitutes true loyalty to the State.

Borogov assisted me in hauling my sculpture down to the courtyard, then outside the gates to that trampled field of snow where the prisoners stage their icy battles by way of sport. We set it in the center, and I twisted the thing for a while, trying to catch some of the feeble rays from our enervated winter sun. Eventually I was forced to leave off by dint of the skin ripping from my fingertips to remain behind on the chilled brass of the telegraph keys. I laughed to consider it my signature, work of my hand.

"You have gone beyond strangeness, my friend," Borogov said to me, "into some dark country of holiness."

I told him the only dark country was that pathless waste of the human heart, and that loyalty to the State and obedience to the precepts of good citizenship were the lighted path out of such a desert.

"You only prove my point, Citizen J___," Borogov told me, then he hugged me.

I sometimes wonder if he is my friend mostly because the Hostiles will not fire upon me.

▲▼▲

July 11th, Year of 99.

The Warden is dead. He was found in bed by his orderly, one Shadrach McKiernan of the first ward, an Irish-Jewish murderer originally hailing from Constantinople. I can scarce believe that this bedrock of our lives has passed. He seemed as if he would live as long as the mountains that surround us.

As commissary and therefore by implication second officer of the prison I instructed Borogov to convene a meeting of the trustees to establish the will of the men. We have not seen the dallying Sergeant F___ since the year of 96, and have thus received no guidance from the State concerning the affairs of the prison. I find it unlikely another Warden will be assigned us in a timely manner.

While Borogov met with the trustees I visited the Warden on his deathbed. He had a sad smile upon his face, and McKiernan had laid two coppers upon the Warden's eyes. Close examination revealed one to be a kopeck and the other to be an Albanian lek, so I suppose the Warden will see two different visions of paradise, should his soul ever find its way free of our mountainous home.

At least he died in the warm season.

I searched his files, but found no record of the Warden himself. It has occurred to me that I can no longer recall his name, but only his title as a servant of the State. As a servant he lived, as a servant he died.

Surely I knew him when I came to this place.

Borogov comes. I must attend to his news.

▲▼▲

July 11th, Year of 99. Second entry.

The trustees have asked me to take on the duties of the Warden. I do not know what to make of this request. They fear me, for the most part, and those who do not fear me hate me instead. I know their superstitious dread of the Hostiles has somehow bound itself to me, and so I have kept apart from the society of the prison these past years.

How can I, outside all their hopes and desires, lead them into the future?

Borogov has pointed out that this makes me the perfect candidate to replace the Warden. My peculiar relationship with Hostiles might extend to all of them. Furthermore, I have no interest in the petty squabbles between the Wards, but as commissary have served only the interests of the institution as a whole. He put the matter to succinct words in his colorful way, "Your cock ain't got no spurs in this ring."

I told Citizen Borogov that was well said. I will not take the title, though, for that would be presuming too much of the powers of the State. I shall call myself Acting Warden, and make Borogov commissary in my place.

▲▼▲

July 13th, Year of 99.

The Warden was buried today. We made a grave for him among the apple orchards, picking the broken cornices and cobbles out of the ground for hours to widen the trench sufficiently for even his poor coffin. Borogov surprised me by having some of the barrators and usurers haul my sculpture of the telegraph keys up from the forecourt onto the mountain to stand between the trees as the Warden's marker.

No one else could recall his name, either, so I said the service only to the Warden, as if we buried the office rather than the man. After calling on the beneficence of the State and enjoining all my prisoners—for they are indeed now mine—to good citizenship and hope of rehabilitation, I closed the ceremony with a moment of silent contemplation. Those among the men who follow God, or some god, deserved their moment of prayer, though the precepts of the State enjoined me from calling it so. Instead I clutched the white deer's bone and thought as little as possible.

When I raised my eyes I saw a band of Hostiles among the trees farther up the slope. One of them smiled at me, and they all bowed, whether to me or to the late Warden I cannot say, before they moved off like the shadows of clouds will do.

I said nothing to the men, wishing not to spread alarm.

▲▼▲

February 2nd, Year of 05.

One of the main gates collapsed this morning under the weight of snow. We have not the timbers to repair it, which means these walls will never more stand closed against Hostile assault.

I have come to a certain knowledge of their ways. They battle us from time to time because we are here, the same way they battle winter snow and summer storms and the hard, tough life they wring from the stony soil and vast forests clothing these mountains. It is something of a sport and something of a prayer for them when they ride against our walls and fell our men. They stand off from me because for them I am like that tiny white deer prophesying great houses and phantom success—somehow I am a symbol of the life within, or perhaps beyond, their everyday world.

I have not sought to turn them to the loyal service of the State. There seems little point. Wild nature serves a purpose as well after all, standing as contrast to the structured life we lead. Without the Hostiles, we would not know ourselves as civilized.

▲▼▲

June 11th, Year of 09.

Borogov is getting old. We all are. The youngest of the inmates is well over forty years of age, and we now lose more each year to senility and the diseases of advanced years than to cold or hostile attack. We all live in the second ward, those three dozen or so of us left, querulous old men cheating one another at cards and hunting rabbits in the spring with snares in order to conserve ammunition for the occasional shooting matches with our neighbors. Always we observe the precepts of the State, enjoined by time and these stone walls to a narrow, correct form of citizenship.

But I am concerned for my commissary. Borogov has spent the past week abed, now when it should be his best time of year. He is a lying, thieving old peasant bastard, and my best friend in the world. I went to visit him in his cell today, where he lay wheezing, and asked him if he was wanting of his grave just yet, for we have dug all that will yet be needed, and each picked them for ourselves so that some men have even chiseled their own memorial stones.

"I'll not lead you underground," Borogov said with a gummy smile. His teeth had finally fled him several winters ago. "I'll throw the last spade on your grave, you Capital dandy." Coughing took him away to a faded place of pain where I could no longer reach him.

I clapped my commissary on the shoulder and commended his spirit, then went to the trustees and told them to ready his coffin.

▲▼▲

July 23rd, Year of 09.

After Borogov's funeral, I determined to set the inmate files in order. I had never paid them much mind, as no person has been committed to or discharged from the prison during my tenure as Acting Warden, but it seemed a fitting thing to do. I could bring the death lists up to the date, and mark each man's file with the manner and date of his passing, so that when the State finally turns its beneficent regard once again upon our prison, agents of the Ministry of Justice will find the records in order.

Today I finally opened my own file. I have avoided the temptation for years, in the interests of setting an example for the prisoners, but it was the last one left to me.

Inside there was a record of my sentencing, some notes upon my early years in the prison, a complaint from one of the lawyers in the first ward about my being a danger to myself and others. No different from any other file.

Except for the letter which lay within.

The outside was dated May, Year of 89, that written in the Warden's hand with a charcoal pencil. Shortly after my sentencing. The address was to the Warden, written in a fine copperplate script that I recognized as that of my attorney from those long ago days in the Capital.

I turned it over. The envelope had been opened, then resealed with wax and an impression of the Warden's seal. He had read it, then set it aside for my files.

The enveloped crinkled as I held it tight in my hand. What did it say? Was this the secret of my endless incarceration?

Who was I to doubt the wisdom of the State, acting through my attorney, the courts, the Warden? If this had been meant for me to read, he would not have sealed it again.

Everything I had wondered, my fears, my hopes, all of it could be answered inside this envelope. It trembled in my hand like the wing of a cliff swallow.

I am a servant of the State, I told myself, both in my person and in my office. Who I once was, what I once feared, have vanished in the crucible of my loyalty. I laid a tiny fire in the stove and burned the letter unopened, though I confess I later tried to read some wisdom in the unknowable ashes.

▲▼▲

June 6th, Year of 15.

We are ever fewer, thirteen now. I fear the last of us shall have to lay ourselves in our own graves and trust the curious Hostiles to shovel in the remaining dirt from beneath the grassy mounds that stand beside each shallow pit.

There are no more doors in the prison. We only stay because it is our home. I have difficulty imagining what duty old men such as we still have, but until we are discharged we will do that duty to the State even if only by shivering in the common room of the Warden's old apartment where we all now dwell.

Except for me. I want to see the three golden statues once more, follow the blue-veined walls, and climb that ultimately airless road so that when my soul finally flees my body it can readily find its way among the dagger-sharp stars of our mountain sky.

I will not last another winter. Already I hear Borogov's footsteps in the hall, as if he has come back to fetch me onward. Petit Cochin still lives, and of late has begun to mutter at length, words none of us have ever heard from him in all his years in the prison.

We are undone, all of us.

Though it makes of me a rebel to the State, I would be the white deer in the woods before I die. I whispered my plan to Petit Cochin, who muttered and nodded, then told him he had charge of the prison in my absence. I will take no weapons nor gear, save only my boots and a decent wool blanket not too far eaten by moths.

It may be that in truth at the far end of the Vale of V____ there are only more slopes leading down to Slavic villages and surly guards lining the border of a neighboring country. It may be that the Hostiles will slay me as I walk and leave me to feed the ravens and eagles that haunt these heights. It may be that the ghosts of the people who lived here long before the prison will haunt me to a stumbling death in shallow water.

But I will leave my sentence and the State behind. Wherever I die, the golden statues will stand gleaming before me, and my thin breath will gasp free in the unforgiving light of the sharp stars.

For my crimes, whatever they may have been, I beg forgiveness. For my soul, I beg no pity at all. Envy me my freedom, you who read this, as I envy myself.

Achilles, Sulking in His Buick

Not much to say about this one. I wrote it just for the fun of the title, which popped into my head one day for no particular reason. (I've never owned a Buick, for one thing.) The best of the Achaeans seemed to lend himself well to a streets of fire vernacular, with a dash of Johnny and the Golden Fiddle thrown in for the sheer joy of mixing my historical metaphors.

Consider Achilles and his cherry ride, a 1947 Buick Roadmaster Fastback, chopped and channeled, lowered three inches, enough chrome to garnish Olympia itself, windows smoked dark as a Spartan's heart. The ride shines under fourteen coats of gold paint, hand-rubbed, custom plates reading 'TIMÉ.' Don't ask how much pull it took to get *that* from the DMV. Achilles has the finest wheels in the Achaeans.

He's parked on the blacktop behind Illium High, pissed. Agamemnon Atreus, street general for the Achaeans, two-timed off with Achilles' girlfriend Brisei. Aggie's squeeze Chryseis was grounded by her old man, and Aggie couldn't rumble the Trojans without a doll in Capri pants and ice-pink lipstick riding shotgun in his baby blue 1951 Lincoln Continental with the 'KLEOS' plates.

Aggie wants the Buick, too, but even though he's the leader of the pack, big as he is he's not quite tough enough to take skinny little Achilles down *mano a mano*. Which would be the only way to get the keys. Brisei was a different story, turned with some fast-talking and couple of lids of primo California Red.

Girls is girls, but cars is cars.

Now Aggie's revving the Lincoln up, fixing to play chicken with Hector, chief enforcer for the Trojans. Hector's got a German ride, customized by Schliemann's down in Culver City, not even a Mercedes for Apollo's sake, but a weird make called a Prinz with a banker's paint job—maroon and blacked-out trim. This ain't the main event, not by a long shot, but the Achaeans and the Trojans like to start off their rumbles with a lot of noise and some flash. Let the leadership show some investment, take a few scrapes. Then the street greasers will shout and shove, somebody will lose a few teeth, some more high-rev dragging and chicken racing, and on a really good night, crunch-bang-boom.

What every race fan lives for, Saturday nights behind Illium High.

Aggie's got his rod smoking on the line, Brisei leaning back and looking cool with a Camel in her pale lips and a tank top strap falling off one bare shoulder. Hector's two hundred yards away, at the ragged edge of the blacktop past the rusty hoops of the rec basketball shooters, German engine almost whining. The Trojan doesn't believe in burning rubber—he likes to show some class, some control.

Hermes, back from college and now above partisanship in these small town Olympian frays, drops the flag and the boys are off. Aggie lays some smoking rubber, while Hector smooths off the line like a goose on Maalox. Achilles in his Buick pretends not to be watching, but somehow no one's obstructing his view of the short track, no one wanders too close to the Roadmaster.

There's a shudder of metal and squeal of brakes as Aggie and Hector miss by a hair, just close enough for each to claim the other one veered off first. A chrome mirror spins in the air, trailing shattered glass like a comet's tail, prize off one of the king cars, though in the flash of the moment, no one's sure which.

After a few moments of disorganization, the rumble starts in earnest, motorcycle chains and tire irons flying. Achilles lights up a Gauloise—he's that kind of guy—leans back against his windowframe, and blows viscous smoke rings around the interior of his car.

"Hey, buddy." Someone raps on the Buick's fender, nearly a capital offense.

Achilles leaps up, bumps the wheel hard enough to sound the horn, and curses in the language of his fathers, something about goats and olives.

"Easy, easy." It's Patroclus, a kid who'd watched Achilles' back since fifth grade for no better reason than Pat liked to see the little guys win. Achilles was the toughest son of a bitch in Olympia, but he was small. Bantam weight, fighting far above his class, and winning every time.

Sometimes he could get tired of honor.

"Pat," says Achilles. "Don't be sneaking up on people like that."

Pat leans in the window, no wine or dope fogging *his* breath. "Look, there's going to be another round of runs later. Hector's stepping in, gonna flatten some of our boys. Aggie really wants you in. Those Trojans are scared spitless of the Roadmaster."

"Screw Aggie," Achilles says with his usual eloquence.

"I know, I know. So I got this plan. Let *me* drive the Buick, put some water in their leadfeet, those boys will fold like yesterday's paper."

Achilles takes a long drag on his current Gauloise. He hates the damned things, actually, but the imported French cigarettes annoy almost everyone else with their stench and their expense. Keeps people jumping. "I don't know, Pat. Nobody drives the Buick."

"Exactly," says Patroclus. "That's why they'll think it's you."

"What do I get out of it?"

Pat grins like he just discovered sex. "You get to put one up on Hector and Agamemnon at the same damned time."

"*Até.*" Despite himself, Achilles begins to chuckle. "That just might be worth it."

▲▼▲

About an hour later, the Buick rolls up to the line. Achaeans and Trojans, they're doing a head-on, six on six. At the sight of Achilles' Roadmaster, two Trojans drop it into reverse and chicken out of the race. There's consternation in the crowd, on both sides actually, Agamemnon giving the Buick a dirty look from his place in the stands.

But Hector's still down there in the Prinz, a car half the weight of the Buick, and he's ready to rumble. Somehow the six-on-six turns into a one-on-one, and no one cares. This is the main event, the big rumble. Big man Trojan against big man Achaean.

Achilles is in the stands, too, wearing a grease monkey coverall from Western Auto and a fedora pulled low. No one looks at a little guy, not in this crowd. He's getting worried, actually, about the Buick and even about Patroclus. This was supposed to be a stunt, but it's turning into a grudge match.

Then it's too late, Hermes drops the flag, the dolls are screaming, Pat lays a twenty-yard scratch as the Prinz flies like a bullet from a gun and they meet a hundred yards from their starting places, dead center in the middle, only at the last moment Pat loses his nerve and heaves the Buick over, which you can't never do that with a car heavy as the Roadmaster, and the Prinz shoots by, home free, straight as an arrow, while the Buick rolls and slides into the bricks on the back side of Illium High's dining hall, and there's Hector standing on the doorframe of the Buick and he's trying to help Patroclus out, or maybe he's pushing Pat back in as the car catches fire and sweet Apollo she's going to blow!

Hector barely makes it away from the explosion. Pat is so much pavement paste. Dishonored, Achilles is far gone into rage, where the whole world goes as red as his hair and every moment in time is a world wasted, leaping down from the stands, literally jumping onto guys' shoulders to get past them, a crescent wrench swinging in his hand to clear the way.

But there's Hephaestus, another customizer from Culver City, standing in the fist-fighting crowd as unconcerned as a summer day in Crete. He's leaning on a hot rod so black it's almost a metal shadow, custom body work down to the frame and maybe custom all the way to the pavement, looking like the bastard child of a Ferrari and a Cadillac hearse. Achilles charges forward with murder in his eye, on his lips and in his hands, and Hephaestus tosses him the keys.

There's one of those moments, when the gods decree that time's arrow shall stand forfeit and entire lives are gathered like an upholstery stitch. The keys glitter in the air, a star snatched from heaven and sent to Achilles' open hand even as his crescent wrench spins toward the pavement.

This is it, his destiny, time to show Hector and Agamemnon both who's the best man in this one-horse town on the edge of the sea, time to be a real fighter, define his own damned weight class, by Apollo. The keys hit Achilles' hand like a stage weight, their heft staggering him in place. Hephaestus touches something secret and a door eases up on the black car, opening gull wing style to a paradise of black leather and pale green lights.

It's like looking into Hades.

Hades looks back.

Achilles stands beneath the upswung door, keys straining forward, hearing the distant sirens of the Olympia Fire Brigade. Hephaestus' black car reeks of leather and oil and, somehow, blood. Achilles glances up to see Brisei staring at him, shaking her head, crying. Even in the shadows of the evening he can see that. He thinks that's Aggie's handprint on her face too, where the Atreian bastard slapped her.

Patroclus' pyre lights the night, the Roadmaster taking him to Hades in style, and probably Illium High's dining hall with it. Glimpsed through the struggling crowd, a tired Hector, singed, bloodied, discouraged, trudges back toward his abandoned Prinz.

This is Achilles' moment. This is what he sulked all afternoon at the back of the parking lot for. His honor. His destiny, to be a hero.

Was it ever worth the lives?

The smell of Hades hard in his nostrils, Achilles drops the keys, kicks them under Hephaestus' sin-black hot rod, and walks out to the street. His heel burns like fire. Someone has the nerve to toot a horn at him, but it's just Odysseus, that odd stoner, in a chartreuse VW microbus with curtained windows and enough dope lit up inside to power a small town. A man who always takes the long way home.

Odd, ever the wily trickster, waves Achilles over. The greatest fighter of the Achaeans climbs in shotgun without a word, accepts a joint the size of his thumb, and motors off in a cloud of burnt oil and sweet hemp to a different destiny.

Behind them, unnoticed, Hector stands weeping at the curb.

Crossing the Seven

Editor John Klima invited me to contribute to his Logorrhea *project, an anthology based on winning words in the National Spelling Bee. He even sent around word lists for the authors to pick from. I, of course, based an entire novella on a rather crappy pun. The astute reader may note echoes of both* Green *and* Trial of Flowers *in this story, but in fact, the seven cities are in no continuity but their own. It's been suggested I write a novel in this setting, but so far, my poor messenger of the blackstar seems to be content to remain at rest from his labors.*

When Halcyone was queen in Cermalus the blackstar first came into the sky.

With the coming of the blackstar, tradesmen and civitors alike cried for protection from the throne. The working people of the city paid no more attention to the shouting on the hill than we did to the lights in the sky. The end of the world might be at hand, but there was still bread to be baked and dogs to be fed and gutters to be cleaned.

I myself was most concerned with the state of the tiles on the roof of the villa belonging to the first mistress of the Civitor Tradelium. I was called Andrade, slave of the city.

The civitor was not an unkind man, in that he sometimes managed to remember that his slaves and servants were human beings with needs and desires. It was more than most of that august class could keep in mind, who had been born amid a cloud of attendants and would die there, either of old age or bloody assassination.

Kindness or no, his sweet mistress had experienced an inpouring of water, ruining a set of silk sheets and some quite expensive leather intimates brought at significant cost from decadent Oppius. This had sent her into a rage of epic proportions. In turn, the Civitor Tradelium experienced no little irritation as the mistress had accosted his wife.

In accordance with the fundamental principle that feces flow downward, all became my responsibility for having failed to divine in advance of the need for repairing the roof. And thusly, while the second sons of the wealthy were rending their garments in the streets for fear of the blackstar, I was up on the roof resetting glazed tiles across my carefully built grout-and-plaster. I had no intention of coming down from my perch for the sake of flood, fire or barbarian invasion, not after the civitor's mixture of threats and promised bonuses.

I was standing on that roof with the long-bladed file in my hand, balanced on the slick curved tiles, when the high priestess of the Temple Regina rode astride her white ass down the cobbled street below. She wore only the three veils of propriety and the seven beads of virtue. Her Worship being about ten stone and forty years to the far side of lissome, the three veils were as effective as a sneeze and a promise. It was a large ass. Both of them were, in fact—the one attached to her and the one beneath her. The high priestess's avoirdupois was of no moment as all good Cermalians knelt in prayer facing away from her line of procession. The bad Cermalians turned away too, out of a sense of good taste or possibly sheer self-preservation.

Even her temple guard marched with their eyes averted.

So it was that when the blackstar discharged its bolt of unholy violet lightning, mine were the only eyes hers chanced to meet.

Given that I stood a good fifty feet above her on the roof line, limned from behind by the blinding light—and I thank the stars themselves I was not looking into the bolt—what the high priestess saw was a purple angel descended from the heavens, harbinger of the blackstar.

What I saw was her great maw opening for a shriek. I figured it was me for a goner, on account of profaning the sacred form of the high priestess by casting my base eyes upon her. I'd have gladly given that vision of pulchritude right back to the pond from whence it flopped, if I had the chance.

She yelled, a second bolt struck the long-bladed file, my hair caught fire, and I was blown off the roof.

After that, things got bad.

▲▼▲

It might have gone better for me if I had not landed on the high priestess. She broke my fall, but together we broke the ass's back. I wound up with my face buried perilously close to her heavenly gates, which smelled of old shoeleather, while the poor, screaming animal had somehow collapsed upon my buttocks and thighs.

In very short order an impressive collection of ceremonial brass spear points pricked me, while an angry man with a face like a tamarind monkey was screeching for me to get on my feet immediately upon pain of sudden and excruciating death. I rolled my eyes at him above the quivering curve of her Worship's belly, contriving to indicate that I could neither move nor speak in my current situation, but he was clearly not a rational fellow.

"Raise up the heretic," he shouted.

The spear points fell away, the screaming ass was levered free, and several pairs of rough yet ungentle hands yanked me off the sacred person of the high priestess, who was promptly covered with a guard's sable cloak. Three cloaks, actually, it took to ensure the requirements of modesty were met.

I dangled in the air as someone finally put the poor beast out of its misery. The officer leaned close, his anger somewhat better under control. "Any confessions before your summary execution?"

"I didn't—" I began, but obviously I had. Dropped from the sky, interrupted the parade, seen her Worship in the forbidding flesh, harassed her Worship's person. There were doubtless a dozen more crimes of which I was guilty. Having neither wit nor patriotism to sustain me, I merely shook my head.

"Wait," bellowed the high priestess.

Half a dozen stabbing spears paused with a shiver. My gut was in such a pucker I almost wished they'd finished it.

She struggled to her feet, a titanic wave of loose sable and pale free-swinging flesh. "Somebody bring me my robe," she snapped to the world at large. Then, to the guard captain: "Don't you know who this is?"

His mouth worked, but he obviously made the same calculus so recently completed by my own panicked mind. "Madame," he said.

The response of cornered guard captains everywhere, I thought with sharp satisfaction. Though I had no idea what she meant either.

"He is our messenger from the blackstar!" she shouted.

An entire street full of people, rushing out of doors for the exciting prospect of an imminent execution, immediately cheered this news that one had come who could speak for, and presumably protect them from, the dreaded blackstar. While most of them cared no more than I did for the heavenly apparition, their masters or their masters' masters, or their masters' masters' masters certainly did.

There was a general riot of cheering. I quickly found myself lifted upon the shoulders and hands of a mob, and borne toward the Cermalic Palace. The high priestess bobbed somewhere behind me, moving at a slower pace and, if she was lucky, drinking heavily.

It was certainly what I wished for in that moment—a stout drink, followed by a nice, safe execution.

▲▼▲

So I came before Halcyone, borne by temple guards and a mob of plebes and proles and slaves who under normal circumstances would not have been allowed through the main gates of the palace. Somewhere in the course of the mad rush I discovered that all the hair on my head, and indeed even my eyebrows, had been burnt away by the violet bolt. Perhaps no one would know me.

Even as we muddled to a halt before the throne, a hasty delegation of civic dignitaries rushed in, lead by none other than the Civitor Tradelium.

Once more I found myself wishing for that drink.

The throne room of Halcyone is lined with two rows of pillars each ten times the height of a man. Between them is a peaked clerestory, with colored glass that lights the floor far below in a pleasing array of shadows. I cannot tell you what is behind the pillars, for bright braziers set before them blinded my eyes to the deeper shadows. The floor is some complex mosaic which I never saw clearly.

Halcyone was a slim bird of a woman, sprawled sidewise within the Cermalic Throne. The chair itself was gilded, in the shape of a giant lotus only partially opened, so that the queen resembled nothing so much as an overthin infant pushing its way out from betwixt its mother's womanly parts.

Though she might look the spoiled child, when confronted by an armed mob in her own throne room, Halcyone had the mind of a ruler. "What is your purpose?" she called out to me in a cool voice which should have been able to stop a battle.

It certainly stopped the mob.

"Majesty," said the guard captain, dropping to one knee as he swept off his helmet. Everyone else took this cue to kneel, which resulted in me being dumped on the floor. "Her Worship the high priestess of the Temple Regina has declared this man to be the messenger of the blackstar."

I stood, bowed, and tried to brush myself off. My tunic was singed by lightning, rent by spears, stained with blood, and covered with crisped strands of my hair. "Majesty."

She raised a hand to forestall further statements from me. The queen slithered out of her throne and stood tall. She wore only a simple white chiton, pinned at the left shoulder, leaving her right shoulder and most of her right breast bare.

"It is known to us," she said slowly, "that the mighty of our city fear the coming of the blackstar. We are not an astrologer, nor are we a mathematician, but even a queen must give nod to a messenger from beyond the heavens. Here is the source and solution to our problems. Speak, and tell us what you will."

She gave me such a hard, calculating look that I knew I was being set up for a fall worse than the one I had just taken from the civitor's rooftop. I drew a great breath and said the only thing I could imagine which might save me. "I am come from the heavens to cross the seven cities. When I leave this greatest of cities, I will take your fears with me. Convey me now to Cispius."

Halcyone quirked a smile, and gave me a tiny nod. As I was swept up again by the mob I could hear the Civitor Tradelium saying, "But that's the slave who maintains my rooftops."

▲▼▲

When Sterope was queen in Cispius the messenger of the blackstar began his journey across the seven cities, the peregrination that in ancient times had been called the Transept.

The high priestess's guard officer, one Leutherion, was assigned to be my own guard captain, a duty he liked no more than I. The rest of my attendants were likewise selected at random from those in the throne room the day of my elevation—servants, plebes and soldiers who were not pleased either. They considered my heavenly mission to the seven cities nothing more than a criminal deceit. The fact they were correct did nothing to ease my fears or my conscience. Instead I played the haughty, as if I were a civitor and they no more than slaves.

We rode forth mounted on brown asses from the queen's stables, Leutherion bearing in my honor a black-on-black banner affixed to the haft of a spear. No noble destriers for us—her majesty was nothing if not practical. In our train we bore a great chest filled with slips of paper on which the great and plebian alike of Cermalus had written their greatest fears for the blackstar, to be carried forth by me, the messenger of heaven.

I was already mightily missing my rooftop duties.

Our journey passed with varying rounds of bickering and silence across a demon-haunted scrubland, in which old bones stood taller than my head and shadows gibbered, chuckled and howled by night. I might have thought myself in the lands of the dead save for the blackstar which stood overhead day and night. In sunlight it was a hole in the sky. In darkness it crackled a baleful purple.

I could only be where I was thanks to its inimical agency.

After six days of infighting and shivering in the dark, we approached Cispius. Much like Cermalus, the city was situated upon a hill, proximate to open water and arable land. Unlike Cermalus, where wealth and power had migrated upward, the Cispians had built themselves a sort of circular palace, a circus of the mighty which ran the circumference of the base of the hill, leaving stables, huts and slave camps for the upper slopes.

I later understood this had to do with the availability of water, and lack thereof, on the slopes of the hill. Cermalus is blessed with springs all the way up its heights and so I had in my naïveté assumed that all the Seven Cities were so arranged.

Flanked by two of his men, Ironpants and Pelletier, Leutherion stopped before the brass-bound great gate. The pair of doors were perhaps three man-heights tall, each a third as wide. Though a smaller wooden trade gate stood wide open nearby, out of which flowed a succession of carts and fieldhands bound for the farms, the formal entrance was closed to us until we stated our business and presented our credentials.

"The messenger of the blackstar is here," Leutherion called loudly. "Come to carry away the evil which descends from your skies."

Had we possessed a trumpet amongst our little caravan, I am certain he would have blown it.

An armored man leaned out the shadows of the trade gate. "I knows a Cermalian accent when I hears one," he shouted. "Your embassy's done come and gone for the season. 'Less you got a caravan permit, be off with you."

Some of my attendants snickered as I glanced behind me at the dayslong trail through the scrub, but my guard captain was made of sterner stuff. He and his outriders kicked their donkeys over to the trade gate. I did not deign to follow, but awaited negotiations. These appeared to be part bribery and part threat.

A few minutes later, we were waved through the lesser gate. Ignominious perhaps, but a better fate than being forced back into the wilderness. I suspected I would not long survive being turned out.

▲▼▲

Once we were within the marble-floored street-halls of Cispius, our reception improved dramatically. Here I was not the villainous ex-slave that my attendants gossiped against by campfire. No, here I was an exotic dignitary from a distant city, come to save them from the blackstar.

The well-born and the wealthy were not the sort to throng their city in celebration. As we traveled toward the Palace Circumferential, the top level of this ring-city where Sterope dwelt, silent servants emerged from ornate doorways to offer presentation trays of flowers, fruits and cunning folded paper dolls meant to resemble mythic figures. After a false start, I found we were not intended to take the trays or their contents—indeed, these were "eye-gifts," offerings of beauty which did not subtract from the mundane wealth of the giver, but only called for an investment of time.

I immediately conceived of a handy business packaging such offering trays in advance and storing them in chill chambers beneath the city, to be delivered at a premium when need called.

It was also passing strange that this city smelled of little but clean stone. I could only imagine the efforts at bringing up water and taking out waste which attended these people. On the other hand, it was in effect a single enormous house, and so less susceptible to litter and filth than any ordinary street in Cermalus.

We wound around the diameter of the city three times in the ascension. The inner street was built as a gently-graded ramp, rising one level per full transit of the circle, and lined with houses, shops, and ateliers. Where in my home city the wealthy showed their taste and resources with extravagant gardens, wild variations in architecture, and baroque rooflines, here all was invested in the front door and the facade which surrounded that portal.

For the wealthy, Cispius was a city of doors. One could live within this arrangement and easily never see the sky.

▲▼▲

The Palace Circumferential was the rooftop of the ring-city. Even here there were many sheltered passages, overgrown bowers and wide-eaved buildings. I was pleased to see some fine examples of the roofer's art.

Under a shelter of grapevines, we dismounted as silent servants brought blue bowls of water for us to wash in. "Don't screw it up," growled Leutherion. His men snickered.

"Fear not. I value my life at least as much as you value yours."

We were soon enough brought before the court of Sterope, Queen in Cispius. She sat on a glittering throne cut from one enormous crystal. Fires had been lit behind her throne so that the crystal gleamed along many facets and the queen was wrapped in a flickering glow. It was very hard to make out her face or form. Anyone could have sat upon that throne.

I bowed low, then rose to indicate the great chest which my attendants Pelletier and Finnric had brought up from our pack train.

"Majesty," I began, but someone immediately struck a huge gong. Brass thunder reverberated.

"Her Brilliance is to be addressed correctly," shouted a tiny man in pink silks. He was no taller than a small child, though there was stubble on his little chin. His face displayed a certain natural inclination toward violence, and he obviously relished his role in rectifying my errors.

"Uh...Brilliance." I was off my pacing now, carefully prepared words jumbled in my head. "Halcyone Queen in Cermalus—"

There was that damnable gong again. It would give me a headache quite soon.

"Her Brilliance is the sole Queen upon earth, and sovereign of all beneath the sun!" The little bastard was grinning now. I could see his teeth were filed to points. Did he wrestle otters in his free hours? "Others rule elsewhere only at her sufferance!"

My thoughts were even more tangled, but I was determined to proceed.

"Brilliance," I said, rushing to get ahead of the next strike of the gong. "Halcyone by your grace styled ruler in Cermalus bade me come before you, being—"

The gong rang out once more. The little man drew breath to correct me again. "Silence," I screeched in frustration. "You mistreat the emissary of Heaven at your peril!"

There was a pause, punctuated only by the last dying echo of the gong. Then Sterope shifted on her throne. "We will hear the messenger in his own words. The court will be silent."

And silent they were, scarcely even breathing, with no more noise among them than a flock of paper birds.

Still I spoke too fast, spitting my introduction in one breath. "Brilliance, Halcyone in Cermalus bade me come being declared messenger of the blackstar and here to relieve the evil which has descended upon your people."

There. I hadn't quite taken personal responsibility for the claim of divine sending.

A long pause followed, the court still quiet as lice on a dead man's head, while the queen sat cloaked in light and—presumably—considered my words. Finally, she raised one arm upward. The hand which I could actually see above the glare of her throne was slim and pale and finely wrought as Halcyone's had been.

"The blackstar stands high in the heavens. Our servants on the hill have cried fear, and our priests burned great offerings on the rooftop temples. Here now is a messenger from the blackstar, graciously sent on to us by our daughter ruler in Cermalus. He will hold court in the Plaza of Punishment for a day and an hour. All will bring their dreads and fears to him. When that day and hour is done, we shall commend him to our daughter ruler in Fagutal. After that, we shall hear no more fear, for he shall carry away our evil."

The entire court turned to face me—servants, nobles, soldiers, priests all mixed together. Every one of them had a starveling look. Leutherion hooked an elbow into my ribs. "Nice going," he muttered.

"Our heads are not on pikes."

▲▼▲

I never did sleep during my time in Cispius. With astonishing alacrity my entire train was brought to a plaza on the ground level of the ring-city. We had of course passed through this area on the way in, but I had not remarked the high posts topped with chains which surrounded the plaza, nor the barred doors of most of the establishments—prisons, oubliettes, and houses of pain.

Another great chest was procured, and a row of scribes was set out before me. The people great and small came. If they had their prayers already written, they were waved on to me by rough men in the uniform of the city. If not, the scribes took down their words. I received every one of those folded slips and silk-bound sheaves, while Leutherion and the others crammed them into the new chest.

This took the entire day and night, and into the next day. While I was kept well supplied with wine and delicacies, I was desperately exhausted. We were turned out of the city with remarkable efficiency at the appointed hour, there to be met by the tiny man and an enormous eunuch carrying that damnable gong.

"Her Brilliance has graced me with the honor of being your herald," the tiny man said with venom in his voice and face. "My gong accompanies me on its legs."

I leaned close. "If I hear that thing struck even once out here in the wilderness, I will have it fed to you. Do you understand?"

Leutherion beside me nodded. "And I will ensure the messenger's orders are carried out."

That was news to me.

▲▼▲

*When Celæno was queen in Fagutal the messenger of the blackstar
made the third stop of his Transept.*

We traveled now over a higher, broken country of purpled rocks
stained with the empty glyphs written by lichen. There were a myriad
false paths that ended in blind walls or drop-offs, so Leutherion was
forced to send outriders ahead to plot the way. Even so, we spent three
days following a road that ended before a shattered temple with no
way beyond.

The little man, whose name proved to be Osmio, had no idea of this
country—he was born and raised in Cispius. His eunuch, who had no
name at all save legs-of-the-gong, seemed bereft of ideas whatsoever.

The blackstar glowered and spat above us. It seemed to have come
lower in the sky, as if following me. For the look of the thing, I made
pretense at prayer, but no one was fooled.

Before we ran out of water we found a man standing at the edge of
a high cliff. He was a squat fellow, wearing a high, square leather cap
with matching armor. He carried a tall bow crafted from horn and hide.
He appeared to be guarding rock and empty air.

"Make way," said Leutherion, "for the messenger of the blackstar, come
by grace of Halcyone Queen in Cermalus and Sterope Queen in Cispius."

The gong rang loud, causing the armored stranger to flinch.

"Her Brilliance—" began Osmio, but was cut off with a squawk as
Pelletier caught him in the ribs with a spear butt. There was a general
muttered cheer. No one saw fit to discipline the eunuch. It seemed pointless, and besides which he could have broken any three of our heads.

Leutherion continued: "We seek admittance to the noble city of
Fagutal there to present our words to the Queen Celæno."

The guard stared at us all, no doubt taking in our numbers and
the composition of our train. "None pass within the walls of Fagutal,"
he said, "save those who have paid the toll and sworn the tributary
prayer." After a moment he added, "You must lay down your weapons
as well."

Leutherion bristled at this, but I raised my hand to speak. "I am the
messenger of Heaven, and have no care for weapons. But I will swear
tribute to no one and pay no toll. Better that I pass on to another city
and relieve them of their evil than that I bend to Celæno in Fagutal. I
enter free, or not at all."

The sentry looked at all of us a moment, then came to a decision.
"The messenger may go freely within, with one guard, and submit to the
judgment of the queen. The rest of you must remain without."

"I accept your terms," I told him. "Leutherion, will you accompany me?"

There was some delay while Leutherion reorganized the train in our absence. I walked over to the guard's post, expecting some declivity in the rock beyond, but instead realized that we stood on the edge of a very high cliff. The ground below was quite far down, verdant with jungles and open prairies, and stretched miles away toward distant ridgelines. Silver glinting rivers wound among the expanses.

I saw no city, only an endless horizon and a country broader than any I had ever thought existed.

Finally the guard led me and Leutherion to a hidden notch in the cliff face. Stairs descended toward the open air.

"Follow this down. You will not be challenged until you are within."

"What if we lose our way?" I asked.

The guard laughed. "There are only two ways to go. You may follow the trail, or you may try your wings in the empty air. In either case, you will know where you are going, though each journey is of a different length."

Down we went.

▲▼▲

The less said of the descent, the better. Suffice to say that I did not have a fear of heights before, but I shall never work the rooftops again. Leutherion liked it no better than I, but his bearing as a soldier compelled him forward.

Fagutal is a city carved from the face of that vast purple cliff. I suppose that if one were to ride astride a dragon or air-demon one might see the whole thing in one sweep of the eye. It has the architectural detail familiar to any ordinary city dweller—columns and fascias and friezes and great facades—but every bit of that is carved from living rock high above the jungles below, and faces out toward the domain of birds.

Being a city of the cliff, these buildings are arranged in a haphazard manner. If one did have a flying view, one would see the building faces stacked as if by a child of the gods. The trail wound among these, never quite reaching an entrance or window through which we might escape inward to safety and a horizontal floor. At last it came to a landing where more square-helmeted soldiers lounged.

"Ah, messenger boy," one said. "We're to take you to the queen."

"Birds," whispered Leutherion. "A letter came a-wing before us."

The enclosure of the ring-city of Cispius was nothing to the carved caverns of Fagutal. All was lit by torches or lamps or a glowing fungus which clustered on the walls like pale green scabs. The architecture within was much like that without—elaborate imitations of an ordinary city. Like Cispius, Fagutal smelled clean, though there was an undertone of molder and earth. People moved quietly, cloaked against the stone chill, avoiding our little party.

We were led deeper and deeper within the cliff, ever further from the sun, until we came to a sort of leather tent. "Her majesty's through here," said a grinning guard. The flaps were laced closed behind us, then we were whispered onward to pass a set of stone doors that pivoted at touch and so into deepest shadow.

Queen Celæno's throne room was dark as the inside of a cow. There was nothing to be seen, not the faintest eye-gleam, and I was seized with the sudden thought that I had tumbled over an edge and was falling into a chasm. My head spun as if I were being tumbled by toughs. Leutherion lay his hand on my arm.

"Breathe deep and slow," he advised softly. "It might help to close your eyes, for then the dark will seem more sensible."

"Advance," said a voice which echoed from all around.

We shuffled like addled pensioners.

"Halt." It was a woman's voice, or perhaps a child's. "Who comes before us, untaxed and unsworn in violation of all our laws and customs?"

We both knelt. I nudged Leutherion with my elbow.

"The messenger of Heaven," he said. "He is here to bring surcease from the ills of the blackstar, sent by the grace of your sister queens in Cermalus and Cispius."

"What fear do we have of the blackstar, who live beneath a roof of living stone?"

"Majesty," I said. I waited a moment, lest another of those damnable gongs ring out, or some similar mischief. "Your wisdom doubtless knows no fear, but there are those among your people who pass outward under the light of day and the gloom of night. To them I offer the opportunity to cast away the evil of their fears, that I might carry it with me back to Heaven. In return, I ask nothing of you or your city save a rest for my train, and possibly a few supplies."

Silence for a while, then the voice again, querulous. "And so those biddies have foisted you on us?"

That did not sound so good. "It was never our wish to burden you, majesty."

She laughed. Bitter, cold. "It is no matter to us. If our subjects wish to unburden themselves to sky-dwellers they may do so. We will direct the mayor of our palace to provide such provisions as he sees reasonable. There remains only the matter of the toll and the tributary prayer. As you did not pay on the way in, you shall forfeit the freedom of one of your traveling party. We are generous, we invite you to make your own choice."

Strong hands grasped both Leutherion and me to pull us away from the audience. "What do we do now?" I asked him when the guards had pushed us past the leather flap and into the light.

"You choose," Leutherion said, disgusted. "You have never bothered to learn the names of most who follow you, it should be easy enough."

▲▼▲

Accepting prayers for the blackstar was easy in Fagutal. Leutherion and I sat upon a bench near a cave mouth, with a view of the jungle basin below. We kept a bucket between us. People came, singly or in small, furtive groups, and dropped tiny scrolls in. Most were soldiers, who would have of course seen the blackstar for themselves. None spoke, few smiled.

We waited on that bench two days, sleeping in a spare little house that seemed to have been set aside for guesting. The fare consisted mostly of mushrooms and cheeses. I did not inquire as to the source of the milk. There were no fruits nor fowl nor fish as might be hoped for from the vast jungle below.

On the third day, another high-helmeted soldier came with a small force at his back. "You have been invited to resume your journey," he said.

"What of our train?"

"They have been brought down the Second Trail to the lands below. Their provisions have been seen to. They await only your return, and your selection of the one who will stay here and serve our noble Queen Celæno."

It was on my lips to say Osmio, for the little man had done nothing to endear himself to me. But legs-of-the-gong would have been lost—I had marked how they slept curled together—and I conceived of a certain sympathy for the eunuch. Besides which, I might someday be called upon to return him to Queen Sterope.

"I will choose when we are a caravan assembled," I said, imagining that we might perhaps simply get underway. Perhaps the weakly Pincus would prosper here. He had been a palace servant in Cermalus. Or the adventurous Pelletier.

"Of course," the soldier replied blandly. "My men and I will accompany you to assist in your selection."

▲▼▲

This time we walked down winding passages inside the cliff. There were occasional windows, or even natural cracks, that helped me gauge our progress. Otherwise we saw by the light of the torches we bore. The better part of half a mile passed before we reached the bottom.

One of the soldiers carried our bucket of messages. Leutherion would not speak to me. Angered, I suppose, by the penalty the Queen Celæno had laid upon us.

We debouched from a gap in the rock to a high-walled corral made of close-set tree trunks. The jungle rose beyond. The caravan was assembled there, men mounted on our donkeys. I could not see a gate from the enclosure, which was more than passing strange. I realized there were more of Queen Celæno's men atop the walls. Therefore a rampart ran behind those logs.

"This is a trap," said Leutherion. "We are not a fighting force, nor do we carry war or disease in our packs."

"No." Our escort commander's voice was almost sympathetic. "But no one who has stood before the Queen is allowed to once more walk beneath the light. She is blind, you see, and jealous of the eyes of others. As almost all visitors refuse to be blinded, we find it easier to offer a quick, clean death." He stepped back from Leutherion and raised one hand to signal.

Bows appeared all around the wall top.

"Inside!" I screamed. The gong rang loud, the asses whinnied, and the air was full of the buzzing whir of arrows as I sprinted back toward the gap, Leutherion's labored breathing hard behind me.

▲▼▲

I lay panting beneath a spreading bush with leaves the shape of a woman's hand. I still held the hacked stub of a torch with which I had fought. There were eight of us who had escaped. Finnric and Ironpants, and a third soldier whose name I was unsure of, as well as Pincus, myself, Leutherion, and somehow both Osmio and legs-of-the-gong. The Fagutalii soldiers had refused to pursue us into the jungle, so we had not been forced to run far, merely out of sight and range of the arrows.

There were eighteen more dead, including Pelletier and the rest of the guardsmen. We survivors were exhausted and bloody. The reek of smoke from the burning stockade stung my nose, mixed with the roast pork smell of burned flesh. I could at least hope the prayers of three cities had burned and found their way to the blackstar.

It was an ill sign in the heavens indeed.

"I suppose it ends here," I said.

"Ends?" Leutherion dragged himself up on one elbow from where he had been lying. He was missing two fingers on his left hand, but hadn't seemed to notice yet. "No, it does not end." The guard captain leaned close. "I'm going to take you home and hang you for the murdering mountebank you are. And I cannot do that until we find our way out of here and onward to Oppius."

"Do you know where Oppius might lie from here?" I asked sweetly.

"I know," said Pincus.

"Lead on," I told him. "Lead on."

▲▼▲

When Electra was queen in Oppius the messenger of the blackstar came down the river on a greenwood raft, bearing a promise of hope from Heaven and the memory of the smell of smoke.

We tended our wounds and rested in the hottest parts of the day. Had the journey been upriver from the jungles at the foot of Fagutal, we might well have perished. But Pincus' knowledge of geography, gleaned from his work in the cartularium of Halcyone's palace, saved us.

Armed with two spears, three knives and a broken sword, we made our way along the current of the great river through jungles infested with beetles the size of cats and snakes too large for any rational vision of the world. I had never understood how many colors of green there were, either. After the views of the open desert, and the stark world-edge of the cliff at Fagutal, it was almost a relief to travel amid the jungle's close confines.

Even here, the inimical blackstar was a close presence, undenied and undeniable. The violet rays of nighttime colored the sky even by day now, and in those moments when the world fell silent, I could swear it hummed.

Oppius, when we came to it some days into our passage downstream, was a city built upon the water. This jungle river was a wide, slow beast, languorous as the giant crocodiles which lazed upon its banks. We missed the first few houses standing stilt-legged like marsh birds as we passed them in the dawn, but when we came to a larger array of buildings, we took note.

The channel divided and subdivided to flow between rock foundations like stone prows. Other buildings sat, or floated, on great mattresses of logs, or rose in stilts as the little houses did. Rope bridges danced between the islands and islets, and sometimes more substantial structures arched, so that the whole city was an accretion strung from one bank to the other by half a hundred ways and paths. Flocks of birds the color of bright jewels flittered between the building-islands, and green monkeys chattered from the high trees growing out of compounds and courtyards. Waterwheels creaked at all sides, while boys and girls fished from tiny flat-bottomed skiffs, grown men working in the faster shallows with throw-nets.

I fell in love in that moment.

Our raft had the crudest rudder, and responded like a mother-in-law on a wedding night, and so our arrival in Oppius was via a slow but destructive encounter with one of the stone-prowed islets.

Leutherion and legs-of-the-gong were able to pull the rest of us and our few remaining possessions to safety. We all clung to the top of the foundation on a narrow ledge before a white-washed wall. Pincus stared about in awe, Osmio simply closed his eyes and rested, while Leutherion's three remaining men kept their weapons ready.

"We're not assaulting anything today," I said. "They're going to have to come fetch us out."

With some good-natured grumbling, the guards stood down. Children gathered in the river and along the roof of a low structure just across the channel, hooting at us and laughing. It was some time before a man dropped out of the air on a springy rope, a harness about his shoulders, to dangle before us and ask our business. He was nearly naked save for a sort of leather clout, and a matching mask which covered his entire face down to the neck, leaving openings only for his eyes and mouth.

"Take us to your Queen Electra," I said, tired of protocol and the strangenesses of rulers.

Then, by the stars, the eunuch rang his gong. Every bird in the city leapt screaming into the sky at the sound, a colored rain streaming toward the sun.

▲▼▲

The court of Queen Electra was an open yard, surrounded by a three-story palace of bamboo—a wondrous wood thin as a pipe, not much heavier than grass, but seemingly strong as iron. Pools steamed, with that eggs-and-fart smell which indicated hot springs below.

Everything else was people. The queen had furnished her court with bodies. Some were entwined to form couches upon which others lay. Slaves crawled, mobile tables with food and drinks upon their backs.

Men and women stood or were bound in positions of naked receptiveness, used for sexual release or casual amusement as the users continued their conversations with others who stood idly by. The pools were filled with slick, squealing flesh as sport was taken within and beneath the water.

And to think that in Cermalus we believed Oppius decadent for the intimate leather goods that came in trade. The greatest perverts of my home city would have been as bumpkins with goat manure in their hair compared to any of the sybarites writhing in this place.

Our man, spry as a cat but still carrying himself with the authority of age, led us to the center pool. A woman lay in a patch of open water, though many thrashed and groaned nearby. She could have been sister to our Queen Halcyone, young and slim, save she was clothed only in water and sunlight. Her small breasts floated nicely in the water, pink nipples standing just at the surface. The thatch between her legs was the same glossy black as the long hair which spread around her in the pool.

The guide stopped before her and bowed low. "These men asked to see you, Elegance."

She looked from face to face before settling on me. I rubbed my chin stubble, then glanced up at the blackstar glowering dark in the daytime sky.

"Would you join us in our pool?"

My cock voted yes, but after my dealings with Queen Celæno I was loathe to trust anything. It seemed quite possible to me that these men and women at their sport were condemned, or slaves, forced to stay there til they rotted or drowned or expired of expended lust.

"With profound thanks, your Elegance, I must decline. I am on a pilgrimage, bringing a message of hope from the heavens to all seven cities. I am making the Transept."

Osmio and the eunuch had the blessed good sense not to strike the gong, which somehow continued to survive the journey despite all our setbacks.

"No pilgrim has made the Transept in generations," she said, her interest obviously piqued. "We each have our diversions, and some small trade passes from city to city. From the look of you, we would presume you fared poorly in Fagutal."

"Indeed." I was reluctant to criticize Queen Celæno, for I did not know if these women were truly sisters. "Misunderstandings all around, I am afraid."

"Yes. She is ever jealous of those who live beneath the sun." Electra raised her arms and stretched, a pretty sight which nearly cost me all my dignity. "We further presume your message of hope from the heavens did not suit our sister queen's ears."

I tried to regain command of my words, and shift my stance so my ardor would not be so obvious. "That I cannot say, Maj—Elegance. Each must decide for themselves. I say only this: I have been named by Halcyone Queen in Cermalus to be the messenger of the blackstar. I have come to bear away whatever evil or ill that may have befallen your people."

She considered that a moment. "Are you in fact such a messenger? Or only so named?"

Beside me, Leutherion stirred uneasily. I understood his fear. We had done far too poorly for ourselves and our train on this journey.

I tried my best. "I was an ordinary man, Elegance, until the blackstar struck me down. When I rose again, a High Priestess named me messenger, and my queen sealed the epithet. I cannot tell you what to believe, only what I believe."

"Hmm. And how will you carry away our evils, assuming we have any?"

I looked around at falling whips, bodies in chains, children crying bloody-legged in quiet corners, and wondered how to answer that. Habit served. "It has been our custom thus far to take the fears and prayers of the people written on slips of paper, and carry us away with them. We lost our chests to fire at the foot of Fagutal's cliff."

Her voice was soft. "And what do you charge for this wondrous service?"

"We ask only safe passage, Elegance," blurted Leutherion. His voice was heavy, thick with lust.

"See them to rooms in the hyacinth wing," she said to our guide, who had remained crouched at the edge of our conversation. "Except for this brave soldier." She pointed at Leutherion. "I would have him stay and tell me more of his ideas of safety."

I bowed and took my leave, taking my party with me save for Leutherion. My last sight of them was the queen stroking her left nipple and my guard captain standing with his tongue between his lips like some wooden-headed beggar boy.

▲▼▲

Our guide, still nameless, returned in the morning. He did not remark on our reduced numbers, but led those of us who remained down halls with sprung flooring, lined with billowing silk tapestries and strange pieces of riverdrift on little stands, until we were in the queen's court again.

Most of the people were gone. A line of several dozen men and women waited their turn at a frame where someone—Finnric, I realized—was strapped with legs spread wide. I tried not to hear his keening as one at the front thrust violently. There was no sign of Usall, but I had a dreadful suspicion that the nude man floating face down near the queen in her pool was Leutherion.

"Welcome," Queen Electra said.

I knelt again. "Indeed, your Elegance. My thanks for your hospitality."

"And our thanks to you for not abusing our hospitality."

I strained not to glance over at Finnric. "Indeed."

She smiled, sweet as an adder. "We have considered your message. Our people live beneath a canopy of leaves and fog. The blackstar to us is no more or less a cause of panic than the crocodiles in the river, or the illnesses that breed in the slow-flowing swamps. Some die, most live, life continues like the river itself. But we will package our evil safe and sound for you to carry away, as you have so kindly offered. As well we shall grant you a guide, and such supplies as a small expedition might require. Be ready to leave at dawn three days hence."

Bowing low, I thanked her profusely.

▲▼▲

There were girls and boys awaiting us in our apartments, oiled and nude, in ages from scandalously young to maternally old, but I sent them away. We barred our little door, for all the good it would do with these puzzlebox bamboo walls, and set a watch. There was no choice but to eat the food the Oppians brought us. We were fully in their power, but there was little else we could do.

On the third day our guide led us along more bamboo corridors to a landing stage on the downstream side of the palace-island. A sleek, swift boat was tied there. A man sat in the prow wearing a mask much like our guide's, save there were no holes for eyes or mouth. His skin was pale and wrinkled, and he was too still, as if wired in place. There were two fingers missing from his left hand.

I did not need to ask where Queen Electra had set her evil to journey forth with us. There was not enough money under the sun for me to watch him take his mask off.

Panniers of food and gourds of water lined the boat. Unless they meant to poison us, the Oppians had seen us well on our way.

We threw ourselves at the mercy of the current and departed gladly, each alone with his thoughts. As the boat bobbed through the city, the eunuch stroked his gong until it began to hum softly, muted by his knees, the faintest metal tears for what we had left behind.

▲▼▲

When Maia was queen in Palatium the blackstar's messenger came toiling up the slopes from the feverlands, bearing his message of hope.

We spent six days shooting down the river, pulling into mid-current islands or snags at night to rest out the dark while the blackstar's violet light crackled in the sky. Pincus tried to calculate our position as he watched the cliffs march in from the east, at first merely dark lines on the horizon just above the tree tops, then closer and closer.

Our guide at the prow never ate, never slept, never spoke, never pissed. Never moved.

On the morning of the seventh day I had the tiller, while Ironpants tried to spear some fish for the sake of fresh meat—our supplies were in fact plentiful, but ran heavily to cured fruits and fowl. I looked forward to see the guide had lifted his arm and pointed at the east bank.

"Time to put in," I said softly. I steered the boat, while Ironpants and legs-of-the-gong put paddles in to help. Osmio was much too small to do that work, and Pincus had a tendency to dither when action was required. How the man had survived this far was past my understanding.

We cut across the current and found a landing hidden in an inlet, one we would have sped right by without noticing had our guide not pointed us in. I gave silent thanks to Leutherion's shade, which I hoped had found better rest than his body seemed to have done.

From there, the trail was clear enough. Obviously trade came this way with reasonable frequency. Someone had even invested time and effort in improvements to the path. It was two days of dreadful chest tightening, leg-burning climbing to follow the path up the nose of the cliffs. There were little way stations every hour or two, wide spots to pause without clinging to a cliff face or dangling legs over a drop. Only the guide seemed to need no rest, following when we walked, standing immobile as stone when we tarried.

No one wanted to sleep in his presence, but we had no real choice. Still, we kept our night watch, more against him than against any imagined predators.

Eventually the slope gentled out, then I realized my legs hurt less. Ahead the trail came to a sort of wide flat spot, with a low wall in the middle. Anyone besides Osmio could have stepped over the wall, or walked around it easily enough, but I halted our little column and studied it.

The trail continued on the far side, but less worn. Whoever came up here stopped at this point, turned around and went back.

Why?

I looked ahead. There were crags in the distance, a sort of crown atop these cliffs that might have been a city. I turned and looked back. The trail meandered a bit, a stone ribbon on stone, before disappearing below the line of the slope. The jungle basin was visible far below. Wind whipped dry and chilly around me, making little complaints.

"Have people camped here?" I asked.

Ironpants and Pincus wandered about a bit. "Yes," called the guard. "There's a shitpit over here, not well-filled in. There's been more."

I had to admire anyone who went to the trouble of hacking a latrine out of the barren rock.

Pincus came back with some broken iron spikes. "Tent stakes."

"So they come all the way up here, they stop at this little wall which wouldn't slow down a good-sized rat, and they wait...for what?"

"Brass," said Osmio.

The eunuch rang the gong.

▲▼▲

An hour later Osmio spotted two men coming down the path from the other side. We stood on our side of the wall, even the guide. He was beginning to smell up here on the stone, like a raw fish left out too long.

When they arrived, the strangers were clad entirely in brass armor. They showed no skin, no eyes, nothing other than their mobility to mark themselves out from empty metal. The two stopped, paused for about half a minute, then turned and headed back up the path.

I stepped over the wall to follow. One by one my fellow travelers came with me, Osmio scrambling with the aid of legs-of-the-gong. Even the guide came, trailing the rest of us.

It was a strange silent journey toward the crown of crags. There was no huff of breath nor stink of sweat from our two escorts. They were like the guide, wrought in metal instead of leather and flesh. I wished mightily for Leutherion back, in his old self. He had not liked me one bit, but the old guard commander was both sensible and trustworthy. None of my current companions met those two criteria save possibly Ironpants, of whom I simply knew too little.

The crags resolved to walls, albeit crumbling. Palatium was a fortress, pure and simple, though I could not imagine what she had been built to defend. There were no fields around her, no town outside the walls. No roads led to or from.

This was by far the most desolate of the cities I had yet seen.

We passed from chilly sunlight to cold shadow through a shattered gate. The architecture was cyclopean. Great red-brown slabs laid together formed the walls. Other slabs stacked to make the inner halls of the fortress. There was no detail, just gaps for openings and incidental cracks which let a bit more light in. Everywhere was dust, with rubble on the floor save where little paths led from room to room.

The armor escorted us through a good mile of corridors, occasionally passing through narrow stone courtyards. It was a strange sort of maze. I was certain we crossed our own path several times, but eventually we were in the great hall. The place stank like a barn—the first smell of life which had hit my nose since abandoning the river for the heights.

A throne, made of the same huge, crude stones, stood in the middle of the hall. Light from overhead touched the foot of the thing, leaving the queen seated upon it in shadow.

"You come from the river." Her voice creaked and whistled, as if she didn't speak much.

"I come from much further than the river, Majesty," I said.

The gong echoed again. I turned to snap at Osmio and legs-of-the-gong when I realized we were surrounded by the brass-armored men, all silent as the guide.

"Ah," I said, turning back.

"There is no law to protect you here." The queen's voice was sad.

"Are you not the law, Maia Queen in Palatium?"

"No more. There is no law."

"I come…" I began, then stopped. I was tired of the charade, tired of the stupidity and deaths. I wished I was back in Cermalus fixing roofs and dodging beatings from old Tradelium's overseers. "I'm just trying to go home, Majesty, only I seem to be doomed to walk the Transept. Palatium is the fifth of seven cities, and I'd like to see Cermalus again before I die."

"That is an unfortunate wish."

That made me angry. After all I'd run from, fought, and lost, her hopelessness fired my anger. "Where is the law in Palatium, then? Did you burn the books and turn out the judges? Does no one care for custom, or for contract? What became of you that you should discard my life so easily?"

"Don't you speak so to me," the queen snapped.

"Why not!?" I jumped into the light at the foot of her throne. "Who are you to tell me not to speak?"

She stood, and I saw how half her body trembled and shook. Her left eye drooped, and that side of her mouth trembled. "I am queen in Palatium, and I tell you not to speak."

I knelt. "If you are queen then you are the law, Majesty. The law and the judge of the law. As the judge, you are free to choose mercy."

The gong echoed again. I risked a look to one side. All the brass men were kneeling.

"They have not taken a knee since I was struck down," Queen Maia whispered.

"They heed the gong, majesty," I said. "For it rings with a heart of brass. And the gong heeds you." I stood and turned, staring at the eunuch. "Legs-of-the-gong, would you stay here and serve the queen as the master of her brass?"

He stared back at me a while, then turned to Osmio with a puzzled expression. The little man shot me a venomous look before nodding at the eunuch.

"He is yours, majesty. What says the law now?"

She smiled at me, and reached out with her trembling hand. "Go, before I forget myself once more. What is your name, sir?"

"I…" I stopped a moment. Andrade the slave fixed roofs in Cermalus. He did not revive queens in Palatium. "I am the messenger of the blackstar, and I have taken your evil from you."

▲▼▲

We passed into an upland forest, so Pincus called it, populated by tall, narrow trees with needles on high, upswept branches. The tall, dry cliffs gave way to slopes running across our line of travel. Snow and ice gleamed on the heights. The blackstar cast purple shadows, so close none of us dared look skyward.

There was yet a trail here, though not quite so well-kept as the one from the river to Palatium. Still, we did not have to force our way through the underbrush and thistled meadows.

Sullen and bitter, Osmio walked with us. At the last moment he had elected not to stay with legs-of-the-gong. Pincus was happy as a child at festival time, exclaiming over rocks and trees and the most ordinary insects. Iron-pants and I stayed close together but spoke little. The guide trailed behind, his function served, but still presumably carrying the evil of Oppius with him.

Was I to burn him, as the prayers were burnt?

It was a matter of some days before our supplies gave out, but none of us had the least idea what could be eaten in this high country, save the squirrels and birds and woodchucks which we would need a bow to catch. No one thought that eating flowers and leaves would be wise, and the little flashing fish we could snatch out of the pools were so tiny as to mean nothing to our rumbling bellies.

Three days into the hunger, Pincus slipped and tumbled down a raw slope, slamming again and again into rocks until he fetched up against some trees some sixty yards below us.

His cries for help echoed up the mountainside.

Without the eunuch, the duty of a rescue seemed to fall to me or Ironpants. I looked at the soldier. "I'll go get him. You watch for…whatever."

We both knew I meant the guide.

"Bad idea, messenger," Ironpants said.

"I can't leave him!"

"Look at him. He's lying funny. Broken bones for sure. He's already done for. We got no food, the only water is from those streams, you got no way to fix him up even if you do pull him out of there without hurting yourself in the bargain."

I felt horribly sick. "He'll *die.*"

Ironpants shrugged. "We'll die if we try to save him. How many of us have died already? He was a useless man, anyway."

In that moment I hated the soldier. But I hated myself, too, for I knew he was right. We didn't even have a rope. The chances I could climb down there and drag Pincus all the way back up without hurting myself, and him more, were small.

We didn't even have a bow to give him a mercy.

There was nothing to be done. It was the ill luck of the blackstar, taking another of my people.

When Pincus saw us turn to walk on, he began calling, "Messenger, messenger."

My gut roiled hot with shame. My heart was hot iron in my chest. How would I feel in his place? But what could I do for him now?

As we walked, I realized the guide had stayed behind as well.

"Oh, holy hells," I whispered.

"With luck, he'll never catch us," said Ironpants.

Osmio made a sort of barking shriek. "What about me? I'm useless, too. You going to drop me down the next ravine?"

I looked him up and down, tried to think like Ironpants. "You don't eat much, you'll last."

The soldier snickered, I just felt shame.

▲▼▲

When Merope was Queen in Sucusa, the blackstar messenger came to her sore of foot and tired from his travels.

Two days later, my stomach hard and beginning to swell, we came to a grove of enormous trees in which a city was strung. Swaying walkways, platforms high and low, people climbing ropes. It was a bit like Oppius, except built within trees instead of along a river.

We came to what might have been a gate, in the sense that the path slipped between two great trunks growing quite close together some little ways inside the grove. Three lithe women met us there. They wore rough homespun tunics and carried small bows unslung. The one standing in the center set her hand toward me, palm up.

"You are the messenger," she said. There was an odd lilt to her voice.

"Yes."

"You come by the light of the blackstar, walking with the soldier and the fool. Where are the scholar and the dead man?"

There was a question I didn't want to answer. The taste of my choices was still quite bitter in my mouth. I glanced at my traveling companions. Ironpants just looked tired, Osmio had a bitter fire in his eyes. "The scholar fell, and had to be left behind. The dead man stayed to care for him."

"You have strange notions of care in your country," said one of the other women.

The first extended her hand sideways. "Merope Queen will see you."

I dipped my head. "Thank you."

▲▼▲

The queen did not rule from a high bower, as I had expected. Nor did she have some seat of polished timbers amid the center of the grove. No, Merope Queen in Sucusa was crouched among ferns spearing fish in the swift current of a stream when we were brought before her.

Behind her, really.

She stood and scrambled up the bank. Again, she could have been sister to the other queens. Young, lithe, though her skin was berry-brown and her hair the color of walnuts.

"I see some of you are here." Her voice was bright bells.

"How did you know to mark our coming?" I asked.

"Your Transept has been the talk of wanderers for some time. Every trader, tracker and footloose younger son we have seen here of late has mentioned you in some way or another. Did you know that you fly upon a cloud, messenger? And your fool travels in the arms of a giant."

"I did once, Majesty," muttered Osmio. "Messenger boy here gave my greatest friend away."

She cocked her head at the little man. "Was your friend the messenger's to give?" Then, to me: "I have no great brief for you, messenger, nor any against you. Our laws here are simple and just. You will only swear to do no harm while you stay within Sucusa, and you are free here as long as you wish."

That sounded simple enough. But I had seen too much already. "What do you define as harm, that I should avoid, Majesty?"

The queen laughed. "Well spoken, messenger. The obvious sorts of things."

"I will swear willingly not to lift my hand against anyone in your city. But beyond that…if I were to tell the children of your city the strange truths about Fagutal and Oppius, would that be harm? What if I described the hard choice I made when the scholar fell down the mountain? Is that harm? Is it harm to seek the bed of a woman, or a man, here? At what age or time of life may they give consent, and is their consent sufficient in the eyes of your law?"

"Enough, enough," she said. "You see the trap better than most. Though it is not meant for a trap. Rather, if we would not have books of the law binding us like chains, we must rely on the good sense of everyone who dwells here or passes through."

"Then I will swear to use good sense to the best of my ability, but only if you swear to respect and honor my good sense, Majesty."

"Enough swearing," she said. "Go find food, and rest, and when you are ready to speak to me of your purposes, ask after me. Almost anyone will be able tell you where I am. In our city, the queen serves all."

"Good day," I told her.

▲▼▲

Rested and refreshed, I wandered a bit to learn more of this place. Eventually I came across a young man whittling arrows from birch twigs. I spent time watching him smooth them, testing their balance on his finger and rolling them to check the true.

After a time he looked up at me and smiled. His teeth were bright in a face as pale brown as the queen's. "Greetings, messenger. Does my work please you?"

"I find the mastery of craft in others to be fascinating," I said. Both polite and accurate.

"I am scarcely a master, but it is true, my arrows are said to fly well."

"It is no wonder."

He offered me a birch shaft. I tested it as I had seen him do, though the result meant little to me. "How are the winters here?"

He shrugged. "I would not know."

"Really? Why not?"

"We sleep, of course. Don't you?"

"All winter?" I blurted, then wished I hadn't.

"Ask for the heart trees. Someone can show you."

Soon enough, someone did. I found myself down beneath the soil, having passed through a narrow hole between two great roots. A giggling girl stood with me, her fingers brushing suggestively against my thigh. I wanted none of that just now, with a sick dread stealing upon me.

They had hollowed out wells, down amid the root systems of the forest giants. Each was perhaps fifteen feet deep, the walls combed like a beehive, but the cells were large enough for a man to climb into. Barrels of wax and pitch stood ready at the bottom of the wells to seal the sleepers in.

"We dream together," she said. "It is another life. A few stay out each season, to breach us in the spring, but the rest dream together." Her hand slipped inside my tunic, seeking my cock. "You have never known anything of the like."

Horror stained me. I wanted nothing to do with their soulless, inhuman dreaming. I fled up the ladders and out the hole, racing till I found Ironpants.

"We must go," I told him. I was panting, sweating from my run.

"Why?" His voice was mild.

"These people…are not like us."

"Of course not," said Merope, stepping into the little circle of sunlight where we spoke. "No people are like another. How did you find my sister's subjects in Oppius? Or the wall-dwellers in Fagutal? If you want people like you, you must go home and hope they have not changed overmuch in your absence."

I bowed. "It is time for me to go, Majesty."

"Scouts tell me the dead man comes. He bears the scholar on his back." She smiled. I noticed for the first time that her teeth were too many and too small in her face. "Would you not abide for a reunion of your party?"

"They have their own concerns," I said roughly. "I have done no harm here, as we swore. I would find my way to Velia now and finish my Transept."

"And will you take your evil with you?" she asked me softly.

"Evil follows me wherever I go. I am the messenger of the blackstar."

"Then he goes," she said with a nod to Ironpants. Her voice was hard, a blade. "Three women he has bedded here, and in the heat of passion taken each of them in the manner of a boy without their permission or the good sense to use a little grease. They will all pass blood for days yet. And your fool, who asks disturbing questions and tries to incite murder against you. Take him as well. The dead man, too, is your evil. You have my permission to leave once he and the scholar have departed these woods."

She turned and stalked away. A number of her young women, with their little bows, remained close by. The strings were taut this time.

Ironpants shrugged. "We keep walking. It's been months, what's another walk?"

"You...bastard," I said, thinking of the women. "We swore an oath to do no harm."

"They weren't complaining when I shoved it into them. Besides, you don't seem to think they're human. What do you care?"

I lay close to a tree trunk and wept into the moss, wondering when I had become so vile.

▲▼▲

When Taygete was Queen in Velia, the messenger of the blackstar danced out of the night with the soldier, the fool, the scholar and the dead man in his train, coming together to sing the blackstar down.

It was a long hike down and east from Sucusa, bending ever toward the north. Velia lay that way, and beyond it Cermalus should I ever choose to return to the city of my birth. The lower woods were warmer and leafier, with an abundance of game.

The Sucusans had patched my tunic and given me better boots. Osmio had traded the last of his silks for child's leathers. Ironpants still wore his old temple uniform, albeit patched and supplemented with bits gathered along the way. The guide remained naked save for the leather clout and his featureless sack. Pincus...breathed.

He rode now on the guide's back, clinging like a baby scorpion to its mother. His legs were twisted, his flesh slack and pale, and though nude he seemed as human as a spider's egg sac. Only the fact that he yet breathed kept me from grasping hold of Ironpants' spear during some nightwatch and plunging it into his quivering, leathered flanks. Pincus was worse than what had become of Leutherion. I could make a pretense about the guide, forget a few hours at a time who he had been. It was not my choice which had killed him.

But I had abandoned Pincus. Every shuddering breath accused me.

The cruelty of Queen Merope was exquisite.

My only solace was that the blackstar seemed to be finally diminishing. Perhaps it had followed the course of my Transept, giving truth to Queen Halcyone's lies.

We marched on.

This trail was well-traveled. From time to time we saw caravans, hunting parties, adventurers. Even a few foreigners, exotics from beyond the seven cities. These we knew by their skin color—blue-black in one party, fire-red in another—and their strange beasts and stranger dress.

All had heard of us, to be sure. We were marked to be respected and avoided. If they saw us coming, they hid in the woods and left offerings of food, wine, and clothing. If they didn't see us coming, they pulled to one side of the trail and muttered prayers, sometimes tossing coins or flowers as we passed them.

Osmio cursed continuously. Ironpants said nothing that was not strictly necessary. I could not bear to look at the guide or Pincus, so I walked alone.

In time we crossed a gentle ridge. A valley spread wide and shallow, a series of little lakes strung along the small river than ran down it. Autumn was settling upon the trees there, underneath a sky that was almost wholesome once more. A city spread around the lakes, without walls or towers, more a town that went on for a mile or two. There were ruins rising from the middle of three of the lakes, ancient metal towers that gleamed with glass and rust and the afternoon sun.

This must be Velia, I thought. My Transept is done. All I need do is present myself to Taygete the queen, then I could go die of shame in some lowlife tavern. I stopped, turned to my companions. "You are released from any obligation to me. Go find your own interests among your own kind."

Osmio never stopped cursing, just kept walking without a backward glance.

Ironpants hefted his spear. "Figure I'll go see who's hiring. I'd never be able to explain *him* back home." He jerked his chin toward the guide. "Try not to get anyone else killed. Including yourself."

The soldier loped down the trail toward Velia, quickly passing Osmio.

I reached out and with trembling hands touched the guide's hood. The leather was wet, rotten, and the brush of my fingers raised a horrid stench. "I release you, too, old friend," I said softly. "Care for Pincus, and when he's done see that his death is decent. It's what I should have done. For both of you."

Slowly I set off downhill for Velia, taking care not to overtake Osmio.

▲▼▲

There were no gates nor guards, so I wandered quiet streets a while. Eventually I worked up the courage to ask a woman where I might find the palace of Queen Taygete. She looked at me as if I was foolish, then sent me to the next lake upstream.

I found the ruined metal in mid-lake was in fact the palace. The people on the waterfront gave me odd glances as well, but one man said, "You're that messenger, ain't you?"

"Yes."

He scratched at his bald scalp, then tugged a drooping moustache. "I can row you out there, I reckon. If you don't want to just swim."

The sun was sloping into the afternoon, and I really didn't wish to get wet. "Please, if you'll just drop me."

"Ain't nothing there no more," he said pleasantly. "But if you've got the hankering, why, you're the messenger."

As he rowed I looked up at the sky. The blackstar was gone, for the first time in many months. "Where did it go?"

"Figured you'd know," said the boatman. "You being the messenger and all. She was still up there this morning."

I climbed out of the boat on a metal landing, and realized I had nothing to tip the boatman with save the clothes on my back. Even the coins and oddments of the trail seemed to have been lost to me.

"I would offer you my blessing…" I began.

"No." He smiled. "You just go on."

Inside the hallways were metal—floor, wall and roof. Everything was wet, rotting, damp, with mold blossoming in a hundred colors muted by the deep shadows. I wandered a while as the light failed, before finding myself on a balcony high up the wall in a open chamber with a great chair at the center.

Not open, I corrected myself. There was a glass roof.

The chair was on a dais made of seven six-sided figures linked together. Much like the cells in the ground at Sucusa, but laid sideways instead of vertically. I climbed down a rusted ladder and walked up to the throne. Each of the hexagons had a clear cover. There was a sort of cushion within, hoses, little buttons. A tiny cell of a different sort.

Queen Taygete lay curled on the big chair. She looked to have died very young, and had since become a sort of leathery corpse. I could see how her face resembled her sisters. I wondered if she had come out of a seventh cell beneath this throne.

Were they better off in Velia, ruled by a dead queen? No kindness, no cruelty, the law being whatever made sense to the people. I did not know.

"You freed him, you know."

Looking up, I saw Osmio on my balcony.

"I should not be so angry," the little man said. "Legs-of-the-gong is happy now." He turned and vanished.

I waited to see if anyone else would appear. Who, though? Ironpants was off drinking and whoring. As far as I knew, Pincus and the guide were in the woods finishing what they should have done long ago— becoming honestly, truly dead.

Would that I could speak to the High Priestess back in Cermalus. I had taken her for a fat fool, but I now suspected she knew a lot more than I'd ever realized. Maybe this had all been my miracle, the blackstar and my journey of the Transept. Maybe it had been the queens' miracle. Maybe no one's at all.

I sat thinking a while at Taygete's feet before I finally fell asleep.

In the morning someone had left three apples and some cheese near me. I put one apple on the throne for Taygete and ate the rest. As the day grew older in the glass roof above me, blessedly clear of the black-star, the boatman came climbing down the balcony with two young men following him.

"They been fighting, messenger," he told me. "Won't stop. Over a girl. I told 'em you'd give a fair judging, being as how you don't know no one involved."

Hope, I thought. This man finds hope in me.

Maybe that's what the blackstar meant. Place your hope in what you don't know. I'd done the Transept after all, first in generations. Maybe I'd found wisdom.

I could only hope.

"Tell me about the girl," I said.

Both young men began yelling at once.

The Leopard's Paw

There is a fine line between pastiche and parody. I'm honestly not sure which side of that line this story lies upon, but my channeling of Robert E. Howard worked well enough to see this into print at Subterranean Online. *At any rate, this piece was smashing good fun to write.*

Standing against a deafening roar, Jacob Ervin slammed his fists, hardened weapons as powerful as any product of the metalsmith's art, into the head of the leaping cat. Fangs longer than his index finger brushed so close to his face that he could smell the rotten meat on the creature's breath. But his shattering blow had done its work. The head was already stove in.

He moved quickly, unsheathing his ancient poniard. The weapon kept a marvelous edge that belied the brutish neglect of its late owner. Ervin worked the point in under the sabretooth leopard's front right shoulder and gutted the beast in one great swoop. Long practice in the woods of Colorado stood him good stead under the alien sun as he skinned the cat.

The meat he abandoned for the carrion eaters already circling close. Let the hyenas and the vultures have it. Ervin had taken his trophy in single combat, a fair fight of muscle against muscle, backed by a superbly trained human intellect set against highly evolved predatory instinct. He could afford to be generous to those who would someday clean his own bones.

Carrying the bloody hide, he smiled into the glare of the setting sun. It would be a long run to his current camp, but the moon was rising and the smell of the cat upon him would ward off all but the most foolhardy animals.

▲▼▲

He spent the next few days scraping and curing the hide. Ervin had picked this particular cave for his campsite because of the saline deposits nearby. He was not sure which of the local plants would be a good source of tannin, so he'd fallen back on the old frontier method of salt-curing. The thing stunk enough to bother even his prodigiously indifferent nose, but Ervin stayed the course.

This sabretooth leopard was key to his plan to enter the lost city of Redwater.

The Borgan tribal king had broken his word to Ervin. Betrayed by a savage! No American man could stand for such treatment, not if he wanted to look himself in the mirror again. Not that Ervin had seen a mirror since coming to this world, but the principle was the same.

The mountain-walls to the north were a boundary to everyone save those black buzzard-men who raided all the local tribes. He had yet to find a way across the rocky barrier, but he would. In the meantime, Ervin needed to settle his position among the savages once and for all. He had no ambition to be their king, but neither would he be subject to their whims and foolish taboos.

The leopard was coming along nicely. He'd boiled the skull, for the sake of being too hurried to bury it. Ervin had never chanced to study the taxidermist's art, but he had some notion of what he was about. He'd already set aside a pair of opals stolen from the Borgans to use for the leopard's eyes. Shame that he had no flashlight or other way of making them glow from within. Now that the skin was drying under its load of salt, Ervin worked on the wicker frame that would make it stand out from his body. This would transform him into a great cat padding through the night.

Redwater was where the last temple of the leopard priests had stood, before the savages had rebelled and thrown them down amid fire and blood. The curses laid upon that benighted place were legendary. But curses meant nothing to a man as hard-driven and unforgiving of self as Ervin was.

▲▼▲

A week to the day after he had hunted and killed the great predator, Jacob Ervin was ready to wear its pelt. The Borgans and their fellow tribes believed that the leopard priests had been skin changers, walking the night with claws and fangs to punish the disloyal and slay the unwary. Ervin knew the secret of skin changing right enough—it was here in his hand.

He slipped the wicker frame across his shoulder and lashed the legs to his upper arms. The skull fell down over his forehead, while he had left the skin of the neck open to provide additional concealment as it dangled. The leopard's pelt was heavy, but he knew the aspect he presented to any man or beast watching was ferocious.

Ervin padded into the night, using a sort of crouched run he had practiced. It was as close as he could get to the bounding gait of one of the great cats, but he reckoned that not many were going to stick around to criticize his errors.

Only a man could stand against the leopards of these hills, and not many men at that.

He made his practice run by night, to avoid betraying details out of place. Tall grass which Ervin the man could simply look over swatted Ervin the leopard in the face. A real cat would have stopped and sat up, or maybe taken a great leap, but neither was an option for him. He cursed the slashes the sharp plant blades opened in his skin, but kept running. He was not a man to shirk or set aside a task once committed to it.

Jacob Ervin was a near-perfect specimen of human development. His physique had been the envy of anatomists at the university in Boulder when he attended college, before all the trouble started. But the human body is not designed to run long distances bent double, especially not with forty pounds of wicker and hide pressing down upon it.

By the time he reached the little creek which marked the edge of what Ervin thought of as his front yard, his hips were like to kill him, and his hands were bloody from supporting his weight. He knew he'd need to take a few days to let the palms heal, and make some sort of hand-shoe. Running gloves.

He stopped to drink, careful to bend down and lap like a cat, his face to the water.

When he looked up from his refreshment, Ervin saw another sabre-tooth leopard watching him carefully from the other bank, not ten feet distant. An easy pounce for such a creature.

This was peril indeed! His poniard was back in his cave-camp. With the wicker bound to his upper arms, Ervin could not throw the bone-crushing punch he'd used to kill the cat from which he'd taken the skin. That had been a carefully-set ambush, too, baited with a wounded antelope staked out and crying. He had been at his most prepared.

If the other cat leapt now, he was dead. By God, he'd show it a thing or two! Ervin tilted his head back and roared, the astonishing projective power of his massive lungs creating an unholy screech that woke the night-roosting birds amid the nearby reeds.

The other cat roared back at him, then turned to pad off into the moonlight.

Victory, even without force of arm, was still victory. Ervin's steps were lighter on the way back to his fire, though he took more care with his hands, avoiding the tall grass as much as possible.

By damn, he *was* the leopard, wasn't he? Sometimes a man had to allow himself a little pride, he thought.

▲▼▲

Six days later, at the new moon, Ervin stood on a ridge and looked down upon his goal. Redwater's cyclopean ruins were no more than bulking shadows by starlight. The river that threaded out of the shattered city was a darker line amid the black grass.

Ervin had brought his leopard skin here by travois, two day's march. It had taken him the days between to heal his hands and make the hand-boots. Now he shrugged his way into the wicker frame with practiced ease, lacing the arm stays. He saved the hand-boots til last. He was rather proud of the leopard spoor he'd worked in the palms.

Now, he thought, to the city.

The Borgans had believed with a passion that no man walking upright could enter Redwater. It was surrounded by curses, and everyone knew the ghosts of the leopard priests had the cold jealousy of the dead. Ervin himself had seen three Borgan youths race toward the walls in broad daylight, passions aflame with dares and counter-dares, before dropping dead in the grass. Older warriors had crawled in upon all fours to drag them forth.

The boys had no marks upon their bodies.

He reasoned that while the idea of a curse was plain foolery, it was possible some strange weapon from the ancient days existed within the ruins. Perhaps it threw a line of force at the height of a running man's beating heart. Perhaps it knew the shape of a man, through the workings of some dimly clever electromechanical eye. The Borgans and their brother tribes were charmingly primitive and downright obtuse, but it was clear enough to Ervin that an industrial civilization had once stood here.

Someone had the means to raise the great slabs which comprised the ruins of Redwater, after all. It would take more than crowds of slaves to do such work.

By going crouched within the skin of a leopard he would twice over fool whatever defenses lurked within. Further, if the Borgans were spying on him as they so often did when he descended from his solitary hills, they would see him go in as a leopard. To be known to those savages as a skin changer could only stoke their fear of him. That in turn would build respect in their simple minds, and give Ervin the freedom of action he required for his longer-term plans.

He slunk through the grass, moving in his best approximation of a leopard's loping bound. The hardest part of this rig was seeing right before him. He accomplished this by tossing his head and looking beneath the fearsome teeth which framed the opening in front of his face.

The walls were close before him. Ervin's sense of direction had not betrayed him. The hand-boots were saving him great trouble and pain as well.

He loped onward, through the massive gates which had stood unbarred for three generations since the downfall of the city.

▲▼▲

The streets were paved, which was strange for this world. Few went mounted and there were no carts or carriages here, let alone motorcars. Stranger still, the pavers were hexagonal. The effect was that of running across a vast stone honeycomb.

Ervin's goal was to steal the leopard's paw. It was the most sacred relic of the leopard priests. Legend said that the attack on the city had failed to breach the great temple, which was defended by skin changers. The Borgans and their temporary allies had burned out the city instead before retreating as the curse was laid down.

He reasoned that the paw would still be inside the temple. The priests were certainly dead, and their savage cult with them. There had been not so much as a balefire inside Redwater since the city was destroyed. With the widespread belief in the curse, no one would have come to steal it. With the leopard's paw in his hands, Ervin could bring the tribes to his word. Not to mention extract satisfaction from the troublesome Borgans.

He found his way to the center of the city, stopping only for the briefest glimpses from beneath his mask. The streets were clear at the centers but the verges were a jumble of rubble and dirt. Redwater seemed to be built on a radial plan. This was just as he had expected from looking at the city from a distance. Not to mention being consistent with the psychology of a religious center.

Running on all fours, Ervin found that he was more adapted to the curious gait. He trusted his finely-honed body to meet any challenge required of it. This was near his limits, though. He was pleased how well he was settling in.

Let the Borgans fear the leopard!

Soon enough he was in the central plaza. The dim light of the moonless night meant the temple bulked large as if it were new-built. It was difficult to see the signs of ruin here.

He bounded up the wide, shallow steps toward gaping black maws which had once been doors. Inside he would shed the skin and move deftly on two feet, as man was meant to. Ervin paused at the top of the steps, turned to face the empty city, and on an impulse released a great roar which echoed over the stone rooftops.

Much to his surprise, there was an answer to his challenge from nearby.

His blood ran hot. His vision flashed red a moment, while the hair on his body stood up. Once more he was confronted with a true leopard while unprepared to fight like man or beast! He had not considered that the scene by the creek might repeat itself.

There was nothing for it but to roar out his challenge once more.

This time the animal trotted into the square. The creature was a lighter shadow in the inky pools of blackness. He could see it pause, settle onto its haunches and issue another mighty challenge. The cat was insolent, he would give it that.

Then it leapt forward, racing up the stairs. Ervin stood to meet it and found he could not. The wicker and the pelt bound him too tightly. He snarled and hurled himself down the stairs on all fours, tail lashing.

The two sabretooth leopards collided in a snarling ball of fur and claws and teeth. They rolled back down into the plaza, each seeking a grip on the other's throat. Ervin slashed with his claws, laying open his attacker's flank. Then he realized what was happening.

He had *become* the leopard.

Skin changer indeed.

Even in another body, his spirit was a finely-honed weapon, his intellect dedicated to fine and brutal arts of combat. His muscles seemed to know what was wanted of him in this new form. His human self within did not know how to lose. Someday, when death claimed him at sword point or bloody-toothed, Ervin would die winning.

She (for he was suddenly all too keenly aware that the other was leopardess) caught her foreclaws in his chest. His great back legs came into play and he hooked her in the belly.

They rolled again to fetch up against the broken base of some fountain. He snapped at her neck, just missing, as she tried to wiggle out of his hold. Then she bit at him, catching the skin.

Their muzzles nearly touched in an eerie feline imitation of a human kiss. With that thought he found himself in his own form once more. The sensation of the change was elastic and electrifying, much like the touch of arcane scientific forces which had first projected him to this world.

Was skin changing nothing more than some ancient weapon? Perhaps the same which imposed the strictures of the curse.

In that same moment the leopardess writhed and changed to a woman. She was voluptuous, with bosoms each bigger than the span of his outstretched hand. Her female form was completely unclothed save for a bath of sweat and blood from the scratches he had laid upon her.

As distracting as her scent and proximate nudity might be, Ervin did not for a moment lose sight of the fact that they had just been fighting a battle to the death. He pinned her, his strength in human form far superior to her distaff physique.

"You have the advantage of me, ma'am," he growled, some trace of the leopard's roar still in his voice.

"You are the outlander," she replied.

"Jacob Ervin, at your service."

She thrust her groin against him. "Truly?"

"Later, perhaps." He grinned. Ervin was not a man to be distracted by the rushing of blood to his nether parts. "Why did you seek to kill me?"

"It was you who gave challenge."

"Truce?"

She nodded. "Truce."

They both stood, stretching sore and wounded muscles. Ervin's own carefully constructed wickerwork and hide was shredded. The woman seemed to have nothing but her skin. She also possessed the refreshing unselfconsciousness of the primitive. Her beauty was clothing enough.

"It is my plan to go within and retrieve the leopard's paw," he told her. "Are you set on stopping me?"

"I am afraid I cannot allow that," she said.

"Why do you defend this place? It is nothing but dead stone and ashes."

She shrugged. "Why do you attack it?"

"Because those who care about it are too craven. I would make them an example of my courage."

"Then be brave," she said. She touched the bottom of his chin. "Do not throw away your life, Jacob Ervin."

He stepped back, admiring her sweat-slicked form gleaming in the starlight. Had there been a moon this night he might have seen every curve and fold of her glorious body, but this was enough. Ervin thought he understood who this woman was.

Turning away from her, he ignored his own turgidity. She would follow or not. He would deal with her or not. His hearing was as superb and finely honed as the rest of his physique, and so he listened as his foot touched the first step.

There was a sort of rustle. She was returning to form.

A second step, and he heard a rush of air as she sprung off her back feet.

A third step, and he knew she would drop to bite the back of his head, as these cats did.

Ervin spun around, swinging his mighty fist at the spot in the air where he knew her skull must pass. She snapped her great fangs, her breath hot and close enough to fill his nose, but the blow of his hammer hand broke her skull.

The leopardess collapsed into the steps in a steaming heap. She kicked twice, then melted, fading to old bones and tattered fur.

"No clothing, no fur," he told the corpse as it receded through the generations of time back toward the sacking of the city. "A man needs scraps to become a leopard. But when a leopard becomes a man, well... You should have been less quick to fight."

Such a waste, he thought. She had been beautiful in both her forms.

He turned his attention to the temple, stepping into the shadows within to search for the leopard's paw.

▲▼▲

Dawn found him walking from the ruins of Redwater upright as a man should. The leopard's paw was heavy in his hand. It was a large nugget of gold, roughly in the shape of its namesake, with three white crystals where the claws might be.

His greater treasure, though, was the weathered skull he'd found on the bottom of the temple steps when he exited. She had aged her years in dying, and so this bone was three generations old. But when Ervin raised his standard and took the tribes north to make war against the buzzard men from beyond the wall, the leopardess would watch over him.

A shame, he thought. He should have sampled her kiss when he had the chance. Ervin was certain he'd never meet her like again.

He turned, looking at the city as it rose in dawn's red glare, and gave one last, echoing roar. Thanks, apologies, tribute to a fallen foe. It was of no real account. Only the next battle mattered.

Coming for Green

When we were putting together this collection, Bill Schafer requested that I provide an original work of fantasy and an original work of science fiction. Green *has been much on my mind, being my trade hardback release for 2009 when we were assembling this collection. Additionally, I'd been working on* Endurance, *the sequel to* Green. *I had some extratextual material from* Green *that I'd been wanting to find a way to use, to bring another view of the world into play. That source material eventually became this story. Interestingly, my insights into the character of* Green *from this piece had a significant influence on the way I framed her in* Endurance.

Samma stared at the water knifing off the bow of the coastal trader *Atchaguli*. The edged curl of white reminded her of the way skin split beneath a blade, lips of flesh curling back in blooded shock. So this ship opened the skin of the ocean.

"Morbid, morbid." She shook off the reverie to look up at the shore passing close by. The little ship's captain—a gross ape of a man, named Padma—ran them along a channel between the mud banks half a mile out to sea and the close-set tangle of vines, trees and narrow-mouthed creeks that made up the shore on their left.

Portside.

Why these sailors couldn't call everything by its proper name was beyond her. They had to have a special word for everything. Except Lily Blades. *Captain* Padma had been quite clear on who and what a Lily Blade was when Mother Vajpai had approached him in that dreadful dockside tavern back in Kalimpura, Samma trailing in her wake.

"I meant no offense," he'd whined, sidling away from his table. Samma's purpose there had been to listen, but she let him see the hilts of her knives. In truth, all any sane person needed to see of Mother Vajpai was the set of her eyes.

"Your offenses are not my concern." The older woman's tone made it quite clear they could *become* her concern at any time. And so the two had bargained for a while, buying passage for Samma (that she did not wish to take) to sail searching for news of the fate of the girl Green (whom she did not wish to find).

"Reluctance is your armor," Mother Vajpai had said to her that midnight on the docks. "Too many of your elder sisters have been thoroughly charmed by that one. Still, the Lily Goddess cares for Green."

"She was my bedmate for a long time," Samma said quietly. "We were each other's firsts. I know her charms quite well, and also how thoughtlessly cruel she can be. I don't wish Green ill, but I hardly wish her back among us."

"The greatest good comes from the greatest trouble. Cooperation rarely transforms." Mother Vajpai laid her arms on Samma's shoulders. "You know her best. Furthermore your long absence will be less remarked."

Samma knew she could be most easily spared from among the Lily Blades. She was painfully junior, generally deemed too reflective for decisive action, and not nearly so gifted at sheer violence as Green. The girl had always been positively supernatural in her power and ferocity.

"In any case," Mother Vajpai continued, "you are not expected to drag her back in chains. You are only to learn what those pirates with whom Green sailed away have done with her."

Or what Green might have done to the pirates, more to the point.

"We are giving you a rich purse. Utavi of *Chittachai* is the sort of man whose fear of us will wane with the leagues, as his own greed waxes. Use the funds for him and him alone." She'd passed over a small leather bag that was strangely light.

Under her questing fingers, Samma realized it contained not coin, but gems. This was so very strange. She broke one of her own rules and questioned the orders. "Why, Mother? Why not just let her go?"

Mother Vajpai would not meet Samma's eye, which gave the girl all the answer she truly needed. Still, her words were curious: "Because Green has passed beyond the view of the Lily Goddess, and there are those in Kalimpura who find themselves with a powerful need to know her fate."

"Mother Meiko," Samma whispered without thinking.

"I should chide you for speculating on this," said Mother Vajpai sadly, "but sooner chide the moon for setting in the west. And to no greater effect."

"So I am to find her, and simply report back."

A long, slow sigh, followed by words chosen with obvious and pains-taking care. "If you find her, you may *invite* her to return with you."

The Lily Goddess wants her back. Despite Green's banishment from Selistan for her manifold misdeeds. She had grown very still at the thought. The Goddess wanted something with Green, and Mother Vajpai was not going to tell Samma what that was. Nor was Samma to bring her back, only to *invite* her. That smacked of magic, or legalisms, or both.

"What if I do not find her," she finally asked.

Mother Vajpai's voice was as final as a dropped stone. "Keep looking."

"Yes, Mother," Samma had said miserably.

Now she was aboard *Atchaguli*, a miserable wallower of a vessel which could turn a surprising speed at need but for the most part crept from muddy beach to muddy beach to trade squalor for more squalor. Samma wasn't sure if she had more to fear from the random violence of the sea or the mindless thuggery of Padma and the three of his cousins who crewed this boat.

"Mistress."

Samma jumped, recalled to the present moment by the too-close voice and hot breath of Aiko, Padma's youngest sailor, who stood imme-diately behind her.

He could have slain me, she realized. *I let him inside my guard.*

"The stew is ready," Aiko added.

What was frightening about this one wasn't that he was a self-centered idiot—in Samma's experience, all boys were—or that he was a murderer in the making—again, like all boys—it was that Aiko fancied himself quite the ladies' man. He appeared to consider his sexual conquest of Samma to be inevitable.

She followed him to the little hearth just below the bow platform. The stew smelled abominable. None of these men could cook. Neither could Samma. So mostly they put in bits of whatever they had and boiled it to the point of slime, then hoped for the best.

Somehow, she was certain that Green had eaten well on *her* voyage.

▲▼▲

Whatever Padma had been running from did not materialize off the stern, and soon after they ate, the captain had put *Atchaguli* out into deeper water through a channel in the mud banks, moving at a more leisurely pace. He called Samma up to the wheel with him.

She went reluctantly. Aiko was a buffoon, but Samma could tap the boy out any time she needed to. Fatally or otherwise. Padma was larger, cannier and mean. Sooner fight Mother Gita back in Kalimpura than tangle with this man's long, strong arms.

Still, he was the master of this vessel, and the one Mother Vajpai had chosen to convey her on this mission.

Trust, always it is about trust. Samma had trusted Green when she shouldn't have, in their early days together at the Temple of the Lily Goddess. And later she hadn't trusted Green when she *should* have, when the foreign girl had grown difficult and dangerous, only to be pushed away by those who ought to have loved her best.

Including Samma.

She just didn't see how there was a lesson of trust to be learned from this fool Padma.

The captain sat on the steersman's bench with his hand braced upon *Atchaguli*'s tiller. He was dominated by his moustache, which had colonized his face like a fungus covering a tree trunk. His cheeks were rounded almost to puffiness, folding into his eyes until they glinted like raisins in a suet pudding. Dark hair swept away from his forehead in a manner doubtless intended to be dramatic. Samma thought he looked as if he should have worn a hat before going out into the wind.

"Hello, pretty girl." Padma always called her that, aboard ship. He'd been nervous and fearful on the docks of Kalimpura, but here at sea where his word was literally law, Padma fancied himself a big man.

Samma knew what happened to big men at the point of a knife— the same thing that happened to men of any size, if the knife was fast enough. "Captain." She steeled herself for the usual evasions. "Any news on *Chittachai*?" No word had come of the vessel in the months since Green's departure.

Padma grinned. "Captain Utavi's brother's wife's cousin sells palm oil and hardwoods where we are soon to come. They may know of him."

That was the first positive word she'd heard in the two weeks since Padma's assurances to Mother Vajpai had faded with their departure from Kalimpura. "The coast is not so large," she said softly.

"Hundreds of leagues from Kalimpura to Cape Dulai." His grin widened, gold teeth flashing. "And then there is the north coast."

One thing that Samma had already learned was that for a man with a small ship, the Selistani coast was infinitely long. She despaired of finding *Chittachai* before someone aboard *Atchaguli* got ideas too big for her knives. The fierce reputation of the Lily Blades fell miles further behind her with every passing hour.

▲▼▲

Late that afternoon they eased into a shadowed harbor. The little bay was protected by a spit of land dotted with palms and heavy shrubs, so that someone standing even a bit offshore might never even know the anchorage was there.

Half a dozen fishing boats were drawn up on a muddy strand—more vessels than she'd seen in one place since they'd left Kalimpura. More to the point, a ship was moored to the single decaying dock. It was nearly twin to *Atchaguli*, a fat-bellied, single-masted coastal trader with a lateen rig—she had been learning more of the sailor's words. A set of louche eyes glowered in faded paint along the prow. She had once been red with yellow trim, but was mostly now the color of old wood.

Somehow, in the fading light of day, the battered little ship looked exquisite, romantic even. Samma noted from the lack of smoke or screaming that Green was likely not aboard, assuming this was *Chittachai*. She resisted the urge to ask Padma. The captain thrived on such small power plays.

More to the point, he seemed neither surprised nor alarmed at the sight of the other vessel.

The knife of water was gone from the bow, replaced by a slow, syrupy ripple so green it was almost black. Pale fish lounging just below the surface flicked away from *Atchaguli*'s progress, leaving faint trails behind them. Great trees spread wide over the edges of the harbor, and stole the sun early from the western horizon. Samma might have enjoyed the cool shadows if she'd been here under other circumstances, but mostly she saw the rise of biting flies in the evening dark, and a mean collection of shacks and hovels above the old dock. Those signified only more copies of Padma, Aiko and the rest.

As if summoned by her thought, the boy appeared. "You will regret missing me," he said with a theoretically winning smile.

"I will regret many things," Samma said. "But if I aim for you, I *will* not miss." She wasn't the fighter Green was—few were, or could hope to be—but she could account for herself well enough, and was a dab hand with a thrown knife. "Missing you will never be among my regrets."

He frowned, trying to puzzle out the insult, then Padma was shouting for the crew to bring *Atchaguli* to the dock.

▲▼▲

Utavi was a skinny, sour man with a heavy Bhopuri accent and a deep suspicion of Samma. "You're one of *them*." He spat into the water.

"I found her on the docks in Kalimpura," said Padma helpfully.

Samma could hear the smile in the captain's voice, but she would be damned if she would take her eyes off Utavi. The man looked ready to fight. They hadn't even made it to shore—darkness had fallen upon them meeting on the pier.

The locals were scarce, too, she noted.

"That damned Mother send you after me?" Utavi demanded.

"Mother Vajpai charged me to find you," Samma replied. This would not be easy, she knew. Wherever Green was, her old lover and enemy was not *here*. Not with Utavi behaving this way.

"You might be a trick. Some chit dressed up in those leathers they wear." He glanced past her, at Padma just beyond Samma's right shoulder. "Where did you really find her?"

She stole a glance of her own, while Utavi's attention was distracted.

The other captain was where he should be, and none of his cousin-crew were poised to jump her.

Good. Still, she eased a knife into her palm.

"Look," said Padma, "the hummingbird has a sting. If you don't believe me, try her yourself."

"Don't be a fool," urged Samma, but she knew the words were a mistake as soon as they left her lips. Utavi took that as a challenge.

"If you are truly one of those bladed women, then you know how to fight." He whistled loudly, then shouted, "Tullah!"

The man who clambered up onto the dock from their deck was bigger than Mother Adhiti, so heavy that the ship rocked behind him even as the boards beneath his feet groaned and popped. His head was small, his face a baby's over narrow, round shoulders, but his body sloped outward from there like the bottom half of a calabash. His arms became huge, and each fist was bigger than the two of Samma's. Likewise his legs, trunks that ended in enormous feet that would have kept him standing in the face of a typhoon. His skin was winter-pale and slick, and he wore only a length of dirty canvas wrapped around his waist and up between his legs.

This was *not* how Samma had intended to meet the man who captained *Chittachai*. Not by fighting some troll on his behalf.

How would Green have handled this, she wondered.

Green would have done something outrageous—stripped off her leathers or attacked Utavi or dove into the harbor—before making one of those strange leaping kicks only she could do. Samma would need to rely on doggedness and solid training, and the nearly-confident assurance that none of these bumpkins knew their way around a fight.

"Come along, big man," she said to Tullah in her softest voice. Samma didn't do sweet very often, but this one might react to it.

The giant looked at his captain in obvious confusion. Utavi nodded, then stepped away to leave them alone on the darkening dock. Helpfully, someone to her left lit a torch.

That only served to make her eyes ache briefly as shadows scattered. Tullah flinched as if he'd been hit.

If she were fighting for real, Samma would have gone right for his knees. He was too damned tall to go for the throat, not at her height, but he would fall like an undermined tree. She already knew this fight to be a set-up, though. She would have to find a way to defeat him without humiliating herself or her opponent, if she hoped to get any further with Utavi. This was as bad as one of Mother Vajpai's teaching traps.

Samma flicked her fingers, beckoning the giant toward her. In the same motion she leaned forward, to keep her balance but also to distract him with the curve of her breasts—men could not help looking at such things.

A giggling snort erupted from her left—Aiko, surely—but Tullah was prudish. He stared above Samma's head and slightly away as he advanced toward her with a sliding shuffle. Those great meat-sides he had for hands quivered before him.

This horrible giant is supposed to make me run in fear, she realized. Samma knew she had been right not to hurt him in the first move. No side-strike to the knee, nothing to the groin. This called for something flashy, something which would count with these rough men, however much the teaching Mothers might despise putting on a show.

She danced to his left, toward the center of the dock. That would draw Tullah to face the torch which some fool had just lit.

"Take him!" someone shouted from behind her. Not Aiko.

Tullah circled as expected, now squinting into the torchlight. He shuffled slowly, obviously confused. Samma wasn't sure he knew how to close and grapple—who would ever have sat still long enough to let him learn?

Time to play it like Green would have.

She sprang up to the top of one of the supporting posts of the pier, landing with balanced heels. The wood shivered beneath her weight, but Samma did not give the post time to reconsider its position. She kicked off hard with her left foot, bring her right up to aim a solid touch with all her weight behind it in the center of Tullah's chest.

A very, very dangerous move against even a slightly competent fighter. Someone of any quickness could grab her ankle and break it, or control her with the threat of that. Samma banked on Tullah's size slowing him down.

He swatted her aside like a drover confronting a horsefly. A great groan arose from the two crews as she spun and barely managed a controlled landing. Samma rolled across the pier and fetched up at Utavi's feet. *Chittachai*'s captain jumped back as if snake-bit.

Her back twinged but this was no time for pain. Nor was it a moment for grace and subtlety, not if he was going to hit her like *that*. She sprang to her feet, spat at the captain, then turned to run the four steps and cannon shoulder-first into Tullah just below his crotch, at the top of his thighs.

As she'd expected, he moved to cover his penis. His arms folded down. That put him off balance. Samma grabbed his knees and pulled toward her, butting her head into his gut where she might have gone for the chin of a smaller opponent.

Tullah swept forward with all the grace of a toppling wall. Samma rolled out from under before he hit the dock so hard two planks cracked loudly in succession. He lay there for a moment, then began to sob.

She found her feet once more. The world wavered and her head felt strange. A few of the mixed crew called out appreciatively.

"You are one of them," Utavi said sullenly. "Fierce women with no sense of how to hold themselves in."

Samma was not so fierce that she would let this enormously oversized child lie there and weep. She knelt to pat his shoulder.

"Up, big man," she whispered. "I can teach you to use your strength if we should chance to spend time together."

He rolled his tiny head sideways and looked at her with eyes the color of slate. "Tullah fight."

"Tullah fight." Samma helped him to his feet.

With her hand still on the giant's arm, she turned to Utavi. "Will you now believe I am who I claim? And you will cede me my right to know of Green's fate."

Chittachai's captain looked around at the mixed crews gathered near. Samma followed his gaze. Padma smirked. Aiko appeared stunned—smitten or terrified, she couldn't tell which. The rest shared a common amazement.

None of them had believed her. Not *Atchaguli*'s crew, not *Chittachai*'s, even though they'd known Green. She could have cried with frustration, saved from tears only by her own anger.

"Please," said Tullah.

In that moment, Utavi looked away with flushed face. Samma knew another secret, one she wished she hadn't.

"We'll take you where she is," the captain said roughly. "But you'll pay for your passage or work it like anybody else. Then you can talk to that girl yourself. She and her pet cat were never worth the damned trouble."

He turned and shouldered past the torch-holder toward the cluster of buildings on shore. One by one the crews followed him, Aiko lingering for a last, long glance at Samma, until she was alone in the moonlit darkness with the weeping giant.

His mouth was wrinkled, dark and toothless as he smiled at her. "Tullah home," he said, and clambered heavily down into the waist of *Chittachai*. Samma followed him, though she found a folded cargo net to rest upon while Tullah wormed his way through the small hatch into the captain's quarters beneath the tiny aft deck.

Resting, Samma felt a sense of accomplishment she had never managed before, not ever. Standing to an unfair fight and winning on her own was something. She'd meant to wait for the crew to return from their revels, to bargain shrewdly with Utavi, but sleep took her too soon, riding on the rails of her aches and pains from the brief, brutal fight, especially the horrid ringing in her head.

▲▼▲

She came to herself sometime later amid bales and barrels of cargo. A half-moon stood pale in the night sky. Sitting up seemed a terrible idea. Samma's head might shatter if she did. It felt lumpy from within.

Tullah brushed her arm. Had she seen him there before? The giant handed her a cup like a thimble in his great hand.

Something very green and dank. Either the world's worst tea, or someone's idea of medicine. Samma was thirsty, though. She balanced the cup on her chest and tipped some into her mouth.

The flavor that bloomed was worse than the smell. She very nearly spit it out. Tullah clapped his hands with a delighted expression, then mimed drinking more.

What else was there to do? Samma drank, wondering if this was meant to be a purgative. It certainly threatened that effect. Somehow she kept the stuff down.

▲▼▲

The next morning *Chittachai* put out to sea. Monkeys screamed in the dark trees along the shore, where the jungle came down into the water behind a great bar of sand. The breeze carried jungle rot and the sickly sweet odor of fruit going bad. No wonder the monkeys howled. They were drunk on ferment.

Samma was still aboard the little ship, without yet negotiating for passage. She was also certain that a meaningful portion of the truth about Green was being concealed. And yet she could hardly pry the girl's fate from Utavi at knifepoint.

Much as with *Atchaguli, Chittachai*'s deck was open, except for a small space under the poop and an even smaller space under a little foredeck, which the crew used as an equipment locker. The ship either had a hidden, shallow hold, or truly enormous bilges. Even more so than the casual criminals aboard Padma's vessel, Utavi's men were smugglers, moving goods past whatever taxmen or customs officials worked the port towns of this coast.

Utavi hid from Samma. Embarrassment, perhaps. Tullah hid as well. From the nudging giggles of the other two crewmen—Little Baji and Arvali—she was sure her understanding of the night before was true. The two were lovers. Who was the catamite, Samma could not say, and did not want to ask. She did wonder how a man with a head so tiny, with so few words in his mouth, knew what it was he desired in the skin trade.

That day passed in slow progress further east. Samma was an uneasy sailor at her best, though she'd handled herself on *Atchaguli* well enough. Here on *Chittachai*, as she looked surreptitiously for evidence of Green's having been aboard, each smack of the waves, each trough of the water, seemed more immediate and abrupt.

The captain remained below all day, along with his giant. No midday meal was served. The other two sailors seemed unconcerned, so Samma tried her best to follow their lead.

Around sundown, as they remained out on the open water, Utavi finally appeared on deck wearing only a pair of grubby white linen trousers. He stretched and yawned and affected a casualness so blatantly posed that Samma was forced to laugh at him. He glared, then stalked toward her.

"Why do you want that dreadful girl, anyway? The bunch of you went to a fair amount of trouble to run her out of Kalimpura."

"That is not for me to say." Samma kept her voice as bland as possible. *As if she knew.* "She is a Lily Blade. The Blades care for our own."

"Huh." Utavi squatted on his heels next to her. "You have money for your passage?"

"When I see Green, we will discuss payment."

A grin, predatory and feral. "No captain who wishes to stay afloat will offer passage on such contingent terms."

"I have coin, you will not see it until I see her." It was the best Samma could do. But she knew she needed to sweeten this man, soften him; and she would be damned if she would do *that* through the skin trade. "I can make you another offer. To work my passage, I shall teach Tullah to fight properly. He will be unbeatable if he can learn to hold himself." She had no idea if this were true, but she could say nothing else. "I will trade daily instruction for your sailing *Chittachai* to where I can meet Green."

Or at least learn of her fate.

Utavi turned this over for a while. Samma had no bargaining position except the implied threat of the eventual, and distant, displeasure of the Lily Blades. Only this man's curiosity and greed would sustain her.

Samma knew which she would bet upon. She dangled her only other bait. "The Goddess' favor is worth much, but solid payment is worth more."

Utavi chose to regard this as a great good joke. He threw back his head and laughed. Then the two of them pressed their hands into their hearts, before clasping palm-to-wrist. That was the seal of a street bargain in Kalimpura, and the manner in which people who had no letters affirmed their agreements. A contract for those without justiciars.

▲▼▲

Chittachai anchored for the night on a shallow bank some distance from shore—the better to discourage raiders in small boats, Samma knew from conversations aboard *Atchaguli*. Swimmers were not so much of an issue, given the creatures lurking in these waters. The little crew reefed the sails, then spent the first watch of the shifting cargo to clear a large enough space on the deck, the full four-yard width of the midships, and almost as much length.

"If we are having strong seas, there will be fast work needed to better balance the cargo," Utavi told her, but he looked pleased.

"Tomorrow morning," Samma promised him. "I will spar with Tullah the first hour of the day, and then we decide how much more to do, and what he stands to learn."

"So early," the captain groaned. Then with another of those easy smiles that told the whole world it was joking with him, "The time is being good enough."

Samma lowered her voice. "How well does Tullah take instruction?"

Utavi blew air through his teeth with a faint whistle, then plucked at his lip. "He is as simple as a bedpost. Surely you are knowing this."

"Yes. Though I prefer to think of him as a child," she added. "He speaks very little. Does he understand more?"

"Sometimes." Utavi shrugged. "He is gentle enough. Too gentle. So I am liking this arrangement."

"I am not going to make a killer of him!"

The captain laughed again. "Just a great child who is having more toughness."

He seemed far too jolly about the whole business, but Samma was not sure how else to manage this. There was nowhere to go but forward. She could not exactly walk home. That night she lay curled on her cargo netting, watching the crew watch her, and wondered why she was doing this.

Tullah was happy enough, it seemed. Who was she to transform him?

▲▼▲

By the time the sun came up, Utavi had stumbled out of his little cabin. Tullah lumbered close behind him. "Mornings are a horror," the captain announced with a bleary voice.

Samma swept the open deck where she would be working with the gigantic simpleton. He needed room to move, and frankly, to fall. No one wanted to go overboard in the waters around Selistan, not if they wished to return to the ship in possession of all their extremities.

Chittachai had nothing to serve for the straw mats on which the Blade aspirants learned and practiced their sparring. Likewise, a fetch up against the rail could crack a skull. She took note of the cargo netting and canvas covers, in case Utavi might be willing to let some of it be used as bolsters.

Tullah stepped into the cleared practice floor, looked at her, then put up his hands and tried to step back out. He nearly crushed Utavi and Little Baji.

"Come," Samma said to the big man in her sweetest voice. "We will only dance a while. No one will be hurt."

He covered his groin with those enormous hands. "You hurt," he mumbled in a voice as small as his head, high as a child's.

For a moment her imagination was belowdecks with Utavi and this strange man, wondering what it was they did. She vigorously shook away the pictures that formed. "Not hurt," she told the big man.

Then Samma realized Utavi was smirking. He'd never meant this bargain to hold any meaning. All was just a game to him. Samma clenched her fist, wishing she had a Blade handle at her back, half a dozen women to school this crew.

Even one more besides herself, and she could take them.

Samma stepped back and drew her knives to set them point-first into the deck. Little Baji and Arvali flinched, but Utavi mostly looked interested. Tullah appeared fearful.

"No tricks," she said softly. "No weapons." She beckoned him as she had done when they'd first fought on the dock.

He lurched toward her, then stopped with another long, nervous look.

Interesting, Samma thought. She had beaten him once, barely, but now he was afraid of her. *How many had laid a hand on this man, ever?* Simple or not, he was enormous. Perhaps Utavi had once confronted Tullah, then discovered his secret.

Was she teasing a child to the edge of his endurance, or training a man? The question made her a bit sick at the stomach.

Samma offered Tullah her hand. He leaned forward to take her fingers, then stepped close with his shoulders hunched. The two of them began a shuffling walk, circling one another. Thinking of how the Blade aspirants had trained as very small girls, Samma stamped every third step, first one foot, then the other, marking a time that Tullah picked up after a few uncertain moments.

They moved around slowly to make a smaller circle within a larger. She increased the tempo a bit. Tullah followed. Utavi's men began to clap out the time. Soon the two of them were dancing, the big man smiling shyly over shining cheeks. He followed her as she changed step again, then changed direction. The sailors kept with the rhythm, which had come to match the rocking of the low swells that nudged at *Chittachai* so that it seemed as if the ship herself were part of the pavane. The faded prayer flags on the mast ropes fluttered in the morning breeze. Even the crying seabirds ceased their endless plaint to circle overhead with the measure of the dance.

Samma felt as if she were watching a flower bloom. Tullah was crying, but his face was joyful as any priestly Mother in the transports of godhead. The two of them glided about the deck with the grace of evening stars on the rise.

"Enough!" shouted Utavi. The sailors lost the beat and sputtered to halt, as did she and Tullah. The captain jumped onto a crate and continued to yell. "This is not sparring, this is dance. You are a foolish woman to teach—"

"No," said Tullah.

Utavi stopped and stared at him. Tullah stared back, then reached for the Samma's hand. Together they began to shuffle about the deck once more.

The moment was gone, the little magic of people and place fled. Utavi shut his mouth and squatted down facing away from them with a resentful hunch to his shoulders. She and Tullah circled a while longer. Samma then set the dim giant to exercises, leading him through steps for balance, for speed, for control.

Afterward the sailors applauded. Utavi shouted a course and retreated belowdecks. Tullah's tiny baby's smile grew even wider. The big man held out his enormous fist. Samma reached to clasp it with her hands when he opened his fingers. A lily bud dropped out, crushed to a sodden mess. She caught the flower.

"She gave." Tullah's mouth stretched almost painfully around these simplest of words. "For you."

Then he followed Utavi down into the dark of their den.

Samma stood staring at the lily. The Goddess had never come to her, never touched her the way She seemed to touch the senior Mothers, had almost followed Green about.

Even now, the Goddess had not touched her, Samma realized, but had spoken through this...this...*man*. She knew she should see it as a blessing, but at the moment, the flower was more of a torment.

Little Baji stepped close on his way to the poop to unlash the tiller for the day. "He has rarely spoken so many words in a day, lady." Gratitude shone in the sailor's eyes.

They set their sails and hauled in their anchor as *Chittachai* groaned into motion. Her beams complained until they found the rhythm of the sea. She settled into tacking back and forth across the southerly breeze, heading ever eastward. Samma sat at the waist of the ship and stared out at the passing shoreline, wondering where Green was, and what message the Goddess had intended with this flower crushed in the hand of the simplest of men.

▲▼▲

They sailed on for a half moon, and a few days more. Tullah's fear quickly subsided as they trained in the mornings. Samma soon came to see that he was so gentle as to be almost impossible to provoke to a real offense. She did not understand how a man who could not stand to gut a fish worked on such a gray-souled ship as this.

They sailed east, slowly. Twice the boat stopped to trade at little river ports she would not ever have spotted. Utavi timed his arrivals carefully in order to be well away before dark, despite the invitations to feast and offers of women. Pirates were a constant danger, which made Samma wonder in turn how Utavi had come to command *Chittachai*.

The whole time, she wondered of Green. Whenever she raised the question, Utavi would look mysterious, touch his lips, and whisper, "Soon, but not yet." Samma was all too conscious of being utterly in his power.

Finally, she could take it no more, and braced Utavi on the poop. Little Baji and Arvali rapidly found business elsewhere on the ship, while Tullah stood at the aft end of the main deck and whimpered at the two of them.

Samma did not bother with idle chatter. "We have been over two weeks on a eastward course, and you always promise me 'soon.' Where is Green, and when will I see her?"

"This is not so easy." Utavi's jaw was clenched. He would not look at her.

"I have made great progress with Tullah. He has steps and practices to keep him improving."

"You are being charming enough, for all your homely face. You are still a fool. A woman being abroad in a man's country, where swift ships sail by night and some powerful courts hold grudges back in Kalimpura."

So he had stalled her with purpose. A certainty which had been borning within her since she first set foot on this deck erupted into bloom. Samma let herself fill with rage. "There is no grudge more powerful than that of a vengeful Goddess," she snarled.

This was what it must feel like to be Green, coursing with power, stopping people with the force of your anger and the hardness of your glare.

Then she heard the unmistakable sound of baring steel behind her. When she looked, Little Baji and Arvali stood with blades in hand. Neither would meet her eye. Tullah began to blubber.

Samma touched her own hilts. "So you have been paid to slit my throat and cast me into the sea? To what end?"

"If you can pay more, make your offer." Utavi smiled grimly.

"Why?" she flared. "So you can take my money and then kill me? Did Green end this way, cast bleeding into the waves?" That could *not* be so. The Goddess would have known of the loss of her favorite.

"Your crazed slut and her cat-woman cost me a crewman," the captain snarled. "Her enemies in the Bittern Court and elsewhere in Kalimpura will pay well for you, as a tie to her."

Dead!? Had they killed Green and the cat-woman? "Then they are greater fools than even you," Samma said, her anger driving her to a white-hot calm. "For they are within easy reach of those same Lily Blades whom you are so willing to scorn out here on the open seas."

His eyes flickered to the west, and so she did as well. A sail stood there. *Atchaguli*, Samma realized. Padma and Utavi had been in league the entire time. She recalled the knife of water under *Atchaguli*'s bow early on, and realized how slowly they had sailed since she'd boarded *Chittachai*.

Stupid girl. You deserve to die now.

"No," Samma said quietly. She was much closer to Utavi than either Little Baji or Arvali was to her. She came at him across the tiller with a single leap.

To her surprise, Utavi had a hidden blade, which she was forced to block with her forearm. He laid a dreadful cut that shocked the bone. Samma bit back her cry and jumped up onto the beam to blind him with two swift kicks with a toe in each eye. He dropped screaming, so she sprang down and made a hammer strike to his temple with the butt of one of her knives.

Biting back the urge to vomit, she took a moment to tear off his ragged shirt and wrap her arm before the bleeding became too much. She had never fought so brutally in Kalimpura, not even while running with Mother Manni's handle.

She turned to see Tullah twisting Arvali's head from his neck. Little Baji danced around the big man, pulling at his arm and shouting. The betrayal Utavi had intended was failing most bloodily.

Little Baji pulled away from the big man even as something inside Arvali snapped with an echo that made her wince. Samma realized that the other sailor had a boning knife in his hand. She leapt the two steps to the low rail at the fore of the poop and threw herself toward Little Baji.

He took Tullah in the kidneys and across the spine before Samma could reach him. She bore Little Baji down to a head-cracking impact, but it was too late. The big man toppled, keening his pain with a high, piercing sob.

She scrambled to grasp Tullah's hand. Blood spewed from his back. He cried in the voice of a wounded bird.

"Oh, my sweet man," she whispered. "I never meant for it to be like this." Samma tried to soothe him, but the pain was too great. Little Baji groaned nearby. Utavi howled from his clutched knot of pain on the poop. And *Atchaguli* was growing closer.

To her amazement, Tullah's feet rocked a bit.

He was trying to dance with her.

Samma leaned close and whispered again, singing a song for the littlest girls in the Temple. As he quieted and began to smile, she snapped his neck.

Tullah died with the faintest whimper. Samma leaned away and vomited on the deck, then swallowed the sobs that threatened to overwhelm her.

▲▼▲

Little Baji touched her shoulder. She whirled and nearly cut his throat. He stumbled back, hands empty and spread wide. "They come."

Samma looked up from the body of the quiet giant. "I will not go with any of you. Sooner swim with the monsters in the ocean."

"No..." he whispered.

They both stared at the approaching *Atchaguli*.

"You want to be taken by Captain Padma?" she asked.

"I don't want anything," Little Baji said. "Not if it comes like...this."

"Too late." Samma slapped him. "This is what your choices cost." *This is what all our choices cost.* The Goddess had given Tullah Her favor, and Samma had allowed him to be killed. Just as the Goddess had given Green Her favor, when Samma and everyone else in the Lily Temple had allowed the girl to be driven forth into the hands of these pirates.

"She's not dead, you know." Little Baji rubbed his cheek. "We put her on an iron ship, and Chowdry went with her because he would not plot against the girl for Utavi."

"Then we go now," she said. "To the iron ships."

"You are crazy. We will perish out on the open sea."

She looked back at *Atchaguli*. "We will not live much longer when Padma sees what has been done. Set the sail. Then take yourself overboard or stay, I don't care."

"No!" he shouted, but her knife pressed into his gut now.

"One more body will not weigh my conscience. And we are far from the Death Right of Kalimpura."

"I-I will set the sail," he said. "But I will not go overboard."

"Suit yourself." She stepped up to the tiller, ignoring Utavi's groans and pleas to unlash the bar and steer them out to sea.

Green would have done no less, Samma thought, and wondered when she had become so ruthless.

▲▼▲

Atchaguli changed course to pursue them out into deeper water, but Samma hoped they had enough distance to hold their lead. She had been told over and over that these coastal traders were not designed for the big swells. No matter, she would follow where Green had gone. The Goddess would see to her.

The lily crushed in Tullah's hand had been proof of that.

Unbidden, Little Baji threw Arvali's body overboard. He tried to move Tullah as well, but was defeated by the sheer size of the corpse. Samma, standing on the poop with the whimpering Utavi, considered what to do with the former captain.

"You are blind," she told him. "I should shove you into the ocean for your treacheries."

His whimpers rose to a shrill sob. "Please, please, kill me first if you do."

She bent close. "You would have not done so much for me."

He sobbed again. Samma took pity and slashed his throat. After his breath stopped heaving, she grasped his arm, lofted him to the rail, and shoved him overboard.

She looked down at Little Baji, who stared at her open-mouthed. In chasing Green, she was becoming Green. She swallowed another heave of violent regret.

▲▼▲

The wind plucked at the faded prayer flags on *Chittachai*'s stays. The sails boomed as she began to dip her bow back and forth. With an inexperienced hand on the tiller, the ship was losing her heading. Samma knew how the poor hull felt.

She looked at Little Baji. "I will find an iron ship, and leave you. Then *Chittachai* will be yours."

His eyes rolled. "I cannot sail her alone."

"Your dead will keep you company. And *Atchaguli* is not far behind."

Samma chivvied him up to the tiller. He came, mostly to get away from Tullah's corpse. She handed Little Baji the beam, then pointed south across open water. He nodded as he settled in.

Down on the deck, Samma regarded the great, dead child before her.

Tullah must go into the sea, she realized. Though she intensely disliked the idea of feeding him to the water monsters, she could hardly bury him any other way. Leaving him aboard to rot seemed more disrespectful than letting him be eaten beneath the waves.

Samma found an axe in the forward locker. She went back to the rail nearest Tullah's body and began hacking, though the blows nearly numbed her wounded arm. Before long she had not only cut down the rail but also sheared off the top of the scupper. *Stupid sailors' words.* There would be no need to lift Tullah in order to push him overboard.

The path now opened, she used the axe handle to lever the enormous body toward the gap. Prepared for the pain, Samma pushed with her off arm. Tullah rolled over onto his damaged back. Peace blessed his tiny face.

She levered again, pushing him onto his right arm, then back onto his great belly. Now the wound faced her once more, an accusing red mouth full of shattered teeth that had been ribs or spine.

With another straining effort, she shoved him next to the rail. Samma eased back to rest her muscles for a moment. "He had no sins or sorrows," she shouted to the wind. "Only grace in his heart. Maybe he dreamed of dancing, or just speaking his mind."

With a final burst of bitter effort, she rolled Tullah overboard. He splashed great as any leviathan, and bobbed in the waves. Samma threw her axe after him for a funerary offering. Lilies blossomed around the largest child she'd ever known, stabbing her heart with passion, but then she realized it was foam being teased from the waves by the wind.

He sank on his own, without being pulled down by some dead-eyed mouth full of ivory knives. That felt like a mercy.

"Thank you," Samma told the Goddess. She stood and wept a moment, then went to the poop to bully Little Baji some more.

▲▼▲

In the end, all there was to do was sail south until Bhopura was a dark line on the horizon, then set the ship's shallow keel wallowing eastward and hope to be overtaken by some larger, faster vessel meant for this ocean. *Atchaguli* lurked in the distance, but seemed reluctant to pass too far from land.

Green had gone this way, according to Little Baji. Samma knew she could do no less.

Padma's reluctance to follow her onto the deeps soon became easy to understand. *Chittachai* might be the very daughter of the coast, but out there she was little short of nightmare. They had a fine day for weather and only modest swells, but even that much overwhelmed the ship's seaworthiness and the pair of fools crewing her. Little Baji refused to give the tiller back to Samma. Instead he directed her to tend the sails as best she could. It was as well they were set, she had no notion how to shift or furl them.

They were committed to their course until the seas drove them under or someone happened by to pick them up. The day drifted past without sight of a single ship.

Samma had never trusted so thoroughly in fate. In truth, she had never trusted in fate at all.

Had that been the difference between her and Green? Perhaps this was why the entire Temple of the Lily Goddess had been willing to bend every rule they had for one girl, while Samma and all the other aspirants had been forced to follow the strictest regimens without exception.

Fate loved the fearless, it seemed.

Sunset brought rain showers that unfolded into a storm. Confronted with heavy chop and contrary winds, *Chittachai* skittered like a cat in a millrace.

Little Baji told her where to find more ropes, and the two of them lashed the tiller. He came with Samma down to the maindeck where they tossed cargoes overboard. Lightening *Chittachai*'s load accomplished little that she could see, but Little Baji was frantic that it be done.

Somehow they passed the night without losing themselves overboard. By dawn *Chittachai* rode so low she was halfway to sinking. The sea was calm and the sky the pale pink of the inside of a girl's sex. The ship had only part of her sail left. Everything else had ripped or been cut away.

"There was being a pump." Little Baji sounded bitter.

Samma looked at the water standing ankle deep on the main deck. Her wounded arm had stiffened up in the night, and would barely move this morning. "Where?"

"You threw it overboard in the storm."

"We have too much water for it anyway, I am sure."

The one bright spot on the day was that *Atchaguli*'s sail no longer fouled their northern horizon. Still, Samma was certain that if they somehow put back in toward shore, Padma would find her. And once Padma found her, well, her choices would become quite limited indeed.

The day continued hot, with barely a wind. Very little food remained. *Chittachai* was doomed, and Samma with her. They would sail east until the water swallowed them up, and then Samma knew that she would haunt the boat's remains, crying beneath the waves for an iron ship that never came.

Little Baji cried out.

"Wh-what?"

"Something is on the horizon," he said. "To the north and west. It moves across the wind."

Samma shook off her dreadful fantasy and looked. A lump, or maybe a small cloud. It rose and fell as the sea moved. "A ship?"

There was no point in hailing. She was leagues distant. *Chittachai* had no signals, no rockets. Samma shook Little Baji for answers, but he just blubbered about dying too far from home.

She realized they gone past the sea lanes and further south into the emptiness of open ocean. Their last hope steamed past. *Chittachai* had no smokestack to answer theirs with.

Smoke.

Samma knew what Green would have done now. She could do no less, not if she was to serve her charge. She raced to the little locker that was the kitchen. It had broken open during the storm, but the punk pot was still clipped tight. Trembling, she took that out and cracked the lid. The coals within yet smoldered. Samma splashed through the flood on the maindeck to the tiny foredeck.

She was able to set a bit of rope wrack to burning fitfully. Carrying it with care, she climbed the damaged mast.

"What are you doing?" Little Baji called from below.

"Setting fire to our ship!"

The remains of the sail burned well enough, and the mast besides. When it toppled after a while, *Chittachai* was a mess of steam and smoke and stench. Little Baji whimpered his own death-song.

Around sundown the ship came out of the north. Not much was left of *Chittachai* above the waves, but Samma and Little Baji clung to the sinking poop until men swarmed down a rope and took them aboard a high-sided iron vessel filled with pale-skinned people who spoke no language she could understand.

"Stone Coast," she kept saying, words she'd learned from Green during midnight whispers by moonlight. "Stone Coast."

"Stone Coast," they agreed, then yelled at Samma for a while in their strange language.

She was permitted to stand at the rail and stare at *Chittachai*'s remains. This was Tullah's grave, to be sure. And Green's legacy. They sailed away from the pooled ashes and debris, the smell of smoke close on her Lily Blade leathers. Samma wondered whether she had done well. She still had the bag of jewels, and for good or ill, Little Baji.

A lily petal blew on the wind to land on the back of her hand. Samma looked around. Leagues from land, only a bored sailor watching over her, and Little Baji slumped next to the rail with misery writ large upon his face.

"Thank you," she whispered, and watched the water spread behind the iron ship, a widening wound in the ever-healing sea.

"Thank you," Samma told the Lily Goddess.

Then: "Green, I am coming for you."

Promises;
a Tale of the City Imperishable

This story was commissioned for the Paper Cities *anthology by Kathy Sedia. I'd recently been working on* Madness of Flowers, *the sequel to* Trial of Flowers, *and had the City Imperishable much on my mind, so I explored the backstory of one of the most powerful and subtle of the supporting characters in those two books. She proved a more difficult, complex woman than even I had imagined her to be.*

Girl

She'd had a name, when she was little. All children did, even if it was just Grub or Little Jo or Sexta. But for some living on the brawling streets of the City Imperishable, names were like cloaks, to be put on and taken off. And for some, a name might be cut away like a finger crushed beneath a cartwheel, lest rot set in.

The lash cracked past Girl's ear, so close she felt the sting, though without the burn of a rising welt.

This time.

Girl held her pose splayed against the wall, dipping her chin as best she could with her face pressed against the rough stone. She waited while Sister Nurse studied her. Right now, there were five of them under Sister Nurse's care. Each of them was named Girl. Each of them was taller than the broken hinge set in the wall stub along Pyrrhea Alley. Each of them was shorter than the rusted iron post in front of the Fountain of Hope where the alley let out on Hammer Lane. That was how long they had under Sister Nurse's care, from hinge to post. It was the way of things in the Tribade.

"What's your name?" Sister Nurse asked, looking up from just below Girl's feet.

"Girl," she whispered, though a woman's voice in her head spoke another name.

"Where are you bound?"

It was the catechism, then. "From hinge to post."

"You've my count of thirty to gain the roof," Sister Nurse said.

Not the catechism after all. Girl scrambled, knowing the task to be impossible—there were at least five body lengths of wall above her, and the other Girls had been climbing quickly while she was stopped for questioning.

She came to a window at Sister Nurse's slow eleven. Scrambling up the side of the frame, it occurred to Girl that Sister Nurse had changed the rules. She was no longer climbing the wall, she was gaining the roof.

With no more thought than that, Girl tumbled into a dusty room. The lash cracked against the window frame, but missed the soles of her bare feet. She scrambled, taking up the count in her own head, looking for stair or ladder before time ran out and she was beaten bloody for both failure and insubordination.

Never again, she told herself. Not while she drew breath.

▲▼▲

Each of the Girls had made a scourge. The six of them, for there had been six at the time, had gone into the River Saltus to land a freshwater shark. One Girl had been bitten so badly she was taken away bloody-stumped and weeping, never to return. The rest skinned their kills, cured the strange, rough hide, and cut it into long strips for braiding. They used human shinbones, found or harvested at their own discretion—Girl had cut hers from a three-day-old corpse—for the handles. The sharkskin braids were anchored to the handles by copper windings. Those, mercifully, had been provided, though Girl supposed only because the City Imperishable lacked mines for them to descend into.

She'd wound her old name into her handle, setting gaps in the copper in the places where the letters might have fallen. It was a code known only to Girl, a secret message from her former self to her future self in memory of silent promises of revenge and betterment. "You are you," she'd said, a message being drawn out of her with red hot tongs by the Sisterhood.

Whenever Sister Nurse landed a blow or cut across her back, her neck, her ass, her thighs, Girl knew it was with the power of her lost name behind it.

She'd never asked the other Girls if they'd somehow done the same. Perhaps they bled in vain. She did not.

▲▼▲

The Tribade did indeed beat her bloody before a fire that roared in an iron grate. The metal glowed like eyes in the darkness of a summer night. Skin came away in narrow red flecks, while sisters shouted at her. Is this your name? Who are you? Why are you here?

"Girl," she told them, until she could no longer move her jaw. That was all she said, no matter what they asked her. She would give them no satisfaction. Instead she remembered every cut and blow, for the future.

In time Sister Nurse cut Girl down and slung her across her neck like a haunch of meat. They trudged through moonlit streets, surrounded by beggars and whores and night soil men, none of whom lifted a face dark or pale to acknowledge Girl as she watched the world upside down through blood-dimmed eyes.

Stairs after that, stairs on stairs on stairs. They were climbing the Sudgate, the great, monstrous, empty castle which anchored the southwestern wall of the City Imperishable, brooding over the river and the poorest districts and the vine-wrapped forests that slunk away to the south. She could tell from the scent of the dust, too—this was cold stone crumbled with age and disuse, not scattered dirt and flakes of skin and pollen borne on bright winds from beyond the walls.

Even if Sister Nurse had remained still and silent, Girl would have known where she was. Then, and always.

On the roof—a roof, rather—for the Sudgate was ramified and ramparted like some palace of dream—the moonlight was almost violet. The heavy grease-and-shit scent of the Sudgate Districts moiled below them somewhere, miscegenating with night humors off the Saltus and whatever flowed down from the Heliograph Hill and the Limerock Palace. Sister Nurse set Girl down so that they stood on a narrow ledge, looking back across the City Imperishable to the north and east as a curious, abrasive wind plucked at them both.

The great ranging complex of the Limerock Palace in the middle distance was the most obvious structure. Gilded and tiled domes of the Temple District gleamed in the moonlight. The Rugmaker's Cupola on Nannyback Hill punctuated the northern horizon, its candy striped walls shadow-on-shadow now. Smokestacks and factories and mansions and commercial buildings stood all across the City Imperishable. This close to the top of the Sudgate, they were as high up as all but the tallest of the buildings and hilltops.

Sister Nurse said a name. It was a familiar name, one borne by hundreds of female children in the City Imperishable. It was the name worked into the handle of her scourge. Girl said nothing, did not even blink or turn to face the half-familiar sound.

"Are you taller than the post?" Sister Nurse asked.

At that, Girl turned and looked. Her own length of leg had not grown in the last day or two.

"Are you taller than the post?"

As always, there was no hint what the question might actually mean. Sister Nurse set exercises, asked questions, made demands, meted out punishments. Waking up each day was always reward enough. It meant she had a future.

It was more than some had, in the alleys and flophouses and mucky attics of her part of the city.

"Are you taller than the post?"

No question was ever asked more than thrice.

"I am taller than the City Imperishable," Girl said.

Sister Nurse smiled. "Then you are free, if you can fly away."

This was something new, something outside the boundaries of pain and promise. Girl looked down at the tiled roof sloping sharply away from the ledge beneath her feet, the angle so steep that the missing pieces were scarcely visible. It was a hundred body lengths and more to the pavement of the wallside alley.

"But I have not been given wings," she whispered.

"Then we have failed you."

It took Girl a moment to understand what had just been said. Not that *she* had failed, but that Sister Nurse, and the Tribade, had failed her.

I will not back down, she told herself. Girl spread her arms, stared at the pale moon a moment, whispered a name, and toppled forward into empty air and the broken-toothed mouth of the cobbles far below.

▲▼▲

Little Mother

"Run it again, Little Gray Sister," urged Sister Architect.

She considered that. The baby shifted in her belly, making her heavy as a cotton bale, and just as ungainly. There had been pains in her groin, too, pushing the edge of what was permissible. She could not lose the child, but she could not lose herself either.

Little Gray Sister looked over at her partner in this effort. It was another rooftop, another nighttime, another Tribadist, but she was very much in mind of the night she'd been reborn. "It's not a matter of trust," she said. "Nor casting away."

"No..." Sister Architect smiled, her eyes glimmering in the pale moonlight. "Pride, I suppose. You've already made your goal." Her goal, in this case, was a scale across the rooftops from the bakery on Forth Street to the Cambist's Hall on Maldoror Street a block over, and there up the false steeple on the old Water Bureau office to make the jump across Maldoror and down to the edge of the Limerock Palace's south wall. From there, it was trivial to slip over the wall enter the building—the real work was in the run up and the leap, the parkour-pace practiced to deadly precision by the Gray Sisters among the Tribade. The false steeple was one of the two or three hardest runs practiced by the sisterhood.

To run the false steeple days before a baby was due was the hardest way to make the run. *No one* could scale and jump with her usual speed and precision while her belly was distended and full of sloshing life.

Little Gray Sister had, and fetched out the Third Counselor's privy seal to prove it. Not for the sake of the theft—the Tribade had their own copy of the seal, accurate right down to the wear marks along the left edge and the three nicks in the bottom petal of the rose—but for the sake of doing the thing.

Pregnant and due.

In this moment she was already minor legend. If she did what Sister Architect suggested, and she succeeded, her legend would grow.

"Vanity," said Little Gray Sister, leaning backward to ease her spine. "I have already proven all that I need to."

"Hmm." Sister Architect sounded disappointed, but did not press her case. "Perhaps you are not quite so much flash as some of the younger sisters claim you are."

Another test, she realized. But true. There were many kinds of sisters in the Tribade—red, white, blue, black and more. Sister Architect was a blue sister, one of the professions, though her skills were mostly put to plotting and revising the rooftop runs, rather than any new construction.

Only the grays were trained to die and to kill. Only the grays were given the bluntest and sharpest weapons and trusted to use them. Only the grays were trained between hinge and post in secrecy and ignorance, that their true mettle might be known.

Only the gray sisters became Big, Bigger or Biggest Sisters, to lead the Tribade into the uncertain future.

She smiled with pride at the thought.

Her abdomen rippled, a muscle spasm that caught Little Gray Sister by surprise so that she sucked in her breath.

Sister Architect tugged at her arm. "Sister Midwife awaits within the Quiet House."

"I—" Little Gray Sister stopped cold, fighting a wave of pain so intense it roiled into nausea. She took a deep, long breath. "Yes."

▲▼▲

Big Sister—like all Big Sisters, a gray sister—sat on the edge of Little Gray Sister's cot. Big Sister was almost a heavy woman, unusual in the Tribade, with roan hair fading to sandy gray and glinting gray eyes. "You're a mother now," she said. "Would you like to see the baby?"

Little Gray Sister had thought long and hard on that question. Her breasts ached for the child, weeping a pale bluish fluid. Her loins felt shattered. Even her blood seemed to cry out for her offspring.

Like everything, this was a test, though of late she had been her own examiner more and more. "I would, but I shan't," she told Big Sister.

Big Sister took Little Gray Sister's hand in her own, clenched it tightly. "You can, you know," she whispered.

Little Gray Sister fancied she heard a burr in Big Sister's voice, some edge of old emotion. It was possible—the Tribade were neither monsters nor ghosts, just women of a certain purpose living within the walls of the City Imperishable. "I could hold her—" She stopped again, realizing she didn't even know if she'd birthed a boychild or a girl.

A girl, she decided. The baby had been a girl. Just as she had been, once.

"I could hold her, but I do not think I could let her go."

"And would that be so bad?" The emotion in Big Sister's voice was almost naked now, a shift from control to a raw wound that might be decades old.

She held on to that hurt, knowing she must own it too, if she were ever to set things right. "Not bad, Big Sister, not if it were my ambition to take the red and care for her myself, or even train among the Sisters Nurse."

"Well." Big Sister's voice was controlled once more. "Will you take the hardest way, then?"

That was the other choice. The Tribade had many sisters of the brown, the street toughs and money bosses. They shook down good merchants and shook down bad merchants far more, kept rival gangs in line, maintained some semblance of order in streets and districts where bailiffs were rarely seen. Those women were the most public of the hidden faces of the Tribade, and they did most of the public work.

Little Gray Sister could run rooftops, tackle criminals and watch over her city for the rest of her life as a brown sister. But the only way to become a Big Sister, a Bigger Sister or even—and especially—the Biggest Sister, was to take the hardest way.

She cupped her leaking breasts in her hand, regretting the feeling of both tenderness and joy. There had been a man at them once, too, for a few hours, the night she'd gotten with child amid tearing pain and weeping and a strange, shivering joy. She still wondered who he was sometimes, but at least he'd been kind.

"I am ready."

"I'll send for the fire and the knife."

"The ink, too, please," Little Gray Sister said. "I'd prefer to have it all at once."

An expression flickered across Big Sister's face—unreadable, save for context. Most women waited for the healing before they took the ink. Tattooing the Soul's Walk across the flat, puckered scars on a Big Sister's chest was one of the greatest rites of the Tribade. It was also one of the most painful, for the poppy given for the fire and the knife was not given for the ink.

Little Gray Sister would do it the hard way, cutting away her womanhood in the first blush of mothering to join the ranks of the sisters who protected their world.

Still, she was surprised they had the brazier ready, and the long knife, and there was even no wait at all for Sister Inker.

Someone had known. Perhaps all of them had known. Just like they'd known to be standing on the rooftop just below, the night she'd jumped into the violet moonlight.

Even though it was the Quiet House, her screams set dogs barking three streets away. It was the only time in her life Little Gray Sister screamed.

▲▼▲

Big Sister

She looked at the long, narrow velvet bag Biggest Sister handed her. The two of them were in a rooftop cafe in the Metal Districts, a place where women in gray leather with close-cropped hair received no special scrutiny. There was an electrick lamp on the table which buzzed and crackled, shedding pallid light against the evening's gloom. The wind was cool, bearing mists and distant groaning booms off the River Saltus.

"You know there is one more test," Biggest Sister said. The woman was compact, a walking muscle more reminiscent of a bull terrier than the fine ladies of Heliograph Hill.

"There is always one more test." Big Sister shrugged. Even now, a year and a moon after, her chest ached whenever it was chill, or when she moved certain ways. Sometimes she awoke with the pain of her breasts still full of milk, and for that brief muzzy instant between sleep and alertness treasured the feeling, false though it was. *Never again* kept slipping into the future. "Life is one more test," she added.

"Yes, yes, that's what we tell the girls. It makes nice philosophy for them to whisper over after lights-out. But really, life is for living. After this, only you will set yourself to more."

"Have you ever stopped setting tests for yourself?" she asked Biggest Sister.

"No." Biggest Sister smiled. "But my Sister Nurse always did say I was a fool and a dreamer."

Big Sister held the bag. She already knew what was in it, just by the feel—her old sharkskin scourge. With her old name coiled in copper round the handle.

"There've been three sisters take the hardest way these past two years," said Biggest Sister. She folded her hands around a cup of kava, but did not lift it to her lips. "Four have gone to rest beneath the stones, and one has taken the blue in deference to her age." The cup twirled slowly in her hand. "I am sure you have studied arithmetic."

"Yes," said Big Sister. "I can count."

"We are not dying away, far from it." Another twirl. "We are at some danger of losing the edge of our blade, becoming in time nothing more than an order of monials ministering to the poor and the victims of the state."

"And if we did not run bawd houses and guard the dark pleasure rooms and take money from the cash boxes of the petty merchants?"

Biggest Sister sipped this time before answering. "We *protect*, and we aid. That is not the same thing as bettering. If we did not do these things, someone else would. Someone else always will. Someone male, who does not care for women, who will not trim the balls off men who prey on children and break the pelvises of whores. Someone who will simply count the money and throw a few more bodies to the sharks. And they would not give hospice or teach beggar children to read or make sure the potshops have meat in the soup kettles."

They would not beat bloody the girls growing between hinge and post, either, Big Sister thought, but she kept her words within. As she had always known, there was a sad wisdom to everything the Tribade did.

"There is...more," Biggest Sister said. "You have not reached this lore yet, but believe me, there is more. Much sleeps beneath stones and behind walls in this City Imperishable that is not seen in daylight. And for good reason. Along with others, we guard those secrets. Only the Big Sisters, though. And you must past this final test before your title is more than honor."

Big Sister drew the sharkskin scourge from its bag. Though it loomed huge in her memories, the thing seemed small in her hand. A toy, almost. She'd used worse straining at pleasure with some of the other sisters who had a taste for the rough trade.

But never used such a thing on a child.

"This," Big Sister began, then stopped. She took a deep breath. Her hand shook as it held the scourge. "This is what is wrong with us."

"No." There was an infinite, awful gentleness in Biggest Sister's voice. "That is what is wrong with the world, that we must raise some of our Girls so in order to be strong enough to stand against it."

They were quiet a moment as a waiter passed with a basket of hot rolls, spiced with cardamom and sea salt. He didn't see the scourge lying in Big Sister's hand, and he never would. It was why some among the Tribade met here to talk from time to time.

"Hear me now: there is a greater wrong to come," said Biggest Sister. "This last test. A distillation of our way. You must give life before you can take it. This you have done. You must take life before you can have power over the life and death of others. You must kill for the City Imperishable, for the Tribade, for yourself."

"With this?" Big Sister asked. "It would be a sad and messy business."

"With that. So you come full circle, releasing the last of your name." Biggest Sister put down her mug. "If you do not come to do this thing, you will still be a Big Sister. In other times you would have remained a Gray Sister, but our need is too great. But you will never rise to Bigger or Biggest Sister, and you will never see the inner secrets that we guard. And you will never wield the blade against someone's neck, either in your hand or by your word." She stood. "Come to me when the thing is done. Tonight, or half a lifetime from now, come to me."

"What thing? Who am I to kill?" Big Sister hated the fear that trembled in her tones.

"The child who you would have been," said Biggest Sister. Her voice was distant as the unknown sea. "Bring me the head of a girl-child, that you have killed yourself, and you are done with tests forever. Beggar or daughter of a Syndic's house, it makes no matter to me."

She was gone then, her cup shivering slightly on the tabletop.

Big Sister walked to the edge of the rooftop, where a wrought iron railing worked in a pattern of roses and snakes marked the drop. She stood there, watching a pair of heavy horses draw a scrap cart quietly through the late streets. The moon was slim this night, but still it washed the streets in a purpled silver.

There were a hundred thousand people in the City Imperishable, she thought. A third of them must be children. Half of those would be girls. Would a hive miss a single bee? Would a tree miss a single apple?

Her breasts ached, and she thought she felt milk flowing across the spiral tattooed scars as she wept in the moonlight. There was no way to stop this save to become what she hated most, no way to keep promises made to herself in the earliest days save to break them with blood.

It was not what was wrong the Tribade, it was what was wrong with the world.

Slowly she picked at the copper windings on the haft of the scourge. The name of that young girl smaller than the hinge dropped away as flashings into the street below, where beggars swept daily for the scrap. She picked until she'd forgotten forever the name, and with it the promises, and there were no more tears in her eyes to follow the copper down.

Big Sister dropped over the railing to a three-point landing on the cobbles. If she was going to hunt a girl, the child would be taken from the highest, greatest houses in the City Imperishable. No mere beggar was going to die for her.

And then, never again, she promised herself. Big Sister ignored the hollow echo she could hear ringing from the future.

Witness to the Fall

In the late spring of 2007 at Walter Jon Williams' Rio Hondo writing retreat, Maureen McHugh and Karen Joy Fowler held me down and beat me about the head and shoulders with a thesaurus until I admitted that I was hot dogging too much in my writing process, and that I really needed to take a careful look at how well I was using my narrative powers. As it happened, we experienced quite a violent dry windstorm over two days of that week high in the mountains of New Mexico, which is where the opening scene of this story stems from. As for the rest, it took me longer to write this short story than any other I've ever written, because I was thinking so very consciously about what they (and so many others) had been trying to tell me for some years. They were right, of course, and I am very glad I finally listened. To my eye, "Witness to the Fall" has a very nice flavor in both the magic and the worldbuilding, making a place I'd like to come back to at some point.

The bottles shiver quietly in their rack on the kitchen windowsill. Wind gnaws at the house like a cat worrying a kill. Rafters creak the music of their years fighting gravity's claim. Outside a groaning window, trees dip in a dance likely to break a back and give me kindling for half a season.

Most strange is the sound. The weather hisses and spits, a long-drawn ess slithering from one horizon to the other. I can yet see the water-blue of the sky, furtive clouds hurrying along the wind's business. This will not bring rain, no relief of any kind. It is only the hands of angels pushing the house (and me) toward our eventual ashy dissolution.

Down in the town there has been a murder. People will say it was the blow, five days of wind so strong a man could not stand facing it. People will say it was an old love gone sour, the harder heart come back for one last stab at passion. People will say it was a baby, never an hour's rest since the poor squalling mite was first born into this world.

Me, I listen to the quiet clatter of the bottles, a tiny sound beneath the roaring lion of the air, and hear the song of death as clearly as if I'd played the tune myself on the old piano in the parlor.

Knowing the truth, I turn out my cloak, fetch my bag and inkwells. Soon enough the preacher man or old Cromie will call for me to sit judgment. It has never hurt to be prepared, to remind them of their own belief that I can hear the hammers of their hearts.

That's not all true, but I never lost by letting them think such a thing.

▲▼▲

I am surprised when Maybelle turns up for me. She is the preacher's daughter, a pretty peach borne off the withered branch that is Caleb Witherspoon. For every glint-eyed slight and patriarchal judgment out of him, she has a smile or a warm hand or a basket of eggs and carrots. Of such small economies are the life of a town made.

Still, she has not before called at my gate on business such as this. A Christmas pie, or a letter come by distant post over mountains and rivers, yes, but she has never come for blood or sorrow.

I open the front door before she can raise her hand to knock. "Hello, child," I say, though in truth I do not have even ten years on her new-grown womanhood.

The wind runs its fingers through her braids, sending hair flyaway around her in a pale brown halo. The hem of her dress whips wompered about her shins and calves. The practical countrywoman's boots beneath are scuffed and too solid to be pulled by air. There is a smile on her face, belied only by the worried set of her pale gray eyes.

"Master Thorne," she says, with a fumbled curtsey that is withdrawn before it can truly take hold. "Please, sir, the beadle and Mister Cromie have asked you come right quick."

I nod and step out on the porch, my cloak seized in the dry gale as soon as I pass the door. "Death's a sad business," I tell her, more loudly than it is my wont to speak, "but there's rarely a hurry once the thing is already done."

"Yes, but 'tis my daddy with blood under his nails this day. We need a Foretelling." She holds her silence a breath, then two, before blurting, "I know he ain't done it."

Interesting. The bottles had not spoken clear, or I didn't listen well. I'd have thought it was a child died for love, not a preacher taking literal the murderous word of God. "All will be well."

My words are both a lie and a truth, depending on how far away from the moment one is willing to stand. Together we set out down the track amid summer's brambles and the wind-flattened heads of wild grass caught gold and sharp beneath the noonday sun.

▲▼▲

Neverance is a town of small blessings. There is enough of a river to water the horses and fields in all seasons, though it will not sustain navigation from the metropolii far downstream. There are groves of chestnuts and hoary pear trees to lay forth autumn's windfall and provide children with ladders to the sky come spring. The first white men to settle here had possessed more ambition than sense, and so laid strong foundations of stone quarried from the surrounding hills for the city which never came.

In sum, Neverance is a town typical of these mountains—nestled in a valley between tree-clad peaks, sheltered from winter's worst excesses, surrounded by bounteous fields bearing hay and corn and the small truck grown on hillsides by farm-wives and those too old to harness a team to work the larger plantings. The cattle now standing with their faces away from the remorseless wind, clumped like crows on a kill, are symbols of sufficiency as surely as the great beeves of ancient myth.

Wealth, no, but neither is life is too difficult here. Some, especially women fallen on hard times, live at the edges. Most people in the valley show their faces in church on Sunday with a smile. A turnpike might come someday, or even a railroad ushering the restless through the ever-moving Western Gates, but for these years Neverance slumbers amid its quiet dreams of pumpkins and smokehouses and the peal of the school bell.

Not this day, though.

There is a crowd outside Haighsmith's Dairy. They huddle like the cattle against the wind. Despite the name, the dairy is a co-op serving farmers and townsmen alike. Maybelle leads me to the back of the kerfuffle, intent on pushing through the mass of shoulders to the door, but I tug at her elbow to halt our progress.

At my touch a spark passes between us with an audible crack, tiny lightning raised by the dry wind. Her face flickers with a fragment of pain as she turns toward me.

I cup my hand and speak close to her ear. "I should like to remain out here a few moments, to observe."

Maybelle scowls, an expression which suits her poorly, but she nods. Taking that as my permission, I study the people who crowd the door of the dairy.

Most are known to me. Farmers in their denims and roughspun blouses, townsmen wearing wool trousers and gartered cotton shirts, a scattering of women bustled and gowned for the sake of their appearance before one another. The wind has stolen a few hats and sent hair flying, so this assembly bears an unintentionally disrupted aspect, as if some tiny demon of disorder has descended upon Neverance's well-starched citizens.

What I do not see in evidence are firearms or ropes or shovels. This is not a lynching awaiting its moment. These people are worried, frightened even, but they have not turned to hunters of blood.

The bottles would have told me if they were.

I listen now for whispers in the windows, echoes of truth, but the wretched wind snatches so much away out here in the street. Instead I nod to Maybelle and we push forward.

To my surprise the crowd parts like loose soil before a plow.

▲▼▲

Thin as a fence rail and with a face just as weathered, Caleb Witherspoon sits upon a coffee-stained settee in the co-op manager's office. In here the howling wind is little more than a murmur, a substitute for the voice of the crowd waiting outside for justice, or at least law. The room reeks of male fear and rage mixed in a sour perfume all too familiar to me.

The manager has absented himself, but in his stead is Ellsworth Clanton, the elderly beadle from Neverance's sole church. Clanton stands shivering with age beside Witherspoon, hiding a hard smile which he cannot keep from lighting his eyes as he clamps a hand on the preacher's shoulder. Mister Cromie is also present, who would be municipal judge if Neverance had the formality of a city charter. Still he wears black robes and mounts a bench to pronounce marriages, hear suits and sign the certificates of death. Though not smiling, he too seems strangely pleased for someone officiating over a murder.

I am witnessing the fall of a man.

Clearly it matters nothing what Caleb Witherspoon has actually done, whether Maybelle has the right of her father's innocence. His years of uncompromising rectitude have layered old scars in everyone around him, the memories of which still burn within angry hearts throughout Neverance.

Though I have not lived here so long, being one of the few immigrants in recent memory, I know well enough for what sorts of sins these countrymen punish one another. They can be read so easily.

Clanton the beadle always craved the pulpit for himself. He nurses a coal of resentment in his heart for Witherspoon as the faith holder who took the word of God from his mouth. There is old blood between them, a thorn prick scarred by time and never healed.

Cromie rushes to judge lest he be judged himself. Of his misdeeds I hold more certain knowledge, having emptied the wombs of two of his daughters by the dark of the moon in my years here. Soon after my attentions, his Ellen Marie drowned herself in the mill pond. Jeanne Ann is long since married to Fred Sardo's son, and lives at the high end of the valley where they tend nut orchards and rarely come to town. I doubt Cromie will ever see his grandchildren except in church.

Caleb Witherspoon has measured both of these men time and again, and found them wanting in his holy scales on each occasion. Now that the preacher is caught on the point of justice they have no more mercy than ferrets on a rat.

Maybelle has requested a Foretelling. Even so, I know without asking that these men desire a Truthsaying which they might use as a cloak for the vengeance each nurses in his heart.

"Do not tell me aught." I address Cromie, for he is the power in this room. "I know there has been a murder, and I know where the blood is found. Let me first do my work untrammeled by testimony, then we shall see what we shall see."

"He is guilty, Thorne." Cromie's voice is cold as a child's headstone. "There does not even need to be a trial, except for the form of the thing."

I meet Cromie's slate-gray eyes. "Then why did you trouble to send for me?"

"I did not."

Though I do not glance at Maybelle, I know she blushes like the fires of dawn. I ask the next question, the true question. "If I am unsent for, why did you await my coming?"

Though the words seem to choke him, Cromie manages to spit an answer. "I could do nothing else." This time *he* looks at the girl.

There is no more to be said. I shed my cloak, sweep the dairy's business journals off a small table, and set out my inkwells.

▲▼▲

These are the essential inks with which I sketch the visions of my art. You will forgive me if I do not tell the precise secrets of their processes of creation.

Culpability—Made from lampblack and the ashes of a hanged man's hand. It smells of a last, choking breath.

Vision—Made from the humors of an eagle's eye and the juice of carrots, much reduced. A sharp scent of nature.

Realization—Made from photographer's chemicals and the bile of a dying child, strained through pages torn from Latin Bibles. Tingles the sinuses like an insult not yet forgotten.

Action—Made from paraffin and the crushed bodies of bluebottle wasps. Stings the nostrils as if to sneeze.

Regret—Made from grave dust, the tears of a nun and the juice of winter apples. A musty odor which will close your throat if you are careless.

I tip them from their wells by drop and gill, and mix them in proportion to the need which I have at the moment. A scrivener's greatest works are meant to be drawn on vellum scraped from the flayed skin of kings or presidents, but most purposes can be inked onto any paper to hand. Always, it must be something which I will eventually burn. Fresh wood, living skin, or stone are therefore not ideal.

All children draw, if the stick or coal or pencil is not snatched from their hand. All children represent the world they see in a language which reflects the essentials of their vision. For most, growing up means accepting the way the world is said to look. But a few cling to their craft. A few hang on to their lidless vision the way ants cling to a rotting apple.

Very few find their way to the essential inks.

Very, very few find their way to someone with the wit and craft to instruct them further.

Someone, at some time, must have been the original autodidact. There was a first teacher. Perhaps more than one. In the lands across the ocean where little yellow men write their thoughts in tiny pictures, mine is presumably a powerful art. Here on the country frontiers of America where no one recalls that 'A' stands for ox, the forms of the words themselves do not mean so very much.

Here is the trick to the craft: consider that there is no present moment. We have anticipation, then we have memory. The present flees our grasp at least as fast as it arrives, slipping from future to past before we can take note. Everything we experience can only be a memory of what has come immediately before. Try to find the space between the earth and the sky—that is the present moment.

If you can see that space between earth and sky, if you can find that present moment, then you can craft a Foretelling, or a Truthsaying, or a Sending, or any of the dozens of forms granted to me and my fellow scriveners to render.

▲▼▲

Today I set to scribing a Passage. I spread out a sheet of birch bark pounded with quicklime and thrush's bile, anchoring the edge with my inkwells. I lay down the jade tortoise which has come from the lands across the ocean. There I begin to mix my recipe in the shallow cup upon its head. As I pour, each tiny ring of glass on jade tells me something, in the manner of my art. Even while listening, I begin a speaking to Caleb Witherspoon. The truth is already with us, after all, waiting only to be discovered.

Three drops of *Regret*. I guard my breath.

"Have you ever wondered on the brown of Maybelle's hair?" The floorboards settle as the dairy building shifts in the wind.

Three drops of *Realization*. The burn touches me deep within my face.

"Your child's eyes are most gray, though your own are oaken dark." Something rattles on the roof. A few stray hailstones, perhaps, or the claws of a mighty wingéd creature.

Caleb Witherspoon begins to shiver. Rage, fear, the chill of mortality. Cromie stirs behind me.

"A prick of your finger, Mister Cromie." His breath hisses his surprise. Amid a sweaty stink of fear, he struggles to answer me. "I..."

Reaching out without looking, my fingers find the judge's wrist limp and dangling. I tug him toward my mixture and stab him carelessly with a silver needle. This does not have to hurt, if I do it better than I have bothered for him.

Three drops of an angry man's boiling blood, reeking hot and metallic.

"Caleb, where is her mother?" Though his long-lost wife is said to have died in childbirth, this time the preacher groans as though freshly stabbed.

A drop of *Vision*. A tiny gust of forest scent.

"Who cries on the wind?" I am answered only by silence.

A drop of *Culpability*. Airs from the grave.

I dip my brush and begin to paint.

▲▼▲

I know even before I begin that I will render the portrait of a woman. I have already seen her on the wind. She is not who I might have expected. Witherspoon's reach was long.

The bones of her face, the curve of cheek and jaw, are an older echo of Maybelle. Her hair falls differently, lighter in hue. This shows on the wet birch bark even though I do not work in colors beyond what my mixture gives me. Their hairline is not the same—despite my speculations about the beadle, Maybelle's is more the shape of Cromie's.

The eyes come to me, half-lidded and bright with standing tears. The secret of portraits is in the eyes. If people can see themselves and those they love peering back from the scribing, they will be convinced.

The outlines now, as if she is growing from a center. She becomes real. This has only taken minutes, with the passion and power that makes the room crackle as electric as the hot, hard wind outside.

It is about a woman. It is almost always about a woman.

"That is Alton Miller's widow Chastity," mutters the beadle behind me. "What lives up behind Corncrib Hill."

The words choke from Caleb Witherspoon's mouth as if dragged on chains. "She is my daughter's mother."

"No," Maybelle begins. She bites off whatever words were to come next.

Cromie's voice is bitter with hollow satisfaction. "*Was*. Now we know who Otis Blunt saw floating in the river today."

"You knew all along," Caleb Witherspoon says.

A woman no one would have mentioned had gone missing, even here in Neverance. Not their grass widow. Who would want to claim to have noticed her? I wonder whose back door the preacher had seen her stepping away from, checking the buttons of her dress.

Does it matter?

I finish the portrait of Maybelle's mother. Caleb Witherspoon's young love. Cromie's conquest, that Alton Miller had taken as a cast-off after she'd borne her child in secret. Well before my time here, but even I knew that the preacher put out that his absent wife had died while the daughter was being sent on to be raised by him. All these men should be in the picture, as well, staring over her shoulder, daring their neighbors to sin.

There must have been a ruse, a carriage or a rider in the dark, in the last moment of friendship between the preacher and the judge before the child took the stage at the center of their lives.

It is a hurt nearly two decades old now, but never really done with. Especially not for Chastity Miller.

I look at Caleb Witherspoon. There is no need to ask him why. The reason has been written on his daughter's face every day of her life in the lines of another man's jaw and cheeks. Still, it does matter, I realize. If only for the sake of her memory, that no one wanted to account for now. "Why now?"

"The wind makes madmen of us all," he says.

"Hardly," mutters the beadle.

I think back on the song of the bottles, my vision of a crying baby. "You saw her hurrying, to Mister Cromie once more perhaps?"

Caleb Witherspoon clears his throat. "From Cromie's back step, actually." He turns his face away from Maybelle, whose breath hitches in her throat.

I have it right, I realize. This is a thing to be finished.

Cromie appears uncomfortable, as if he now wishes for silence.

"Was there to be another child?" I ask him. He does seem short on daughters these days, and the widow Miller was not so old.

"It doesn't matter now." The judge's voice is blurred with tears.

So there were two murders today. Did Witherspoon know? There is nothing else to say. The wind pushes at the building, sending dust spiraling down mote by mote from the grubby ceiling. I pack my inkwells in my satchel, carefully avoiding Maybelle's distress.

"Mister Cromie?" It is Clanton, the beadle, practically creaking in his excitement. "Might be a good idea if I preach this Sunday's sermon, don't you think?"

I take my leave, wondering as I go where the river has taken Chastity Miller and her quickened child. Perhaps I should follow them away from this place. Beneath my arm, the bottles shiver a little hymn that I lack the wit or courage to understand.

Number of the Bus

Though I can't remember quite why any more, I am almost certain that this story is Ray Vukcevich's fault. That man could inspire a flatiron to write fiction, so this should be unsurprising to you if you're familiar with his work. If you're not familiar with his work, I suggest you remedy that flaw in your reading. In the meantime, however, here is the first in a story arc that I think of as "the Portland wizards" series.

Eleutherio knew the buses the way some people knew their own bedrooms in the dark. He'd been born on the number 12, during the late night run. The bus number had been 4517. That coach had been retired the day of his fourth birthday, leaving only the 517, three primes which themselves added to form a fourth prime replacing the four which had been traded away. This meant great luck and skill to Eleutherio.

Fourteen months later Tri-Met reassigned the number to coach 4422, which had been involved in a fatality collision on SE Grand Avenue with a drunken pedestrian named Pretty McTeague.

No reason, the drivers had said over coffee at Niki's on the corner of SE Grand and SE Morrison. Niki's sat right at the west end of the Morrison Bridge where the roadbed climbed skyward on concrete pillars and the routes crossed over both each other on the streets below and, more importantly, running water. Morrison Street, of course, did not actually cross the Morrison Bridge, a circumstance of great benefit to the downtown wizards in the confusion the naming caused.

But everyone knew that spirits were drawn to even numbers, because they could live in the cracks left behind by the influence of 2, the only even prime. And so after a series of shattered mirrors and two driver heart attacks in the months following the pedestrian's death, 4422 became 4517.

Eleutherio's bus, complete with the restless spirit of Pretty McTeague. And the death coach took back the four-prime magic of his 517, too.

When 4517 started running the number 12 route again, Eleutherio had to ride the bus, out of sheer self-preservation.

Every wizard—downtown, grassland, or transit—knows that magic comes from stories. They just find their stories in different ways.

Downtown wizards use the numbers of money, scrying in the stock pages of the *Wall Street Journal* and *The Oregonian*. For their kind, the serial number on a chance-discovered five-dollar bill can call spirits from the not-so-vasty deeps of the Willamette faster and better than any hoary tome of old Europe. Numbers talk to a downtown wizard.

Grassland wizards watch the patterns of sheep in the fields in the Willamette Valley, and wait for rabbits in the morning mist. Their kind read tracks and the flocking of crows to move the ways of old lady Earth, and it is Her children who speak their stories to grassland wizards. They bring the rains when the sun has been too kind, and soothe the harsh gait of winter's passing.

But Eleutherio was a transit wizard. Or would be, someday, if he was allowed to finish growing up. Transit wizards get their stories from drunks trudging shopping carts under bridges, and the rumble of truck tires on I-5. A good transit wizard can weave a worldchange from the jeremiads of a bus-riding Korean War vet high on Sterno, and save the lives of dozens of children suffering from diphtheria in a North Portland slum.

And buses were nothing but giant story sieves, passing through crowds of illegals, junkies, the desperate and the driven. Happy and prosperous people rarely rode the bus.

Eleutherio was neither happy nor prosperous. Instead, he was twelve. The age of his route number. He sometimes wondered what it might have meant to ride the 66X bus—would he have been forced to grow old before claiming his place in the world, or would some *nombrejo* have made a ciphering for him to break his route number into something younger.

Twelve, on the number 12 bus which carried a portion of his powers, where the past few years had done nothing to quell the restless spirit.

Pretty McTeague sat down next to him while Eleutherio was scanning the license plates of passing traffic for three-digit primes and felicitous sequences. It was summer in Portland, uncomfortably warm except in the air conditioned space of the bus.

"Hey, kid," the dead woman said.

This surprised him. McTeague usually ignored Eleutherio. She could spend days sulking in 4517's cooling system or down in the growly darkness of the drive train. When she was on board, she usually spent her time irritating passengers who had dozed off sufficiently to glimpse her, or shrieking inaudibly at other spirits trying to board.

"Hello, ma'am." It always paid to be polite to spirits. You might have to summon or banish them someday, after all, though neither of those tasks was taken lightly.

"Whatcha doin'?" She'd died drunk, and she always seemed a little drunk to Eleutherio. *State permanence*, that was called. He thought of it as stubbornness.

"Riding," he said. Eleutherio gave up on license plates. This woman, after all, was the reason his powers were so closely bound into the bus. As he'd grown older, 4517 had become an increasingly powerful bus. It rarely met red lights, and even the mighty locomotives of the Union Pacific hesitated to pull into its way at the 11th/12th Avenue grade crossing.

Some people had said this was McTeague's doing, but Eleutherio always knew where 4517 was, even if it was at the Powell garage, or off on event shuttle service. When it ran the number 12 route, 4517 was as close to him as his beating heart.

"Nah…" She would have spit on him as she talked, had she been corporeal enough for spittle. Pretty McTeague hadn't been, despite her parents' apparent hopes. Death had not improved her. "Ridin' people…get off." She winked at him. "Ever'body who gets on gets off. Get off, off on the bus. Get it? *Come* on." She brayed a drunken laugh that caused several drowsing passengers to jerk awake and stare around in confusion.

"No," said Eleutherio, who did in fact know what she meant. He'd been told, over and over, give nothing to a spirit that wasn't bound to you. Not even the time of day. Time was numbers, after all. Numbers were everything, the order of the world.

She leaned over so close her face started to merge with his, then whispered as if anyone else on the bus could hear her anyway. "I got me a problem, kid. You ain't ridin', you watchin'. Good brown eyes on you, like a dog on the hunt. You hunt out my problem, I'll make it worth your while."

There was little enough Eleutherio wanted from a spirit, especially at his age. Older, with hair on his chest and wrapped in life-numbers, he might take a servant. Now…she was nothing but the idiot whose death had given him his powers, then tied them to this bus.

But problems were why wizards existed. Wizards swam in problems the way some people swam in meth, or sex, or fast cars. Because problems always came with stories.

"So what's your problem?"

"Heh. You'd like to know." She settled away from him, crossing her arms as she transformed to a truculent drunk. "Nobody gets nothing from pretty little me."

That was random, even for a spirit. He tried the smallest summoning—a naked name. "It's all right, Miss McTeague."

Something sparked around her face. She jerked in her seat, shouted unintelligibly as the bus cornered onto NW 5th.

"What's your problem?"

She shifted through multiple phases, her face flickering in and out of expressions like a runaway factorial. A sad-eyed young woman settled out of the blur, Pretty McTeague not as she had died, but as she might have lived some years before that date. "Someone's calling me back, kid. I don't want to go."

Calling her back? That was big magic, especially after all this time. She'd been dead, what...four years. The longer they were gone, if they hung around at all, the more fragmented the spirits of the dead became.

"So what do you want to do?" he asked softly. "You want to move on?" Eleutherio controlled his sense of excitement. If she were unbound from the bus, he should be able to get his strength away from bus 4517, carry it within him. As it stood, he was only powerful on this coach, on the number 12 route.

"No." The truculent drunk filtered back into her face. "Want to stay here. My bus. Comfor'ble. Takes care of me. Don' want to be called back nowhere. Don' want to go on nowhere."

Hope faded, his chest growing heavy. Still...to help her could be right. And it might do something to address his relationship with the bus and his bound powers.

"So you want to stay here." Statement, not question. Don't challenge the drunk.

"Yeah." She glared at him, her eyes bloody-red as they must have been at the moment of her death.

Eleutherio had seen a number of spirits in various dread guises on the buses, but this still gave him pause. "Who's calling you?"

Now her face was so mournful as to be comic. "I am."

Eleutherio closed his eyes and counted to seven. She was crazed. All spirits were crazed, to some degree. Death was not a state that overlapped much with sanity. But Pretty McTeague had lost all logic, even the logic of story.

When he opened his eyes, she was still there. "I am sorry," he said, "but I cannot help you." He closed his eyes again and began to factor nine-digit numbers in the wizard's quietus within his head.

Later, when he got off the back of the bus to find some lunch, he saw Pretty McTeague getting on at the front. A living woman, who looked just like his bus spirit. In the flesh, she wore hip hugger jeans and a blue-and-white striped halter top. Eleutherio raced after the bus as it pulled away, but the driver had grown tired of him and wasn't cutting any slack.

A lot of the Tri-Met drivers knew the wizards kept their buses quiet and safe, but either this one didn't know about the transit wizards, or he didn't know Eleutherio was in the process of becoming one himself.

"Damn," he said quietly, though the *nombrejos* would whip him for disrespect once the wind told them of his transgression.

▲▼▲

All through his taco from Pardo's, Eleutherio tried to follow the bus in his head. 4517 was *his* bus. He *always* knew where it was.

Not today.

After he'd finished eating, he waited for coach 4517 along the number 12 route until the sun dipped below the West Hills and evening's damp chill crept over the city, but the bus never came back. And he still couldn't find it in his head.

Which was wrong.

First of all, he knew the routes intimately. 4517 shouldn't have gone out of service right after lunchtime. It would have rolled until shift change 3:38, then either headed for the Powell garage or done another shift until the route went to the evening schedule.

And besides that, it was his damned bus.

The dead woman had come to life, climbed on board, and the bus had vanished.

He could go ask for help, but Eleutherio knew that if he went to the *nombrejos* with a problem, it would cost him. They'd grumble and complain and fart and scratch themselves, then tell him what he shouldn't have done, then demanded tribute, then maybe, if he was lucky, do something helpful. Mostly they'd just grumble and fart.

Wizards solved problems, they didn't create them.

Sitting on the bus bench in the failing light, Eleutherio turned a Jack In the Box napkin over against his thigh and made a list.

0. Spirit on the bus—Pretty McTeague, killed by this coach
1. Spirit asks for help
1. I say no
2. I get off bus
3. McTeague gets on bus, alive
5. Bus vanishes

It made no sense. But the numbers *always* made sense. So Eleutherio spent some time thinking about explanations. The trickster 2 was always a threat—had Pretty McTeague been twins?

Possible, he thought, but unlikely. Too simple, too pat. Besides, McTeague had said "I am" when he'd asked her who was calling her back. Not "my sister is," for example.

How could a dead woman live to call herself back?

Try the problem from the other end, he thought. How would he call a spirit back?

Well, Eleutherio thought, he wouldn't. But if he had to...

Calling back was a form of binding. Numbers could bind, in certain sequences and patterns. Some numbers were wicked powerful—perfect numbers, where all the divisors taken as a sum formed the number itself. 6, 28, and 496 for example. But he'd need a mighty big perfect number to wrestle a spirit back into the corporeal world. 2,658,455,991,569, 831,744,654,692,615,953,842,176 sprang to mind. With sixty-one prime factors, the ninth perfect number would give him a goodly supply of anchor points.

Anchor to what, though? He could only call a spirit back if there was a vessel to call it back to. The newly-dead—Eleutherio had once seen it done with a stroke victim, filled with the spirit of a slain girl. She hadn't lasted long, turned out crazier than a bridge troll trapped in the body of a fat, dead ironworker, but she'd been able to identify her killer to her mother and the *nombrejos*. Justice was served.

Sometimes people used big dogs, making them into servants and guardians. But that was mostly grassland wizard business. They cared about the land more than justice. Boundaries mattered to grassland wizards.

Him, he'd call a spirit back into a bus. Which, in a sense, was what had already happened to Pretty McTeague. Her spirit never got off coach 4517.

Maybe what she meant by "called back" was different. Maybe she just meant someone was trying to get her *off* the bus.

He stared at his napkin.

Where had the bus gone?

Somewhere that Pretty McTeague didn't feel in danger of being called back from. The bus had gone wherever the dead went to hide.

It was time to take the story of his problem to the *nombrejos* and see what they could conjure from the arrays of the world. He hoped their interest would trump their irritation.

▲▼▲

The number 17 bus—nicely, safely prime, that route number—took Eleutherio back to the transit wizards' roost where he had lived since he could remember. He got off at the intersection of SE Holgate and 17th, walked to the vine-wrapped hole in the fence of the intermodal terminal, then slipped between the parked trucks and across the tracks to the ancient engine turntable and the round house beyond. Inside, the *nombrejos* had an ageing, elaborate space in the servicing pits beneath the tracks.

The long, dark bodies of three retired steam locomotives filled the track-level space. Trains were good numbers, better than buses in some ways, but harder to use for transit magic because of their frozen routes. If the track patterns were felicitous, that was powerful good fortune, but most of the early surveyors had not been sufficiently aware of the significance of numbers.

Here the locomotives were the guardians of the *nombrejos*, their decades-long accumulation of numbers and time overlaying whatever might go on like armor against the forces of the night.

Eleutherio nodded at the two old men working on a Walschaert gear. One hawked and spat—a folk warding against a wizard, useless as it was—but the other was more courteous.

Then he climbed down the ladder into the pit, dreading what might come next.

There were narrow benches or bunks all around, hammered together out of salvaged boards ripped down to odd-numbered dimensions. No two sections were the same size, to keep the numbers from aligning too well. Little rows of bottles, flowers, candy, spread in Fibonacci arcs away from the bunk pillars.

Offerings, from the grateful and the fearful.

Many of the *nombrejos* were sleeping yet. The powerful transit wizards did their business under the countless stars rather than the unitary sun. Only the young or the brave were sent out by day. A few were awake already, early risers or the day watch—Old Kevyn, Maria de la Luz and Sailorman, playing their endless, clicking game of dominos.

Eleutherio stood quietly, hands folded, waiting to be noticed. These were the true wizards, the men and women he was trying to become.

Old Kevyn finally looked up. He was an Anglo, but his face and body were covered with tiny tattoos of numbers so that he was mostly shadow-colored, the hue of ancient tattoos mottled by too much sun and cigarette smoke. Old Kevyn had a towel printed with a map of the London Underground wrapped around his waist, but Eleutherio could count the wizard's ribs. The numbers almost glowed where the thin skin laid over the pale bone.

"Boy's got a problem," he announced.

Maria de la Luz let a domino slip between her fingers to clatter on the moldy, oil-stained concrete. "*El muchacho tiene un problema...*," she whispered through a toothless pucker of lips. Older than sin and twice as dark, Maria de la Luz could call fire. That was a rare and mostly useless talent in a transit wizard—the numbers had little affinity for such physical manifestations, usually preferring to work through the flow of information, ideas and the intangible. Her eyes glittered with something Eleutherio hoped was sympathy.

"P-p-p-problem," echoed Sailorman in his delayed babble. Pasty, pudgy and pale, nobody knew what Sailorman called himself, but his lips were always wet, his chin always glistening. He didn't have any water magic, Sailorman, but he could spot patterns in the tread wear on bus tires, or the sequence of brake lights on I-5, and was a fearsome fighter when the real trouble came calling.

"I have a problem."

Maria de la Luz nodded. "*Maldecido el viento.*"

Eleutherio bowed his head. "Yes. I am sorry."

Sailorman hiccupped, then chewed out another word: "D-d-d-d-dead."

Eleutherio lifted his head as the other two *nombrejos* gave Sailorman a long glace. Sailorman rarely spoke on his own initiative, but that was an answer of sorts.

"Dead, yes," Eleutherio said. He told his story, quickly and succinctly as he had been taught, wishing he could literally speak in numbers like some of the oldest transit wizards did.

Old Kevyn chewed his lip, a domino flipping in his hand. 6, 1, 6, 1, 6, 1, Eleutherio's eye followed the pattern, the dots blurring into a cascade of prime 7 that trapped his attention.

"Is there a wrong been done here, boy?" Old Kevyn finally asked.

"I'm not sure." Eleutherio's voice was nearly a whisper. "I think so, but I cannot state it clearly, cannot write out the balancing numbers of the problem." He stopped, then blurted, "My bus is missing."

"Missing how?"

"She has taken it, hidden from herself, somewhere the dead go to be safe."

"Where are the dead safe?"

"I don't know, sir." Eleutherio felt frustration and fatigue creeping up on him in equal measure. "Their bodies are safe in the cemetery, the morgue... in the urns of their ashes. But their spirits are safe once they have departed, moved on. Where would a spirit hide, and where would she take my bus?"

"No puede conducir un autobús al paraíso," grumbled Maria de la Luz. All the *nombrejos* as well as the younger transit wizards were perfectly clear on Eleutherio's special relationship with coach 4517. But Maria was right—no one could drive a bus to Heaven. Not even Pretty McTeague.

Especially not Pretty McTeague.

Where would a dead woman feel safe?

Old Kevyn worried at the problem some more. "Your bus, it's a mighty powerful bus. Could it just be hidden from you? Cloaked in its own numbers?"

That thought made Eleutherio's gut tighten. Those were *his* numbers. Where could the bus be hidden, that he would not see it?

"Where, boy?" Old Kevyn asked, staring close. Maria de la Luz's eyes glittered more brightly, while Sailorman blubbered his way toward some thought. Dark shapes stirred in the bunks around them, burping and yawning toward wakefulness, or propping themselves up to listen in.

"Into the undecidable," Eleutherio said slowly. All numbers had a secret flaw—Gödel's Theorem mandated unprovable propositions. In transit terms, there were places the buses could not go. Not for lack of roads, but because the routes couldn't bend around to reach. "The blind spot of my numbers." He gasped with relief. "Can you see it?"

"Oh...probably," said Old Kevyn.

Maria's eyes roiled with fire now. *"Es su problema."*

"S-s-s-s-solve," Sailorman spat out, then appeared pleased.

"Look where you cannot see," Old Kevyn added, not unkindly.

Worn out from his day, Eleutherio decided he would look first in dreams. Wherever 4517 had gone, it wasn't on the streets of Portland tonight.

▲▼▲

The Dream of the Bus

I roll down familiar paths, picking up energy the way a new tire picks up sparks on a winter morning. The stories slip into me by ones and threes, commingle and miscegenate, fertilize and cross-pollinate, so that each leaves a little richer, a little deeper, a little more powerful. I know my place, an extended, attenuated home inhabited in slices of time and motion, a thin house of my self and soul.

Some stories come to me fire-bright and glittering, some come age-dulled and dying. Some stories are so packed inward they cannot be told, not even to themselves, while some turn so outward they become thread-worn and translucent. Some stand before and proclaim themselves, and some are ghostly as my own exhaust when I am in good tune.

But they are all mine. Everyone that passes my fare box, touches my steps, breathes on my windows, settles sweat-tired into my seat is mine. Even the invisible ones, the ancient ones, the lost angels and the searching shadows. They are mine, and I will bear them with me even to the scrapyard and beyond.

▲▼▲

Eleutherio woke knowing that his bus had passed into story. Whatever that meant.

Tri-Met probably had different opinions, as did the City of Portland, but numbers were tricky. Number magic raged inside computers in a river of blue-green fire. The transit wizards didn't work with that—they worked with, of and for the street—but Eleutherio could believe that a powerful bus like 4517 might be able to jigger the numbers in the dispatching computers.

He could even bring himself to think that Pretty McTeague's body had gotten on the bus her spirit rode, and they'd journeyed onward together to the next life. Despite what Maria de la Luz had said, perhaps the bus had driven to paradise.

But what about the driver, the other passengers? There had been nine people on that bus when he got off, as the other Pretty McTeague had gotten on. Tri-Met might be tricked into not noticing a missing bus, but Amalgamated Transit Union Local 757—all three digits prime, as was the local number itself—certainly would notice a missing union brother. Though people routinely fooled themselves in a thousand ways, it was much harder to use the numbers to rewrite people's memories than it was to rewrite electronic records.

And Pretty McTeague's spirit had asked him for help, asked not to be called back. This was not a peaceful transition, not with nine other bodies and souls and the entire corporeal mass of a city bus.

The bus might have passed into story, but it hadn't gone to heaven.

Eleutherio slid out of his hard-board bunk and stumbled out past the morning watch, the almost-snoring Mersenne triplets. He climbed through the now-empty round house and into the glare of morning. It was time to look where he could not see, in the heart of story.

The number 17 took him back downtown. It was coach 4680, a curious number in its own right, but he was trying to find the place not to look. Hunting for ideas, Eleutherio tried the main branch of the Multnomah County Public Library. There were a million stories there, all dead and frozen to their pages, but numbers abounded there too—stuck to book spines, on shelf ends, running in endless repetition at the corners of the printed pages.

He ghosted the vast central stairwell a while, feeling foolish and unfocused. Certainly no one had tucked a missing Tri-Met bus in the upstairs book stacks of the library. 4517 was still missing from his sight.

Why couldn't he see it?

Because it wasn't there.

Eleutherio considered the number 4422. There was a number riddled with 2s—two 2s, two more 2s raised to the second power. They added up to 12, which was one 2, symbolically. It was a killer number, had almost literally killed Pretty McTeague. And it had been the number of his bus.

4517 had gone into Pretty McTeague's story, drawn there by her body walking like a dream in broad daylight seeking her spirit. 4517 had become 4422.

Everyone had gone home last night. They just hadn't ridden 4517. They'd ridden 4422.

Eleutherio almost whooped for joy. He raced down the stairs, burst out the doors of the library onto SW 10th Avenue and slammed into Pretty McTeague in her denim hip huggers and striped halter top.

"Hey, Lefty," she said, folding him in as if for a hug.

"What...?"

"Play nice," she whispered in his ear, cramming his face into her breasts. "I'm sorry, hon."

"Sorry for what?" His voice was muffled by her chest.

"Not coming back for you sooner." She pulled him to one side, her hand pinched tight on his upper arm. They started walking south, Pretty McTeague dragging him along.

"Coming back for me?" Eleutherio felt stupid. Wizards were never supposed to be *behind* the story.

"Who's your momma, little wizard boy?"

"I..."

"You was born on a bus, I died under a bus. I drank too much between times, but I was there at both ends. Traded my life for yours, finally...son."

At Taylor she tugged him onto an idling Tri-Met bus.

4422, Eleutherio realized.

His bus. Always his bus. Not because they'd changed the number. Because Pretty—his mother—had died of this bus, and the power of her spirit flowed to him.

She hadn't been keeping his power from him on the bus these last years. She'd been keeping it *for* him.

Until now. "What next?" he asked.

Pretty sat herself in the driver's seat, shut the door, and buckled up. "I'm back," she said simply, then gave him a tight smile. "Your power is mine. I never was no wizard before, but I got to say, I already see the world differently."

She was as homely in the flesh as her spirit had been, but she didn't have the pale-rot look of the grave, nor the slick-plastic look of the embalmed. That body hadn't been in the ground these past years, he realized.

"You're not Pretty McTeague," he said slowly.

"Right, kid. And you're the ghost of Elvis."

"No. You're not. You're someone else, glamored to look like her. To fool the spirit on this bus."

Her knuckles were anger-red where she clutched the bus' big wheel. "I'm back, damn it." She looked startled at her own words.

This was wrong. Completely wrong. Eleutherio reached out for the numbers around him. The odometer on the dashboard, the second odometer on the right rear wheel hub, the license plate, the speedometer, the incidental numbers printed on the fare box and in the telephone numbers of the bus signage. He thought of his 61-divisor perfect number, rolled 2,658,455,991,569,831,744,654,692,615,953,842,176 around in his head. He cloaked himself in numbers, clothed himself in numbers, anchored their power points and let them stream around him.

Driving, Pretty McTeague couldn't fight him off. "I'm your mother, kid," she shouted, though the air inside the bus wavered and crackled.

They crossed NW 13th Avenue—another prime—then the viaduct over I-405. Air under the bus, cross traffic, a number with a zero at its heart, void and amoral. Eleutherio swung his trailing stream of numbers and wrapped them around his mother.

"Go on," he shouted in her ear. "Pass on. You are done here. Rest."

He reached for her spirit, into the body which was dissolving into a nest of 2s. She fought, Pretty McTeague fought him hard, but over the emptiness of the Interstate bridge, away from the grounding earth, her spirit was weakened.

Shrieking, she fled.

Her body collapsed into a tangle of rats and pigeons and weather twine and shopping bags and old shoes, which exploded all over the bus. 4422 ground to a halt just at the light at 14th Avenue as the panicked animals fled.

Gathering the quivering remains of his powers, Eleutherio opened the door and stepped to the curb. None of his spirit remained behind this time.

He walked a while, away from the sirens and the horns honking at the stalled bus, then eventually sat down and made another list. This time he wrote on the back of a used Starbucks napkin.

0. I was born on a bus
1. Pretty McTeague died under a bus
1. She was my mother
2. She stayed to watch over me
3. Someone called her back and set her against me
5. Wizards

He looked up to see Old Kevyn standing in front of him, wearing an enormous wool coat and a ragged sombrero, though it was already close to eighty degrees. The *nombrejo* leaned on a Fred Meyer shopping cart filled with old combat boots. Lots of numbers in any well-worn laced shoe, Eleutherio knew, but the multiple eyelets of a combat boot increased that even more.

That cart was like a battery of number power. And because it was wheeled, it was accessible to a transit wizard.

"Glad you're still with us, kid," Old Kevyn said.

Eleutherio was tired all over again. Had he just killed his mother? She'd been dead for years. "You don't come out in the daylight often."

Old Kevyn nodded slowly. "New wizard don't come to his power often."

"Sure. Did you make all...that...happen?"

"Some of the *nombrejos* worked together on it. It was time, kid. You're getting older."

"I'm twelve. That ain't old."

"Old enough." Old Kevyn hunkered down next to his shopping cart. "You ever wonder why we're such a bunch of weirdos, kid? Us *nombrejos*? Misfits in the third degree."

"Never thought about it, really." *Nombrejos* were *nombrejos*. He'd always assumed their powers had eaten through them, changed them, made them something else.

"Most of us don't find numbers until it's way too late. Wizard stuff... magic...it changes a person. Not many kids come to it." Old Kevyn sighed. "We was kind of hoping you'd grow up straight and clean and true and smart. Get a job at a bank or something. Use the power of your numbers to do more than kill off rats and keep poor kids breathing a little longer. Save neighborhoods, cities." He leaned forward. "We believe, kid, but we're...busted open. Us wizards. No one comes to it whole. Me and some of the others, the ones who still think halfway straight, we thought...hoped." He sighed. "You, kid. You're the next big thing."

Eleutherio started to cry, startling himself. He couldn't remember ever simply letting go and sobbing. "I just killed my mother. I never knew her, never knew she existed. And you made me *kill* her."

"She's been dead for years, kid. And now...now you don't have to ride that bus all day long to have your power. It's inside you." A few rattling breaths. "Right?"

He thought about the bus. It was just a bus again, stalled out of place in an intersection a few blocks away. The transit magic was in him now. "Yeah."

"Everybody has a trial to come to their powers, kid. Yours was just a little better organized."

Eleutherio was quiet for a while. He studied his fingers, refusing to look up at Old Kevyn. He didn't know what he wanted, but nothing felt right now. He was too big, overfilling his skin with grief and power both.

Was this what it meant to be a grown-up? Responsible for things you hated?

"I want to go home," he finally said. Eleutherio got up.

Old Kevyn put his arm around Eleutherio's shoulders. "Come on, kid."

They stashed the cart and took the bus. Route 17, coach number 4471. Eleutherio didn't think about the numbers at all. Instead he let the old man keep hugging him all the way back to their stop.

A Different Way into the Life

Another one of the Portland wizards stories, this from a very different point of view than "Number of the Bus." Written to commission for Loren Coleman and the anthology Wizards, Inc.

Sunday the 15th, evening

The exhausted wizard cupped her hand around the dog end of a hand-rolled cigarette and tried to get one last drag out of the wretched thing. Cold, wet wind snatched the trail of sweet smoke into the evening air.

"Bugger it," she snarled and flipped the butt with a practiced snap of her fingers. It spun away on the breeze, trailing a tiny spray of extremely short-lived Heisenbergian butterflies. Diamond dust wings glittered in the shadows before exploding into lacy clouds of ash.

The street glistened with damp. The air smelled rotten wet. It wasn't quite raining, one of those Northwest evenings where the sea had come down out of the sky to soak the world without ever quite precipitating into identifiable rain. Chilly, too. Amid the joys of Portland weather, she had toiled through another long damned day of badgering everyone on the street—krusties, transients, janitors, taco wagon drivers, professional bus riders, you name it. Anybody from the subeconomy or the underclass she'd found, she'd talked to.

Nothing to show for it.

Nada.

She pulled a crumpled photo from the pocket of her Gore-Tex coat. Portland in winter was no place for substandard clothing, and no one in their right mind used magic just to keep warm. That would be like setting your house on fire so you could have light to read by. The picture hadn't changed in the hours she'd spent showing it to people, looking for a spark of recognition, or even better, the dull glow of a lie. A girl, Cauc, mid-teens, pale brown hair falling over one eye, a smile that could buy her way through life if she used it right. Sunlight in the background over one shoulder, image cropped in tight to the right of her face.

"Have you seen her?"

"*¿Usted ha visto a esta muchacha?*"

Even Cantonese, a few times, though she'd had to cheat to reach inside that language. Sparks flared when she did that, trees in sidewalk planters creaked, and once in a convenience store, two wine bottles had exploded.

Magic sucked.

She took the number 19 bus home and tried to figure a different way into the life of Maisie Potter. The easy way wasn't working too well.

▲▼▲

Monday the 16th, morning

The wizard sat in her cubicle, looking blankly at spreadsheets. Melançon stuck his head around the corner, already talking before he could even see what she might be doing. "I need your end of the Buchanan proposal before noon Wednesday."

He wasn't a bad egg, for a vice president. There was some quintessential quality of assholery which seemed to be a prerequisite for promotion in corporate America. Melançon mostly kept it under control. He had rich guy habits—skeet shooting, overpriced clothes and cars—but he was okay.

She smiled at him, still worn out from her weekend of working the streets. "That's mostly up to Jason, boss man. I'm just doing the competitive analysis on that one. Besides, I've got the Varicorp and United Metathemics bids going too, on tight deadline." Deadlines he'd given her. It was a very short to-do list, but very wide. Everything was top priority.

"You'll get it done." He smiled back, capped teeth bleached to appliance-like perfection. "You always find the time somehow."

Steal it, the wizard thought with a trace of worn-out bitterness. All the work she'd put into her trade, and what she did was steal time and look for the lost. There weren't three other people here at Gierloff, Williamson and Closson with magical skills. Bartelme in accounting, who was a wizard with numbers—saints and madmen, she hated that phrase!—and that intern who worked with the copy writers. The kid didn't know it, though, completely raw. Had the glow, but no more focus than an old CRT.

That was it. Them and her. In her little cube.

The walls were that horrid carpet fabric used in low-end cubes everywhere. Most of her colleagues had covered theirs with birthday cards, fuzzy scans of unfunny cartoons, photos of vacations to Crater

Lake or Disneyland, and mountains of stupid plastic toys. Not the wizard. She had her pouch of tobacco and rolling papers—no smoking in the building, not here in green Oregon—and the little skull from one of *them* that she kept inside a Japanese paper box, but that was it.

Well, there were office supplies, files and whatnot, but those came with the cube, not with her.

It was difficult to focus on the Buchanan response. GWC had files on all major direct and indirect competitors, but she still had to go through each proposal, looking for nuances. Was there an offshore angle? What about mom-and-pops cutting into the business with lowball pricing? Did they know who was running the sales effort on the competitive side?

That was why GWC put up with her. Paid her in cash, even, which was damned near illegal these days. The wizard never wrote her name down on anything, anywhere. She was, as they said, unbanked. Undegreed. Uneverything, really.

But she could reach out and see what the other guys were doing. No one could figure out the insides of a deal like her. No one without her talents, at any rate.

"Time to set the house on fire," she whispered, and took the tiny skull from the Japanese paper box.

▲▼▲

Monday the 16th, evening

That evening was a little warmer than the weekend had been. After taking the bus home to eat and rest a while, she chose to walk back downtown, taking the Hawthorne Bridge. It was an old lift bridge, one of the first of its kind, she'd read, recently restored to a sort of industrial age beauty. The name had magical associations, of course, reaching back to Joseph of Arimathea. It was old, built in 1910, named after the director of Oregon's first mental hospital. Iron over running water, ancient Grail mysteries, and twentieth-century lost souls—it was a miracle the bridge didn't lift itself up out of the riverbed and dance under a gibbous moon.

The buses from her part of town, the near Southeast, generally ran over the Ross Island Bridge. It should have been a double cross-roads—the bridge carried US-26 over I-5 and over OR-99E—which would have been very powerful indeed. Instead the designers had gone to great lengths to ensure that neither cross-roads actually met, instead extending the spans well onto the bluffs set back from the Willamette River on each side. The result was a monstrosity, a sort of giant magical trap, impairing the energies of the river below, which was already sluggish from the dam at Oregon City. To make matters worse, Ross Island itself had been gutted, the heart literally torn out by a gravel pit.

The wizard idly wondered as she walked how much of the effort at the distorted bridge design and the destruction of the island was aimed at the widow Rebecca Ross who'd once farmed there. One of Portland's founding witches, perhaps.

She paused as the Hawthorne Bridge passed over from water to land. Sniffed. The air smelled crisp, almost hot, as if the doors had been opened on vast yet distant ovens. Downtown was different tonight. The cluster of high rises by the river gleamed as their lights fought back against the encroachment of darkness. Red beacons blinked at their tops, warding the structures from sky-borne evil and incidentally warning off aircraft. The streets gleamed this evening as well, with a dusk dewfall beneath a sky clear enough to see stars even against the city's glare.

The energies had shifted substantially from the day before. Perhaps the change of bridges had been sufficient. The wizard promised herself she'd keep away from the Ross Island Bridge for a while, and look into the history of Portland's other bridges as well. Had the office of the city's bridge engineer been in a state of magical warfare for the last century?

She sat on a bench in Tom McCall Park, right along the waterfront, and rolled another cigarette. Her right hand was stiff, so she used it to hold the thing while pinching and forming with her left. The tobacco was a particular strain of white burley which came from a grower in the King's Valley area who much like the wizard herself worked on a cash basis only. Tobacco was just a form of nightshade, after all, and carried many of that poison's magical associations. Hers was harvested by the dark of the moon, and cured over a fire of smoldering rose petals.

The smoke didn't give her a buzz. Rather, the cigarettes opened the doors of her mind. Different doors than the little skull on her desk. Or rather, different keys to the same lock.

Use the skull, see the world of numbers, businesses sliding like icebergs on the ocean of commerce, individual executives and salespeople sailing dreamlike through the air as small black clouds. Dreadfully mundane, but it kept beans on her table and shoes on her feet.

She rolled her cigarettes in papers torn from old blackletter books of English statute written in law French. She generally stole them from libraries and antique dealers. Lighting one of them let her focus in on the world of energies, what some called spirits. These ranged from the sad and simple thoughts of trees to the great, slow, vengeful musings of the rivers wounded by dams and bridges and sewer outflows.

People, as well, of course.

Like Maisie Potter. Living or dead, she would have energy. If Maisie had spoken to someone, been somewhere, walked, eaten, shat or died, the wizard should have been able to see her.

Yesterday the city had fought her, the energies twisting wrong. In retrospect, she supposed she couldn't have found a penny in the street under those conditions. Today she'd approached from a different portal, walking the span laid down in honor of Joseph of Arimathea's hawthorn bush at Wearyall Hill.

The wizard puffed her smoke into the gathering gloom. It sparkled a moment, then hissed away to the north.

She shivered. The smoke had moved against the wind.

"You're out there, aren't you?"

The wind gave her no answer, only direction. The wizard walked north, following the sparks. Behind her, the grass around the bench crinkled in a new circle of dark, dehydrated rot.

▲▼▲

Monday the 16th, morning

The Buchanan proposal had been choppier than she expected. The numbers sea was in a froth, much as it had been back when Enron was gaming the California power crisis. The wizard sometimes wondered why more of her kind didn't play Wall Street the way the energy traders had.

Or maybe they did, and their efforts were mutually canceling.

Her home iceberg, GWC, radiated stability even amid the rough weather. That was Bartelme in Accounting keeping the company steady. The wizard gave him a sort of mental nod. Unremarked, no doubt. Bartelme had long ago made it clear he had no use for her.

Wizards were an unstable lot at best. Asperger's syndrome if not full-blown autism seemed to be almost *de rigeur* for her kind of powers. She had no illusions about herself—someone who refused to ever divulge her personal name bore no claim to normalcy whatsoever. Bartelme's indifference to her was as natural as breathing, for him.

The wizard's curse was that she *did* care about other people.

She set that thought aside. It belonged to the other part of life, the part that was currently wondering where Maisie Potter was. This part of her life was important now. Give Melançon his sales information. Every time GWC closed one of her deals, she got a thousand dollars in old, mixed-denomination bills. Above and beyond her weekly payouts.

She knew she showed up on the books as contract research. Her cube was listed as "Miscellaneous, Visitor/Contractor." She was nothing but a ripple that sometimes tossed up critical nuggets of fuel for the engine of commerce that employed her.

The wizard skimmed low over the rough seas, following the threads back to the iceberg that was Buchanan Sales and Services. It was much bigger than GWC. A glowering dark gray fog shrouded the upper shoulders of the berg. That would be their competitors. Though it was a strange presence, more of a mantle than the little cloud of an account executive sniffing around the deal.

When silver lightning crackled, she realized the competition was using a wizard, too. Someone much bigger and rougher than her.

She kept a distance, orbiting Buchanan and watching the fog. Shapes moved within. Rats, perhaps, gnawing at Buchanan. Definitely rougher than her. The wizard preferred finesse, a light touch, the magical equivalent of peering through windows. The competition was actively invading their sales prospect, turning Buchanan into a target. A resource to be exploited.

A big boy then, from the East Coast. Or possibly Chicago or Los Angeles. One of the really high-end consultancies, the kind that had attorneys on the sales staff and quiet men in dark cars to do the street work. Most people didn't operate this way. Couldn't afford to spend the magical power, couldn't effectively manage the consequences if caught by the temporal world legal systems or press.

Melançon was not going to be happy.

The wizard backed away. She thought maybe she'd follow the cloud's track across the sea of numbers, give Melançon a name to work with at least.

Competitive analysis, her skinny brown ass.

▲▼▲

Monday the 16th, evening

Just before she passed under the Morrison Bridge, the wizard stopped. The east bank of the Willamette was a glare of streetlights, Interstate and warehouses, but she peered across the slow, muddy water anyway. She relit the hand-roll and took a deep drag. When she released it, the smoke rose silver into the moonlight.

Nothing was pulling now.

Morrison was a strange bridge, too. It didn't really connect to Morrison Street at either end. The street was interrupted, energies of transit simply grounding off into the Willamette and the open air. A lie, this bridge. If you looked at the waterfront retaining walls in daylight, you could see the scars of the old Morrison Bridge, that had united the east and west extensions of the street.

More magical truncation? Or just the exigencies of traffic engineering in a city so inconveniently bisected by a major river? North-flowing at that, in violation of the southward trend of water in the United States.

She should pay more attention to geography, the wizard thought. A *lot* more attention. She'd never focused on places in her magical work. Businesses, which were of course abstractions, and people. She resolved to take up the study, once some of her time came back to her.

The wizard looked carefully at the bridge. Much less decorative than the Hawthorne Bridge. Not so unnatural as the Ross Island Bridge with its broken cross-roads and rape of the namesake island. No, Morrison was low, with two squat piers holding the counterweights required to lift the center span. Unremarkable concrete structures, save for the control towers clinging to them on the south side, where she also stood.

Carefully the wizard extracted the photograph of Maisie Potter. She held it out at arm's length in the reflected streetlight and stared at both the image and the bridge beyond. The faint curl of smoke from her cigarette wreathed Maisie and glittered once more.

"You under that bridge, girl?"

She took the stairs leading up from the park's esplanade to the bridge deck passing over. The wizard needed to find the middle of the bridge, look out across the water, see what the night could tell her.

▲▼▲

Monday the 16th, morning

The dark cloud was unquestionably the cause of the chop in the sea of numbers. The wizard followed it some goodly distance, past icebergs, longships, little islands with steaming hills, silver-backed beasts rolling just beneath the surface of this strange ocean of metaphor.

Time and distance were artifacts of the observer here. Arguably this was true in the temporal world too, but she couldn't take short-cuts through either of those dimensions without expending considerable effort and creating noticeable side effects. In here the transition was only a matter of will and word.

She expended the will and mouthed the word.

Immediately the wizard was at the base of a black glass tower rising up out of the twisting sea of numbers. It seemed to plunge directly

into the depths, while the upper reaches vanished into the sky. Not a
tower then, but perhaps a line drawn perpendicular to the plane of this
inner world.

That took more power than the wizard had ever seen. Even the great
banks in New York and London and Hong Kong, massive and stable as
they were, had bounds and limits to them. Islands, or bergs the size of
islands, but finite. This was a dagger stabbing through both sea and sky,
faced with a million windows in which she could see million workers
toiling over a million desks.

A name. She needed a name to take back to Melançon.

The wizard circled, looking for a way in. She kept her distance.
Simply coming up next to one of those infinite windows struck her as
a supremely bad idea. Her lower back tingled at the thought. Clouds
seemed to roil around various levels of the tower, close cousins to the
one which even now gnawed at the Buchanan berg. Rats or worse lurked
within those dark fogs. She wanted nothing to do with them.

Finally the wizard had to conclude that there was no obvious
entrance. No spiritual equivalent of a building sign either. Just this
overproud tower filled with people.

Where had they gotten all those people, anyway?

Ordinarily she would have thought this illusion, as everything was
here in the sea of numbers, essentially, but there was too much solidity.
The thing practically vibrated.

They couldn't be real. Everything here was a metaphor. How could
this not be a metaphor?

People as a metaphor for what, she wondered, closing in slowly on
the tower despite her fears.

The wizard noticed something odd. No matter how much she moved
toward the tower, it remained the same apparent distance away. She circled, trying to get closer and closer, setting aside her caution, but there
was no "closer."

Finally, she closed her eyes and extended her hand. (The wizard
believed firmly in keeping her own body shape at all times—it created
far less confusion for her.) She reached right into where she would have
sworn the building stood, until her fingers closed around something
narrow, cold and sharp.

Stifling a shriek, the wizard pulled her hand back. There was a
bloody line scored on the palm.

The clouds filled with rats moved quickly toward her. The wizard
abandoned her mission and fled into the roiling darkness, low over the
troubled waves of the numbers sea. She needed to be far enough away

from the tower—Blade? Wire?—to release her hold on this world without being followed home by agents of that terrible entity.

▲▼▲

Monday the 16th, evening

Out on the Morrison Bridge, the wizard flexed her stiff right hand. The scar was bright there, though she had never been cut in the temporal world. Not on the palm, anyway.

She stood on a sort of balcony, a place for pedestrians and bicyclists to wait while the bridge was being raised and lowered. She leaned over the railing and tried to see the pier beneath her. Where was Maisie Potter?

Another question occurred to the wizard in that moment, standing over open water on a bridge with a false name.

Who was Maisie Potter?

Her hand throbbed at that thought, her head aching in near-harmony. Right in the center, where the third eye would be if she had one.

She tugged the photo from her pocket. No Gore-Tex tonight. Instead the wizard wore a fleece zip-up over an old wool sweater and two oxford shirts. Layers, always with the layers. Keep warm and confuse others. She studied the picture of Maisie Potter once more.

"Why am I looking for you, girl?" she asked the night.

Maisie had a pretty smile, the wizard thought with a twinge in her gut. But why should she care? The wizard was still a virgin. It wasn't a requirement of her craft, but sex was messy and powerful and took too much away from what she could do. Should do. Needed to do.

She knew for a fact how overwhelming sex was, and she had the ache in her groin to prove it.

Who had given her this photograph?

She had been downtown the day before, looking in the rain, working against hard opposition from the energies of the city. Sunday, that was.

What about Saturday, the day before that?

The wizard tried to focus her memory. Nothing came clear. Hunting Maisie, maybe, in the warren of post-industrial streets on the east bank of the Willamette.

A problem, then. She wasn't born yesterday. She had a mother. Must have had a mother. A face, the wizard thought. What did her mother's face look like?

A name, then. Her own. Her mother's. The name of someone or something not connected to work. The only name she knew outside the walls of Gierloff, Williamson and Closson was Maisie Potter.

Shaking from cold and fear, she rolled another cigarette, then lit it from a matchbook with a Matisse painting on the cover. She knew who Matisse was, for the land's sake, she wasn't ignorant! The wizard puffed on the cigarette and tried to let go of the birds of her fear.

They fluttered close, but they left her chest.

Was *she* Maisie Potter?

No. That couldn't be true. She would have noticed her own face in the mirror. Besides, the wizard told herself with a look at her hands, she was far too old to be the girl in the photograph. And rather the wrong color, too. Coffee-with-cream, the wizard thought of herself as being, though she drank neither. A pleasant enough skin tone, belonging to all races and none.

The walkway beneath her feet thrummed. The drawbridge pier was surely full of machinery, counterweights, the apparatus required to lift one hundred forty feet of span to the vertical for the passage of ships.

How could Maisie Potter be down there in the machine-darkness? Surrounded by iron-as-steel, and oil-the-blood-of-the-earth.

How could a million people fit inside the blade of a sword plunging from dark heaven to the darker heart of the sea of numbers?

Memories were beginning to break up in the wizard's head, to reassemble, finding new configurations.

Anger, too.

Someone was *using* her.

That made the wizard very angry indeed. With will and word, she set about cutting across time and space.

▲▼▲

Monday the 16th, morning

Her face slammed into the work surface of her cube, narrowly missing the Macintosh keyboard. The wizard sat up groaning and rubbed her forehead. There would be a goose egg later, right in the center.

She stared at her hand. The skin of the palm was an angry, raw red. She'd grabbed something ugly, then.

She'd grabbed a *building*.

That didn't make any sense.

The wizard felt a sense of anger coalescing inside her. She didn't understand where it was coming from, but she knew enough to let it gather, to see where the impulse would lead. There were different ways into everything. A wizard had to be ready for locks that turned the wrong way, doors that opened against their own hinges.

What pulled the sky and sea together, she thought? Nothing, they just were each what they were. What kept them apart? Again, nothing. It was all a matter of perspective, and perhaps the density of the water in air.

The secret of knowledge was little more than a matter of perspective, then. Knowing where to stand and how to look.

She glanced up to see Melançon frowning at her.

"How's the Buchanan proposal coming?"

The wizard had never quite noticed the way her boss's eyebrows met when he was concentrating on something unpleasant. On her.

The small of her back tingled. That meant trouble was at hand.

"Big competitor," she said, sticking to the narrow truth. "Someone who's actually working the deal from inside Buchanan."

"Interesting." He made his frown go away, but the wizard could see that was an act of will. "You've sussed out who the players are, right?"

"No…" Careful, she thought, feeling the heat blooming within her. "They've got some pretty heavy coverage. Nothing for me to read."

"Come on, you can read anything."

You can find anything, he'd said once, his voice echoing from behind a locked door in the palace of her memory even as he handed her a photograph of a pretty girl. *Just keep looking.*

"Just keep working."

"I…" Careful, careful. "I think I'm going to lunch."

He made a show of looking at his watch in surprise. "Barely ten in the morning. You should try eating breakfast more often."

"Right." She forced a laugh. "I'll have more on the Buchanan competitor this afternoon."

He walked away, looking over his shoulder.

The wizard followed the thread of her anger. She knew she was at the other end of the burning strand, but where and how? There were many ways to do this, many reasons, but her other self had sent only anger, not a situation report.

She stood to leave her cube and found Bartelme squatting on a stool just outside.

"Back to work, missy," he said with a brown-toothed leer.

"No," said the wizard. With will and word, she set about cutting across time and space.

▲▼▲

Monday the 16th, night

The wizard dropped about six inches to a filthy concrete balcony in a large room. She scanned quickly, hands up to ward off any attack. The space was huge but claustrophobic, filled with enormous machines barely visible in the light of a few distant bulbs. The ceiling groaned and popped and hissed.

She had to be inside the Morrison Bridge, in one of the piers with the draw equipment.

She snapped her fingers and a cigarette butt spun out into the dark well of the pier. It flared, leaving a trail of brilliant butterflies which in turn burst to glowing ash.

Nothing out there but weights and wheels and gears. Like the inside of a massive engine. But iron, so much iron it even gave her a headache. And grease, too, immense amounts of blood-of-the-earth spread here.

All squatting on the bed of the river outside these concrete walls, another insult to its free-flowing energy.

"Maisie!" she said.

The wizard was rapidly coming into possession of more and more of her memories. Melançon, offering her a job by letter hand-couriered to her little southeast Portland sublet. Arguments over where and how she should apply her skills. He had given her the Japanese paper box for her little skull, the bones themselves coming from a mossy grave in the Garden Beneath, a relic of the Bright Days.

What had the paper been? The wizard was horrified. She'd put one of *their* skulls inside paper, where anything could have been printed or written.

Melançon must have already begun to snare her then, in a web of cash and inattention cast by that bastard Bartelme.

The wizard found her way down a ladder to the metal floor that gave service access to the great counterweights. This was a place of power, where *they* would have been nothing but cries on the wind in the presence of so much iron amid running water.

It wasn't that the world needed the Bright Days again. *They* had been terrible masters, cruel as cats, vicious as badgers, indifferent as the sweet songbirds in *their* apple trees. But *they* had given magic to humans. The first keys to the wizard's doors. *Their* path had been a different way into the life of the world.

Why was she thinking so much of *them* now? Not simply the memory cascade in her head, either.

The wizard rolled a fresh cigarette. Even in the shadows the word "maleficum" caught her eye on the torn page. Another one for the fire, she told herself. Good enough.

She lit the hand roll, took a deep drag, let the smoke open her own doors.

The picture. Maisie Potter.

The wizard took it out of her pocket once more.

The photo glowed.

"Maisie." She looked at the bright background over the girl's shoulder. *Where* had this been taken?

Truth dawned on the wizard. The Garden Beneath. Maisie Potter had been smiling somewhere Under the Hill when some wizard or fool had brought a camera past the stone doors.

And armed with that proof, Melançon had set the wizard to looking for the way back to the Garden.

Maisie. Not far from Maeve. Also known as Queen Mab, mistress over all of *them*. The mead-queen of the Garden Beneath, feeding blood to her lords and servants. Her own, in drops, mixed with that of children stolen from the temporal world. Potter for the Potter's field, no doubt, the traditional cemetery of the poor where the nameless dead returned from beneath the earth were buried.

Melançon wanted to bring *their* madness back into the everyday light.

That must have been the shaft she had found plunging into the numbers sea. The sword of *them*, reaching out from the Garden Beneath, needing only someone to open the door.

"Not by all the fires in Gehenna," said the wizard. She wedged the photo of Mab in the teeth of one of the great gears that drove the lift span of the Morrison Bridge, took another drag on her cigarette, then used the glowing tip to set fire to the photo. It flared, then burned sputtering bright as if made of magnesium.

That was good enough for the wizard. The next time the bridge lifted, the ashes would be ground between tons of cold iron, then fall beneath the grating of the floor to rot amid grease and leaked-in river water.

Now she had to deal with Melançon. And Bartelme, too, most likely. The wizard discovered she had neither the will nor the word to step across space and time now. That had been exhausted, and it would be some hours before she could find that part of herself again.

So instead she climbed, up the ladder to the balcony, then up the iron stairs to the locked door at the top. There she was defeated by steel locks on the outside, with a spell laid upon them. Though the wizard worked an hour or more, she could not budge the door by strength or spirit. Here in the room of iron and blood-of-the-earth, she could not call out for help. This pier was as much a magical trap as the Ross Island Bridge, only this one was folded in around her.

Eventually she curled up by the door and slept. There was nothing to do but wait, and she might as well be rested when the door next opened.

▲▼▲

Tuesday the 17th, morning

The wizard awoke to a deep groaning rattle. The bridge was going up. She looked across the space at the lift machinery, counterweights descending down the depth of the pier, and realized that the far end would be exposed to air as the deck members lifted.

Moving quickly as she dared, the wizard slid down the stairs and the subsequent ladder to the grating that served as a floor. She was all too conscious of the massive weights shifting just by her head as she passed them, but still she sprinted to the inspection ladder bolted to the opposite wall. The wizard scrambled up that ladder as the bridge reached its lift angle.

The interlocking hinges of the bridge deck and the lifting arms towered above her. She could be crushed here as easily as the ashes of Maisie's photo beneath her feet. The wizard scrambled up the exposed edge of the stonework and looked down.

The Willamette was perhaps seventy feet below here, dark brown in the early morning light. A small boat, certainly not what the span had been lifted for, bobbed in the water.

Melançon and Bartelme stood in the boat. Melançon waved cheerfully at her, then lifted a rifle.

Lacking any other choice, the wizard leapt into the open air, dropping toward them.

The fall, as such things do, seemed to stretch time like taffy. Much ran through her head as she plunged. The will and the word were back, but it would do her no good to send herself away. She needed to stop these two, now.

Melançon smiled, his perfect teeth gleaming, as he pulled the trigger. A skeet shooter, she remembered. The wizard was much bigger than any clay pigeon.

She summoned the will and the word and sent the bullet away from her. Though it had been aimed true at the wizard, the round cut across time and space to plow into Bartelme's ribs from the left side. The shock sent him tumbling with a shriek into the Willamette where the water now boiled from the pull of her magic.

The wizard burned the last of her will and word to land smack on top of Melançon, neat as jumping off a ladder. She then used a very old fashioned and decidedly non-magical elbow to break his perfect teeth. His weapon had gone flying into the river when she hit him, so the wizard settled for striking Melançon's temple hard against the side of the boat, twice, before she slipped into the warm river and let the water carry her away.

▲▼▲

Tuesday the 17th, night

The wizard sat in a coffee house in Southeast and listened with half an ear to the news. She hadn't been able to get back in to Gierloff, Williamson and Closson to retrieve her skull. Security had turned her away with a shake of the head, doubtless sometime before Melançon's disappearance was known. The wizard was willing to let that little problem slide. She wasn't so sure she wanted to be near one of *them* anyway, not at this point. Not even *their* bones.

Now the television was talking about the murder-suicide of a local businessman and one of his employees. The coroner's office had reported a silver bullet was used. The newsblonde made a werewolf joke.

The wizard stepped out into the evening dark, taking in the scent of the air and wondering what she should do next. She never had enough money, but she never quite ran out either.

Somehow, another job seemed out of the question.

The wizard lit a cigarette and walked into the shadows, confident she would find a different way.

Green Grass Blues

This is the third of the Portland wizards stories, written as an emergency replacement for "Fat Man" when that story sold to Steve Jones and had to be dropped from the planned table of contents for The River Knows Its Own. *I used the opportunity to tie up some of the ideas I'd developed in "Number of the Bus" and "A Different Way Into the Life." I've occasionally contemplated writing a novel within this continuity, but there are many people who do urban fantasy much more effectively than I, and the shiny has not yet been strong enough to draw me into a book.*

There wasn't much in the world stupider than sheep. Except more sheep, perhaps. T.R. wasn't inclined to test the theory. In any case, the summer was warm, the meadow was green enough to hurt his eyes, and the chimney swifts that lived in the ruined mill were writing omens in the Oregon sky.

He sat in a deck chair with a Little Oscar full of Mountain Dew propped next to him and an air rifle on his lap. T.R. had found that potting the ewes with the air rifle was good way to get them to pay attention. This deep into the summer, their wool had regrown enough that the pellets didn't hurt them.

Something was bothering the sheep, though. The same thing that made the swifts write glyphs of warning in the air, presumably. Sighing, T.R. put down his copy of *The Chymical Wedding of Christian Rosenkreutz* and picked up the rifle.

With luck it would be a coyote, or a stray dog off the Interstate. Without luck...well, there was a reason the grassland wizards liked good, solid basalt beneath their soil.

He popped open the chamber of the air rifle and dumped out the orange plastic pellets. T.R. then reached into his pocket for an old Red Man tobacco pouch filled with an entirely different sort of pellet.

It always paid to be prepared.

Of course, now his rifle stank of myrrh and old blood.

The Chymical Wedding fluttered to the grass as T.R. left his chair behind and walked his field, following the restless tracks of the stupid sheep, guided by the swirling calls of the swifts.

▲▼▲

"A.P.!" T.R. shouted as he slammed through the aluminum door of his master's trailer. "There were footprints in the grass."

His master was stretched on the fraying plaid couch. Snoring, as usual, with mustard stains on the old man's wife-beater undershirt, while the fishing channel played in Spanish on the television.

At least he's wearing pants, T.R. thought.

Distracted from his excitement and fear, T.R. took a deep breath. When A.P. was meditating—at least that's what the old man called it—he didn't like to be woken up. The working to summon him back was simple enough, but they had an iron rule out here on the grasslands.

No magic in the trailer.

You never brought the stink of work into your home.

Without the working, there wasn't much T.R. could do. He knew from experience that even firing a starter's pistol next to A.P.'s ear wouldn't have much effect. Not til his master was done.

T.R. stepped back out onto the little pine deck. The afternoon was wearing on. Exurban commuters from the government agencies in Salem were filtering down the county road in ones and twos. A thin finger of clouds was working its way over the Coastals from the west. There wasn't any scent of trouble in the air here, not at all.

No footprints in the yard, either.

He stepped off the porch to gather the three identical grass blades he'd need.

"Who's watchin' them sheep, boy? You're early."

He jumped slightly, before hiding his grimace as he turned to face A.P. Some days the old man just wasn't worth it. Most days, lately. "Bobbie Krausner is penning them for me, sir."

"And so you come runnin' back, drivin' like to draw somethin' down out of the mountains just to see what the hurry was."

"Sir." T.R. took a deep breath. "Footprints, sir. In the sheep grass."

A.P. locked stares with him a moment. His master was looking... thin. "Not your'n, I reckon."

"Big footprints, sir. *Big* footprints."

They both glanced east, to where the foothills of the Cascades dropped into the flat Willamette Valley floor.

"But nothin' there?" A.P.'s voice was soft as a shadow now.

"No sir. No feet at all."

"Walkin' backwards, they are. Well, we can't be havin' that. *Basta*." He stretched. "Here boy, get on with that grass. I'm projectin' right now. I reckon you need to wake me up."

"No magic in the trailer, sir."

A.P. gave him a look of profound irritation as he began to fade away. "Then open the damned door first and do it from the porch."

▲▼▲

They headed back out to the meadow in the evening dewfall. Grassland wizards mostly used pickup trucks for a variety of reasons, none of them esoteric. Vanished makes were strongly preferred, for reasons which *were* somewhat esoteric, so T.R. drove a rust-covered 1947 Hudson Big Boy with a redwood bed. A.P.'s vehicle was even stranger, a 1965 Mercury Econoline E100 with a spray-painted pattern of flowers and marijuana leaves all over.

Naturally they took A.P.'s Mercury, but T.R. still had to drive. He hated the old man's clutch. While he horsed the transmission and strained his knee, A.P. lit a twist of kind bud and stared out at the stars.

"You don't remember the last time, do you?" the old man asked.

T.R. jammed it down to second for a tight turn. The drive wasn't ten minutes, but still that was going to be too long in this monster. "Feet? No, sir. Before I got the call."

"Before you was old enough to know the difference, I'm thinkin'." A.P. laughed. "What'd you tell Bobbie K. when you asked him to bring in the sheep?"

"Told her there was a problem I had to hotfoot it out to take care of. I didn't figure something invisible was going to eat her just then. Besides, the sheep weren't that upset, and neither were the birds."

A.P. took a deep long drag. "Well, you'd be wrong about not being eaten by the invisible, but you was right about the signs." He stubbed the joint out in the Mercury's ash tray. "Probably."

They clanked to a halt along the west fence of the sheep meadow.

As promised, Bobbie had driven the sheep to their pen across the way. It was a smaller enclosure, fenced high to keep the coyotes out and with a shelter against the inevitable Oregon rain. A.P. got out, faced the pen with his arms spread wide, and just stood. T.R. stayed in the truck and listened to the ping of metal as the engine cooled. He knew his master didn't want to be interrupted while he read the flock.

Much more quickly than T.R. might have thought, A.P. dusted his hands together, then walked around the back of the truck. Never walk in front of a vehicle if you had the choice. Another grassland wizard rule, that was, one that made crossing city streets a significant challenge. But there were things which could see out of headlights which hadn't been properly treated. The front end of the Mercury stank the same as T.R.'s air rifle, when the air wasn't full of gas and burnt rubber.

T.R. slipped out the driver door and followed A.P. into the sheep meadow.

The old man walked toward the footprints as surely as if he had made them himself. He quartered around the track—three steps, two left and one right—staring at the ground in the moonlight. The dew had given texture to the shadows on the grass. The sheep had not stepped on the prints, either.

He wondered if that were a sign of intelligence or simply natural selection in action.

The footprints were roughly the same shape as a human print—as opposed to, for example, enormous chicken feet. Which was another possibility out here, depending on the season of the witch. T.R. estimated that the prints measured almost three feet from toe to heel.

A.P. bent down. "You look at these with any care, boy?"

"Came for you, sir," T.R. answered truthfully.

"Hmm." The old man fished a mechanical pencil from the pocket of the yellow Brake Specialists work shirt he'd donned on leaving the house. He reached down and touched the first of the footprints with it. "You ever ride in an early 1970s VW?"

"What?" That non-sequitur caught at T.R.'s wandering thoughts.

"Headliners were made of white vinyl. They had little pinholes in them. Don't know why, maybe kept the glue from coming loose from the heat. Who the hell knows why Germans do anything? If you stretched out in the back of an old VW and stared at the ceiling, after a while you couldn't tell if the pinholes were in the fabric, or floating above it."

"Did it help to be stoned?"

That earned him a sharp look. "Of course it helped to be stoned. It always helps to be stoned. There's more than one reason we call ourselves grassland wizards, boy."

"So..." T.R. tried to divine the point of A.P.'s ramble.

"So, look at these here prints, boy." He jabbed at the disturbed grass with the mechanical pencil. "See the grass? They's coming *up* out of the earth, not pounded down in."

T.R. bent down. Damned if the old man wasn't right. Despite himself, he shivered.

▲▼▲

A. What They Tell the Young Ones About Remembering the Balance

The thing you got to remember is we're not about fighting some battle between good and evil. The downtown wizards in Salem and Portland, they can balance the numbers and dance on the workings woven into GAAP and play games with the SEC and call it what they want. Down here in the valley, we're just living with the earth. Them volcanoes, them trees, them streams and rivers and elk and coyotes were all here long before any of us, and they'll be here long after we're gone.

But everything has a pattern. Actions that cause change in whatever's around them. And I don't just mean with feet or fingers or fins. Even a stone makes a dimple in the world. The thoughts of a squirrel or a trout mean something. Those purposes add up. Rock thinks slow, but there's a god damned *lot* of it on this planet. Salmon think in cycles, and if you don't think the river knows a fish's mind, then you're not paying any attention at all.

None of this has a purpose. Not in the way you and I do. It all balanced out, like cats in a sack too tired to fight in any more, til we came along. The ones before, the Indians, they weren't as bad as us. They didn't bind the rivers with iron and walls of stone. They didn't tear down the old forest and scar the land with roads and towns and cities. But they were like a fresh cat, stuck in that sack.

Us, with our cars and feedlots and silos, we're like a tiger stuck in that sack.

The land pushes back because that's all it knows how to do. It ain't evil, it ain't trying to hurt us any more than it's trying to help us. It's just seeking balance, like water seeking its own level.

Our purpose, us grassland wizards, is to help that balance along without giving away too much of what people need, nor taking away too much of what the land needs. Remember balance, and you'll never go completely wrong.

▲▼▲

They sat on the tailgate of A.P.'s Mercury and shared another joint. This one was a real spliff, fat as T.R.'s thumb, but they were on working time now. T.R. didn't toke on his own account, only when the magic called for it.

This was a night for magic.

The high-altitude cloud cover had moved in from the west, covering the sky and making a rainbow-dogged glow out of the moon. There was a will o' the wisp fog confusing the frogs and insects, though knee-high the air remained clear. The temperature was a bit more crisp than usual for July.

A.P. let a stream of smoke slip from his lips, staring upward. "We know some things it ain't."

"Not one of the Sisters," T.R. said. "That would be chicken feet."

"Right. You're thinkin', boy."

"Besides, it's the wrong season."

A.P. choked. It took T.R. a moment to realize his master was laughing. "You don't think a woman can't come out of her season? You got a lot to learn about girls." His voice trailed off into giggling.

"As may be, master, but there is a time for witches. This isn't it."

"Fair enough." He took another long drag, held it for a while, then let it slip away without ever releasing another stream. T.R. was impressed with the fact that A.P. never seemed to cough. "Ain't a witch. What else ain't it?" He passed the spliff back to T.R.

After a slow drag of his own, T.R. talked around the tingle in his throat. "Not a Skookum. Feet too big for bigfoot." That set him to giggling. He *hated* giggling. There was little enough dignity in being a wizard. This was just stupid.

Funny, but stupid.

A.P. seemed to agree without giggling. "No, no, not one of them. If it were, he'd have left a trail or not as he chose. 'Sides, they're polite. Whatever did this wasn't polite. Ain't neighborly to frighten the sheep. What else?"

"Nothing walked out of a river to do that. This meadow's too far from free-running water, and it would have left a trail."

"Right again." His master took another draw. "Damn, boy, who trained you up? They done a good job."

T.R. giggled again. He just couldn't seem to help it. "I wouldn't care to say, sir. Just a damned old fool."

"Reckon it was. Not one of the Sisters, not one of the brothers, not a water walker, no wise an air sign neither."

"Either the grass itself, or something of the earth." T.R.'s memory tingled. "You mentioned walking backwards, sir? I don't rightly know what that signifies."

"Walkin' backwards." A.P. hitched himself back on his elbows, despite the hard cold metal of the bed. "It ain't none of it magic, boy. You know that."

T.R. did know that. 'Wizard' was just a way of looking at things. "It's not magic, sir. You've taught me that time and again. Just nature by another path."

"Right. Well, some of them paths run backwards. Some things walk them."

▲▼▲

After that pronouncement, they passed the spliff back and forth in silence a while. T.R. reflected that silence had always been A.P.'s favorite teaching method. Or perhaps strongest weapon. Silence could just as easily signify support, questioning, disapproval or nap time. Sometimes all at once. It was almost always up to T.R. to break the quiet and fill the silence. If he didn't do that well, there were consequences. Usually starting with more silence.

The old man drove him crazy. But here he was, years into being an apprentice wizard. He could always go be a shepherd, he supposed, but that was basically what he did now. Still, all that grass could drive a man crazy.

T.R. turned his thoughts to the subject at hand.

Nature by another path. That was one of the catchphrases the grassland wizards used, when talking about the world. As with anything oft-repeated, the literal meaning was worn as a stone in a riverbed.

T.R. privately thought that words were another field waiting to be plowed, much as the transit wizards and the financial wizards did in the cities. Just as water flowed home to the sea, to be lifted into the air by the fire in the sun before returning to the soil and stone as it fell from the sky, so words flowed through the entire world of men. It wasn't that he disagreed with the balancing ethic of the grassland wizards—far from it—he just thought there were more ways to influence that balance.

It all came down to words, after all. Without words, the beacon fire of thought never bridged the gap from one consciousness to another. The world's purposes were powerful but wordless—no volcano ever wrote poetry, no forest ever told its children a tale of heroes rampaging amid quiet folk—and words were how the wizards tipped the balance back into place.

Even the little workings were no more than ways of making those words sensible to the land.

So T.R. turned the words over in his head.

Nature by another path.

Another path by nature.

Path by another nature.

Walking backwards. *Path another by nature.*

Passing by nature, passing in reverse.

Under the grass, of course. That was the key. That whatever had come had pushed *up* out of the grass. As if it walked beneath the earth, and for a moment stepped too deep, like a man treading more heavily than intended on mud.

He turned that thought around some more.

"It came from below," he finally said.

A.P.'s response was uncharacteristically quick. "Think so, do you?"

"How else could the prints be the way they were?"

"Our magic is almost always the art of the obvious, boy."

"So what would we find if we dug up the turf?"

A.P. took another long drag off the burnt-down nub of the spliff. "Shovel's in the toolbox. Knock yourself out."

▲▼▲

T.R. spent some time carefully quartering the prints. The grassland wizards needed some money, after all, and often the sheep weren't right to sell. So they raised a lot of turf. The Willamette Valley was the leading source of both lawn grass seed and live turf in North America, so this was normal enough. It meant he'd had a lot of experience with turf cutters, rollers and little square shovels.

None of which A.P. seemed to carry in the toolbox behind the cab of his Mercury. Why would a grassland wizard carry grass tools, after all? T.R. made a note to add those to the collection of equipment rattling around in the bed of his Hudson, for future use.

So he chopped the turf with the round-point shovel A.P. did have, the world's most generic utility shovel and not especially well-suited for the job. Lacking gloves, he accepted the blisters and splinters the old wooden handle gave him. At least the dark of the evening was cool.

There was even a kind of magic practiced around turf cutting—turbary, they called it. T.R. had spent his time studying sheep and birds and the movement of wind on grass, but he knew there was an entire clan of wizards that based their divination and power on the patterns of roots and tracks of worms.

He was no turbarist, that was clear enough, but still he'd worked the grass farms sufficiently to understand what he was about.

Eventually the first of the prints came up to only slightly bloodied palms. There was a strange clicking noise from the soil, as if someone had buried several dozen ticking clocks. He wasn't sure what he was looking for, so he didn't know what he'd found at first. Even with the veiled moon there was light enough to see by for his night-adjusted eyes. The lifted section of turf showed him churned soil writhing with large black beetles. A moment's gingerly inspection showed that they were concentrated in a rounded mass of loosened soil.

Where a leg might have extended downward from the upward-forced print.

It was the insects which were clicking, louder now that he was close. When T.R. tried to pick up one of the beetles to examine it, the insect bit him hard enough to make him bite off a shriek. He shook the beetle away and looked at the first knuckle of his middle finger. A drop of blood welled, black in the attenuated moonlight. The skin was already visibly pale in a ring around the wound site.

Even as he raced back toward the truck and A.P.'s assistance, T.R. wondered if the black beetles were really the color of blood.

▲▼▲

"Damn, boy, you really fucked that one up." A.P. had T.R.'s wrist in a grip so tight it hurt, while he probed the fingertip with the mechanical pencil.

T.R. held his breath behind his teeth, not trusting himself not to scream. His finger was *cold*, which was almost worse than being numb. The ring of pale skin had already grown past the first knuckle joint, and he couldn't wiggle that finger any more.

He wanted to protest, to say that his master had sent him into danger, had allowed him to fuck up, but…so what? T.R. fell back on logic. "What about my finger?"

"I'll look to draw this out." A.P. gave him a quick, hard look. "Fire will be best, but you'll need to be ready for it."

"Ready how?"

A.P. pulled another spliff out of his shirt. "Light this, and don't watch what I do."

That was the first time since he'd been apprenticed to the old man that T.R. had heard his master tell him to look away. He lay down in the truck, stared at the sky and sucked on the joint. He ignored everything he could. The cold in his finger. The fear that the frigid cramping would extend to his entire hand, wither his arm, even stop his heart. The noises of A.P. rummaging in the tool box, metal clanging as the old man cursed quietly.

When a blow torch hissed to life, T.R. nearly swallowed the spliff whole.

When the cold in his finger was swallowed by a bright sun of heat-driven pain, he still didn't look. He just toked and stared at the veiled moon and tried to keep enough of his thoughts in order to wonder what walked beneath the soil and left deadly black beetles in its wake.

The last thing he heard before the combination of dope and pain put him to sleep was A.P. saying something about not letting the sheep back into the meadow.

▲▼▲

B. What They Tell the Young Ones About Why We Live Here

You ever wonder what's so special about the Willamette Valley? Why we live here, and not along the Truckee or the American River, or the Missouri back east? That's because here the thoughts of the lands are both hotter and simpler.

This is all volcanic rock here. Not marine rock, which is full of old slow life that's angry about being locked down for a hundred million years. Nor the stuff squeezed from the earth cold and hard with the complaints of gravity and geothermal stress. No, this here's scabs on the earth, simple stuff from a simple time.

Easier to do what we do without the ghosts of time groaning in the bedrock beneath the soil.

Likewise, this piece of North America has a mind of its own. The mother continent swallowed Okanagan completely, and has been chewing on California for long ages. All them volcanoes over there? Death cry of a land being swallowed into the fire far down below. This place remembers oceans and eons of life on its own. Kindly echoes, if land can ever be said to be kind.

So we live in a simple balance, compared to most. Water, soil, stock and stone, fish and bird and fur, we work with them without also contesting against older, stronger, slower wills out of the abyss of years.

Different places have different concerns. The land might as well be dead beneath the streets and rails of the old eastern cities. The Midwest sleeps beneath a deep blanket of soil, tickled by plows but not enough to wake from its windswept dreaming. The deserts of the Southwest have their own thoughts, but when men enough go there to wrest the balance loose, they fence it in with watered lawns and a grid of streets. Here in the Northwest we can still live in the dynamic balance.

So here we live. We count the blades of grass that rise in the spring and watch the mindless sheep. It's not that we must. It's just that we can.

▲▼▲

When T.R. woke up it was daylight. He was in his room at A.P.'s trailer, not much larger than a closet in a normal house, with a single louvered window, a tiny bed and several bits of cheap furniture. G.D., one of the few female grassland wizards, sat next to him on a wobbly dinette chair drinking coffee from a giant plastic Sapp Brothers mug.

At least he assumed it was coffee—that's what he smelled.

She was an old woman, old as most of the masters were. Where A.P. had the indefinable dissolution of a rummy who'd spent too many years on the couch, G.D. was still a head-turner. Her long hair flowed salt and pepper, the arch of her brows was dark and perfect over gleaming pale eyes, and she dressed like a Deadhead who'd gone into color divination. The flowing silks and South Asian prints suited her trim form well.

"Hello," he said.

She cocked an eyebrow. "Not good morning?"

"I doubt it, if what I remember from last night holds true." His right hand lay beneath the covers. It ached abominably. T.R. was in no hurry to tug it into the open air and count his fingers.

"So you are thinking clearly."

"Clearly as ever, I suppose."

She chuckled. "Not that he'd ever tell you any such thing, but I have it on good authority that A.P. thinks highly of you."

The words were out of T.R.'s mouth before he could stop them. "If he does, he does so in silence."

"That man does nearly everything in silence, T.R." The tone of G.D.'s voice made it clear what she thought of his disrespect toward his master.

"Well, yes..." He decided he wasn't sure he wanted to know the boundaries of 'everything' insofar as A.P. and G.D. were concerned. "I'm sorry." *Time for a change of subject*, he thought. "What was that last night?"

"The Western deathwatch beetle. *Xestobium rufovillosum maximum*. Not something we normally find here in the valley."

"I didn't think we had any poisonous insects in Oregon."

"We don't."

"But the deathwatch...?"

"Is not generally poisonous." She set her mug down and leaned forward, moving her hands to her knees. "That was imbalanced."

'Imbalanced' had a specific meaning among the grassland wizards. Things—animals, plants, weather, the land itself—acting out of character.

He tugged his right hand from beneath the covers. The entire hand was swathed in cotton, but there wasn't a familiar tenting finger at the middle. T.R. gently pinched the cotton there until his left thumb and forefinger met.

With that, he began to cry.

▲▼▲

A few minutes later as he settled down to a rattling, stressed breathing, G.D. stared over the rim of her mug. "Are you finished?" she asked.

It was more kindness than he would have gotten out of A.P. Though perhaps A.P.'s greatest kindness was to let T.R. come to terms with his missing finger without the old man having to watch his apprentice grieve.

"I'm..." T.R. stopped and took a deep breath. The sobs threatened to return. "It's missing."

"Sucks, doesn't it? Want some coffee?"

"I lose a finger and you offer me coffee. That's it?"

Her eyes narrowed. "If I had a finger to spare, I'd offer you that. What I *have* is coffee."

Chastened, he said, "Yes, ma'am. Please." T.R. turned his wrist back and forth, looking at his bandaged hand from both vantages. It didn't hurt, really, except for a deep, dull ache which seemed to throb from somewhere down in his forearm all the way up to his hand and where the stump would be, if he could see the stump.

The stump itched horridly.

Carefully he poked at the bandage, almost wishing he had A.P.'s mechanical pencil. Nothing. Not even down past the point where he could swear the itch was coming from. T.R. sucked in another sudden breath.

"The nerves don't know the finger is gone," G.D. said as she poured some coffee from her mug into a Flintstone's jelly jar.

"I *do*." He tried not to let the horror into his voice. His revulsion was already mingling with a sense of mourning. Middle finger, at least. He could still push elevator buttons and point at people. He generally didn't do either one of those things very often, in point of fact.

Not a lot of elevators in the grasslands of the Willamette Valley, and wizards were trained early not to point. A lot of power could flow through a finger. In either direction.

At least I'll be more polite now, he thought. No more flipping the bird.

T.R. reached for the jelly glass. It was hot, of course, but he wanted the caffeine. More to the point, he wanted something to do.

The coffee within was as hot as the glass promised, and burned his tongue on the way down. Apparently G.D. took it black and unsweetened.

He'd probably tasted better motor oil. Still, coffee was coffee, and the trembling he hadn't even noticed in himself seemed to subside.

"Where's A.P.?"

"Out with half a dozen others burning turf in your sheep meadow. Pretty much everyone else is looking for more footprints."

"Burning turf?" Given the moisture content of both the grass and soil, T.R. found that difficult to credit.

"Pest extermination. You of all people should appreciate why."

He tried to make a fist of his right hand, but the fingers were bound tightly under the outer bandage. "Shouldn't we also be out looking?"

She smiled sweetly at him, though T.R. could see the daggers hidden behind G.D.'s expression. "In point of fact, yes. Some of us, at any rate."

He rolled out of bed, wincing at the pain in his back. Of course, he'd been out shoveling last night as well. "Let's go."

"You might want to put some pants on first."

▲▼▲

T.R. drove his Hudson, slowly, and divided his attention between the little rural roads and the flocks of sheep, mixed occasionally with cattle, horses or even llamas. Cattle were too stolid to be useful for their work, horses too skittish, and llamas too smart, really. Of the three, he'd put his money on the South American bastards, but by preference it was sheep every time.

G.D. kept her head tilted out the window to stare at the sky. He knew she was watching where the birds flocked and wheeled, because every now and then she'd call a halt and point something out.

Working the gears turned out to be difficult with his wounded right hand, so T.R. kept it mostly in second. The stiff linkages in the three-on-the-tree shifter required more leverage than he could reasonably deliver with an open palm. The old six banger labored as he alternately lugged and raced it, but the truck kept on.

"Everyone in the valley's out today," she said after pulling her head in so they could cross a major junction with Highway 99. "Can't recall last time all the grasslanders came out on the same summoning."

"How dangerous is this…thing?"

"It's not the backward walkers they're worried about. It's the beetles. What they did to you? Imagine that happening to the sheep."

"Ah." He should have thought of that. T.R. drove on in silence, still watching the grazers. After a while he asked the next logical question. "What are we doing about the backward walkers?"

"You know the Trouble Rule." Her voice was too mild, a form of rebuke much as A.P.'s silences could be.

He did indeed know the Trouble Rule. Whoever the trouble found was the one to lay it down again. That was one of the basic commandments of the grassland wizards.

"Right. So why are we out looking at birds and cows?"

"It's what some of us should be doing," she said mildly.

He turned the truck around. "I'm heading back to my meadow. Can you watch the birds on the way there?"

"Surely as I can anywhere else."

▲▼▲

There were half a dozen trucks parked along the road by his sheep meadow, including A.P.'s Mercury, along with two post-war Studebakers, a 1948 1-1/2 ton Diamond T and a 1930 REO Speedwagon. Unfortunately, one of the other vehicles was a late model Dodge belonging to the Marion County Sheriff's Department.

Grassland wizards and law enforcement didn't mix much. Other than the little matter of industrial-grade marijuana consumption, there was no reason to. The wizards were law-abiding citizens, and their trailers and farmhouses tended to be in the center of a fair amount of peace and quiet. Rural crime was sufficiently irregular in its distribution that no sharp-eyed demographer had noticed this yet, but an occasional topic of conversation among the wizards was whether some genius with a computer model would some day notice them by that trail of peace.

Still, a lot of their activities didn't bear close examination. The haruspicators among the grassland wizards especially were at risk, for example.

T.R. pulled up behind the sheriff's truck and made his way out into the field where a group of people were gathered around a smoldering mess. As he got closer, he could hear the discussion.

"...care if it's wet...burn out here without a permit."

"...pest control..."

"...not much trouble, but..."

He stepped up into a circle of silence. T.R. didn't recognize the deputy, but the deputy apparently recognized him. "You're the one Bobbie told me about."

Kearns, his name tag read. He was a big man with a beefy face who was perspiring even though it wasn't seventy degrees out here.

"Deputy Kearns," T.R. said politely, nodding.

"Look, I don't care what kind of cult you fellows are running." Kearns glanced at G.D. "We got enough old hippies out here to start another revolution. I'd have to move to Malheur County to get away from your kind. I don't even care what you're smoking, long as I don't have to watch you and you're not selling meth to the kids. Which you aren't. But you *cannot* go setting fires in the summer." He hooked his thumbs in his belt. "People complain."

"I'm the one was hurt by the bugs here," T.R. said. He saw the wizards around Kearns tensing. "Dug 'em up without realizing what I was getting into."

The deputy scowled at T.R. "You couldn't call the extension agent like everybody else?" Out of the deputy's line of sight, A.P. was working a Banishment with a hank of black wool and three dried clover flowers.

Stall, thought T.R. "Can't say I thought of it, sir. Little buggers hurt like fire. I was worried they might be like the fire ants down south, or those killer bees."

"I can see where a fellow might panic." He looked down at T.R.'s bandaged hand. "Hurt you bad, huh?"

T.R. winced. "Yeah. Bad enough."

"Let me guess. You folks don't believe in doctors, neither."

"We live in harmony with the land, sir." Utter bullshit, but it was what the deputy was expecting to hear. The wool in A.P.'s hands smoldered, then blew away to ash, just as the deputy's radio squawked an incomprehensible gabble of code.

Kearns looked around. "All right fellows, that's my number. No more fires, though, or there will be more trouble. People looking into barns and things. Which I reckon you guys don't want too much of."

"No sir," said L.F., another of the senior wizards. He was a chubby man with a moon face pocked by old acne scars. "No trouble."

"All right then. I'm not going to file a report, this time."

With that, Kearns lumbered back to his truck.

A.P. glared at T.R. "Come to fix it, boy? What took you so long?"

G.D. started to say something, then changed her mind.

"I've come to fix it, sir," T.R. said. "And I came as quick as I could think it through."

"We was a long time waiting," mumbled L.F. The senior wizards headed back toward their trucks.

▲▼▲

"It had been headed east," T.R. said. He stood behind where the last—or first?—of the footsteps had been, visualizing the line of travel. The area stank of kerosene, burning and turned soil.

"Into the Cascades," said G.D., still sipping her coffee. She and A.P. were the only wizards who'd stayed with T.R.

The Cascades indeed. Which was a bit odd, since when trouble did come, it usually came down out of the Cascades, from the east. Not toward the east.

T.R. turned and faced west, toward the line of the Coastals cropping up on the horizon a few miles that way. "How far are we from the river here? A thousand yards?"

"About right."

"So...say it came out of the Coastals, heading for the Cascades. The brothers live in both places. So do the Sisters. This...whatever it was... could do so too."

Silence this time. T.R. glanced at A.P. His master wasn't frowning, at least.

That meant continue.

"If it walks backwards..." he stopped, thinking about the paths of nature. "Not backwards. Not exactly. Inverted. Earth as air to it, our air as the rock beneath the soil. Like a..." Elemental was the only word he could think of, but that wasn't right, he was sure. "A pattern, a push from the soil. A sending. Carrying a purpose from the Coastals to the Cascades. It crossed the Willamette, from beneath, and came up here to do the equivalent of a man wiping his wet feet after wading a stream. It broke through."

A.P. grunted. "Is it dangerous?"

"No, not in and of itself. This is land business, the land talking to itself. I don't even think this is a push. Not like some of what passes. We just happened to be where it wanted to go. Like people in the path of a mudslide. But what the sending leaves behind is dangerous. Those deathwatch beetles. Not dangerous, in and of itself, but still trouble. Under the Trouble Rule."

A.P. turned to G.D. with exaggerated delight. "The boy does remember a thing or two."

"The boy does indeed," snapped T.R. "Now how do I keep this from being trouble?"

"How do you cross a river?" G.D. asked softly.

"Use a bridge," T.R. responded without thinking.

If he was right, if this made sense, if there was a way to get the sending to cross whatever arrangement they made.

Guide the land, set the balance, keep people safe and the land as whole as it could be while infected with humans.

▲▼▲

The only bridge which made sense was the crossing at Independence, Oregon. It was a concrete deck bridge, a very typical highway bridge. T.R. would have strongly preferred wood, but wooden bridges were long gone, except for a few creek crossings and the odd historical structure. Concrete wasn't his natural medium, not at all, but it would have to do.

The bridge was accessible from open fields, that was one strength. They couldn't have done much in the middle of Salem, for example. The bridge also ran almost directly along an east-west axis, each end pointing at one of the mountain chains. That meant if T.R. could set the proper wards and signs, it would be a path that the sendings would not resist.

He'd parked the Hudson in the woods below the eastern end of the bridge, where an odd little circular interchange linked Riverside Drive to the highway. No one would question the old truck parked in the brush just north of there. They walked west, picking their way through the riverbottom brush under the bridge itself. Traffic passed overhead in an occasional hot, thumping whoosh.

"It walks beneath the soil," T.R. said. "We can't just direct it to the underside of the road deck."

"There are piers every few dozen yards," G.D. pointed out.

A.P. growled, muttering something that might have been "Trouble Rule."

T.R.'s finger itched. He massaged the palm and back of his hand, trying to distract himself from the sensation of what was missing. "The far side isn't built up, either. As long as we can get them to pass close to the town over there, this may well work. These piers extend below the soil to be stabilized. They can use them as stepping stones."

G.D. laughed lightly. "If you can get the land to pay attention."

"If not, I'm not very well going to solve the problem, am I?"

"How you going to do it, boy?" demanded A.P.

"Draw the sending in here with some kind of beacon, and set wards further out to keep it from trying another way."

"What kind of wards?"

T.R. noted that his master had abandoned silence. He felt obscurely vindicated. If A.P. felt the need to push, T.R. was going in the right direction. "This is a sending of soil or stone. We'll alternate fire and water wards. Smoldering Wool, I think, and Jar Water. One every quarter mile in a line opening out from here dozen miles in both directions." He grinned at A.P. "A lot of work, I know, but not any more than going out beating the meadows for deathwatch beetles."

G.D. snorted.

"Meanwhile, we'll set a beacon here. Something that will call to soil and stone." He paused, took a deep breath. "Bright Grave would work well."

"You planning to bury someone, boy?"

That was a flaw in his plan. T.R. didn't think this was worth a bit of grave-robbing. "I don't believe Bright Grave needs to be a person. It just needs to be bright."

A.P. pushed harder. "And if you make all this? What next?"

"I'll have to watch for another sending, and lead it in. The land learns, after all. The world was never stupid."

"So you're going to kill a sheep to fill that grave, and then go calling deathwatch beetles on yourself while the rest of us are out planting wards?"

Suddenly T.R. was very tired of A.P., the old man's cranky ways and damning with faint praise. "No, no sir. I'm going to help all of you plant wards, then send you home before I kill a sheep. Trouble Rule makes the bad part of all this mine, surely enough."

▲▼▲

C. What They Tell the Young Ones About Our Names

When you were born, someone called you Tanner or Mary Lou or Enrique. Your parents gave you names. When you come to the wizards, whether you're a babe in arms or an old woman who's finally heeded the call, that changes.

We still carry driver's licenses, most of us. Only a few drop off the rolls completely. It's an advantage to be able to see a doctor or take a trip, after all. So we've got those names. But they're not ours any more. We gave them away.

Without those names, we're harder to find. More difficult to pin down. Neither the power of the land nor feuds of the hand have the same effect. Think about it. Trees don't give themselves names, any more than rivers or mountains do. A name is just a label.

So your master, or at least some master, will take your name away when you're read, and give you another one. We like them to have meanings, then we remove the meaning by only using the initials. Pro Bono, for example, becomes P.B. Used to have a wizard named A.V., for Ad Valorem.

You might think those kinds of names sound stupid. And if you're an Enrique or a Mary Lou, they do. But those names, they're real words with real power that still can hide in the chatter of the world around us. No one calls themselves Geometricum Demonstratum but one of us, yet the words are out there.

And no one knows they're names. Not even the land. Especially not the land.

Sooner or later you'll be an H.O. or a B.B. Take that name with pride. No one but your master will ever know, except if you choose to tell them. It's all about hiding in plain sight.

▲▼▲

It took T.R. the better part of a week to organize the setting of the wards. At the same time he had to prepare the Bright Grave, a greater working than he'd ever done before. All of it was in service of turning nature to another path, which seemed fitting to him.

His finger ached, though. All the time. With everything he did. It was as if his hand were crying for its missing child. T.R. tried telling himself to be grateful that A.P. hadn't taken his thumb or forefinger. This was merely painful and inconvenient, as opposed to debilitating.

He couldn't work Bright Grave at the trailer, of course. No magic in the trailer. So he moved out to the sheep pen by the meadow. A.P. had done some sort of land swap with Bobbie to keep the sheep away from what they'd had to burn. That meant it was quiet and calm. The smell he didn't mind, save for the whiffs of kerosene and ash from the burnt spot.

The final part of Bright Grave would be worked under the west end of the Independence Bridge, of course. But he needed time to carve the ash poles, weave the grass ropes, and soak the dull knife in stale wine.

T.R. still wasn't sure about how to call another sending down toward the Bright Grave in the first place. He figured on spending some time camping over at the west edge of the Willamette Valley until another one came out of the Coastals.

If one didn't come, he wasn't sure how the wizards would determine the trouble had been settled. The Trouble Rule didn't address that. Whatever would come, would come, but the land's sense of time in no way corresponded to how human beings in general and the grassland wizards in particular saw things.

He smoked a lot of dope, too, to put him in the right headspace for Bright Grave. Killing a sheep would be difficult. He'd done slaughtering before—that was part of rural life, after all. But to bring one to the pit he'd dig and use that dull knife to cut its throat over the fir boughs and the grass ropes was another class of ritual entirely than the slow progress of the food chain.

Counting birds in the sky was one thing. This was another.

When he was waiting for the elements of his working to cure, to set up or set down, T.R. continued to read *The Chymical Wedding*. It made more sense when he was stoned, he realized. The air rifle was never far away either, with its blood load.

If he had to drive something away for which he had no working of Banishment, that silly little weapon would be his only friend.

Meanwhile the wizards came and went. Their old trucks wheezed up to his fence line, while they approached by ones and twos and, occasionally, threes, to give and take counsel. T.R. found himself exercising his proposed word wizardry through the medium of the old-fashioned art of discussion. So much time spent in the laconic company of A.P. had left him out of practice.

"You'll be setting your wards out along the rail line where it runs just west of south," he told F.Q., a woman wizard who was one of the youngest of the masters. "The steel will help drive the sendings along the wards."

"It will turn away from the metal bindings," she told him.

"The last one had to cross the rails somewhere. Several times. Find a culvert just south of Independence, leave some Openings there. That will help draw it to the Bright Grave."

And so it went, both the sympathetic mostly younger wizards, and the grumpy old men like L.F. who were friends of A.P.'s and distrusted everyone under the age of sixty. He talked, parried, crafted the workings, looked over maps of where the wards would be laid.

Somewhere in the process, his finger came to matter less and less.

▲▼▲

The night of the Bright Grave working came. T.R. had already told Bobbie he'd be taking one of the ewes out of the herd to pass on to a buddy over in Lincoln County. G.D. drove up around sundown in her 1975 Plymouth Trailduster as he was checking the ties in the bed of his Hudson and loading the materials for his working.

"Bright Grave's a dead man working," she reminded him without any preamble of greeting.

"You know anyone planning to die tonight?"

"No. But L.F. put it around the working might go best if you cut your own throat."

T.R. jerked hard on a bungee, so that it snapped away and stung his left hand. His right he kept in a work glove, the middle finger stuffed with a scrap of wool. *"Why?* Why would he say that about me?"

G.D. shrugged. "You were here the day the sending came through. It was you the beetles bit. Some of the old guys are mad that you didn't stop it at the time, and convinced they could have done better."

"There was nothing to see that day, I assure you. Just circling birds and nervous sheep. I could have been standing on the spot and it wouldn't have made much of a difference."

"You're making a difference now," she said.

"Just following the Trouble Rule." He threw a satchel in the front of the Hudson. "Most of the grassland wizards are out watching tonight, aren't they?"

"It's a big working. The problem could be big, too. Especially if your plan doesn't work."

"Who gets the Trouble Rule if I fail?"

Her teeth flashed in an aggressive grin. "A.P."

"Then L.F.'s an idiot, making book against me. Those old men don't want to be creeping around under bridges at midnight. They should be doing everything they can to help me."

"Tell me," she said slowly. "Are you ever motivated by anger?"

He opened his mouth to answer, but G.D. just turned and walked away.

▲▼▲

The ewe, ear tag 24-017, wasn't happy about the truck ride in the dark. It was more difficult to find a discreet parking spot at the west end of the Independence Bridge. A bawling sheep did little to improve that situation.

Still, he whispered a little Quiet in her ear and loaded up his duffel bag as she moaned softly. T.R. had bundled his shovel with his ash poles and his fir boughs. He shouldered his bag, grabbed the air rifle and the bundle and led the ewe down the embankment and along the west bank floodplain beneath the bridge. The combination was too heavy and too balky both, but he only had to drag all that junk a few dozen yards. Somehow he got the ewe out of sight without being blown out by passing headlights, and the attendant questions.

She was a soft-eyed, dark faced merino that he recalled having a pleasant enough disposition in the flock. 17 had never been a trouble-maker, unlike some of the other ewes. He'd picked her for tonight's business due to her relatively tractable disposition. Fighting a ram down here was almost beyond his imagination.

The river sulked nearby in the dark, burbling to itself. Some night hunting bird meeped and flew just outside the range of his vision. There were water and grass smells, and the stink of the frightened ewe. Other than the occasional rumble of traffic on the bridge deck above him, it was an Oregon summer night.

T.R. tied her off to a pillar and set up a little electric lantern from his bag, then began digging the Bright Grave. He had brought A.P.'s shovel, the same one he'd used to cut the turf and find the beetles. Down here was an odd mixture of shifting sand and hard clay, the result of decades of intermittent flooding and occasional shifts in the river bank. He had gloves for both hands now, so while his back ached and his hands hurt, he wasn't collecting splinters and kept his blisters to a minimum.

By the time he was done with the hole, sweating and gasping, the ewe had settled into chewing her cud. The traffic above him seemed to have stopped passing somewhere in the process, so the night had fallen silent save for the river itself.

Even the birds were quiet.

Was it coming again? He wasn't ready. The Bright Grave was a beacon, not a protection, but it was meant to set the path.

T.R. pushed the fir boughs into the grave, then grabbed the ash poles. After a second of thought, he picked up the air rifle as well and jumped down into the grave to prepare the working.

As he arranged the boughs, the ewe bleated once, softly. T.R. looked up to see A.P. His master was between the lantern and the grave, but T.R. would recognize that stance anywhere.

The old man was carrying a weapon—rifle or shotgun, in silhouette, T.R. couldn't tell.

The real meaning of the old men's griping and betting against him suddenly came clear as T.R.'s breath caught in his throat. His master intended T.R. to fill the Bright Grave. He grabbed at the air rifle, wondering what good the blood load would do when used against another grassland wizard.

Less than whatever his master had chambered in that other weapon. His only chance was that A.P. wouldn't want to kill T.R., for fear of ruining the working.

"You want some help there, boy?"

Just as T.R. brought the air rifle up, A.P. bent over and set down the shovel he'd been carrying. T.R. managed to jerk the barrel aside in time for the blood load to spang against the bridge deck above them.

A.P. grinned maniacally. "Damn, you are nervous." He extended a hand. "Come on out of there."

T.R. mostly wanted to throw up, but he climbed out instead, arms and legs shaking. "You bastard," he hissed.

"Take the damned sheep," said A.P. "I'll hold her, but it's your working, boy."

"I am not a boy," T.R. snarled.

Together they wrestled the protesting 24-017 to the edge of the grave. He'd already laid the boughs and the ash poles. All he needed to do was cut the wool twists from each shoulder, say a few quiet words, and slash her throat.

The dull knife sawed slowly through one bit of wool as the ewe began to buck. The other bit followed. He was breathing heavy now, his gut like lead, not ready to kill an animal so uselessly.

His finger tingled, though, the phantom pain strong. How many would have died if the sheep had strayed into the deathwatch beetles?

The knife went in more easily than he'd expected. The ewe's warm blood spilled across him, but he wrenched her head back and let her bleed into the grave. The words came easily enough, a simple invocation to sky, water, stock and stone, then he shoved the body in.

So much easier this way than with one already dead, he thought. The working sealed itself.

He turned to say something to A.P., some angry denunciation, when the grave began clicking. T.R. whirled back to see a mass of deathwatch beetles squirming out of the sand and clay of the open hole, already almost covering the ewe.

"Fill it, quick," hissed A.P. For the first time in his life, T.R. heard fear in his master's voice.

As they spaded the soil back into the grave, A.P. threw something in with the first few tosses. It was small and dark, and T.R. thought he knew what it was, but he said nothing. He just bent and lifted and thought about the power of anger.

▲▼▲

Later, after they'd washed themselves in the river, they wound up in A.P.'s Mercury. The old man produced two spliffs in an uncharacteristic show of generosity.

"You did well, boy," he said.

"How would you know?" T.R. asked bitterly. The hard words still crowded in his head, fighting for his tongue.

"You wanted me to be nice?" A.P. chuckled and took a long drag. "It was too easy for you. You knew how to do the little workin's just fine, and you liked sittin' with the sheep. Ain't too many come to the grasslands to loaf, but I do believe you did. So we threw you the goose, and made you work for it."

T.R. thought about the finger A.P. had thrown into the Bright Grave. "You called that sending?"

"No, not exactly. Let's just say I invited it your way. It was past time for you to grow up, boy."

"I am *not* a boy!"

"Not any more. That was kind of the point."

He thought about that for a little while. "What about the finger?"

"You were stupid. A stupid wizard doesn't live long. Think of it as tuition."

"Yeah?"

A.P. reached across T.R.'s lap and pushed open the passenger door. "One more thing. You can't keep living in that sheep pen. Time to get your own trailer, *wizard*." He gave T.R. a none-too-gentle push.

T.R. got out, torn between dazed amusement and smoldering anger. A.P.'s truck coughed to life and he headed into the night, east across the Independence Bridge.

Glove off, his hand looked odd. The missing finger was a shout. And it still hurt like crazy.

"I'm a wizard," he told the tiny ghost of part of himself. Whatever that meant. He hardly wanted it now.

Had the Bright Grave been worth the trouble? Had the price of the finger been worth what he'd bought?

Questions for another day, T.R. told himself. He went back to his own truck and headed home to the sheep pen. He could read the rest of his book by the light of the lantern, think about the power of words some more, and burn a little incense for the ewe's tiny, puzzled soul.

Fat Man

This piece was inspired by my various hikings and lurkings in the Mt. Hood National Forest, just east of Portland. In setting, it has a great deal in common with "In the Forests of the Night", my novella which appeared in METAtropolis. In them, it is first and foremost about the agony and joy of being a parent. Or maybe it's about Bigfoot. You get to decide.

Clint Amos and his friend Barley John Dimmitt stalked through the Mt. Hood National Forest, not far from Timothy Lake in southeast Clackamas County. They stalked quietly so as not to disturb the elk they hunted, but more to the point, so as not to disturb the forest rangers. Clint didn't hold with tags nor permits. Barley John generally agreed with Clint on most things. It made life easier for everyone involved.

The two of them hunted this division of the forest because most people avoided it. Hikers and campers had disappeared over the years; unlucky accidents befell loggers. There had been more than one lost child never found, even by legions of search-and-rescue trail runners. The Forest Service had quietly closed down the last of the managed trails about three years earlier, killing what little tourism their town of Sweden, Oregon had still received. Even the most die-hard independent loggers now looked elsewhere for their cutting permits.

No trails was okay with Clint, though, because it meant fewer rangers, and no tourists messing up his hunt. No loggers was hard on the job situation, but he couldn't fix that.

They moved silently amid ranks of hemlocks and lodgepole pines. Rhododendrons grew in the burn breaks, and at the edges of the shadow along the ridges, but deeper in only the smaller plants struggled alongside the doomed offspring of their tall parents. The forest smelled of loam and tingly pine scent and the cold grayness of the mountain rock buried not far beneath their feet. Snow would be there soon, which made the elk easier to find but more difficult to hunt.

Barley John held out his hand, fingers spread down.

He'd heard something.

Clint would allow that while Barley John didn't have the sense God granted to a Canada goose, the man could hear grass growing. It made Barley John a hell of a hunting partner.

Clint crouched, his Ruger Deerfield carbine loose and ready in his hands. The position folded his substantial gut, but it was the only way he could pop up for a clean shot. He could hold it still for a while. Barley John might spot their prey, but Clint always got first shot. He usually got the clean kill, too.

Let it be a big mama elk, he thought, with some good meat for the coming months. They ain't either of them had a job in over a year, since Barger's Sawmill had closed, and his wife's pay had been cut twice at that auto parts place up in Estacada.

He didn't kill, they didn't eat.

Hell, no one in the whole town of Sweden had enough to eat without they went out and shot first. It was like to make a man mad at the government, raising taxes and taking jobs away all at the same time. Clint wasn't sure whether it was the Japs, the Chinese or the al-Qaeda, but somebody that had snuggled up to those damned Democrats had gone and stolen his job. Made his life hell, too.

He hadn't been old enough to serve, but he remembered Vietnam. This country should be so strong again. Sometimes taking a clean shot felt good. He could pretend it was someone whose death would make his life better.

Barley John made a clicking noise to get Clint's attention, then waved his hand to the right, two fingers now up. Clint swung his carbine to the four o'clock position relative to their line of travel and watched for movement. Barley John stepped quietly away, disappearing among the pines to find a covering position. Clint's partner would flush the elk, Clint would take his first shot, then Barley John would drop the animal if need be.

The light was pearly gray, prophesying snow. Clint felt time slow down like it always did when his finger was right on the trigger. Meat, sausage and steaks for the winter. Jobs. Slick Willie in his sights. He shouldered the carbine and slowed his breathing.

Somewhere further off to the right Barley John clicked again, louder this time, then tossed a rock. There was a flash of fur as the elk bolted and Clint took his shot, the old Ruger bucking against his shoulder even as he realized something was wrong.

He must have hit, because there was an unholy screech, like the sound of a really big eagle or hawk. Whatever it was—no elk, he was already certain—it went down in a thrashing of rhododendrons at the edge of a clearing.

"Damn!" shouted Barley John, breaking cover and sprinting toward the bushes. Clint was close behind him, moving fast for a big guy. They both pulled up short, thirty or forty feet from whatever they had hit.

"That weren't no elk," Clint said. "Bear, maybe."

"No. Looked more like an ape."

"Ain't no apes out—"

They stared at each other for a moment.

"Bigfoot," breathed Barley John, real quiet.

Clint nodded. It couldn't be true, could it? "Cover me," he whispered. "If it moves, plug it." Keeping the Ruger low and close to his body, he approached the bushes where a watery beam of sunlight had stabbed downward.

It was big, lying on its side, belly large as a bear's. Clint studied what he'd shot. Belly or not, it couldn't be a bear. Didn't have no fur as such. Rather, it was covered with stringy hair. There were hands and feet instead of paws. This thing also had ropy ridges of scar tissue on its knees and elbows, all around its fingers and toes.

This was the biggest fat man he'd ever seen. But no man was that huge. Clint estimated it at eight feet or more, at least five hundred pounds. Slowly he reached out and nudged it in the belly with the carbine's barrel.

No reaction.

He walked around the thing, noticing out of the corner of his eye that Barley John was still covering him.

"Big fella," Barley John said.

"Bigfoot. Like you figured." Clint poked its head with the carbine, just behind the ear. Nothing. Not even a twitch.

"Think he's still breathing?"

Clint snorted. "Think I'm putting my hands down there to find out? Bastard could fit a melon inside those damned jaws." He shouldered his carbine, his aim point wavering.

Barley John hefted his own weapon. "What you doing?"

"Checking," said Clint, and shot the enormous creature in the butt.

It didn't twitch at all.

"Friend," Clint breathed, "I believe we may be on our way to fame and riches. This here's a real live Bigfoot."

"Actually," said Barley John in a rare show of independence, "this here's a real dead Bigfoot. I got just one question."

Clint was already imagining himself being interviewed on Jerry Springer or 20/20, describing their arduous days-long hunt of the killer ape. "What's that?"

"How we going to haul this thing out here without we cut it up first?"

▲▼▲

In the end they got the body back to Clint's old Wagoneer with a travois, a comealong, a hundred feet of rope and hours upon hours of cursing to cover four miles of trail with such a damned big deadweight load. An elk they'd have just skinned and field-dressed, hauling it out in pieces.

It was dark by the time Clint wheeled the Jeep off the unmaintained Forest Service track and on to State Highway 224, the road that ran through the town of Sweden. Sweden's only road, in fact, except for some gravel lanes running back into the woods on each side of the highway. He pulled over and got out to unlock the front hubs and put the vehicle back into two-wheel drive. It was cold, with no moon, and his breath steamed in the starlight.

They'd lashed Bigfoot to the roof. Glancing up, Clint saw the wind stirring his kill's fur. Looked like the fingers had curled up on the drive out of the forest. Reflex action, he thought. Nobody and no thing took a bullet in the butt without flinching, not even knocked out cold.

Up and back into the truck, where Barley John was smoking a joint and staring into the woods.

"Put that thing away before we get home," Clint said. "Margie'll hate the smell on me as it is. She sees that joint flaring in the Jeep she'll lay into me like crows on summer wheat."

"You ain't the one smoking," Barley John answered mildly.

"Don't make no difference to her. Says we set a bad example for the kids."

Barley John took a deep drag, then carefully stubbed the joint out on the dashboard before slipping it into a pocket of his fatigue jacket. "Clint."

"Yeah?"

"I got a question."

"Shoot." Clint held on through a tight curve on 224. The load on the roof was so heavy the metal creaked, and it pulled the Jeep off balance.

"Did we do the right thing?"

"Does the Pope shit in the woods?" Clint glanced over at Barley John. His hunting partner looked positively distressed. That was unusual. "What do you mean?"

"It was like...shooting a man or something."

Clint laughed. "Just tell yourself he was a damned liberal traitor. You'll feel shitloads better."

Somehow explaining that to Barley John made *him* feel worse. They drove on into the darkness. After a few minutes, Clint said, "Mind if I take a quick pull off that joint?"

▲▼▲

Sweden was a town of three hundred people, with a post office not much larger than a gas station restroom, and a gas station not much bigger than that. There was an old truck stop, diesel pumps long since shut down and ripped out, that hosted Sweden's one halfway thriving business, the Fish Creek Café. Operating in a well-lit corner near the doors, the Café always seemed lost in the immensity of its own building, but it still had the huge walk-in coolers from busier days.

Clint pulled up in front of the restaurant to drop his load. Shelley Mendes who ran the place let folks use her coolers in exchange for a few cuts when someone made a run in to Estacada to have their meat processed. Sometimes people got ambitious and finished dressing their own kills on the concrete apron outside, but that tended to draw bears, so Shelley discouraged the practice.

It was almost nine o'clock when they lurched to a halt outside the Café. The lights were on within, with a few folks scattered around in the dozen booths or along the service counter. Clint noticed a Clackamas County sheriff's cruiser parked out front, the big Ford Crown Victoria gleaming among the collection of primer-colored pickups and rusting Subarus normal for rural Oregon.

"Hell. Damerow's in there."

Clint and Barley John had gone to high school with Elise Damerow. Elise had been a hard-playing jockette then, who never seemed to date any of the boys, and had harbored an intense and dedicated dislike for Clint and his friends. All he ever did was tease her a little.

She hadn't changed much over the years, except for acquiring the badge and the gun and, recently, a tattooed girlfriend who lived in a tree house out in the National Forest somewhere. Certainly her dislike of Clint hadn't diminished at all.

"What are we going to do with him?" asked Barley John, thumping on the roof. "We ain't got no permits."

Clint grinned. "Ain't no such thing as a Bigfoot permit. But I'll park out back. We can go in, talk to Shelley, maybe *Deputy* Damerow will be on her way by the time we need to unload."

He killed the lights and drove around behind the Fish Creek's building, stopping next to the dumpster. Then he and Barley John went inside.

"Evening, boys," said Shelley. She was a handsome girl, blonde streaking to silver over a comfortable figure a man could admire, widowed in Desert Storm and not much interested in close personal company after that. Clint had thrown a pass or two, times when Margie had been out of state visiting her sister. Shelley been nice enough about it, but there were some pass returns even Clint had little trouble receiving.

"Shelley." Clint nodded. Barley John just bobbed his head along with Clint, a silent echo.

She swiped at an imaginary dust spot on the counter. "What can I do for you? Coffee?"

"Yes, ma'am. Both our usuals." Barley John nodded again, though his lips moved slightly this time. "Might want to use your freezer." Clint leaned a little closer. "*Later*," he whispered, nodding toward the deputy who was getting up from her booth.

"You boys ever heard of permits?" Shelley asked with a smile.

Damerow walked up, hip slung out so her pistol was the most prominent part of her. Not that she had much else of prominence, in Clint's opinion. Thin as a fence rail and half as good looking. He had to admit, when the chips were down far enough to actually *need* a cop, he'd rather have Damerow coming around to help than anyone else, but otherwise he didn't have much use for the woman.

"See you had to park out back. Lot too crowded?" Her gray eyes glinted.

Clint shrugged. "You know how it is."

"Shoot something in season, it ought to have a tag. Shoot something out of season, well..." She laid some money down on the counter, pushed it toward Shelley. "Lucky for you boys I'm no game warden. Get it out of sight before I have to notice it."

"M-m-man's got to eat," said Barley John with the stutter Damerow always seemed to induce in him.

She smiled, chucked him under the chin. "What you eat should make you happy, Johnnie." With another glare at Clint, she headed out the door.

He watched until the cruiser pulled out on to 224, then turned back to pick up his coffee. Barley John was blushing red as Shelley's ketchup bottles.

"I do declare," Shelley said, closing Barley John's fingers around the second Styrofoam cup, "that woman likes you."

"He's always had a thing about dykes," said Clint.

Barley John stuttered into life again. "C-c-c-can't use that word n-n-no more."

"Women, then. You got a thing for manly women."

Shelley walked off, laughing into her dishrag.

▲▼▲

Outside with Shelley's flatcar dolly, they unlashed the Bigfoot. Clint wasn't willing to cut or dress it, figuring the carcass was worth a lot more whole. The fingers had curled into a fist, he noticed. Clint rigged a comealong to one of the roof stanchions of the building, then used the Jeep's bumper winch to pull the Bigfoot off the roof, Barley John guiding the load onto the dolly.

After that they wheeled him inside.

Somebody in one of the booths yelped and Shelley turned to look. Her eyes narrowed to about the same degree Damerow had employed to glare Clint down. "What in the Nathan Hale is *that*, Clinton Amos?"

"Game we shot," he said, glancing around the Fish Creek. Walter Arnason had gotten up from his booth to get a better look, as had the Koiichi brothers. Clint was damned glad Damerow was gone.

"Game. Huh." She flicked her towel back and forth, thinking. "You been shooting gorillas in the mist, maybe. Whatever *that* is, I don't want no steaks off it."

Barley John grinned. "Ain't gonna be no steaks."

"John," Clint said with a warning lift in his voice.

"That's no bear," said Freddie Koiichi.

The six or seven people left in the Café were crowding around the flatbed dolly now.

"Bigfoot," Clint confessed.

Walter Arnason laughed. "Duh shit, Clint. You boys are gonna be famous."

"You called anybody yet?" That was Franky Koiichi putting his oar in.

"No, and I ain't gonna until I had time to think it over good. Don't none of you do me no favors in the mean time, okay?"

They all stared for a while at the massive body on the dolly. Shelley finally spoke up again. "You shoot it, Clint?"

He swelled with pride. "Yeppers."

"I spotted it," said Barley John.

What *had* gotten into that boy? Clint wondered. "Our kill," he said with a generosity he didn't feel.

"Sweden's kill," said Shelley. Her voice was decisive. "You put this thing in my freezer, the whole town has to stand to profit. I don't want your sorry fat ass running off to Portland or Seattle with the evidence.

Folks are going to come here, eat my food, buy Koiichi's gas, and mail home postcards from our little post office. That all right with you, Mr. Bigfoot Bigshot?"

Clint didn't have anywhere else to store the creature. He sure as hell wasn't taking it home to Margie. He looked around the room. Seven pairs of eyes looked back. None of them made much money, half of them didn't have jobs at all. Himself included.

"Damn, I hate being public spirited without a reward in the bargain," Clint said slowly, enjoying his moment. "But I'll hold title—I mean, me and Barley John will hold title. I promise, whatever we make of this stays in Sweden."

Everybody in the Fish Creek Café shook on that, like a round of toasts at New Year's. They wheeled the dolly into the number three freezer, which Shelley turned way down cold just for the occasion before sharing out celebratory beers on the house.

Around midnight Clint dropped Barley John off at the little rusted-out Airstream trailer tucked in the freezing damp woods. Then he went home to his huge, rotting A-frame at the edge of town—a converted visitor's lodge from the 1940's—to explain to his wife what he had done.

▲▼▲

Breakfast was tense. Margie slapped down Krusteaz hotcakes and glared Clint Junior, Suzanne and no-longer-baby Hobson out the door to the school bus while Clint groaned through a headache composed of equal parts mild hangover and lack of sleep from being kicked out of bed at six in the morning. He managed a kiss for Hobson and quick hug for Suzanne. Clint Junior just dodged a punch on the arm, too old for his dad.

Then Margie pulled up a chair for herself and tucked into another stack of hotcakes with the same two strips of bacon the family economy allowed each of the children. Clint listened to the clink of her fork and smelled the cloying smudge of her syrup in wounded silence. They never had spoken last night.

That made him a little sad.

"Elise called," Margie finally said. The tines of her fork were squeaking on the empty plate now, pushing dollops of syrup around. "Yesterday evening."

Elise? Damerow, he realized. She was talking about the deputy.

"Said you and Johnnie had been out poaching again."

"You want to eat this winter?" he asked mildly, though angry words boiled inside of him. He was too tired to let them out. "Besides, it wasn't poaching."

"What the hell was it, then? You find enough religion to get honest with a hunting license?"

"No. I shot...something that ain't covered by the Department of Fish and Wildlife."

Margie stared at him, her face somewhere between angry and desperate. He remembered how pretty she'd been twenty years back. Hell, she was still pretty now under all the weight and chopped-short easy-to-care-for hair and them ugly, stretchy Wal-Mart clothes bought up in the city.

"What," she finally asked. "You shoot a space alien or something?"

"Bigfoot," he said proudly.

"Bigfoot?" She sounded like she'd never heard the word before.

"Bigfoot. And I do mean *big*."

"Jesus, Clint." Margie shook her head, tears standing in her eyes. "You were either drunk or stupid, or both. For the love of God, if you're gonna go poach, poach something I can cook."

"Barley John was there when I killed it," he said, defensive. "Shelley seen it when I brought it in. Walter Arnason and the Koiichis too."

"A real Bigfoot?"

"Real as they come."

"What are you going to do?"

"Call a press conference." He grinned. "Go big. Charge admission. Make some money." Clint reached across the table, took his wife's hand. "Big money, Margie. This'll be bigger than...than...I don't know. It will be like the Super Bowl come to Sweden, Oregon, and we'll own the winning team."

She burst into tears, somehow looking prettier than ever.

▲▼▲

There were a lot of people at the Fish Creek Café that afternoon when Clint pulled up to check on his kill. A whole lot of people.

He had to park out back for real.

Every booth was full inside, and most of the seats taken at the counter. Some of the folks were regulars, but a lot were people he saw only once in a while, at Koiichi's buying gas, or maybe passed by on the road to Estacada to do some city shopping. A few he didn't recognize at all.

Shelley was flying back and forth behind the counter. She actually had help, which she hadn't been able to afford since the mill closed and took the last of Sweden's steady jobs with it. Clint stared at the cook, who looked familiar but out-of-place, until he realized it was Damerow's tree-hugger girlfriend, skinnier than Damerow was, her head shaved, with sea green tattoos on her face and a big silver barbell coming out of both sides of her nose.

"Damn lot of people in here," he grumbled at Shelley when she stopped in front of his seat at the counter.

"Three people can't keep a secret unless two of them are dead," she said. "Besides, this is good for business. Whole town profits, right? We shook on it."

"Yeah, we did." He shook his head. "Coffee, when you get a minute. I came by to have a look, but I don't want to crack open number three freezer with all these folks here."

She sounded exasperated, just like Margie. "What do you think these folks are here *for*?"

He sipped at his coffee and thought that one over for a little while. Publicity was good, but they couldn't just start letting mobs in.

This wasn't a mob, though. Maybe he could do something. Definitely no cameras. The photo rights would be worth a lot. Millions.

Could he trust Shelley? Clint really wanted to ask her to let him put a lock on the number three freezer, but he had a good idea what she'd say to him. He wouldn't like having to find a new home for the Bigfoot.

Trust.

"Alrightie," Clint said, standing up and stretching. He felt as fake as he had the first time he'd oh-so-casual-like put his arm around Margie, back in the day. The diner had gone quiet as a schoolhouse in summer. "I'm gonna check on number three."

He walked around the counter and into the kitchen.

"Clint."

It was Shelley.

He turned to see a whole crowd standing behind her, massed at the counter as if waiting to start a race.

"You want to come look," he said, uncomfortable but knowing he had to play it Shelley's way, "come look. Two rules." He stuck up his fingers. "Only if I know you. And no talking to the press. The whole town's got to be together on this one."

There was some muttering, but Shelley nodded.

He went back to number three. The handle was popped loose. Somebody had opened the freezer before he got here, sometime since last night. Clint almost said something, but he didn't want to lose the goodwill of the moment. Besides, it had to be Shelley. She wouldn't have let anyone else in back here, except maybe that little slip of a cook she'd suddenly hired.

Which meant Damerow knew, he realized.

Clint tugged the handle open. The lights flickered on inside. Bigfoot lay where they'd left him last night, still on the dolly, his hair all frosty. People pushed in behind Clint, filing into the freezer like they were going to a funeral home viewing. He stopped one man, a big redhead in a checkered shirt.

"Do I know you, friend?" Clint asked. "We ain't open for the public yet."

"Worked the mill together back in ninety-two, ninety-three," the redhead said. "I drove the log lifter out in the loading yard. Moved on downstate."

"Why you back today?"

The redhead grinned, nodded at the Bigfoot. "Wouldn't you come back for this?"

After that, Clint gave up checking people. He just watched for cameras in their hands, or flashes going off.

They were all crowded around the body in a circle, still in that funeral way, when the comments began. Just like a memorial.

"Big fella," said Janie Watkins who lived with her deaf husband a couple of mileposts northwest of town in a cabin older than anything else in this part of the county.

"Didn't die happy," observed the redhead from downstate.

"Didn't live happy, neither." That was Walter Arnason, back for more after the previous night. "Look at them scars. Like someone worked him over with a k-bar a long time ago."

They went on that way, commenting on his size, details of his body, like high school students dissecting their class frog. Finally Clint cleared his throat. "It's cold in here, folks. Let's let him rest while me and Shelley work out our press strategy." He was proud of that line.

"What are you going to call him?" asked Janie.

"Swedish Steve," said Clint without even thinking about it.

"Good-bye, Swedish Steve," she said before leaving. Everyone else repeated the line on their way out, until it was only Clint and Shelley left.

"I guess half the state knows now," he said.

Her smile was hard. "Better get to work on your *press strategy* then, Clint."

Clint looked back at Swedish Steve. The corpse's hands were open flat now. He was certain they'd been fists the night before.

▲▼▲

He spent all afternoon at home trying to write out his pitch. Clint knew he'd have to find someone pretty big, fast, to get behind this. Michael Jackson would dig it, but no way he was going near that cross-raced freak. There were some good Oregon conservatives he liked, like that hotel guy Hemstreet, but Clint figured he needed someone from the press, or Hollywood.

No matter who, he had to have a good pitch to deliver when he got his prospective sponsor on the phone. Clint had seen enough TV shows about people who won the lottery or whatever then lost it all on investment scams and greedy relatives. He didn't want to just go to the papers or the TV stations. He needed his Mr. Big.

Margie wouldn't get off work until seven, be home until later, so Clint was by himself when the kids came in around four. Clint Junior—a junior in high school—banged open the door and flopped out on the couch with a burp. Suzanne—seventh grade—followed him in with a flip of her hair and a drama queen sigh before disappearing into her room.

Clint waited for Hobson, but his youngest—third grade—didn't follow.

"Where's your brother?" he asked Clint Junior.

"What brother?"

"*Junior.*"

"Oh, you mean my baby *bother.*" Clint Junior grinned. "He got off the bus same us up by the Fish Creek. Went kiting off into the woods with that freakazoid friend of his."

The 'freakazoid' was Barley John's nephew, Tyler Dimmitt Stephens. Tyler was a chip off the old barleycorn, which Clint didn't figure was good for the kid's future, but Barley John's nephew got along with Hobson like kerosene and matches.

"He's supposed to come home first," Clint grumbled. "House rules."

"I ain't his keeper." Clint Junior flopped open a math book and pretended to study.

Clint didn't feel like arguing the point. He fetched his coat and stepped out the front door to go look for his youngest son. Hobson and Tyler had no more sense of time than a jaybird did, and it was close to dark.

Outside had the crisp, clear feeling of snow about to fall. The sky was pearly gray again, and the wind worried at the collar of his corduroy coat. Clint briefly wished he'd grabbed his field jacket instead, but he figured a quick walk up to the Fish Creek Café to shout into the woods would serve. He lived about half a mile southeast of the town center, so the distance was just right for a warm-up. As he walked, he hollered, "Tyler! Hobson! Come on in, boys."

There was no sign of the kids by the time he'd made it to the Café, so he stuck his head in the door. Shelley wasn't there, but Damerow's weirdo girlfriend still was working behind the counter. It was still busier than normal.

Was she showing people the freezer? He wondered how much profit Shelley could pull into her own pocket off Swedish Steve without him knowing it. Clint realized he'd have to start spending his days down at the Café, have the kids meet him here when they got off the bus.

"You seen Tyler and Hobson?" he asked the girlfriend.

"Nope."

"Two little kids," he added. "Got off the bus maybe half an hour ago."

"Nope."

"Shelley here?"

"Nope."

"You know how to say anything else?"

She shot him the finger. "Nope."

He fingered her back, then went stomping around in the woods that lined the Fish Creek's huge parking lot on the southeast side. On the northwest, it kind of graveled over to Koiichi's gas station, then to the Post Office. If they'd run into the woods, as Clint Junior had said, it was here.

Twenty minutes later, after a stop at Tyler's house confirmed Barley John's sister hadn't seen the boys either, Clint was back at the Fish Creek Café. It was already getting twilight, and he was worried. He banged open the door again. There were a bunch of people inside, maybe half of them locals.

"I don't mean to raise a panic," he said, "but there's a couple of boys missing out there, and I'm hoping some of you folks can come walk the woods and help me search."

"Aw, shit," someone groaned, but the vinyl booths creaked as everyone in the restaurant got up in a hurry. The girlfriend went for the telephone. Calling Damerow, Clint figured, but right about now that was probably a good idea.

"Any of you got flashlights in your trucks, please get 'em out," he called. "It's darker than the inside of a raccoon's ass out there once the sun goes down."

The girlfriend brought him a Mag-Lite from behind the counter, one of those five-battery police special skullbreakers.

"Thanks."

"I called Elise, and Shelley," she said. Then, "Sorry about your kid."

"What do you mean, *sorry?*" he asked, instantly suspicious. And where the hell was Shelley, anyway? a little voice in the back of his head wondered.

She shot him the finger again. "Sorry he's lost. Sorry he's got a loser fuckface like you for a dad."

Clint was shaking with rage then, all in a moment, but he knew better than to slap her down in a room full of worried people. "Come on," he shouted. "We got to go."

They poured out of the Café, splitting up in different directions, calling the kids' names. Clint's heart felt like a fist in his chest, straining to get out. When he ran into Clint Junior in the parking lot, he gave his older son a bone-cracking hug.

"Easy, Dad," Clint Junior said in a soft voice. "Little bother's just off playing with a bird's nest or something."

Neither of them believed it.

▲▼▲

By the time Margie's old Plymouth Arrow came straining up the highway, around 7:40, the whole town was out. Damerow had arrived shortly after the search was launched, and tried to call for backup, but a bank robbery at the other end of the county in Portland's outskirts had tied up all available units. She did get the fire district people out, and a promise from the Forest Service to send rangers. They hadn't shown yet.

Clint didn't want to talk to the Forest Service, not one tiny bit, but he wanted his boy back a whole lot more. It was already below freezing out here and people were starting to say the word 'bodies' when they should have been saying 'kids.'

Margie's Arrow slowed as it passed the Post Office and Koiichi's, then pulled over in front of the Fish Creek Café. The lot was completely full. Clint watched her get out, ask someone what was going on, and be pointed toward him.

He wanted to run away, right then, more than anything he'd ever wanted in his life. He couldn't face his wife and tell her he'd lost their baby boy. Clint knew that all Margie's toughness would be gone like piss in the wind with the news.

He knew he'd be the one to kill her with the words.

Margie walked up to where Clint stood in the glare of one of the Café's security lights. Her face was already a crumpled mess, like God's laundry basket.

"Honey," he said slowly. "We'll find him."

"I....he..." Her words wouldn't come, stuck in her mouth like taffy.

"Everyone's on it," Clint told her, his voice tightening as he spoke. "We've been stopping every car that passes through, getting them to help. The whole damned town of Sweden's out here, Margie."

"Hob...Hob..." She gulped for air, dying as surely as any hard-landed rainbow trout. "Hobson."

He opened up his arms and folded in her tears. They stood in the frigid air, bodies shaking together, while people shouted and called and played lights in the trees all around them, as far as Clint could see. Farther, he hoped. All the way to the end of the world.

▲▼▲

Half an hour or so later, Margie was inside having coffee and crying with Shelley. Clint stayed out in the cold. He wanted to search, badly, but Damerow had ordered him to remain at the Fish Creek. "We've got to find *you* when we find him," she'd said.

Clint had done fire district search-and-rescue work off and on since he was a teenager. He knew the rules. Still he punished himself by waiting in the cold, refusing Shelley's coffee, as uncomfortable as any of the searchers.

As uncomfortable as Hobson or Tyler.

Barley John came sidling up out of the darkness, a fading flashlight in his hand. In the distance, people were shouting. "Clint," he said. "You'd better come on."

Clint knew without asking that this wasn't good.

He followed Barley John into the woods, onto the gravel track where Barley John's sister's trailer was, and maybe another dozen families beyond her. Further down they cut off the track into wooded darkness marked only by a swarm of flashlights. From behind him, Clint heard the grumble of the fire district's old Power Wagon rescue truck.

Whatever it was, they needed the truck for it. That was even worse than not good.

Barley John led Clint to a little crowd of people pointing their flashlights up into a Douglas fir. The lowest branches were forty feet off the ground. A little higher, there was something pale.

"The dog was barking," someone said, the crowd beginning to tell Clint the story in dozens of voices. "My boy heard something." "She never comes out here." "It was like wind said my name." "Who looks up in the woods?" "Walked past here a dozen times." "How would anyone get up there?" "Blood dripping down the tree trunk." "Must have been a wolf." "An eagle." "Bigfoot's revenge."

Then the Dodge was there, easing between the trees, and men were unbolting a ladder and laying it against the tree and strapping on climbing spikes and arranging safety ropes and ascending the bark and shouting and calling for the stretcher and it was like all the time in Clint's life had collected in this one moment, a huge bank of time teetering on the edge of a cliff, an avalanche that would sweep away all the rest of his days in a tide of grief and rage and pain.

The rope came down with the stretcher and there was one tiny body strapped in tight under blankets and people caught it. Clint pushed forward, but it was Stephanie Dimmitt who never would marry Bart Stephens because she didn't want to be Stephanie Stephens who threw herself on the bloodied blankets and wailed. Tyler Dimmitt Stephens lay there, his face swollen, his scalp torn, the color of a ice cube with lips as dark blue as Clint's jeans.

"What about Hobson?" he asked, but nobody heard.

Tyler's eyes fluttered open, a blue as icy as his lips though Clint would have sworn they were brown like his uncle's, and Tyler said in a clear, piercing voice, "Monkey, it was the monkey." He threw up on the blankets, a mix of bile and blood, and began to shiver violently.

The fire district people shoved Tyler in the back of the Power Wagon and backed out, already shouting into their radio for a medevac flight.

A few minutes later, Clint was almost alone. With a dull echo of surprise, he realized he was standing next to Damerow.

"Hobson's close by," she told him. "Whatever sick fuck did this, he can't have gone too far. You started the search quickly enough." Damerow put her arm across his shoulders, which didn't even feel weird to Clint even though she was dyke or whatever he was supposed to call her now. "You did the right thing, Clint. You didn't do anything wrong."

Then the steam of her breath carried her away, chattering into a walkie-talkie, redirecting people and equipment like Eisenhower at Normandy.

After a while, Clint walked back to the Fish Creek Café. He wanted to look inside number three, see if Swedish Steve was still there. He really wanted to see if there was blood on Swedish Steve's hands.

When he got there, Damerow was standing outside the big aluminum door with a digital camera in her hand.

"Figured you'd be along," she said. "I want a look. Care to fess up?"

Clint nodded, tugged open the door. They stepped inside, and he began to tell the story. It was clear Damerow had already heard it, but he told everything he knew anyway, except the part about the freezer door being loose and the hands changing around. He didn't want to sound crazy.

There was no blood on Swedish Steve's hands, but the right one had two fingers extended, like a V-for-victory. Clint figured it was Damerow's girlfriend mindfucking him, but he wasn't about to say that to the deputy either.

▲▼▲

The Fish Creek Café stayed open all night, as home base for the search for Hobson. Clint finally decided to keep indoors, to watch the number three freezer, he told himself. But there was coffee, and company, and occasional kindness. Margie was long gone, swallowed up in that mysterious sisterhood of grieving women. Clint wondered half-seriously if he was ever going to see her again, either.

Clint Junior insisted on staying out with the search parties, while Suzanne had ridden off to the hospital in Portland in the helicopter with Stephanie and Tyler.

That left Clint alone, even when a group bustled in for coffee and burgers and a restroom stop. He gathered from the gossip that Damerow had split the searchers, keeping one half on a wide-ranging spiral, while the other half worked close around the tree where Tyler had been found. They'd maybe located a blood slick near the tree, but it would be tomorrow at the earliest before there could be any reliable crime lab work on that.

Damerow came in around three a.m. She was tired, pale, her skin almost green. "Bad news, Clint," she said, sitting down opposite him and blowing on her hands to warm them.

"What isn't?"

"Hospital called. They did typing on the blood on Tyler's face and clothes. Not real forensics work, mind you, but there was plenty to go around, you should pardon my bluntness. Mix of two types. Tyler's a B negative. You wouldn't happen to know if Hobson's an AB positive, would you?"

"Hell no," said Clint, "I've got no idea. Margie might know." He sighed, a long, shuddering sob of a sigh. "But I'd bet both nuts it's his blood. Whose else would it be?"

"An attacker's," she said, but her face was almost frozen in her lack of expression. Damerow wasn't giving much away right now. "The book says you're suspect number one, but you've got no cuts or bruises, sure as hell not enough to bleed as much as Tyler had on him. Besides which, I've known you longer than I've had my tits. You're a jerk, and an oaf, and you're mean to your wife and shiftless in the bargain, but you'd no more kill a kid than you would fly to the moon on gossamer wings. Beyond that, you'd *have* to be able to fly to put Tyler fifty feet up a Doug fir."

"Well, I can't fly." Clint's voice was flat as an old tire.

"Neither can anyone else. It's what we call a little forensics problem. More to the point, you've got an alibi tight as anyone else's. You left your other kids at home ten minutes before people here saw you hollering for help. No way you ran around in the woods, slaughtered two kids, climbed a tree, cleaned up and got back here that fast."

It didn't surprise him that she'd been talking to witnesses. It shouldn't—it was her job. "So who put him up that tree?"

"Some psycho with a ladder and a hell of a lot of nerve. If I knew who," Damerow said, "I'd know where Hobson is."

"Hobson's body," said Clint.

"That's still Hobson." She stood up, patted him on the shoulder, then leaned over and kissed his head.

"Wait."

"What? You going to confess and ruin all my good policework?"

"No. But it was him. Swedish Steve."

"The *Bigfoot*? He's dead, Clint. You've been up too long."

"He got out before. I found the door loose this morning, on number three. And his hands...they're different every time I look at them."

"Come on, big boy." She grabbed Clint's shoulder, dragged him to his feet. "Let's go look."

The fingers of Swedish Steve were still in a vee. Damerow took more pictures, then got some Scotch tape from beneath the counter and sealed the door at the top, middle and bottom, taping one of her business cards on the handle. "Somebody sneaks in, they'll miss the top tape," she told Clint.

"What have you told the sheriff about Swedish Steve?" he asked.

"Nothing, yet. I don't want to come off like a looney tune here. But the County Attorney's going to be all over this child abduction as soon as it hits the paper in Portland, and I'm going to have to come clean before it looks like I've been hiding evidence." She grimaced. "You want a big score, you've got another eight to twelve hours to make it. In the mean time, keep your sorry ass in here where plenty of people can see you."

She went back outside, to the miserable cold of the search for whatever was left of his youngest. He went back to his booth and cried for a while.

▲▼▲

Later, the kid-sized hole in his heart was really getting to Clint, and the coffee had stopped helping much. He figured a little cold air would brace him up, so with a nod to the girlfriend behind the counter, he stepped outside.

There were still lights in the woods, and people calling his son's name. Every direction, both sides of the highway, like little fireflies. He stood shivering, wondering what he could do. Should do. Should have done.

It couldn't be the damned Bigfoot. It had to be, but it couldn't. Who got up from a freezer, with three bullets in them, and ran around behind everybody's back?

He should be out there, should be one of them fireflies. Hobson would hear his daddy's voice instead of some strangers. Clint knew the kid like no one else but Margie did. He'd recognize the kind of hidey-hole that would appeal to Hobson, running from whatever fucking psycho had sliced up Tyler so bad.

Dead or alive, no one could find Clint's kid better than Clint could.

Tugging his Cat cap down over his forehead, Clint lurched off into the woods, heading toward where Tyler had been found. Damerow had been right. Stood to reason the kid would have run from that point. He was so tired he nearly stumbled with every step, and the cold cramped him up something fierce, but Clint figured that was God's way of telling him he should have kept a better eye on the boy.

What else could he have done?

▲▼▲

Clint wasn't sure where he was any more. He'd lived in Sweden all his life, never been lost once, but this was different. One second he'd swear he was waist-deep in snow that hadn't come yet, the next he was almost summer warm. He didn't recognize the trees, either.

There were still voices, though. He tried to follow them. He couldn't quite make them out. Some funny singsong language—the Koiichi brothers talking Japanese to each other?

"Hobson," he croaked. Maybe it was his son.

Then he heard that eagle screech again, just like it had before he'd shot the Bigfoot. Clint stumbled, throwing out one hand against a pine to catch himself, and had a vision of a little skiff on a river, a huge bearded man firing some old-fashioned pistol up at him, as if he was in the air. A campsite burned along the river bank, people in furs lying face-down in the water.

He stumbled again, collapsed into some blackberry canes that tore at his clothes. The bearded man was screaming now, cursing in some other language, while the skiff turned sideways and his pistol tumbled away to the river below and the biggest God damned osprey Clint had ever imagined in his life beat great, slow wings that sounded like a dying man's heart, its enormous claws dug deep into the bearded man's shoulders.

Right where Swedish Steve had big scars.

Clint gasped as flat-faced women smeared with bear grease sawed at his joints and tendons with sharpened clamshells, then woke up screaming to a flashlight in his face.

"Buddy, we'd better get you back inside," said Barley John, looking sadder than Clint had ever seen him.

▲▼▲

Someone shook Clint's shoulder, hard. His head jerked violently. A cup tumbled with the motion. Cold coffee sprayed in his face and hair.

"I'm awake," he said, almost shouting.

"Are you Clinton Gerald Amos?"

Sitting up, Clint rubbed his eyes. A tall man in a trench coat, with a narrow black tie and Ray Bans, stared down at him. Early morning sunlight glared in the windows of the Fish Creek Café, making Clint squint. The guy was a near ringer for Agent Mulder from that tv show.

"What the hell are you?"

The tall man frowned. "I'm with the Paranormal Investigation Bureau."

"Para…" Clint rubbed his eyes again. "What the fuck? Get away from me, you fruitcake."

The tall man knelt, bringing him almost face to face with Clint. "We're a private foundation sir, investigating paranormal incidences. Ah, X-Files material, if you will. Except in real life. We also compensate handsomely for verifiable information."

"Do you *compensate handsomely* for missing children?" Clint asked, his voice getting nasty. This was the first person he'd spoken with since Hobson had disappeared who he could legitimately punch out.

"Children?" The Paranormal guy looked surprised. "I'm here about your Bigfoot."

Clint jumped up out of the booth, grabbed the glass cylinder of sugar, and took a hard swing. His visitor ducked the punch and began backing off, as a couple of other people came up out of their booths, intent on stopping the fight.

The door banged open so hard the glass cracked. "Clint Amos, get your ass out here *now!*"

It was Damerow, another deputy with her who Clint didn't recognize, big fella with a red face and beefy lips. Franky Koiichi and Bob Watkins were already backing Paranormal guy into a corner as Clint walked out into the frigid morning.

Damerow stabbed him in the chest with her fingertip. "Do you have *any* fucking idea where Stacey Kamerone is right now?"

"What?" Stacey Kamerone was the teen-aged daughter of the postmistress.

"She was missing from her room when her mother went to wake her up this morning. Window was open, a little blood on the sill." The finger stabbed again. "*Three* fucking kids in less than twenty-four hours, in *my* town, and you started it somehow. And Sunfire tells me you fucking left the café last night after I fucking told you to stay the fuck *put!*"

"Elise," said the other deputy, grabbing her elbow.

Damerow took her finger off Clint's chest. "Where the hell is she, Clint?"

"You check the freezer?"

"God damn it, Clint, I will shoot you where you stand if you are fucking with—"

"*Deputy* Damerow!" barked the other deputy in a voice southern as corn pone. "That is *enough!*"

"It wasn't me and you know it," Clint said, his voice low and urgent. "Check the God damned freezer. Take Deputy Dawg here with you."

She looked ready to slug him, but she kept her voice down. "I know it wasn't you, shithead, but I can't prove it because you left the God-damned café!"

"So what's in the freezer, Damerow?" asked the other deputy.

"You wouldn't believe it if you saw it," muttered Damerow, "but it doesn't have anything to do with these kids."

"I'd like to judge that for myself."

Damerow shot Clint a look that probably should have wounded him, then the trio trailed back to the number three freezer.

"Got your card on the door," said the new deputy, Rohan—Clint had finally puzzled out his name tag.

"Tape's broken," Damerow said in a smaller voice. She glanced at Clint. "Who's been in here?"

"Hell if I know. I fell asleep."

"Some fucking father you—"

"*Damerow!*" shouted Rohan. "Enough!"

Damerow got quiet, tugged her digital camera out of her coat pocket, and took shots of the snapped open tape on the freezer door. Whoever it had been hadn't even tried to set the tape back in place.

When they walked in, Swedish Steve's right hand had three fingers extended.

▲▼▲

Damerow was somewhere else, and Rohan was sweating Clint inside Shelley's tiny office.

"Listen to me," the big deputy said. "I know you've got alibis. I know you've been in here since yesterday. But you walked out last night, which means all that good cover is gone.

"You're friends with half this shithole town, and anyone one of them could lie their asses off for you and I'll never know. But you listen to me, Amos. When they realize exactly what you've done, what kind of person you really are, they're going to stop covering for you. Give it up now, and maybe this nightmare will be over sooner. Because I promise you, it will end one way or the other."

Clint stared up at Rohan, his eyes red and rimmed with hot, sandy crap. "You can keep asking me the questions, but the truth ain't changing. It's my fucking kid that's missing, Deputy. What am I covering for? What the hell am I hiding?"

"You tell me, Amos. You're the one hiding the kids from us."

Clint jumped up, banging his head on a shelf and sending a row of computer and food service manuals flying. "How the *fuck* did I kidnap Stacey Kamerone, smart guy? Am I identical twins? Did I fucking hypnotize everybody in this town? Sure I was out for a while, but I came back. I was sleeping in the restaurant booth until Paranormal boy woke me up. Right in plain sight of everybody."

Rohan grabbed Clint's shirt front, murder in his piggy eyes, when the office door opened. "A word with you, deputy," said a tall Hispanic woman in civilian clothes. She laid one hand on Rohan's arm, showing him a badge with the other.

Rohan dropped Clint and backed out. His face promised further retribution. Another civilian, a small black guy in a fruity sweater with reindeer woven into the pattern, stepped into the door. "Agent Moran, FBI, from the Portland field office," he said.

"Thanks for pulling that maniac off me."

"Deputy Rohan was doing what he thought best, I'm sure," said Moran.

Clint was suddenly bone tired. Soul tired. "And what do you think best?"

"Walk the ground with me, Mr. Amos, if you would."

Clint followed Moran out, past Deputy Rohan being read the riot act by Moran's partner, and into the cold morning of a world without his son.

▲▼▲

They walked without talking until they reached the tree where Tyler had been found. It was surrounded by police tape, which Moran brushed past. He and Clint stared upward.

"Don't do a lot of tree forensics," Moran said. "Except once in a while on logging cases. Spiking and what all."

His tone was conversational, even friendly, but Clint refused to be drawn in. "I guess not."

"How would you climb this tree, Mr. Amos?"

Clint stared up forty feet of branchless trunk to where the canopy began to spread wide. It wasn't even all that high, as Douglas firs went. "I wouldn't."

"But if you had to."

He shrugged. "Get a bucket truck, I guess."

"Climbing spikes, ropes…?" The agent's voice was gentle.

"Look at me, Moran." Clint patted his belly. "I'm seventy, eighty pounds overweight, well past forty. I couldn't climb this tree if my butt was on fire and there was water at the top."

"I believe you, Mr. Amos. That's the sad part."

"Sad?"

"Because if you *could* climb this tree, this whole nasty business would be over."

"Damerow said as much last night."

"Deputy Damerow's well past the end of her rope right now. However, I have already developed considerable respect for that woman." Moran paused, as if considering his words. "But you know, don't you?"

"Yes." Clint's shoulders shook as sobs overtook him again. The scars on Swedish Steve matched the places where those Indian women had been cutting on him in his dream. Matched where the osprey had grabbed that great bear of a man. "Bigfoot. I shot the Bigfoot, and somehow he's doing this in return."

"The body in the freezer? He has more witnesses to his good behavior than you do to yours, Mr. Amos. In a bulky coat, you might pass unremarked. That person, thing, whatever it is, would be noticed by a blind man."

"You'd think," said Clint quietly. "But Tyler said something about monkeys. And that's what Swedish Steve is. A big, giant, killer monkey."

Something rattled behind them, that Clint belatedly recognized as gunfire. He was only two or three steps after Moran in heading back for the Fish Creek Café.

▲▼▲

"It was a monkey," shouted Freddie Koiichi. "Outside Walter's house. Just like the kid said."

There was a group of people in the parking lot, angry, a lot of them with pistols and rifles. Deputy Rohan and the Hispanic FBI agent were there, looking very unhappy.

"What the hell happened?" Clint said.

The crowd crystallized around him. Most of them were from Sweden, most of them knew him, knew that his kid had been the first to go. "A monkey," Freddie repeated. "Trying to climb into Walter Arnason's back bedroom."

"His kid Bobby was in there getting ready for school," someone else shouted.

"Well," asked Clint, "did you hit it?"

Somebody laughed, sharp and nervous. "Shot at it," muttered Freddie. "So did a couple of the guys."

Rohan looked disgusted. "They blew out the window and winged the kid."

Damerow stalked out of the Fish Creek Café, walked over to Clint and Agent Moran. She looked like hammered shit, and sounded like it too as she said, "I've got to show you something."

"Not now," said Clint.

"It's something that means I believe you."

He glanced at Moran, whose face was impassive. "Fine," Clint said, and stepped away from the crowd as Deputy Rohan began to harangue them, threatening the whole lot with arrest.

She pulled out her digital camera and flipped it over to the little preview screen. "Look here," Damerow said. "I just took this picture."

It showed Swedish Steve lying in the freezer.

The deputy flipped the little menu button a number of times. "Now look here. My first picture."

Swedish Steve again.

"What's the point?" asked Clint.

Moran frowned. "He looks different."

"He's *thinner* now."

Clint was ready to explode. "How the *fuck* is that possible?" He whirled, charged at Freddie Koiichi. "Give me your pistol, Freddie, *now*!"

Unnerved, Freddie handed the Glock 9 mm to Clint.

"Is this thing ready to fire?" Clint asked.

"Hey there," said Rohan, but Moran touched his arm.

Freddie took the pistol back, worked the slide, and returned it to Clint. Clint headed for the Fish Creek Café, trailing Moran, Damerow, Rohan, the other FBI agent and a dozen of his fellow Swedes. Gun in front, he moved through the door, past the girlfriend back at the counter, and back to the number three freezer.

He stopped there, taking a deep breath. "Somehow that fucker in there is doing this to our kids," Clint announced. "I'm going to put four or five into his head and stop him for good and all."

Rohan really didn't like that, but Moran had a firm hand on the deputy now. Damerow looked ready to shoot either Clint or the Bigfoot. Everyone else just looked scared.

Not knowing what else to do, Clint yanked the freezer door open.

Swedish Steve lay inside, right where they'd left him. His left hand had four fingers up now. "Somebody else is missing," Clint said with sick certainty.

"Rohan," barked Moran and Damerow almost in unison.

Clint heard the deputy's footfalls echoing away. He lifted the Glock, pointed it at Swedish Steve's temple, and rested his finger on the trigger.

Something was wrong, he realized. He had a flashback to the Indian women, cutting away by firelight at the soft places of some man's body. His body, at least in that dream or vision or whatever it had been.

This wasn't the right thing to do. Somehow, Clint knew that. Then he thought of Hobson, and realized he didn't care. He took a deep breath and pulled the trigger.

▲▼▲

All hell broke loose and then some. The bullet shattered Swedish Steve's frozen left temple, spraying Clint and Moran with crunchy pinkish-gray goo. Then the great body split at the seams.

The hair rippled, carrying skin with it, twisting off like a nuclear sunburn. Little monkey men, tiny versions of Swedish Steve perhaps three feet tall, jumped free from his body, sloughing off as if they had escaped from a prison. There were two, then four, then a dozen.

Someone began screaming. Clint wasn't sure, it might have been him. A lot of people began shooting, which wasn't too smart in the enclosed, metal-walled space of the walk-in freezer. There was a lot more screaming as the little doubles of Swedish Steve jumped up on people's chests, gnawed at fingers and crotches, leapt for exposed ears, noses and lips.

Bullets rang and whizzed in a spray of blood and painful shouts, while Damerow shouted for people to get down and stop shooting.

The door, Clint thought, don't let them get the fuck out, and he tried to wade through the press of panicked bodies, but too many of his fellow townsmen were already crowding the exit and little bastards were running across their heads, tearing bits of scalp as they went, and he could hear screaming outside in the dining room of the Fish Creek Café.

Someone, or something, tripped him. Clint went down as a shotgun roared, hearing another screech from some big-ass bird. The floor was cold, but the blood pooling on it was warm, so he waited until it was safe to move.

▲▼▲

Twenty minutes later Clint was in a circle of people out in the parking lot. Every one of them had a gun in their hand. Damerow and Moran were there with Clint. Keeping an eye on him, maybe. A lot of folks were missing. Including Freddie Koiichi, whose pistol he still held.

Moran was talking into a handheld radio. "Clackamas County Deputy Rohan's dead. Special Agent Martinez is dead. We have at least three civilian deaths and a large number of casualties." He glanced up at the clouds. "Confirm that. Highway is closed at both ends. Give us at least twenty-five miles of separation. No one comes in here without my say-so." There was a long pause. "Well if that happens, send in the Army. Hell if I know what else to do. Moran out."

The FBI agent slipped the radio into a pocket of his parka. "We're on our own, people," he announced. "After that honkie firing squad in there, I'm not endangering any more lives until we know exactly what the hell is going on here. I've got a cop or an armed parent standing watch over every child that's still here. What do we do now? This is your town, what the hell was that?"

"Swedish Steve," said Clint. "What I've been saying since yesterday. That Bigfoot fucker did this."

"Nobody splits into a dozen killer monkeys," said Moran. His voice quivered toward panic. "That shit just doesn't happen."

Clint stared him down. "You were standing there."

Nothing had been left of Swedish Steve except the tiny, contorted body of a very old white man, his head blown to pieces by Clint's bullet. What Clint had glimpsed of his body had unnervingly familiar scars. They'd killed two of the monkeys, or whatever they were. At least those little beasts *could* be killed.

Of course, nobody had seen a single one of them since the survivors had swarmed out of the Fish Creek Café and disappeared into the woods.

"So what was that? Or they?"

Damerow's girlfriend spoke up. She'd been cooking out front when the swarm had come out, fought them with a scoop of flaming grease. That's how one of the two dead monkeys had died, though there were a couple of dicey minutes with a fire extinguisher afterward. "They're his fetches."

"Fetch?" asked Clint.

"Fetch. Double. There's probably a Northwest Native American term for it, but I don't know the word. They're parts of him, like, reflections."

"How do you know this?" Moran demanded.

"You have a better theory?"

A horrible idea dawned on Clint. "I want to see one of these fetches," he said. He glanced at Damerow. "Can I go back inside? With her?" He inclined his head at the girlfriend.

"My name is Sunfire."

Right, thought Clint, Damerow had mentioned that name earlier.

"Go with them, Damerow," Moran ordered.

Damerow, Sunfire and Clint went back into the Café, Clint and Damerow with weapons drawn.

"Sunfire?" Clint asked. "Really? Is that what it says on your birth certificate?"

"Shut *up*, fuckwad."

"Shut up you both," growled Damerow. "There might be more of them in here."

There were certainly more dead people in here, Clint thought. It made him sick. How many of them had shot each other? How many had died from the fetches, as Sunfire had called them? He could see Freddie Koiichi lying outside freezer number three, throat torn open.

"I'd rather look at the one Sunfire killed," Clint whispered. He really, really didn't want to go back into the freezer.

They walked slowly across the Café. Tables were overturned, blood spattered on the floor, with flecks of white extinguisher goo everywhere, along with spilled salt, sugar and ketchup. The effect was unnerving.

Sunfire's dead fetch lay curled up between the counter and the kitchen area, its furry back facing them. Clint handed his pistol to Sunfire, who shook her head, so Damerow took it. He grabbed a twelve-inch knife off the prep counter, leaned out and poked the fetch with the point of the blade.

It was too familiar, and too weird. Just as he'd done to Swedish Steve, back in the woods. Clint had an image of the fetch dissolving into a dozen tinier fetches, and so on, until Sweden was overrun with microscopic, hellish imps.

If he was right, that wasn't true.

The fetch rolled over. Its front was horribly damaged where Sunfire had burned it.

"Nice work, girlfriend," Clint breathed. He worked the tip of the knife into the bubbly flesh, wiggled it in, then tried to saw back and forth without actually laying a steadying hand upon the fetch.

The fetch slid back and forth on the fire-scarred linoleum floor of Shelley's kitchen, but the knife caught and dug in deeper, with a scent like fried bacon wafting up from the hairy little body.

"What the hell—" Damerow began, but Sunfire shushed her.

Then something popped and the skin slid open, just as Swedish Steve's had, curling back to reveal a withered, pale body wrapped within the hairy fat.

One of the women behind him began to retch, then threw up.

"All the victims," said Clint hoarsely over the choking and spattering. "Over the years, the missing hikers and vanished kids. He, somehow, he took them in. Each of these fetches is a little bit of Swedish Steve wrapped around one of...one of...us."

Then he began to cry in earnest, because Clint knew where Hobson was.

▲▼▲

"Now what?" Moran had gone into the restaurant alone after listening to their report, and come back out again looking pale and determined.

"We lure them in," said Clint. "They're still human under that monkey skin. That's must be why Swedish Steve went after the kids. We need my Margie, and Kathy Kamerone, and any other parents those lost kids might know, and we need all the kids, and we need them in a big circle, out here in the parking lot where the fetches can see them. And we call to Stacey and Hobson and whoever's in there, bring them out to us." He paused, breath caught in his throat. "Then we kill them. Our lost children."

"No," said Sunfire. "We don't kill them. We set them free."

Clint was just sick. "How?"

"We bring that old man out here, the one you said was still in the freezer, and those two dead fetches. The curse, or monster, or whatever it is, it's about him. He was the first. He pulled the others in. We lay him to rest, heal his soul, the others will follow."

"Heal his soul?" Moran asked, his voice incredulous.

Clint turned on the FBI agent. Maybe, somehow, he could have Hobson back, if he could keep Moran from exterminating the damned fetches. "What's your plan, Efrem Zimbalest Junior? You've got the highway closed. Going to napalm us all to death? Destroy the village in order to save it?"

"If I have to," said Moran quietly. "This is, in my terms, a hot biohazard of the worst kind. I'm willing to give her idea a little time before I go nuclear. So to speak."

Clint grinned. He could feel his lips tight back across his teeth. Anything for his son. Anything. "So to speak. Her idea is mine, Special Agent."

When Clint looked around, he was surprised to see Damerow smiling at him. "I'll go in and get Swedish Steve," he said. Amazingly, his voice didn't squeak with terror. "If two of you will get the other fetches. We'll still need the children here, too."

"And a battalion of shrinks," muttered Moran, "assuming any of them live through this."

"It ain't like the fucking movies," Clint told the agent. He uncocked the slide on the Glock, stuck it into his belt loop, took a big stretch, and headed once more for the bloody interior of the Fish Creek Café.

▲▼▲

Sunfire and Moran followed him in. Sunfire split off immediately to retrieve the fetch that she had killed, while Moran and Clint walked very lightly to the door of number three freezer.

It was still standing open.

Clint glanced down at Freddie Koiichi, and said a prayer to a God he didn't believe in anyway. Then he stepped around the corner and into the freezer.

Rohan was there, face down in a substantial pool of blood which was already a dark, goopy mess. Martinez was slumped against the wall by the door, her pistol in her lap, three bullet holes in her face and neck. Walter Arnason was there too, though Clint could only tell who he was by his clothes.

And a fetch, its head blown almost free of its neck, along with Swedish Steve.

Clint walked over to Swedish Steve, who looked very tiny indeed coiled up on a mass of bloody gobbets on Shelley's flatbed dolly. He was a very old man, his skin wrinkled and loose on tiny bones. The scars were still familiar. Clint thought briefly of Hobson, then lifted what was left of Swedish Steve in his arms like a baby.

On the way out the door, the body flexed. Clint looked down to see the lips moving. He almost dropped Swedish Steve as the old man whispered something unintelligible.

In the parking lot, they laid out the three bodies they had gathered. Sunfire began to walk a circle around them, chanting, as the children of Sweden were herded into place in a wider circle by frightened men and women with guns. Clint looked up to see Margie staring at him, her eyes so deeply ringed that she looked as if she'd been beaten. She shook her head slightly, then stared down at her feet.

He was profoundly glad that Suzanne had gone on the helicopter. At least his daughter would survive.

Sunfire motioned for the circle to open a pathway facing the woods. She kept walking, chanting, waving, her voice sing-songing up and down in a language Clint didn't understand. It was cold as hell, and flurries began to whip down from higher elevations.

They all stood there, their breath hanging in the air heavy as their hopes, listening to some New Age hippie sing.

Then the first fetch crept out of the woods.

"Pray for him," Sunfire said, working the words into her song as she kept circling the bodies. "Pray for them."

Clint found himself wondering exactly how many fetches there had been. Around him, people began to say the Lord's Prayer.

"Our Father, who art in Heaven, hallowed be Thy name."

Sunfire still circled and sang, her voice and hands and body inviting the fetch into the circle. Another came out of the shadows to witness the fate of the first.

"Thy kingdom come, Thy will be done, on Earth as it is in Heaven."

Two more now, and the first fetch crouched next to the old man's body. The snow flurries were picking up. Clint found himself wondering which of these fetches had been his son.

"Hobson," he said quietly, melding his voice in with the prayer. "Hobson Bernard Amos."

"Give us this day our daily bread, and forgive us our trespasses, as we forgive those who trespass against us."

There were nine of them now, moving into the circle one by one. Had there been twelve back in the freezer? With the two dead, was there only one left outside the circle? Still saying his son's name over and over again, Clint couldn't tell which was Hobson.

"And lead us not into temptation, but deliver us from evil."

A tenth fetch appeared. Clint thought maybe there had been thirteen all told, that one more was missing. He wasn't sure how he knew, but he knew.

Hobson had not yet come.

Clint laid his Glock upon the ground, broke the circle, went to sit among the fetches gathered by the body of Swedish Steve, and opened up his arms.

"For Thine is the kingdom, and the power, and the glory, for ever and ever, amen."

"Hobson Bernard Amos," said Clint as his son, twisted and small, wrapped in fur and rage, came into his arms.

Sunfire closed the circle around them, the children holding hands, the adults ranked behind them, and sang a song of sunsets and leaping salmon and birds vanishing over the mountaintops. He heard that familiar raptor screech, then that same enormous osprey Clint had seen in his dream dropped from the clouds, straight toward them. Its claws spread wide as the massive wings spilled air for the bird to come tight inside the circle where Clint sat.

The fetches climbed on to the body of Swedish Steve, like scorpions on their mother's back. In his arms, the fetch that had been Hobson struggled to join its new brothers even as the osprey dug its claws into Swedish Steve's body and beat its wings to gain altitude again.

Clint hung on to the body, not willing to lose his son one last time. Across from him, in the adult circle, Margie's face was twisted, tears streaming from her bruised eyes. Sunfire looked down on him, pitying but hard. Hobson twisted, trying to escape.

He finally looked to Damerow. The deputy shook her head.

Clint let go of his son.

▲▼▲

Clint Amos and Barley John Dimmitt were fishing on the Willamette River, off of Sauvie Island. Neither one of them lived in Sweden any

more. Nobody did, not since the fire last fall had raked the town completely out of season, against all odds burning in the snow. Fire was
a clean end, the problem of missing bodies neatly handled as long as
Moran tied up the forensics.

Margie was with her sister in Idaho, saying she might come back
some day. She had Clint Junior and Suzanne with her. Clint figured he'd
never see any of them again.

He and Barley John were still together because they had nobody
else. They talked less than ever. Clint liked being on the water, in part
because every now and then he'd see or hear an osprey. The center of
the river was also far away from any trees.

Clint cast his line, but the float popped loose, and the weight took
his hook too deep. Pulling it back in, he felt a snag. "Damn."

"Probably," Barley John agreed.

Clint worked the line a little, unwilling to cut it without making
some minimal effort. It came back toward him, still weighted, but dead
weight, not a fish. Curious, he reeled it in.

Crusted in mud and some little shellfish was an old pistol. Real old.
The handle was curved back a bit, and when he rubbed at it with his
thumb, Clint could see an octagonal barrel.

"What do you think?" he asked, showing the thing to Barley John.

"It's damned, too. Just like us."

Clint shrugged and stared across the water. Something screeched,
maybe an osprey, maybe a lesser bird. He hefted the mud-encrusted grip.
He knew who had shot from here, and what they had been shooting at.

"You belong to the river now," he told it, then threw the weapon
back in. "We all do," he added, watching his reflection in the ripples of
the splash. Something big flying overhead cast a shadow on the water
that made Clint close his eyes and think of Hobson.

Dogs in the Moonlight

I've published a fair amount of fiction set in or around Caldwell County, Texas. This story strikes out all the way to Kerr County, Texas, which has a very different geography and sensibility than Caldwell County. Inspired, very loosely, by the Paul Simon lyric, like all my fiction, "Dogs In the Moonlight" incorporates bits and pieces of whatever was going on in my life at the time that I wrote it. I can assure you, however, that this story is not autobiographical in any significant way.

One fine April evening shooting broke out down the hill from me.

I'm pretty firearms-averse, but that sort of thing gets your attention. Ralph Lazard, my only near neighbor, doesn't have much use for me, and I've got mixed feelings about him at best, but neighbors look after each other out here in the Texas Hill Country.

So I waited about ten minutes after the shooting stopped, then push-started my '75 Volvo sedan to rattle slowly down the half-mile or so of steep gravel track and see what was wrong. I came sputtering around the stand of mesquite just outside Ralph's front gate to find the man himself waving a thirty-ought-six at me.

"God damn, Bet!" he yelled, lowering the rifle barrel to point at the dirt.

Better Method, that's me, raised in a school bus by a couple of dropouts with a lot of LSD and not much sense. It hasn't been easy being a boy named 'Bet,' but my sister Crystal definitely got the worst of it.

I killed the headlights but left the engine running, and got out of the car.

"Ralph, you okay?"

We nearly had a full moon, and the stars are always bright out here in Kerr County, so I could see Ralph clearly. He was a big old man with a battered face and a life to match. For all that it was about fifty degrees, he was sweating like he'd been out postholing. The gun trembled in his hands, rattling against the bottle of Shiner Bock he'd got in the crook of two fingers. Ralph wore one of those old man polyester jump suits, and reeked of perspiration and beer.

"You seen anyone on the road?"

"No." It was a silly question—I lived at the upper end of our little road. No one drove between his place and mine but me.

"You didn't see no taillights or nothing heading down for the highway?" He sounded desperate.

"Sorry, Ralph. Um...why don't you put that gun down and tell me what's going on?"

"My dogs." Ralph swung the gun toward the dark woods. "Some crazy son-of-a-bitch cut up my God-damned dogs." He choked back a sob, then loosed another round off into the night.

"The gun, Ralph." I held out my hand. I don't usually handle firearms, but it seemed time to make an exception.

▲▼▲

We stood out by the dog run, me holding the rifle and Ralph holding his Shiner Bock. Three coon hounds were dead at our feet. It was gory, even by moonlight.

"Tore their throats out. God damned kill zone." He rolled the neck of the bottle in his big fingers. "I've seen stuff like this done with a k-bar, in country, but never here Stateside." The beer bottle shattered in his hand. I jumped, startled. Ralph didn't even seem to notice.

Ralph didn't have a lot left to notice. His wife had left him a year or so after I moved into the area—right about this time of year in fact, on their wedding anniversary. People said she was tired of rusty pickups and droughts, broiling summers and scrawny cattle.

I knew she was tired of Ralph, especially, because she told me so personally, with great care and attention, shortly before she ran off with a stock boy from the H.E.B. grocery in town. They stole a fast car and headed west. And Marion especially hated his dogs. Perversely, they always loved her.

As if that wasn't bad enough, a couple of years after that, Ralph's boy Leroy got run down and killed by a Chevy Suburban filled with drunken starters from the high school football squad. Kerrville had a shot at going to state that year, so there wasn't much community interest in serious efforts at prosecution. Ralph's marriage hadn't been worth the effort to his wife, and Leroy's life hadn't been worth the effort to the county attorney.

All Ralph had now was his dogs, and fools like me on whom to lavish his resentment. And someone had just taken his dogs.

I was glad as hell he never found out about me and Marion.

▲▼▲

We provided ourselves with Shiner Bock from an ice chest. As he started to talk, Ralph cleaned his bloody fingers with splashes from the newly opened beer and an oil rag from the back seat of my Volvo, studying the cut dogs in the orange glare of the car's parking lights.

"I was inside when I heard Dimwit whining." Ralph sniffed and paused for a slug of Bock. "Dimwit, he barks, but he don't—didn't— whine much. He was carrying on pretty loud, so I stuck my head out the screen door. Someone was down here in the pen."

"Weren't they barking?"

"No, it was a person."

Lord love a duck. As far as I could ever tell, the damned animals barked at anything that moved and most things that didn't. Same as Marion, they liked me even though I didn't like them very much. My feelings aside, they sure as hell didn't deserve this.

"The *dogs*, Ralph. Weren't they barking at all?"

He shook his head. "Just Dimwit whining. It was like he knew the— the guy. So I cussed real loud, and..."

"And?"

Ralph shifted, looked uncomfortable. I could swear he was shivering. "I never seen nothing like it," he finally said.

The man had spent eighteen months of his youth in the jungles of Southeast Asia killing people, and he was losing control *now*?

"He—it—that thing...it didn't top five foot six. Its eyes were glowing. And Bet, I swear it had *wings*. Like an angel or something. It tore the throats out of the three meanest coon dogs in the county without them giving any kind of a fight."

"Chupacabras?" I whispered. My one regular magazine was *Fortean Times*. I wasn't even sure who the governor was these days, but I was up on a lot of odd phenomena. Including the distinct possibility Ralph was lying—he was acting damned twitchy. On the other hand, who wouldn't be, finding something like this in their front yard?

"What?" Ralph prompted me.

"Goat sucker," I said, as if that explained anything to Ralph.

"Bet," he said in that tone of voice the good old boys reserve for the contemptibly stupid. "These here are *dogs*, not goats."

▲▼▲

Out here among the dry creeks and crumbling stock tanks, the world is brown with flashes of dark green, and it always smelled like dust and cow shit. We're surrounded by rolling limestone hills, cedar and mesquite, whitetail deer, javelina, turkey vultures, red-tailed hawks, cows and country people. There isn't much for a would-be hippie with a tiny trust fund to do except drink a little beer, smoke a little grass, and read up on the wide, weird world.

So I rooted through my pile of *Fortean Times* until I hit pay dirt. Chupacabras—the story started in Puerto Rico, a culture virus that spread all over Latin America within a couple of years. Sort of a junior version of a cattle mutilator—tearing throats, sucking blood and spreading panic among the *campesinos*.

I believe in a lot of things against all evidence or pressure of public opinion—the brotherhood of man, the power of faith to move mountains, the incompetent evil of Ronald Reagan—but I couldn't bring myself to believe in chupacabras. Not in broad daylight in the Texas Hill Country.

Ralph had refused to go get the sheriff—a combination of stubborn pride and redneck resentment of authority. He wanted to handle this himself. Himself and me and a fearsome bloody dog killer, one happy family on our little hill.

I went out on my porch to watch the view and think about dog killing for a while. After a bit, I noticed a new stain on the decaying white paint of my Volvo, one that seemed to be attracting flies. On closer inspection, I realized there were several bloody handprints around the trunk lid. Ralph must have gotten the stuff on the car the night before.

Sighing, I tore a strip of paisley cloth from my porch couch and went to clean the blood off.

▲▼▲

Around two in the morning I woke up to barking. It sure sounded like Ralph's dogs were loose again. That struck me as wrong, then I remembered why.

They were dead.

No one else lived closer than two miles to me. It had to be another damned pack—they sometimes roamed the hills, killing my chickens and tearing up God knew what else. I hoped like hell these weren't feral.

Between this new pack and the dog killer, I really didn't want to go outside, but they sounded like they were on the property, close to the house. I had to check. I went into the kitchen and considered my cooking knives for a minute before realizing I could barely cut tomatoes, let alone knife-fight a dog pack. I settled on my police flashlight, one of those six-battery jobs that could crack a skull. So armed, I stepped outside.

The moon was bright, on its way to the back of the world behind the western sky. The dogs still barked somewhere just down the hill from me, much closer than they should have been unless they were a loose pack—definitely in my yard, although I still couldn't see where they were.

You can tell a lot from a dog's bark. These dogs didn't sound angry, really, and I couldn't hear a fight in progress, so I stepped off the porch and gave a sharp whistle, the kind you use to herd sheep or goats. The barking stopped immediately. I walked around the yard, checking things. Nothing inside the rusted Studebaker, nothing under my Volvo. Nothing in the old metal stock tank lying on its side. As I worked my way toward the gate, I heard whining.

"Come here, boy." I felt foolish, talking to the dark. I didn't know what was out there. Certainly nothing I really wanted to meet. "Come on, where are you?" I whistled a couple more times and slapped my thighs.

I heard panting, and some excited yips, like a dog doing that little dance when they get worked up. I walked over to the gate. "Here, doggie, doggie."

They started barking again like crazy, sounding like they were right next to me, and I still couldn't see them. They sure did sound like Ralph's dogs, though. One hand on the gatepost, I swept the flashlight across some Johnson grass and post oak. When something cold nudged my ear, I screamed.

"What the hell you diddy-bopping around here in the hot zone for, Bet?" Ralph had the barrel of his rifle stuck in my right ear. I couldn't see him at all. "Noisy bastard like you wouldn't last ten minutes in country."

"Me? What the hell are *you* doing?!" I was mad enough to grab the rifle barrel, pull it away from my head. "Jesus Christ, don't point that God-damned thing at me again or I'll stick it so far up your ass they'll need a tongue depressor to find it!"

"I heard Dimwit up here," said Ralph real quietly. "Howling and barking with Dummy and Fleabag."

"Ralph." I sighed. "We buried all three of them last night, remember?"

"I heard 'em, Bet." The tears stood out in his voice. I still couldn't see Ralph—he was crouched in the big wisteria by my gate, but his voice shook. "I know their barking. I heard my dogs."

"Ralph," I said in my gentlest voice. "I don't know what we heard, I don't know why. But your dogs are dead and buried. Come up to the house. I'll make some ham scramble and crack a couple of beers."

He stepped out of the shadows of the wisteria into the moonlight. I backed away—Ralph had returned to the jungles of Southeast Asia. He wore torn fatigues, his face blackened with some mucky, dark crap. He was carrying a lot of gear.

"Whoa, Ralph, this is Kerr County, not Da Nang." I really, really hoped he didn't know about me and Marion.

Ralph didn't answer at first, just stalked me as I trudged back up the yard.

"Bet..." he finally mumbled from behind me. "If my dogs were going to come back, why'd they come to you instead of me?"

I bit off the first answer that leapt to mind—*because they always liked Marion better than you, Ralph, and she liked me better than you.* I thought of a lot of answers, thought of wives gone and sons dead and lives wasted pounding dirt in the hot, brown Texas hills. A lack of honesty seemed kindest right then.

"Because no one would have believed you, Ralph. Not even me." Especially not me.

▲▼▲

We were both somewhere on the far side of drunk, sitting on my front porch surrounded by rows of empties with plates of scramble half-eaten at our feet. I had hidden the rifle inside the house as soon as Ralph was too potted to notice. I figured with the rifle gone, we could work on getting so whacked Ralph wouldn't be tempted to go hunting dog killers in the caliche. My plan seemed a lot safer than finding that gun barrel in my ear again in a few hours.

"Why would a dog come back from the dead?" Ralph addressed his question to the darkened western horizon.

"Hell, Ralph, why would *anyone* come back from the dead?"

"Lots of reasons..." He hurled a Bock bottle into the yard. It shattered on a fender of the Studebaker. He still hadn't wiped off the face paint.

"Man, I walk around out there. With my feet, I mean."

"Everyone walks around out there, Bet."

"In *my* yard?"

"In the world, boonierat. You sit still long enough, everyone walks by."

The world according to Ralph. It was profound, coming from a drunken, washed-up dirt rancher. "You're deep, man."

"Not deep enough." Unexpectedly, he started to cry. "The dogs, Bet...my dogs..."

"I know."

"No. You have no God damned idea." He jumped up out of my second-best chair, knocked it over and broke the scramble-encrusted plate. My grandmother's china, such as it was.

"Damn it, Ralph, I've only got three of those left."

"Come on," he said. "I want to show you something." He staggered over to my Volvo, pawed at the driver's door a couple of times before jerking it open. "You'd better give me a push," he called.

I was too drunk to say no.

▲▼▲

We crashed through my gate. One of the headlights smashed in the process, dimming our already questionable view of the road.

"Ralph!"

He grinned. "We're hitting the LZ hot and hard, man."

We slammed down the moonlit road considerably faster than I drove it in broad daylight. The beer bottles, loose tools and fencing wire in the back seat clattered and bounced with the lurching of my car. Stark terror sobered me up quickly, but Ralph was at the wheel and there wasn't much I could do. Yelling only seemed to endanger his concentration. At least the rifle was hidden in the busted chest freezer in my bedroom.

"You ever think ill of the dead?" Ralph screamed over the spewing gravel and bone-rattling lurches of our progress through the dark. Twigs and brush slapped against the sides of the car as we slewed back and forth.

I prayed for dawn, for sobriety, for patience. Ralph was an entire twelve-step program on the hoof. "I'm gonna think ill of you if you don't slow down," I screamed back.

"No, no, you don't get it." Letting go of the twisting steering wheel, his right hand chopped up and down. "You ever curse the dead, Bet? You ever hate someone so much it just got worse when they passed on?"

I tried to give the question a serious answer. "I never hated anyone that much. Richard Nixon, maybe. I don't know."

Ralph shook his head, stared at me in the glow of the dash lights instead of watching the road. His pale eyes gleamed out of his dark face paint. We clipped a cedar with a crumpling screech of metal. The other headlight went out. It was pretty damned dark out there on the hill. The inside of the car reeked of juniper.

"The road, Ralph!"

"Yeah, yeah, roger that." He settled down over the wheel again, squinting forward into the dark as if narrowed eyes could compensate for a lack of headlights. He was driving by the amber glow of the one surviving parking light. "Bet, you poor bastard, you ain't had much of a life. You never cursed the dead, that means you never really loved the living."

Oh Christ, I thought, *he's popped his twist cap for real now.* As Ralph power-slid my Volvo through his own front gate, I leapt up in my seat. I could swear a dog had just licked my ear.

▲▼▲

We shot by Ralph's doublewide like we were cruising down the highway, busted through another gate and across his pasturage. Damned near hit a Brangus heifer too, which would have been the end of the road for my long-suffering Volvo.

I'd given up talking to Ralph, mostly because I was afraid of whatever crap he might say next. There was *no way* I was looking into the back seat. Not with that warm dog breath panting in my ear. I held on as we tore through a barbed wire fence line. I heard one of the tires go. The car immediately started to pull hard to the right.

Ralph fought the wheel. "Almost there!" he sang out.

We drove up a steep hill, along a track that clearly hadn't been used in years. Saplings taller than me snapped beneath the front bumper to scrape along the bottom of the car. I could hear topsoil spray from the rear wheels. I'd need new transportation considerably sooner than I had budgeted for. Ralph gunned the Volvo up a little switchback and ran it straight at a bank of brush laying against a limestone cliff face.

"Oh God!" I screamed as I let go of the dash to cover my head.

We crashed through the brush and slammed to halt, a much gentler impact than the solid limestone catastrophe I had expected. The engine died with a muttering cough, followed by the pinging of heat dissipation and the hiss of escaping fluids. I looked up to realize we had pushed through the brush into a cave. The stench of overheated engine and scorched brakes twisted through my nostrils. The remaining parking light showed that my Volvo had rear-ended a Corvette convertible.

"Oh, Ralph."

"*Khong xau.*" His grin seemed tight enough to force his teeth out of his gums and his eyes glittered like an amphetamine overdose.

"Huh?"

"Viet—Never mind. End of the line, Bet. Everything you need to see is right here."

▲▼▲

"After all I've done for her, she killed my dogs, Bet. It wasn't no chalupa cabana."

"Chupacabras," I corrected automatically. Marion? What *everything* had he done for her? Ralph was so far gone it had to be him that killed the dogs.

"Yeah," he muttered. "I knew it was her."

The Corvette had been there a long time. The tires were dead flat, there was a thick layer of grime on the car, and the body in the passenger seat was a leathery sack of bones. It grinned at me above a knitted H.E.B. Grocery golf shirt, the kind stock boys wore. There wasn't a matching body in the driver's seat.

Where the hell was Marion? Had she escaped?

I realized I wasn't likely getting out of here. *Stall*, I thought, *stall Ralph, and think hard.* "Was she, uh, here?"

"Oh, yes." Ralph's chuckle echoed in the little cave. "Until she escaped, and killed my dogs. Gets restless every year around our anniversary."

Their anniversary—the day they married and the day she left him. My knees buckled. He couldn't be serious—no way he'd had Marion living up here these past five years, not in a cave. Marion. My heart ached, for a moment, for both of them. She always hated his dogs—was that all he had left of her in his heart?

"She knew I loved them," he added.

"Ah." I figured if I ran like hell back down the track we came up, and he didn't catch me and break my neck on the way, I could make the highway and flag down a ride into town. Ralph didn't have a phone and neither did I, so that was the only way to get help.

"I lost her boy, and no one got called to account for it."

"What?" Leroy died two years after Marion left. Was he crazy, or was she still around?

"Marion was real angry when Leroy died. She knew it wasn't my fault. But when they wouldn't do nothing to those other boys that killed him, she wanted me to take care of it." He shook his head. "I couldn't do it. No more dead boys, not even for her."

God, I thought. Ralph must have walked up to this cave and talked to his wife all the time. No wonder he was crazy.

"She said I'd killed once, it was easy enough to kill again."

"Once?"

Ralph nodded at the dead stock boy. His nametag read, "Jason, Serving the Public for 1 Year." He didn't smell at all. Ralph laughed. "Her boyfriend. I killed him."

Thank God he didn't know about me and Marion.

Ralph studied the expression on my face, then sucked in a breath. "Oh God, Bet, you think I killed my wife, don't you?" He sounded more hurt than anything else.

Honesty, I told myself. It was honesty that killed the cat, not curiosity, but I had to keep him talking. Was she here or not? Where the hell was she? "Yes, the thought had crossed my mind."

"Bet, you know me. I'm not that kind of guy."

Yeah, right. That's obvious.

He reached down into the foot well of the driver's side of the Corvette and pulled out a long dog chain. "She was fine up here until she broke free last week."

He was for real. She'd been up here all this time. His wife, my one-time lover, chained next to her dead boyfriend. I retched, my throat filling with stinging bile as my thoughts spiraled into horrified panic.

I couldn't make it to the cave mouth before my stomach gave out. Ham scramble and Shiner Bock didn't taste any better coming back through the second time. Outside the cave, invisible dogs barked as I heaved, over and over, crying though my eyes were screwed tight.

▲▼▲

"Ask not for whom the dogs howl," I gasped through my stinging, stinking puke breath.

"What?" Ralph was becoming more and more dissociated. I could almost see his head floating free of its tethering neck.

We sat on the hood of the Corvette, deeper inside the cave. In the growing golden light of morning that flooded through the broken barrier of brush, I could see stacks of unopened army surplus C ration cases, barrels of water, manacles bolted to the limestone wall of the cave, and the little nickel-plated pistol Ralph had slipped out of his boot before I finished throwing up.

Outside, Ralph's dead dogs howled. I didn't think about Marion, not for a moment. Not me.

"Your dogs, Ralph, they're talking to you."

Ralph waved the pistol in a vague gesture. "They're dead. You helped me bury them, remember?"

"They didn't stay dead."

"Not like my boy," he sniffed. "I miss Leroy."

"Yeah, well, somebody misses Jason there, too."

Ralph gave me a hard look before staring back at the cave wall. Me and my big mouth. How the hell was I getting out of this? I wasn't about to wrestle Ralph for the gun. The dead dog chorus was like a color commentator on sports-talk radio—interesting but meaningless. I figured Jason wasn't going to do anything for me at this late date.

If Marion had escaped and killed the dogs, she was probably hiding somewhere nearby. Then I remembered the blood on the trunk of my car. The lock never had worked.

She was in my trunk.

Marion had to have climbed into the trunk while I was helping Ralph bury the dogs.

Something killed those poor coon hounds, and it sure as hell wasn't me or the stock boy. And Ralph loved those damned dogs too much, for one thing.

Get him to confront her, I thought. That ought to cause enough trouble for me to escape. I felt sick about Marion being chained up here all these years, but whatever was between them now was far beyond me. "Ralph." My voice was quiet, calm. "I need a drink."

"Plenty of water up here," he said dreamily.

I nodded at the Volvo. "Couple of six packs in the trunk." *Like hell.*

The thought of beer brought Ralph back into focus for a moment. He looked at me with narrowed eyes. "I don't reckon they would of made the trip up here, what with all that bouncing around."

Inspiration soared, or flapped in this case. "They're wrapped in some laundry. They might have survived."

Ralph wandered back through the cave, down the length of the Corvette, past the Volvo, to the brush-strewn entrance. He staggered a bit, looking confused. I wondered if he was having a stroke. Outside, the dogs kept howling.

He stopped behind the Volvo as I stood up to stare across the two cars at him. I ignored Jason's permanent grin to focus on Ralph's increasingly glassy stare.

"Maybe she is and maybe she isn't," he said.

Marion? "Is or isn't what?"

"You learn weird shit in country."

"Weird how?" He was gone, way far gone. *Keep him talking*, that had to be good. *Be cool about the trunk*, I reminded myself, *don't spook the man.*

"There was a Cuban guy in my platoon, used to slice open chickens and spit rum all over the place. Didn't save him from being killed by a beer truck in Saigon, but it did keep the VC bullets away."

The dogs quieted down as Ralph spoke. Perhaps they were soothed by his voice.

"He showed me the line that separates the living from the dead, Bet. He showed how that line could be moved. Thing is, I did kill Marion." I noticed the Volvo rocking on its shocks. He tapped the trunk lid, tears tracing pale gray lines through his black face paint. "Thing is, then I brought her back. Bet, I loved my wife so much I brought her back from the dead. But she still didn't love me, even after all I done for her."

Dead? Brought back? Had he chained a corpse to the Corvette? I heard the squeak of the Volvo's distressed suspension. Whoever—whatever—killed the dogs was in there. My skin felt cold and numb and my gut threatened to heave again. Dead or alive, suddenly I wanted nothing to do with whatever Marion had become. I didn't want Ralph to open the trunk, not even to save my own life.

Tears, modern tears, tracking over the camouflage face paint of a war lost thirty years ago, focused me back on Ralph. Things had gone so very badly wrong in his life. He needed help, a lot of it.

"Ralph," I said, repenting of my plan. I had to get him, and me, away from the cave and Marion. "I don't need that beer. You don't need to open that trunk. You and me, we could just walk down to town together and check in to the hospital. Leave the cars here, no one would ever know."

The sheriff, I thought, *let him come find Marion.*

"I'd know." Ralph cocked his pistol. "She'd know." He reached for the trunk release. "The dogs would know." Gun ready, he opened the trunk. "Happy anniversary, baby."

The howling rose to merge with a human scream. Something man-sized and leathery sprang out of the trunk, knocking Ralph backward and sideways against the mouth of the cave.

"I love you," he yelled as Marion, naked and desiccated, grabbed him by the throat and face and cracked his head against the limestone. Ralph looked like he was being attacked by a giant, four-legged spider.

I scuttled down the left side of the cars, toward where Ralph was meeting his noisy, messy death at the hands of his late wife. My stomach heaved to the sounds of Ralph's bones breaking against the limestone wall—like hearing sacks of meat dropped on pavement. Marion's chain was caught around my right foot. I kept my eyes on the floor, seeing only Ralph's jungle boots and Marion's curled, dried feet.

And his nickel-plated pistol.

I grabbed that pistol like I was grabbing a snake. I hated the damned things, but Marion had passed beyond killing rage and somewhere into the realm of an elemental force. I stood, my right foot tugged backward by the dog chain and raised the pistol braced in two hands just like in the movies.

Marion dropped Ralph's bubbling body and turned to face me. Everything about her was twisted, curved, pulled tight, her tendons drawn backward in death. Her lips were bacon rind, pulled far back from shattered eggshell teeth, her eyes withered black olives. She looked like a rabid bat weeks dead on the highway.

"Marion." There was nothing to say.

She nudged Ralph with one clawed foot, staring at me. Her body trembled like an overtightened come-along—that killing force was held back, at least for a moment. I noticed that she really didn't breathe. "Finish it," she said. Her voice creaked like my porch in the wind. "Please."

I pulled the trigger, putting a bullet into the chest of my one-time lover, murdering her for the second time in her life as her husband's dead dogs howled.

▲▼▲

It took a few weeks for the county attorney's office to decide not to charge me. Shooting a corpse wasn't precisely a criminal act, and the sheriff finally chalked Ralph's death up to self-defense on my part. Lucky for me there was no other remotely logical explanation.

I tell myself it all meant something, but I'll be damned if I know what. Nobody got what they wanted, except maybe the dogs. Sometimes those dead dogs come to my window at night, but I just whistle and call them by name, and they whine happily and go away until the next time the moon is bright. Haven't had any problems with roving packs lately, either.

I like to think those dogs are out hunting dead raccoons somewhere in the woods with Ralph and Leroy.

Little Pig, Berry Brown and the Hard Moon

I was invited to contribute to a Denise Little/Marty Greenberg anthology called The Magic Toybox. *The general concept was along the lines of* The Nutcracker, *to write about toys which come to life in some form or fashion. Being me, I decided this called for a story about a Neanderthal band of hunter-gatherers. Oddly, they published it anyway.*

Little Pig sat in the thin-leaf tree and watched Mother Sun dance upon the water. She-of-the-Sky made silver sparkle in the creek below the bear fur that wrapped the girl in warmth. Little Pig smiled, but folded her laughter within—noise out of place could bring a hungry cat.

Stick, Little Pig's only toy and best and greatest friend, opened her tiny carved mouth. *"Child, child, sitting in a tree, what sort of furry fruit do you be?"*

Little Pig swallowed another laugh, though her body shook and swayed against the thin-leaf's bark. "Silly Stick," she whispered, then put her friend within her own mouth for silence and safekeeping.

▲▼▲

Later Brother Spear returned from his hunt with her mother and the rest of the clan to fetch Little Pig down from the safety of the thin-leaf tree. He was covered in mud and sweat and blood that stank of the Tusk Beast, breath steaming in the evening as the stars cut away his heat in tiny ribbons to feed their secret jealousies. His glittering eyes were narrow-closed, but the axe of his anger did not seem held high for Little Pig. She hugged to his chest as he carried her home, and kept quiet as a nesting mouse, still sucking on Stick and wishing she could ask her friend about the fire in Brother Spear's face.

Soon enough she found the reason, when they returned to the Hard Moon Camp.

Her clan had different camps for different moons. Each was in a place that drew good fortune from the cold skies and sheltered the People from whatever harmed them most in that season of Sister Moon's journey through the year.

The People's Hard Moon Camp was in a shallow bowl atop a bluff near the Biggest River. The bowl was for luck in saving enough food for the Ice Moon and Dying Moon camps soon to come. The bluff kept the People above the animals in the scrub forest surrounding the Biggest River. As they crossed the ridge, she smelled blood, and saw that this night there was fire, big as any prayer-fire, meat on drying frames spread before the flames. Close to the fire, Oldest Woman and Broken-Eye knelt next to someone wrapped in too many furs.

Like the last grub in the sack, Little Pig thought, lonely and unlucky. None of the People should be so sad.

"Stick," she whispered, risking noise as Brother Spear made his quiet way down to the warm light. "Who is it?"

"Child, child, clutching tight, count the People here tonight."

Brother Spear touched her back with his hand, signaling quiet, but she had Stick's advice now and made good. Little Pig wasn't very clever with numbers, but she knew names, and so she sang the list of the People in the voice only she could hear, behind her ears, looking for each one as she named them.

Oldest Woman, hands so bent
Sleeping Sister, dreaming much
Broken-Eye, sees only night
Walks On Rock, feet too big
Berry Brown, mother of my heart

There she stopped, for she did not see her mother anywhere. Little Pig was hungry then, for Berry Brown had always fed her. Little Pig was frightened then, for Berry Brown had always comforted her. Little Pig was worried then, for Berry Brown had always protected her. Berry Brown belonged to Little Pig the way Mother Sun belonged to Daughter Sky.

Brother Spear stopped at the feet of Berry Brown, who was wrapped in the three magic furs and head close to the fire. "I have brought the child," he said. Little Pig felt the rumble of his voice where her head lay against his chest. She held Stick close.

Berry Brown had made Stick for her, carving her friend with a black-stone blade and the patience of rain, lending her breath into Stick's mouth, kissing Stick's hurts. Little Pig's eyes salted like summer-killed meat, as she clutched her toy tight enough to make Stick squeak and shiver.

Oldest Woman took the bear fur robe from Brother Spear and greeted Little Pig with a tiny dry kiss upon her forehead. Then she made Little Pig stand with her close to the fire, next to Berry Brown's face, a soft little hand wrapped inside a trembling old one.

"Who lies before us?" Oldest Woman asked. Her voice was not unkind, but Little Pig knew Oldest Woman could crack rocks with her will, and not even Boar Killer with his temper and his huge muscles would argue with her.

"Child, child, before the fire, answer all Oldest Woman desires," whispered Stick, squirming in her hand.

"Berry Brown." Little Pig stared at the unmoving eyes, lost in the sweating face like leaves in the creek. Her chest shuddered. "My mother."

"What has happened to her?" Oldest Woman asked.

"I do not—" Little Pig began, then stopped.

"Child, child, Berry went hunting, did not hear the Tusk Beast grunting."

Oldest Woman made a soft noise, inviting Little Pig's next words to come out of her mouth.

Little Pig closed Stick to her chest, just as Berry Brown used to hold Little Pig. "She was hurt by the Tusk Beast, wasn't she?"

A squeeze of the hand. Then: "What will become of her?"

Little Pig waited for Stick to speak, but the toy was silent. Oldest Woman squeezed her hand again. *What was she supposed to say?*

"She is my mother." Little Pig's voice was as slow as her thoughts. "She will not leave me behind."

Oldest Woman bent and whispered in Little Pig's ear. As she spoke, Little Pig could feel Stick straining to listen. "Berry Brown has gone beyond the reach of my hands' skill or the depths of Broken-Eye's wisdom. We cannot make her whole. Still, she might come home for you, child. But you must ask the Hard Moon and the sharp stars if this can be, and what words will bring her back."

"I will speak to the moon," said Little Pig.

Oldest Woman released her hand, brushed her hard, crooked fingers across Little Pig's shoulder. "Go find your way, then."

▲▼▲

Little Pig climbed up toward the rim of the Hard Moon Camp's small round valley. She took one of her paths, not the People's trails, so she could visit her special places. The Hard Moon was not so old that she had lost the light. She touched her crystal rocks, the oldest bone, and the brown anthill. Stick always liked the special places, sometimes talked about the magic that dwelt in each, though right now Stick seemed to be silent. Thinking, perhaps. Mice scuttled away from Little Pig as she walked, while an owl sailed overhead, wide-winged and vigilant. Had the night-hunter come to take the last of Berry Brown's spirit away?

She almost ran into Brother Spear. He sat cross-legged, still covered in blood and muck, making tiny sparks as he chipped at the edge of his spear point.

"I am sorry," he told Little Pig without meeting her eye.

She thought about that a moment. "You did not hurt Berry Brown."

More chips of the rock. "I led. Success is mine, failure mine."

"There is meat by the fire, for the Ice Moon and the Dying Moon." Little Pig knew this without turning to look, as the dank blood smell lay upon the entire valley.

Brother Spear finally lifted his chin to her. "There is no magic. Only spear and blood and bone. Tusk Beast took Berry Brown in trade for itself. Blood for blood."

"Child, child, Brother Spear is wrong, Berry has not yet sung her last song."

Little Pig squeezed Stick, a gentle hug of thanks and reassurance. "My mother is alive," she told Brother Spear, touching his knee with her free hand.

A smile ghosted across his face like a crane in the mist. "Go on. Follow Oldest Woman's magic. Ask the moon. I only know the spear. It feeds us but it takes away as well."

"Like the Tusk Beast. Spears are our sharp teeth. You are the strong hand."

He bent once more to his work. Little Pig gave Brother Spear back his silence and moved on to talk to the moon.

▲▼▲

She picked a tree that some great storm had driven down, and climbed the mossy, rotting trunk to sit among the insects and the tiny plants at the top. The perch gave her a view of the Hard Moon Camp and her mother's body—a tiny dark smear before the fire circle when seen from here. If she faced away from the flames, the sky ghosted above her.

The knives of the stars glittered sharp. The Hard Moon was beginning to rot and grow lean, and hungered already for the bed at Daughter Sky's western verge. To the north was the faint, dull glow of the Ice Wall.

"What shall I do, Stick?" Little Pig held her toy up in the moonlight. The tiny eyes squinted. The mouth pursed as in thought. Stick's long wooden body twitched in Little Pig's hand. Then she smiled, ivory bright as any bone from the sand pits of the Biggest River.

Little Pig had never seen Stick's teeth before.

"Child, child, ask the moon, she rules over every doom."

She kissed Stick. Stick kissed back—another first!—though it was a sting, like the bite of a tree ant, rather than the gentle press of Berry Brown's lips. Then Little Pig set her legs apart, as Broken-Eye did when he was called to wrestle spirits from the weed smoke. She spread her arms wide, as Oldest Woman did when asking questions of the southern wind. She titled her head back, as Brother Spear did when calling to the wolves and bears and cats. Stick clung to her outstretched hand, and the Hard Moon swam at the top of her upward gaze.

"Sister Moon," Little Pig said quietly. She did not feel a need to shout. No voice was great enough to reach the moon if the moon was not ready to listen, and any voice should reach if the moon had turned her face to hear. "I have been told three times to speak to you. A thing thrice-told is a thing true through and through. Tell me if Berry Brown may live. Tell me what I can do to make her whole. Tell me what magic there is under your cold light."

She listened a while, to the whisper of the wind in the thin-leaf trees, and the call of a distant nighthawk hunting insects, and the puzzled, nervous snorts of the deer moving through the scrub brush.

Sister Moon made no answer, but Stick twisted in Little Pig's hand.

She listened more, to the rustle of the mice scavenging under cover of darkness, and the mutter of the Biggest River remaking its bed every moment, and the faint ringing of the night's cold pouring off the Ice Wall to the north.

Still Sister Moon made no answer. Still Stick twisted, twitched, demanding attention.

She listened a third time, to the faraway scream of some animal caught up by great rushing feathers, to the cough of a hunting cat, to the scrape of claws on rock.

A third time Sister Moon made no answer. She was silent as she had ever been, edging through the sky toward her meeting with the western horizon.

"What is it, Stick?" Little Pig asked, feeling no hope.

"Child, child, you have grown, lay me down and walk alone."

"No!" she shouted, then swiftly sat to wait in silence. She had made far too much noise for being this distant from the fire and the rest of the People. A cat could come, or a wolf, or even one of the mountain teratornis. Stick twitched but held her peace.

After a time, as the trees creaked and the breeze brought a musky scent of furry hunger, Little Pig whispered urgently to Stick. "You are my friend. Berry Brown made you for me. I cannot leave you behind."

"Child, child, think what she did, when Berry carved me from a twig."

"You're *Stick*," hissed Little Pig. "You watch over me when I am alone. You're always close when the People are far. You protect me."

"Child, child, your mother is in me, and I am part of what she could be."

Little Pig studied Stick's eyes. They were wide open now, a deep, shining black just as Berry Brown's had been. *Were,* she thought as her stomach lurched. Just as Berry Brown's were. The tiny teeth gleamed ivory-bright, and Stick's narrow cheeks had rounded.

"So you are her, and she is you?"

Stick twitched. A nod.

"I could keep you. Hold you close. Never let you leave. You'd always be with me!"

Then Little Pig's eyes were drawn back to the fire down within the bowl of the Hard Moon Camp. Berry Brown lay still upon the ground. Oldest Woman stood beside her, shadow bent and shaking, waiting for Little Pig to return.

She could keep Stick close, always have her mother. But at the same time, Berry Brown would lie by the fire, unmoving and cooling. Like a stunned doe with the slaughter-knife trapped in her throat, leaping up unexpected into the forest to bleed out her pain until the People ran her down again and completed her life.

Or Little Pig could lay down Stick—her toy, her friend, her companion, the always-touch of Berry Brown—and let the Tusk Beast's work be finished.

"I understand what Oldest Woman meant for me to learn from the moon," she said.

Stick lay quiet, as if knowing what was to come. Crying, Little Pig found her way back down the hill toward the firelight, scarcely noticing the bright eyes which watched from above. They were of the same night that had taken Berry Brown away from her, and so she gave them none of her concern.

▲▼▲

Walking toward Oldest Woman, and the rest of the People who watched in shadowed silence, Little Pig could feel years settling upon her shoulders. Though she was still seasons from her own bleedings, she could not be a child when Berry Brown's place among the People was empty.

Her eyes were dry when she passed out of darkness.

Oldest Woman's voice rang with the authority of rock splitting water. "Have you asked the Hard Moon what might be done?"

Little Pig stroked Stick. "Yes, I have." She looked around the fire, where the eyes of the People gleamed little different from the eyes of the beasts around the outer ring of the Hard Moon Camp.

"And what answer did Sister Moon give you?"

"Silence," said Little Pig. She raised Stick above her head, turning slowly so that everyone might see what had become of her toy. If they could see it. "Silence, which told me everything. Silence, which told me that no matter what we do the sky circles onward and the seasons of the moon pass just the same. I can no more ask Sister Moon to turn back Berry Brown's time than I can ask her to turn back the Ice time or the Dying time."

Oldest Woman stared a while at Little Pig, then smiled. It was a thin smile, quick as a lightning stroke, but Little Pig saw it come and go, and like looking at lightning, was blinded for a moment. "And now that Berry Brown is gone where the skill of my hands cannot follow, where Broken-Eye's wisdom cannot lead, what will you do for your mother?"

Little Pig squatted on her heels next to Berry Brown and touched her mother's pale face. The skin was chill, the eyes never moved even as her hand passed before them. She tugged the furs aside—bear, wolf and cat— and lay Stick down in the bruised skin between Berry Brown's breasts. Stick smiled at her, showing not only the new teeth but a tongue and mouth within, far pinker than the black blood which had dried upon her mother.

"I give Berry Brown back the toy which she had made for me," Little Pig said slowly. "I will not be a child anymore, now that she is gone. My mother needs her spirit returned so that she can travel into the lands beyond the horizon where Sister Moon goes every night."

"Woman, woman, letting go, your mother's love is bright as snow."

With those words, Stick became stick—a bit of wood slashed in a few places to make something like a face, worn from endless handling, tips softened where an infant had suckled on the wood in her hunger, split where a toddler had grown her teeth, worn where a child carried it everywhere. Little Pig looked at the bare and damaged wood and wondered what gifts of her mother's remained to her.

▲▼▲

Oldest Woman gave Little Pig her new name, to help her take her mother's place among their little clan. Trembling hands blessed her before the fire, Oldest Woman speaking of the mothers who had birthed the People just as the mountain streams birthed the Biggest River. Little Pig was set upon her own journey toward motherhood, following Berry Brown's path.

Now Youngest Woman, she held Brother Spear close as he wept his sorrow. The tears helped her mother's spirit move onward. In his turn, Brother Spear dug a grave, that Berry Brown might sleep deep enough to stay out of the claws of cat or wolf during the Ice Moon and the Dying Moon to come.

"I will work alone to set the rocks," she said. Three days later, Youngest Woman laid the last of the stones upon the cairn. Berry Brown and the old, chewed stick now rested beneath. Youngest Woman spread leaves and soil between the rocks, and found the secret seeds of flowers for the days of the Bright Moon to come, even though the People would not be camped here then.

She stood silent beneath the pale sun, the ice wind plucking sweat from her head and hands. In that quiet moment, her mother came to her, carrying Stick. "I did not think it would be so beautiful," said Berry Brown in a voice made of the wind sighing in the grass, the buzz of insect wings, the creak of trees on the distant hills.

Stick nodded.

Youngest Woman returned the nod. "The toy you made for me carried me through my years of need, Mother. May it carry you through yours."

Berry Brown smiled, her mouth a glimmer of beetles' wings and shiny pebbles and light on water. "As you will carry me onward through the journey of your heart."

"Always," said Youngest Woman, but she was speaking only to herself and the uncaring sky.

There was time before she had to lay the evening fire for Oldest Woman, and the rest of the People were out gathering garlic and onions. This was what she knew that day: just as the streams become rivers, daughters become their mothers, and in turn make more daughters to spread like rain upon the land. She owed her daughters-to-come the memory of Berry Brown, the wisdom of her mother, and whatever more she might glean from her own life.

And so Youngest Woman went looking for a stick. With Stick had come stories, comfort, safety. Love. She might as well start practicing to carve now. Then she would be skilled enough when her time came to make a toy to carry her own daughters through the years.

On the Human Plan

Back in 2004, I had a story in issue one of Lone Star Stories. *Editor Eric Marin had contacted me asking if I'd like to be part of his new project, and I thought it sounded like a fine idea. Five years and six stories of mine later, he asked if I could be part of his fifth anniversary issue. I had absolutely nothing in inventory, and quite a bit of work on my plate, but I try to be loyal to markets which have been loyal to me, so again, I thought it sounded like a fine idea. I had absolutely nothing in mind when I began this story, was merely following my nose from the very first line, but I'm rather pleased with the result.*

I am called Dog the Digger. I am not mighty, neither am I fearsome. Should you require bravos, there are muscle-boys aplenty among the rat-bars of any lowtown on this raddled world. If it is a wizard you want, follow the powder-trails of crushed silicon and wolf's blood to their dark and winking lairs. Scholars can be found in their libraries, taikonauts in their launch bunkers and ship foundries, priests amid the tallow-gleaming depths of their bone-ribbed cathedrals.

What I do is dig. For bodies, for treasure, for the rust-pocked hulks of history, for the sheer pleasure of moving what cannot be moved and finding what rots beneath. You may hire me for an afternoon or a month or the entire turning of the year. It makes me no mind whatsoever.

As for you, I know what you want. You want a *story*.

Oh, you say you want the truth, but no one ever really wants the truth. And stories are the greatest of the things for which I dig. Mightier even than the steel-bound femurs of the deinotheria bred by the Viridian Republic, which I can show you in vast necropolii beneath the Stone-Doored Hills. More treasured than the golden wires to be pulled by the fistful from the thinking heads which line the Cumaean Caves, screaming as the lights of their eyes flash and die.

Anyone with a bit of talent and the right set of bones to throw can foretell the future. It's written in fat-bellied red across every morning sky. But to aftertell the past, that is another trick entirely.

▲▼▲

They say death is the door that never opens twice. At least, not until it does. Sorrow is usually the first child of such a birthing, though just as often the last to be recognized.

People die. Cities die. Nations die. In time the sun itself will die, though already it grows red and obese, a louche, glowering presence fat on the midsummer horizon. When the daystar opens up its arms, all graves will be swallowed in fire, but for now, the bones of men lie atop older bones beneath the friable earth.

Likewise the skins of cities. All our places are built on other places. A man might dig down until the very heat of the earth wells up from the bottom of his shaft, and still there will be floors and streets and wooden frames pressed to stone fossils to greet him there.

You know that the first woman to greet the morning had gone to sleep the night before as an ape. Some angel stirred her dreams with God's long spoon, and the next day she remembered the past. The past was young then, not even thirty hours old, but it had *begun.*

That woman bred with an ape who didn't yet know he was man, then birthed a hairy little baby who learned she was another woman, and so the world unfolded into history. That woman died, too, laid herself down into the earth and let herself be covered with mud which turned to rock.

If I dig down far enough, someday I'll find that grandmother of us all. But this story you've come for is about another time, when I only dug down to death's doorstep.

It was an exogen come to me, in the twenty-seventh hour of the day. My visitor was taller than a pike-pole, with skin translucent as the slime of a slug. Still, it was on the human plan, with two arms, two legs, and a knobby bit at the top that glittered. The ropes and nodules of its guts shimmered inside that slick, smooth, shiny skin. Its scent-map was strange, the expected story of starships and time's slow decay mixed in with spices and a sweat which could have gotten a rock-crusher drunk.

Dangerous, this one. But they always were. The safe ones stayed home.

"Digger," the exogen said. It used a voder which could have come from before the dawn of technology. Believe me, I *know.*

I'm not one for judging a man by his shape. Metatron knows I find myself judged enough. Still, I'm cautious around one who comes from too far away, for a man distant from his home has no need of scruples. "Aye, and that's me."

Something flashed pale, pallid blue in the exogen's middle gut. "Compensation."

One of them types. I could handle this. Like talking to a Taurian. All syntax implied inside a hyperlimited morphemic constellation. Like playing a game of two hundred questions. "Compensation in what cause?"

"Seeking."

"That's what I do. I seek. By digging. What do you seek?"

"Death."

That one required some careful thought. I didn't reckon this exogen had come all the way across the Deep Dark between the stars just for me to dig him a grave. Not that I hadn't dug a grave or four in my day. It was just that no one spent the kind of energy budget this exogen had dedicated to being here on Earth simply to lay themselves down.

"Anyone's death in particular?"

"Death." My visitor flashed a series of colors, then manipulated its voder. "Thanatos."

"Oh, Death his own self." I considered that. "You must be aware that death isn't really anywhere to be found. Mythic personification doesn't leave behind calling cards for me to dig up. Entropic decay does, but *everything* is evidence of that."

I knew from experience that it would take the exogen a while to assemble my loose stream of lexemes into a meaningful morph that fit its own mind. I'd been working on my sun-altar when it had found me among the dunes of rusted bolts where I make my home. So I returned to my labors, confident that my visitor would speak again when it was ready.

Exogens work on their own timescale. Some are sped up so fast they can experience a standard-year in a few hours, others move so slowly they speak to rocks, and perceive trees as fast-moving weeds. In time, this one would answer.

Two days later, it did.

"Secrets," the exogen said, as if no time had passed at all.

"You want me to dig for the secrets of death?" I laughed. "There's no secret to death. It finds us all. Death is the least secret thing in the universe. I can open any grave and show you."

The traveler's hand brushed down its translucent front, trailing tiny colored flares. "Undying." The voder somehow sounded wistful.

I picked up a ritual axe from the Second Archaean Interregnum, traced a claw tip down the blade edge. "That's easy enough to take care of. Dying is simple. It's living that's hard."

For an awful moment, I wondered if the exogen was going to dip its head and dare me into trying that pulsing neck. Instead it just stared a while. I thought the exogen had slipped back into slow-time, until it spoke again. "Door."

"Door." Death's door? That was a figure of speech as old as architecture. This exogen must have something more literal in mind.

"Door." This time the voder's tones implied an emphatic conclusion. The exogen shut down, sinking into a quietude that took it across the border from life into art. The sense of light and life which had skimmed across it like yellow fog on a sulfuritic lake was gone.

I had acquired my very own statue. Walking, talking, likely intelligent, and certainly fantastically wealthy.

For a test, I poked one tip of the Achaean axe into its chest. About where the sternum would be on the human plan. It was like poking a boulder. The exogen's skin had no give, and the sense of weightiness was downright planetary.

Door. What in all the baroque hells of the Mbazi Renaissance did it mean by *door?*

▲▼▲

You know perfectly well that while the Earth is dying, it's nowhere near dead. Even a corpse on the forest floor isn't dead. Intestinal flora bloom in the madness of a sudden, fatal spring. Ants swarm the massive pile of loosening protein. Patient beetles wait to polish bones until they gleam like little fragments of lost Luna embedded in the soil.

So it is with this world. I can tell by the cut of your suit that you're from offworld, but I can tell by the quality that you didn't ship in from across the Deep Dark. A patient man with an unlimited air supply and a wealth of millennia in his hand can almost walk from here to Proxima Centauri by station-hopping, but anyone terrestrial planning to move between the stars on anything like the scale of a human standard life-time is very, very wealthy. And you are plainly terrestrial in origins, and just as plainly from those boots are not so wealthy.

I'm sorry. Did I offend? Take it from me, after you've riven open the graves of a million generations, you find your sense of tact has evaporated with all the rest of time's detritus. *I'm* poor, poor as a chuck moose, so I see no shame in anyone else's poverty.

Besides, this story I'm telling you may save your life some day. Surely that's worth an unintentional insult or two. Not that I'm planning another, mind you, but Dog the Digger is famously plainspoken as any of his kind, for all that he's not on the human plan.

Here we are, a collection of mortally wounded peoples on a mortally wounded planet, but we yet live. No matter the elevation of our estate. I may be a beetle polishing the bones of the world rather than a bright explorer at the morning of all civilizations, but still I draw breath. (Metaphorically speaking, of course.)

And so it fell to me to search for meaning in the exogen's request. After a month had gone by, his skin was cooled to the color of cold iron, and no one might ever have believed him to be alive. He stood like a man marking his own grave and stared sightlessly at the spot where I happened to have been positioned that night.

At least I understood now how he passed between the stars. The exogen had no life support requirements, and was immune to boredom. He wasn't so much undying as unliving.

I went to my friend Pater Nostrum. A man very nearly on the human plan, as so few of us were in these terribly late days, Pater Nostrum lived in a cathedral he'd built himself as an agglutination of debris, donations and some downright thievery. He dowsed for his cathedral one shard at a time, using a rod made of Gerrine Empire hullmetal wrapped in sable manskin. A time or ten I'd dug and hauled great, broad-beamed members for him, fetched by some unseen-to-me holy mandate from the dank rust-grained soil.

The genetics in that rod's leather grip were worth more than all of Pater Nostrum's earthly accumulations, but as a priest, he was beyond caring of such things. Or so he told himself, me, and everyone else who would listen.

This day I claimed back from him one of the favors owed.

"Pater," I said. It was the season for my third body, which was generally the most comfortable for those with whom I spoke. Not that the exogen would have cared, or truly, even Pater Nostrum.

He smiled, resplendent in his robes of rich vinyl trimmed with donkey fur. "Digger, my...son. Welcome."

We met in his cathedral's Second Sanctuary, a round-walled room with a ceiling line that very nearly described a hyperbolic curve. Armor cladding off some ancient starship, with a look like that. The walls were relieved with 10,432 notches (I am incapable of not counting such things in my first glance), and each notch held a little oil lamp wrought from some old insulator or reservoir or other electromechanical part.

They all burned, which argued for some extremely retarded combustion characteristics. The scent map of the room confirmed that well enough.

"I would ask something of you, Pater Nostrum. I cannot yet say whether it is a remembering or a scrying or just some keyword research in the deep data layers."

Information flows everywhere on this earth. It is encoded in every grain of sand, in the movements of the tumbling constellations of microsatellites and space junk above our heads, in the very branching of the twigs on the trees. Knowing how to *reach* that information, how to query it and extract something useful—well, that was one reason why the world had priests.

Prayer and sacrifice invoked lines of communication which remained obdurately shut to most of us most of the time.

"I will do this thing for you gladly," Pater Nostrum said. "But you must first cross my palm with slivers, to make our bargain whole and place you under my hieratic seal."

This I knew as well, and so had brought a cluster of shattered beast-ivory from a sand-filled sea cave recently explored beneath the Hayük Desert. I scattered it over his open hand in a brittle mist.

Pater Nostrum closed his fist and grimaced. I knew with skin like his that the ivory would cut, burn, slice. When he opened his hand, the usual small miracle had occurred. A tooth with four twisted roots lay whole on the bloody palm.

"Well brought, Digger," the priest said. He smiled. "And of course my debt to you is long-incurred. So speak plainly and tell me what you seek."

I closed my eyes a moment and let my skin tell me the story of the point-source warmth of ten thousand little flames. The framing of this question had been much on my mind of late, with me working at great length to tease it out. Still, no matter what I said, I'd be wrong. Clearly enough the only choice was to address the moment and trust my friendship with this old priest.

"There is a client. A difficult one. It has charged me with finding the door into death. I would know if ever there was such a thing outside the sliding walls of metaphor. If so, where might I find this door, or evidence of its former existence?"

"A door into death." The priest stared up at his hyperbolic ceiling, his eyes following the receding curve into some dark infinity. "I will scry," Pater Nostrum muttered. The air began to swirl around him, dust motes orbiting his upturned face like swallows around a charnel house chimney. His eyes rolled inward until nothing remained within his lids but a silvery glowing sliver. One by one, the flames on the wall niches began going out in tiny pops as the priest drew from their energy in some pattern known only to him.

I settled to watch. The brilliant dust of a thousand millennia of nanotechnology meant the world could describe *itself*, if like any competent priest one only knew how to ask the questions.

So he scried. The flames carried Pater Nostrum inward on a wave of information, a palimpsest of infinitely successive and fractal functional languages, protocols, handshakes, field-gestalts and far stranger, more curious engineering dead ends. I knew there had once been information systems which stored data in the probabilistic matrices of quantum foam, extracting it again in a fractional femtosecond as observational dynamics collapsed the informational field to null. Likewise I knew there had once been information systems which relied upon the death of trees to transmit data at a bit rate so low it could be measured in packets per century.

Pater Nostrum could reach them all. At least on his best days. Each little lamp was a channel into some dead language, some time-hoared data protocol, some methodology which had once swept the world so hard that its fingerprints remained in the noösphere.

One by one, 10,432 flames went out. Slowly we passed through shadow before being cast into darkness. I don't measure time on the human plan myself, and so hunger, micturation, joint fatigue and the like tend not to impinge overmuch on my situational experience, but Pater Nostrum experienced all those and more, until blood ran gelid-dark from his nose and ears as the last of the lights winked away to leave the two of us alone in lightless splendor demarcated only by the priest's breathing and my scent map of his body's sudden advancement into further decay.

Finally he came back to me.

"Well." Pater Nostrum picked his way through his words with an exaggerated care. "It has not been so in more decades than I care to admit to."

"You scry well, Father," I said politely.

"I should not think to scry so well again. Not as I value my own health."

"Surely the gods forfend."

"Gods." He snorted. "I am a *priest*. What does my work have to do with gods?"

"I can't say, Father." After that I waited for him to find the thread of his thoughts.

Finally Pater Nostrum spoke. "There was a movement during the era of the Viridian Republic. Religious, scientific, cultural."

A long pause ensued, but that did not seem to require an answer, so I did not answer him.

He gathered himself and continued. "They called themselves Lux Transitum. This movement believed that life is a waveform. So long as you do not collapse the waveform, life continues. Death was viewed not as a biological process but as an unfortunate event within the realm of some very specialized physics."

"Life is...life," I replied. "Antientropic organization in chemical or electromechanical systems which, when left unattended, tends to metastatize into computers, people, starships, catfish and what have you."

Lighting a candle from the inner pocket of his vinyl robes, Pater Nostrum shook his head. "As the case may be. I only reflect what I have been told. I do not believe it. Sooner argue with the dead than contend with the noösphere."

"Wise policy, every bit of it."

"At least for those of us on the human plan." He tried another grin, but this one failed.

More silence followed, as if Pater Nostrum was now determined to subdivide his attention into short tranches interspersed by gaps of inertia.

Finally I stepped into the conversation again. "Did Lux Transitum have a laboratory or a temple? Is there some place where they addressed this uncollapsed waveform?"

"Hmm?" Pater Nostrum looked at me as if noticing me for the first time. "Oh, well, yes."

"Father." I imbued my voice with infinite patience, something this body was fairly good at. "Where might I find their holy place?"

He woke to my question with a non sequitur. "How long have you been alive, Digger?"

"Me?" I stopped and considered that. "At least 7,313 years, by the most conservative view. Counting since the last cold restart of my cognitive processes."

"How long have I been alive?"

"I shouldn't know with any certainty," I said, "but we met shortly after the Andromachus strike. Which was 4,402 years ago the second Thursday of next month."

"You are not on the human plan, but I am." He leaned close, almost touching me. "Do you think the human plan called for four thousand year old priests? When was the last time you saw a child?"

I tried to remember when I'd last encountered a juvenile of *any* species. Not just human. "Surely people must breed somewhere."

"Surely," said Pater Nostrum. "But not here on Earth, it seems."

"This would not come naturally to my attention," I pointed out. "But you might have noticed it somewhere along the way."

"You know," the priest said vaguely. "The days are bathed in almost endless red light. There is always something to do. So few people roam the world..."

"A thought-block," I said sympathetically.

He seemed shocked. "On the entire human race?"

"What human race?"

We walked outside under the dying sun and argued long over whether Lux Transitum had the right of it, and what *had* been done with people. Most of all, whether to wake them up.

▲▼▲

You're wondering now, aren't you? How long ago did this happen? What did Dog the Digger do next? Did I wake the exogen and what did I tell him when I did?

Look around you. What do you see? Quiet place we've got. That line of hills over there is a linear city from the Vitalist Era. Bury it in a quarter million years of rain and three major eruptions due west of here, and there's nothing left but low hills covered with scrub. Until you go digging.

Now beneath your feet. The red sand dusting your boots is rust accumulation from when teratons of asteroidal iron were brought down by the Wolfram Bund to clad the world in an impermeable metal shell.

Feel how the air tickles your throat when you breathe? You'd be appalled at how much processing power goes into your lungs, and what percentage of that crosses through the alveoli into your bloodstream. There's a *reason* that access to this damned planet is so heavily restricted.

So we live here in our lowtowns and our cathedrals and our shanties and caverns and buried mansions, and nothing ever changes. That was the big secret the exogen was searching for. You can transcend death, but only through stasis. The whole point and purpose of life on the human plan is death. Otherwise you are *us*, grubbing in the ruins of a million years of dreaming.

And you are us, now. Check in with your shuttle. I can promise you it's not going back up in this lifetime. My fourth and sixth bodies have already disassembled the engines and control surfaces. You will live forever, too, my friends, trapped in the same story as the rest of us.

The exogen?

He'll wake up eventually. We're letting him sleep. He's already found the answer. He just doesn't have to dig holes under a bloodred sky to earn it every day.

I am called Dog the Digger. I am not mighty, neither am I fearsome. But I am all you will ever know now.

Or maybe this is just a story, like you asked for. Under the crimson light of a dying sun, is there any real difference between a story and the truth?

Welcome to my Earth.

Lehr, Rex

Back in 2005, Peter Crowther invited me to participate in Forbidden Planets, *a tribute anthology honoring the fiftieth anniversary of the release of the film Forbidden Planet. That's a pretty exciting opportunity for an SF geek like me, so I quickly said "yes" before he came to his senses, then hied myself to the video store for a rental to carefully rewatch the movie. I didn't see much point in riffing on the movie directly, so I decided to rip off another Shakespeare play much as the original screenwriters had with* The Tempest. *The weird thing about writing this story is that under the hood it is a New Wave identity paranoia story, but it's dressed up in the language of Silver Age (or possibly Golden Age) science fiction. Which was damned hard to do, because the prose kept trying to bend more toward Phil Dick than Doc Smith. I like to think that tension is part of what makes this story work.*

Captain Lehr's face had been ravaged by decades under the coruscating emanations of this forgotten world's overbright sun. The angry star, a rare purple giant, dominated the daysky with visible prominences that sleeted hard radiation through every human bone and cell that walked beneath its glare. Still, one could see the spirit of command which had once infused him, present even now in the lines and planes of his face as rough and striated as the great, crystalline cliffs which marched toward the horizon sparkling azure and lavender under the hard light. His eyes were marbled with a blindness which had come upon him in the long years, victim perhaps of some alien virus, until his blank visage appeared to be chiseled from the planet's sinews, much as the very rocks themselves.

How he and whoever yet lived among his crew had survived this hellish gravity well for close to half a human lifetime was a mystery to me, which yet remained to be truckled, but survive they had. The old man was king of all he surveyed with his blind eyes, soul shuttered behind milky shields, ruling from his seat in a shattered palace comprised of the main hull frame series of INS *Broken Spear*. The baroque pillars which had once bounded the great rays of energy required to leap between the stars now served to do little more than support a roof to keep off the rare rains, and cast a penumbra against the pitiless glare. The place had a gentle reek of aging plastic laying over the dank dance of stone on shadowed stone, but otherwise was little different from a cavern fitted out for the habitation of men.

We did not yet know where the rest of his benighted vessel had come to her grave, but she had certainly fulfilled her ill-starred name. Finding the balance of her remains was critical, of course, in the niggardly time allotted our expedition by Sector Control and the unsympathetic laws of physics. That mankind had bent our way around the speed of light was miracle enough, but we had not yet broken past the photons cast so wide in nature's bright net, and so must live with the twinned constraints of relativity and simultaneity.

"Golly, skipper, he's a real mess," whispered Deckard behind me. "Just like his ship."

I waved my idiot engineer to silence.

Allison Cordel, a woman still beautiful amid age and hard use, stood yet beside her commanding officer, loyal as any starman's wife though it was the two of them together lost so far from home. Our own records, copies of dusty personnel files laboriously thermaxed from ancient microfilm, had shown that despite the natural disadvantages of her sex Cordel had risen to Executive Officer of *Broken Spear* before that late ship's collapse from heaven. Most of the girl officers who came into the service under the Navy's occasional outbreaks of gender-rebalancing soon enough yielded to destiny and their biological imperatives and found more suitable work as service wives, competing as hostesses to aid their chosen man's rise to Admiral in the no-less vicious battlefields of the salon and ballroom. Not for Commander Cordel these sharp-nailed sham combats. In the time I had studied her file, I had developed a fond respect for her, nurtured amid the hope that she had been one of the survivors mentioned in the desperate longwave help signal which had finally arrived at Gloster Station after laboring at lightspeed across the echoing darkness between the stars.

Now I cast my eyes upon this woman who had served as a sort of shadow idol to me in the months of our journey to this unnamed place, Girl Friday to the great Captain's Robinson Crusoe. Had it been her footprints which disturbed the bright, brittle dust outside as she found whatever resources had sustained them all these years? At any rate, she was yet slim as any message torpedo, her rough-spun tunic cut in homage to a uniform doubtless long worn to raveling threads but still hinting at womanly charms beneath. Her eyes gleamed bright with genius as any worthy man's, her charming chestnut hair in an unbecoming style fit only for such a primitive place, shot through with a silver which lent her gravitas beyond her gender.

"So, Captain de Vere," she said, her voice like vacuum frost on a lander's struts, "you are come among us. Even in the face of our pleas for you to keep your distance."

Despite myself I nearly bowed, so elegant was her manner. Were there women this controlled, this powerful, even among the silk-walled drawing rooms at the core of the Empire? I strongly doubted it. She might have been a duke's consort had she remained in society, or even dowager-duchess of some cluster of lucky planets. Though I supposed this woman who had fought so hard for the twinned comets of her rank would hardly shed her uniform for the love of either a man or politics.

I settled on a salute. "My orders are all too plain, ma'am."

Cordel favored Lehr with a look in which I fancied I espied the smoldering ashes of prior argument, though the flash in her eyes was lost upon his sightless gaze. She then returned her attention to me, with a focus as tight as any comm laser. "So you have told us. 'Search and rescue with all despatch survivors and assets of *Broken Spear*.' Did it never occur to you that the survivors and assets might have made their peace with fate after all these years?"

Behind me, snickers broke out amid the ranks of my contact team. Those men would pay, later, with a thrashing or a discipline parade depending on how my temper had settled by then. I knew Heminge would rat out the culprit, and satisfied myself with a promise of a pointed discussion later on.

"Ma'am..." I chose my words with care and some precision, allowing for the sort of dauntless ego which had to be in the makeup of any woman of Cordel's achievements. "Commander, rather. With respect, it was your broadcast seeking assistance which summoned us to this place. *Broken Spear* was stricken from the ship list twenty-eight years ago, after she'd been missing thirty-six months from her last known course and heading." I drew myself up, tapping the deep well of pride in the service which had always been an inspiration to me. "The Imperial Navy does not leave starmen behind."

"Nor starwomen, apparently," she said with that chill still in her tone. I did fancy that a smile ghosted at the edge of her stern but striking face, even as another snicker escaped behind me.

It would be a thrashing, I thought, and a good one, down in the ship's gymnasium, something to make those monkeys remember respect.

"Enough," said Lehr. His voice was as ravaged as his expression, a mountain slipface given over to gravity's claims until there was only rough gravel and rude streams left to trap the unwary. "You are here. Perhaps you will profit thereby." He leaned forward on his throne—and throne it was, for all that his seat had been the captain's chair salvaged from *Broken Spear*'s bridge, the toggles and interfaces embedded in its generous arms long gone dark as the spark within their commander's eyes. Rocks, perhaps uncut gems, had been applied to the surfaces, creating strange patterns and half-recognizable friezes which his hand stroked as he spoke. Comfort, or some fingered language, a geological Braille reserved for his special use?

Lehr's blank gaze met my face as if he were still blessed with the gift of sight. That confident stone stare clamped a hard chill upon my spine, which I sought not to show as weakness before the captain's formidable executive officer. "We are upon a time of change here, Captain de Vere. It may be well enough that you are come among us."

It was a voice and manner that would recall any starman to his days as the rawest recruit, all left feet and ten-thumbed hands, much like a man grown and bearded might be yet a quaking boy before the echo of wrath bursting from an aging father. Nonetheless, my duty to my command and my orders sustained me against this unexpected onslaught of primitive emotion. "Indeed sir, and what would this time of change be?"

The captain's laugh was as rough as his speech, a sort of stony chuckle that gathered momentum until another layer was stripped from the gravel of his voice in a wheezing hack. The look with which Cordel favored me would have chilled a caloric insulator, but I resolutely ignored her, awaiting her commander's pleasure.

"I am dying, de Vere," he finally managed to say. "And dying I divide my kingdom among my daughters." His arm, still great-muscled and long enough to strike any man with the fist of authority, swept outward to encompass what lay behind my shoulders—the open end of his hall, where the cataclysm of *Broken Spear*'s demise had left a gap through which an enterprising man could have driven a herd of banths. "These green and pleasant lands which we have wrested from the anger of this world must be husbanded against the days of our children."

I turned slowly, staring out past the strips of thermal cloth and fabric scraps which made a curtain insufficient to hide the glowing glass desert beyond. If anything the color of a Terran field prospered under that hideous giant sun, it was outside my reckoning. My team—Deckard the engineer, Heminge the security man, Beaumont the political and Marley the doctor—stared as well, each then turning to cast a shadowed look towards me.

When I once more faced the captain, Cordel's face was twisted into a mask of silent misery, like a widow's crumpled handkerchief. She betrayed nothing in her breathing, but a slight shake of her head confirmed what I already knew: to humor the ancient, failed madman in deference to his years of service and impending demise was the far better course than to slaughter his final, feeble hopes with the hard light of truth.

"Indeed, sir," I said slowly, holding her gaze with mine. Could this gray-eyed Valkyrie be yet a natural woman beneath the veneer of discipline? "It is a fair world you have brought forth." In that moment, a thought surfaced, blazing bright betrayal of my just-coined policy of polite fable. I am not a man to leave a thing alone, even in face of a desirable woman's desperation, but surely he had not breached the chain of command so horribly as to get children upon his exec. There were no other women among *Broken Spear*'s crew list.

"Who are your daughters, sir?" I asked.

Like a metastable solution leaping to a crystalline state at the tap of a technician's stirring rod, Cordel's face hardened to wrath in that moment. Lehr, oblivious to anything beyond the soft stones of his eyes, said nothing.

A long minute of silence passed, underscored by the whistling of the hot wind outside and the slow, steady hiss of dustfall within, before I saluted again and excused myself and my party. We retreated beneath twin masks of blind indifference and bloody hatred, heading for the forge of sunlight beyond the shadows of this ruined starship palace.

▲▼▲

We returned with all due haste to my own ship, INS *Six Degrees*. As an expeditionary cruiser, she was designed and built for descents into the treacherous territory of planetary gravity wells. The constraints of naval architecture generally kept ships in orbit, safe from weather, natural disaster or the less sophisticated forms of civil disturbance. Not *Six Degrees*. She was wrought as a great disc, capable of sliding through atmosphere layers without expending overmuch power, but now sitting balanced on tripodal struts atop a karst outcrop some kilometer and a half from Lehr's location. It was a natural vantage for defense, with a view of the broken valleys that led toward the crystalline cliffs, and a clear line of sight to the dull bulk that had once been *Broken Spear*.

When aboard, I abandoned my resolve to enforce justice among my officers in favor of a swift council of war with respect to the soon-to-be-late Captain Lehr and the matter of his ship. We had reviewed a dozen major action plans in the long, cold months of transit to this system, but none of our contingencies had included finding any of the crew alive.

I had secret orders, that not even the weasel Beaumont had seen, pertaining to the handling of *Broken Spear* and her cargo. *Six Degrees* carried a planet-buster in her number two hold, most unusual armament indeed for an expeditionary cruiser, but some of the outcomes modeled in the files of my sealed orders suggested that I might be called upon to execute that most awful responsibility of command—ordering wholesale death to be visited upon an entire world. Even if all we eliminated was the buzz of strange arthropods, it would still be acknowledged a great and terrible crime.

It did not rank among my ambitions to be recorded in history as de Vere the Planetkiller. But *Broken Spear*'s secrets needed to stay lost—a determination which I was given to understand had been reached among the highest of the ivory-screened chambers of the Imperial House.

But no one had imagined that Lehr yet lived, king of a broken kingdom, attended upon by Cordel. And who were his so-called daughters?

My sons, as it were, surrounded me. Deckard, wiseacre but loyal, stood at one end of the ward room, his head deep in the hood of an inform-o-scanner brought in for our purposes.

Heminge, stolid as his pistol but equally reliable as both peace-keeper and weapon, sat at the conference table which had been pulled up from the deck and secured into place, a red marker in hand as he reviewed reconnaissance photography of this world, still damp from the imaging engines. The good Doctor Marley, paler and more slightly built than the rest of us, sly and twisty as ever, a master of challenge without quite rising to the level of insubordination, was down in the sick bay, making notes about his observations of Lehr and Cordel with a promise to return shortly.

And of course there was Beaumont. My Imperial Bureau of Compliance liaison, by courtesy holding rank of Lieutenant Commander, and serving without apparent qualification or experience as executive officer on my ship, forced upon me by the nature of this mission. I would have been unsurprised to find that despite my sealed orders he had separate knowledge of my charge with respect to the planet-buster. Here was a man created by Nature to climb the ladders of power like a weasel in a hydroponics farm. Were I free to do so, I would have strapped him to that bloody bedamned bomb and dropped them both into the nearest star. Instead, he currently sat opposite me, his face set in that secretive smirk which seemed to be his most ordinary expression, hands steepled before his lips as if in prayer, his black eyes glittering.

Beaumont spoke into his fingertips: "So, Captain de Vere, such a pretty trail you have set yourself to. Do you plan to offer aid and comfort to *Broken Spear*'s survivors?"

"Imperial Military Code is clear enough," I replied. "We are required to render such assistance as our capabilities permit, and evacuate however many survivors we can accommodate, so long as those left behind are not so reduced in numbers or required skills as to be in peril of their lives."

"Codex three, chapter seven, subchapter twenty-one. Good enough, Captain."

"I'm so pleased to have your approval, *Commander*. I misdoubt me that they will come. They were not pleased to see us."

Heminge interrupted without looking up from his photographs, though he was most certainly listening intently. "Where is the command section? The portions of *Broken Spear* which are identifiably hull down on this world do not include the command section."

"Does it matter?" snapped Beaumont.

Heminge looked up, met the political officer's eyes. "Yes. It does matter. *Sir.* Captain Lehr was sitting in a command chair. That means the command section was either at one time on the surface, having since departed, or that it survived undamaged in orbit long enough for interior components to be removed and brought down by other means."

Deckard spoke from the depths of his viewing hood, his voice only somewhat muddled. "There are several metallic bodies in high orbit. One might assume they represented missing sections of *Broken Spear*."

"Which suggests Lehr allowed the ship to be broken apart in orbit, and made an emergency landing with the main hull section," I said. The cargo-at-issue on board *Broken Spear* had been carried in the captain's safe, immediately behind the bridge on that hull type. Had they landed the command section as well and taken the cargo off? Or moved it to the main hull section before bringing that down?

It had been a terribly dangerous thing to do, whatever the reason. And the nature of Lehr's throne underscored that the object of my search could be anywhere.

I considered my regret for the planet-buster in the belly of *Six Degrees*. Marley bustled into the ward room, speaking quickly as he always did: "Only one woman on that ship, de Vere, which is one more than our lot has got. Don't know why he thinks he has daughters—Allison Cordel hasn't been gravid any more than I have. Not here, she'd never carry to term." Marley slid into a chair. "Lehr's dying, I'm fairly certain. In this environment, one must assume cancer or radiation poisoning. How he lasted this long is more than a small mystery. Delusional, of course, too, seeing green fields beyond his inner horizon. Gentlemen, what are we about now?"

"Shut up," Beaumont suggested.

"We are being signaled," Deckard added, emerging from his hood. He touched the personal comm unit strapped to his wrist. A cluster of microphones and screens and speaker grilles unfolded from overhead.

"Attention *Six Degrees*," said a strange, flat voice, the caller devoid of emotion or inflection. I could scarce determine whether it was a man or woman who spoke. "Do you copy?"

"This is *Six Degrees*, de Vere commanding," I replied in my crispest training academy voice, waving madly at Deckard to indicate that he should track the source of the signal. "Please identify yourself."

"I am Ray Gun."

I exchanged glances with my command crew. Beaumont's face was sour and pinched...he never had either a sense of humor or an imagination. The others displayed varying degrees of thoughtful interest, though Marley was smiling strangely behind his hand.

"And you are whom and where...?"

Deckard flashed one of Heminge's photo prints, an image of one hemisphere of this world as shot from our approach to the planet. He circled it with his finger.

Orbit? I mouthed.

My chief engineer nodded.

How could that be? But an unknown agency of Lehr's in orbit was no stranger than what we had already seen. The associated comm lag explained the strange rhythm of this conversation, for one.

"Ray Gun. I am one of Lehr's daughters. Bound to Cathar, who loves me as the stars love the horizons of evening."

Marley twirled one index finger around his temple.

For a woman, Ray Gun had a remarkably sexless voice. Not for her the tingling tones of Cordel's strong contralto, intertwined womanly charm and matronly discipline that went straight to my gut. And other parts. Ray Gun's strangeness made me wonder about this Cathar.

"And you are in orbit, Ray Gun?" I said. "How may I help you?"

Deckard shook his head, while Beaumont looked increasingly sour. I knew perfectly well what both of my officers were about—trying to puzzle how there were more women in this place. Unless Lehr had begat children on Cordel shortly after their arrival. But who would place a girl-child in orbit, and *how*? Why? This world was a conundrum and then some.

"My father has divided his kingdom between the best of his daughters," said Ray Gun primly. "We who love him most shall carry his standard. It is I who rule the skies above."

Deckard was back under the sensor hood, Marley made more notes, while Beaumont now stalked the deck in angry thought, glaring at me as Heminge watched him carefully. I glared back. Perhaps I could leave him here with the madmen and women.

"I'm very pleased to hear that," I told her.

"Good." Ray Gun's voice fell silent a moment. Then: "Do not listen to Cordel. She will betray the king my father's dream. You should leave. Cathar says so, and he is never wrong."

I was leaning toward Marley's theory. "Thank you for the information."

"Cathar and Kern will move against her soon. Best you stay away. Leave now, *Six Degrees*, while your purpose and dignity are intact."

Who the hell was Kern? "I shall take your remarks under advisement."

"Ray Gun out."

I looked at my command crew. They stared back at me, Deckard emerging from the sensor hood.

"That was very strange," Heminge said.

Deckard nodded. "I got a signal lock. It's one of those metallic objects I found earlier. Command section would seem to be likely."

"So who is Ray Gun? Not to mention Cathar and Kern?"

Beaumont swung around, breaking the momentum of his pacing to face me with barely-suppressed menace, as if he thought I was to be intimidated by a darker sort of passion mixed with the threat of his connection to the secretive political puppet masters of the Empire. "This is stupid, de Vere. All of it. You know what do. Everything else is just pointless theater of the mind."

Heminge's voice was quiet. "The bomb?"

Though my orders were in strictest confidence, the planet-buster itself was hardly a secret aboard my ship. It filled the number two hold, a modified re-entry vehicle designed to be launched from orbit. Any man could deduce its intended use. A smart man wouldn't comment on it. Especially not in front of Beaumont.

"Yes, the bomb, you moron," snapped Beaumont.

"So whatever is in our secret orders," Heminge put his hand up, palm out, "and don't get excited, we *must* have secret orders, since we're not carrying that thing on a cargo manifest, and it is fully commissioned. As I was saying, whatever is in our secret orders must be very important indeed, for you to take such disregard for the lives of *two commissioned officers of the Imperial Navy*. Not to mention crew and dependents, regardless as to their number or sanity."

"They're dead." Beaumont's voice was flat. "They've been legally dead since *Broken Spear* was taken off the ship list. Lehr and Cordel are walking around breathing, but their commissions lapsed twenty-eight baseline years ago."

"So whatever *it* is, this great, terrible secret is worth their lives, without any respect to their legal existence?"

I stood, took a deep breath. "Yes. Though it burns me to agree with my good Lieutenant Commander Beaumont." I cast him another sidelong glare, sickened by the look of triumph on his face. "Our view of the outcomes may be the same, but our view of the process differs. I prefer to dance a few measures in this theater of the mind. Our Captain Lehr holds secrets behind the marble of his blind eyes, gentlemen, and I propose to have them out of him if possible. They might just save his life at that."

Heminge nodded, his eyes still on Beaumont as he spoke. "How long, Captain?"

"On my authority," Beaumont said, one hand straying to the pistol at his belt, "a day."

"No." I stared him down. "I command here. You may have my commission when we get home, but until then the decision is mine." The orders had been clear enough. We weren't to spend time on site, lest we become contaminated too. I'd already consigned *Six Degrees* and her crew to extensive quarantine on our return, simply by landing and approaching Lehr in person—a fact as yet understood by no one but Beaumont, though I suspected Marley of either knowing or deducing it for himself. "As long as it takes."

Beaumont refused to flinch. "A time limit, de Vere."

Sadly, he was right. "Seventy-two hours, then."

Deckard walked across the ward room, slammed his shoulder into Beaumont, knocking the political officer backwards, though they were of a height and build. "Excuse me, *sir*. My clumsiness." He turned back toward me. "If time is short, we should be working."

"As you were, Beaumont," I shouted, before he could spring up off the deck. "We're going back out. I want to speak to Cordel." About these daughters, I told myself. The old man himself was useless, lost in the hallucination of a green world and decades of blind introspection.

"I'll bet you do," Beaumont muttered, picking himself up with a slow, false dignity. "I'll just bet you do."

▲▼▲

We trudged across the dry crystal beds, gravel washed down from the distant cliffs. They smelled like talcum, with the astringent overlay of this world's native organics, stirred by the hot winds to a sort of dehydrated atmospheric soup which would eventually damage our lungs if breathed too long. The sun glinted hot, mauve steel in the sky, hiding the mysterious Ray Gun somewhere behind its glare.

Ray Gun had to be inhabiting *Broken Spear*'s missing command section. I glanced upward, shading my eyes from the daystar's killing brilliance. Where was she?

It.

Of course. Ray Gun was an "it."

"Deckard," I said, picking my way past a shining bush that resembled a fan of coral rendered by a drunken glassblower. "Did *Broken Spear* have onboard AI support?" Intelligence-boosted systems went in and out of fashion over the decades in a sort of endless tug-of-war between the inherent instability of such self-aware entities, prone to mental collapse after a brief, hot life-cycle, and the high value of an intelligence not subject to the disorientations of supraluminal travel nor the stresses of high acceleration.

"Depends," puffed my engineer.

"Depends on what?" asked Beaumont nastily.

I heard Deckard grunt, almost as if struck, but he could take care of himself. He chose the high road: "On whether she was pre- or post-Yankelov Act. Her ship class originally did, but there was a refit wave after the AI regs changed, right around the time *Broken Spear* was lost."

I thought that over. "So Ray Gun might be Lehr's ship's systems. All alone up there in orbit all these years."

"Crazy as an oxygen miner three days after a comet claim," said Marley.

"Indeed. And one of Lehr's daughters."

"Maybe Cathar's the other one," Heminge said.

A stranger stepped from behind a pillar of stacked rubble and glittering silica. "Cathar is a traitor," he declared.

Heminge and Beaumont both drew their weapons. I kept my own hands away from my holstered pistol and the swift death it could deal

like the sword of justice. This was not my courtroom. Instead, I studied the stranger as he studied me, ignoring the armed threat my men
presented.

He was whipcord thin, naked as the landscape and much like the
sullen world around us covered with white dust that sparkled and fleck-
ed as he moved. That coating matched the sparse, silvered hair upon his
head and about his shriveled penis, and the thousand-kilometer stare
in his eyes, which seemed to bore right through me from beneath his
hooded brows. Here was a man who looked across years, and bore their
wounds upon his body. I could count his ribs, and the cords on his neck
twitched as he spoke. He was no better armed than the wind.

"Another one rises from the earth," I said mildly. "Of the crew?"

"Lieutenant Fishman," he replied. His voice was as cracked as his
skin, also a thing of this world. What this place had done to people,
I thought. He raised his hands. "You should go. Before Granny Rail
finds you."

"Surely you mean Ray Gun?"

"No." He laughed, a mirthless chuckle dry as an old bone. "She has
taken the sky from my Captain. Granny Rail has taken the world. Lehr
lives on sustained only by the love of Lady Cordel and myself."

Beaumont shoved forward, pistol in his hand. "Granny Rail. You're
as cracked as that old rummy, Lieutenant Fishman. Go back to your
hole in the soil and count yourself lucky to have any days remaining in
your life."

Fishman shifted his long-range stare to drill through Beaumont.
"You wouldn't understand loyalty, would you, man? Count yourself lucky
to have any minutes remaining in your life."

Three gouts of dark fluid spouted in Beaumont's chest, grim flowers
bringing color to this drab and barren landscape even as his final words
died in his mouth. A smile quirked across Fishman's taut face as the rest
of us dropped, but the great, gray-silver spider thing which erupted from
the ground ignored him completely.

It whirled, clattering, a motile version of the crystalline plants of this
world, except for the well-worn but fully functional Naval-issue assault
rifles in two claws. Rolling up against a back-breaking jag of rocks, I
drew my own pistol, but the blunted flechettes intended for antiper-
sonnel use in vacuum-constrained environments would have very little
effect on this bright, spinning monster.

Heminge moved past me, firing his much more deadly meson pistol.
The rays gleamed with an eerie anti-light, the air ripping as the weapon
sundered the very molecules that sustained us all, dust particles flashing

into component atoms in the same moment to create an eye-bending sparkle which distracted even our ferocious many-limbed assailant.

One rifle exploded, taking the tip end of an arm with it in a shower of glass, accompanied by an ammoniac ordure very much at odds with the gleaming destruction. The other rifle swung to Heminge as he collided with the fast-moving legs, tumbling amid their silver-gray stems like a man in a twisting cage.

I launched myself after him, noting out of the corner of my eye Deckard taking a headshot on Beaumont, even as Marley scrambled for better cover, his medical kit already in his hand. Ever an optimist, the doctor, thinking about who might live to be the recipient of his attentions. The rifle spat again and something burned my thigh with the fire of a solar prominence, but then I was in among the legs, pressing the bell of my flechette pistol against a joint and firing even as Heminge shouted something unintelligible and loosed his meson pistol into the dented, dull ball which seemed to serve as nerve center and balance point for our enemy.

The very air ripped once more and my hair caught fire, then the thing exploded in a clattering shower of legs.

For a moment there was only the patter of debris and the whirl of dust devils, the ammonia scent of local death mixing with the stench of my burnt hair. I looked up, for somehow I was not standing any more, to see the long legs of Fishman above me.

"Granny Rail will be angry," he said, smiling enough to show shattered teeth that gleamed even within the shadows of his mouth.

I was amazed that I could hear him. I struggled for my voice, choking on dust, some thick, pooling liquid, and—though it shamed me—fear. "I want Cordel," I said, my finger crooking on the trigger of my pistol.

Marley bent over me while Deckard gathered pieces of the monster. Heminge, who unaccountably still had all his hair, grabbed at Fishman's arm. "We will find her."

▲▼▲

A few minutes later my leg was bandaged and splinted. Deckard had the pieces of the monster laid out in roughly their original relationship, albeit disjointed and unmotivated now, studying them with the intensity of a mystic at the feet of their god. Marley squatted on his heels and watched me just as carefully.

"What is it we came to kill?" the doctor finally asked me. "Surely not these madmen with excessively high survival quotients?"

I could not be certain that I wasn't dying—Heminge's meson pistol had done more to my head than simply burn my hair off, either that or our assailant had struck me a chance blow there amidst the battle. Beaumont was dead unmourned, and so would not report me for treasonous speech. I could see him, steaming slightly, something wrong even with his blood. "*Broken Spear*," I said, finding the words difficult. My mind formed them well enough, but something was wrong with my mouth and throat. "*Broken Spear*...carried...biologicals. Templates."

Marley's mouth twisted, his eye thoughtful. "Combat viruses?"

I tried to nod, but that was worse than speaking. "Uh-huh. Tactical... population...con...control."

He glanced around. "If they're loose, we're all already infected. We may never go home."

"Planet...buster. We...have...quarantine...arr...angements."

"I can imagine. Well, whatever it is didn't kill *all* of these people. There's at least three of these lunatics left, after several decades. Which makes me wonder if the virus ever got into the wild."

My voice was coming back to me. "Not much...population control... there."

The doctor grinned. "You're returning to us, captain. Had me worried for a minute or two."

Deckard wandered over, a broken crystal rod in his hand. He cocked his head, stared at me as he wrinkled his nose. "You going to live, sir?"

"Yes." I wasn't ready to sit up, though.

"That thing was a highly modified Naval recon drone. Cyborged, if that's the right word, with components from the local ecosystem. Somebody's spent a lot of time over the years."

"Somebody's *had* a lot of time," I managed. Then: "Bury Beaumont, will you? Please?"

They exchanged glances.

▲▼▲

Cordel came to me at last, trailed by Heminge with his pistol still in his hand and Fishman wearing a truculent expression. The ancient Lieutenant seemed to be so much furniture to his superior officer, but even I could see that when his eyes turned toward her, that thousand-kilometer stare came into bright focus.

I knew how he felt.

"I am sorry about your man," she said.

"I'm too tired to fence." My voice was quiet and slow. Marley and Deckard had propped me up against a rock, for the sake of my dignity. I had refused to be moved back to the ship until after I'd met Cordel, here, on open ground. The spider-thing still smoked nearby, evidence of someone's perfidy, and the pulsing sunlight seemed a better choice to me than the oily-aired, whispering corridors of *Six Degrees*. "So I will simply ask, on your life, ma'am. What has become of the biologicals *Broken Spear* was carrying in the captain's safe?"

Her puzzlement was genuine, as best as I could tell. "Biologicals? We carried no biologicals, Captain de Vere. Not beyond the standard cultures in our sick bay."

"You've been here thirty years and Lehr never mentioned this?"

She folded her knees, bending down to speak to me at eye level. I could have watched her legs move, stork-scissors, for hours. And had she opened to me, a little, some sense of engagement in those gray eyes? In that moment, I was ashamed of the reek of my injuries. "Captain," Cordel said. "I emptied the safe the one time Ray Gun landed on the surface. There was nothing of the kind, I assure you. Wherever did you come to think we were carrying something like that?"

I turned her statements over in my head. Why *was* I sent to crack a world to cinders? "What is *Broken Spear*'s terrible secret, then?"

"Ah," she said, her face shuttering. "Perhaps you should speak to my captain once more."

"He is too busy gazing at green fields beyond," I muttered.

"Indeed." She stood. "Fishman, gather this man up with all due gentleness and bring him to Lehr."

Deckard and Marley stepped forward together to object, but Cordel turned her glare, now pure ice, upon them. "Granny Rail will not bother Fishman. Hands free, you two might be able to win through with your lives if we are attacked once more by her servants."

And so we went, my head lolling back as I stared into the deepening colors of evening and tried to remember why I'd ever wanted to come to this world.

▲▼▲

Approaching Lehr's palace, Deckard and Heminge were attacked by another of the spider-monsters. It lurched out of a stand of the crystal-line growth, brushed past Marley and headed straight for the other two. I watched from my curious angle of repose in Fishman's arms—I am not light at all, which gave me cause to wonder at the Lieutenant's strength, especially in his advanced age—as Heminge snapped off a meson bolt which sheared two legs, while Deckard pumped flechettes into a high-stepping joint. Heminge's second shot slagged the underslung central core, proving that the creatures' advantage lay in surprise, which advantage they had now surrendered.

It was almost too easy, though I wondered why the attacker had not gone for Marley first. Perhaps because he carried no armament?

Then we swept through the curtains and into the hall of the blind king of this world. Lehr leaned forward on his throne, chin set upon his hand in an attitude of thoughtful repose. "Welcome, de Vere," he said, staring toward our little party at a height somewhat above my own angled head.

So, the great man did not know I was being carried wounded to be laid before his throne.

I tugged at Fishman to set me down. Deckard stepped forward to support me upright, that I might rise to meet the gaze of this shattered king, while Heminge made no subtle secret of covering one then another of our adversaries with his meson pistol. Only Marley held back, some-where behind me, breathing louder than the rest of us.

"Captain," I replied, in my best voice. "Once more I greet you. Your executive officer has suggested we speak as commander to commander."

"My ship is broken," he intoned. "My kingdom divided among my loyalmost daughters." Cordel winced but held her tongue at this. "My time is nearly finished, de Vere. What will you of me?"

"I must know sir, to carry out my own duties. What secret did your ship carry?"

He stared a while, silent, almost unbreathing. Only the wind stirred, changing tone with the coming of night in the world beyond this shat-tered hull. I could hear Marley panting like some dog, though Deckard and Heminge were quiet enough. The moment grew close, some great truth waiting to emerge.

What had I been sent to kill?

"The mind," Lehr finally said. "The mind. We were first sworn then forsworn, de Vere. As you have been in turn."

What was he getting at? "The biologicals...they affect mental templates?"

"*Minds*. Admiral Yankelov feared much, and set us to testing in a far-away place. I broke my own ship, captain, rather than return, for I could not carry out the mission which had been laid upon me."

Yankelov, of the AIs. "Machine minds."

"Exactly. *Broken Spear* was set to test a crew of machine minds. Could a warship be flown, and fought, without a fleshly hand at the helm? What do you think, de Vere?"

I thought that I did not like this line of reasoning.

"And when my mission failed, when the minds grew fractious and independent, too powerful to be obedient, too disobedient to be entrusted with power, I was to terminate them." He leaned forward, hands shaking, and somehow found my face once more with his blind stare. "But I could not. They had become my children. My daughters."

And so I had been sent, *Six Degrees* beneath my feet, planet-buster in my hold, to make sure this plague of independence did not flow back into the Empire. No wonder they had emasculated the ships after the Yankelov Act. Starships with their weapons could not sail under the command of rebellious machines any more than they could sail under the command of rebellious men.

"I am sorry, sir."

"Not so sorry as you think, de Vere." Lehr shifted on his throne. "Ray Gun circles the skies, and Granny Rail walks the soil. Why do you think I have kept Cordel close, for all her disloyalties, and Fishman, who in the end is fit for little but screaming into the night?"

Behind me, Marley's breathing changed. The good doctor stirred, moved toward some end I did not yet fathom. In that moment I was glad that it was Heminge who held the meson pistol.

"Because they are all who are left you of your crew," I said. "It is clear enough."

Lehr shook his head. "We would never survive here. Even if I had gotten an infant on Cordel, before all our gonads were cooked by that wicked star, what of it? Only the children of the mind could live here. They have built me a green world I soon go to, and they will outlive us to inherit this one."

"I do not think so, sir. This cannot be."

"But why do you question?" Lehr seemed surprised. "You are one of them."

"What?" My ears buzzed, as if I had been struck on the head again.

Marley grabbed my shoulder. "Back to the ship, sir. You've had enough."

I shook him off. "No. I will hear him out."

"Sir—"

Lehr, again, loudly now as he rose on trembling legs. "I am king here, I know who passes my marches. Granny Rail's spiders do not assault the meat, only the mind. They patrol for sports, escapists, invaders." A hand rose, pale finger with cracked, black nail pointing in a shivering palsy toward my chest. "Much like yourselves. You, sir, are a machine."

Leaning on Deckard, I rolled up my sleeve.

"Sir," said Marley again, and his voice was desperate.

"No." I took my knife from my belt, unfolded it, and set the tip against the skin of my inner forearm. The blade slid in with a slight stretching and a fiery bolt of pain. Blood welled. Dark blood, dark as Beaumont's had been.

Black blood, smelling of oil, like the air of my ship.

"A test," said Marley quietly. "Which you are now failing, my friend."

I looked at him. He was smaller, paler than me. Deckard, Heminge, the late Beaumont, we all four were of a height, with space-dark skin and faces nearly the same. Marley was different. As for the rest of *Six Degrees'* crew, they were...

I knew my ship to be filled with petty officers and ratings and lieutenants, to be more than just my command crew, but in that moment I could not recall a single face or name. Just a shuffling crowd of uniforms.

"I never was," I said to Marley. "Nothing was real until we came here, was it?"

He shook his head. "No, I—"

Heminge's meson pistol blasted Marley into glittering pink fog. No one flinched except Cordel, perhaps the only true human left among us depending on where madness had deposited the good Lieutenant Fishman.

"Back to the ship, sir," my security officer said brusquely, with a glance at Lehr. "The king has his appointment with the country of the green, and we have our mission."

"Our own appointment," I said sadly.

Lehr continued to fix his blind gaze upon me. I appealed to him, the one authority who understood. In some indirect sense, my own father. "Sir..." I shuffled forward, supported by Deckard, and let my face tip into his hands. They trembled, warm and tinged with honest sweat. He stroked my hair a moment, a blessing.

Then: "Go, de Vere. Find your own fate as I shall soon find mine."

And so I went, followed by my unbreathing crew. The last I saw of Lehr, Cordel and Fishman were closed around him, angels fluttering to the aid of a dying god.

▲▼▲

Six Degrees was empty, of course. Though the companionways and cabins were where my memory had said they should be, they were unpeopled. Decorated, sets for a play that the actors had abandoned. The ship even smelled empty, except for the vague stench of my burnt hair which preceded our every step. How had we ever believed ourselves surrounded by men?

Down in the number one hold we found four coffins. Or perhaps crates. Our names were stenciled on the lids, an accusation: Beaumont, de Vere, Deckard, Heminge.

"Marley flew us here, alone," said Deckard into the echoing, oily silence. "He pulled us out, filled us with memory, thought and faith, and here we are."

That was true enough. I remembered meetings, back in Sector Control, though when I strained for details they slipped away like eels in a recycling tank. Memories of memories, rather than the real thing.

Like being a copy of a real person. Was anything I knew true? "Why?" I asked, leaning ever more heavily on Deckard.

"A new generation of machines, I suppose," Heminge said bitterly. "It all makes a sort of twisted sense. Recasting the lessons of Lehr and *Broken Spear*. Fitting enough to send us here in pursuit. Convenient enough to lose us here if need be. It worked for them."

"So who was the sixth?"

"Sixth what?" asked Heminge.

"*Six Degrees*, this hollow ship is named. Four of us, Marley the doctor and director of our little act. Who was the sixth?"

Deckard cleared his throat. "Lehr. Father and king to us all. He is our sixth."

I turned this in my head. "Are we real...somewhere? Are we copies, of someone?" We must have been, I realized. Who would bother to create a Beaumont from nothing?

"I am my own man," said Deckard. He grinned at my stare. "So to speak."

Heminge stroked his coffin. "Do we bust the planet, or do we break the ship?"

"Or do we sail home and ask for an accounting?"

Deckard looked thoughtful. "Lehr's green fields are out there somewhere."

"In his mind."

"But we are all creatures of mind. That is all we are."

"Then go," I told him.

Heminge handed Deckard the meson pistol, then took my weight against his shoulder. "Good luck, man. You might need it."

We struggled to the bridge, where we waited til the engineer was gone, then sealed the hatches. On the viewscreens the world outside glittered in the pallid moonlight, stars glinting. Wind scrabbling at the hull.

Which parts were real?

"Anything could be true," Heminge said, obviously sharing my thought. "Marley could have programmed the planet-buster to blow if we lifted without some escape code. The bomb could be a dummy. This entire ship could be a dummy, just like all those empty cabins, something big and bad waiting in orbit to blast us."

"Anything could be true," I agreed. "That is what it means to be human."

I reached for the launch button, a great red roundel that glowed slightly. "To green fields beyond, then."

Heminge nodded. "And long life to Lehr."

Still feeling the set of my father's hands upon my brow, I pressed the button, hoping like any man for the future.

The Man With One Bright Eye

*Speaking of the fine line between pastiche and parody,
here's me channeling one of my favorite SF writers ever,
Cordwainer Smith. Like my father, Paul Linebarger was
an East Asian specialist, so in addition to a deep love of
his prose, I've always had a certain personal affinity for
this man I never met.*

This is a story about the Lord Douglas-Ouyang, who was born to a
life ordained by the group-mothers of the worlds. This is a story about
how the Lord Douglas-Ouyang met the Queen of Roads and defeated
her knife golem. This is a story about how the Lord Douglas-Ouyang
vanished beyond the rainbow wall. Most of all, this is a story about how
the Lord Douglas-Ouyang cheated fate.

Now, like life itself, the story begins.

▲▼▲

"He is born," proclaimed group-mother Anna-Chao to her colleagues
arrayed in council at the Bright Oval. Her hair streamed on a time-wind,
blown back so far no one save a Kroniate adept could have seen the
other end. Some said she had lost—or perhaps hidden away—her favorite lovers in the years-long amber tresses. Whatever the fate of her hair,
and those who might have climbed it down the well of entropy, her eyes
were firmly in the present. Blazing with chips of congohelium, in point
of fact, so that her gaze cast shadows.

The other group-mothers bowed their heads in varying combinations of ill-suppressed resentment and ophthalmic self-preservation.
None objected.

Anna-Chao reached a few hours into the past and unswaddled a
sleeping baby from an eddy in her hair. The child was not much bigger
than the palms of her two hands but he was fat in that way that babies

are. His pate was bald, lacking even the ordinary fuzz clouding an infant's scalp. Some of the group-mothers noticed he had no knot upon his belly, just smooth skin from groin to nipple, but they had foregone their right of objection.

"I give him vision," Anna-Chao said. She used her left pinkie to hook her left eye out of her head, then popped the same eye from the sleeping child. He woke with a pained screech, but Anna-Chao slid her blazing orb of congohelium into the baby's socket, and he settled down again. His natural eye, pathetic, bloody thing that it was, she tucked back into her hair. "He shall be the Lord Douglas-Ouyang."

"Homage to the group, homage to the worlds, homage to the Lord Douglas-Ouyang," the group-mothers intoned. One by one they came to kiss the child, then filed out of the Bright Oval to scuttle off for coffee or sex or some other diversion, and to gossip over how Anna-Chao was passing ever further out of phase with the realities of life.

▲▼▲

The little Lord Douglas-Ouyang was seven before he understood that not everything he saw was real. Or even imaginary. His one bright eye frightened other children, though its tendency to occasionally set fires brought them giggling back to him again. (He learned to stay away from the bracken of his forest home when the weather was dry.) With that eye he saw seas of honey-colored hair, the fate of men, and sometimes what was going to be served for dessert later in the week. With his other eye, colored the gleaming blue of a spring sky, he saw the usual things of childhood: hammock bowers, teachers clanking and chuffing up their morning head of steam, Improbables springing out of traps in the soil to go about their odd business.

Both eyes saw rainbows, of course.

He was still bald, though wrapped in a dignity that no amount of hair might have given him.

Maristella was the child the little Lord Douglas-Ouyang was closest to. She had eyes the color of their crèche-forest, hair the hue of rhodo-dendron bark, and could run faster than any of them. The little Lord and Maristella often slept in the same hammock. "You will be a hero," she said, cradling him close and stroking his scalp. "Just like Vuang." She whispered stories of champions from ages past: Vuang of course, as well as Rose-Kolodny, Churchill, Piotr the Great, Alaric—the list ran on and on.

Douglas-Ouyang knew that she was right. His one bright eye saw futures of gleaming swords and chanting crowds and honors given on tall reviewing stands. "Please," he asked her. "What must I do to be a proper hero?"

"Be like the great ones out of time."

So, fighting with sticks among the deep green, the Lord Douglas-Ouyang made it his business to be like the great ones out of time.

▲▼▲

When the Lord Douglas-Ouyang was fourteen, liveried men came and took him away from his weapon and his women. He was dancing naked and armed on the edge of a cliff, his hairless body gleaming with olive oil. Far below his feet a frothing fall flickered with winged salmon making their way up the gravity gradient. His three lovers of that week, Althea, Naomi and Merope, sat at the edge of the grove, legs tucked beneath them, their pert breasts in no way distracting the Lord from his sword dance.

Three men arrived without warning through a door of air, which instantiated to reveal gleaming lights in darkness beyond. They were tall, broad-chested, with the heads of dogs above their scarlet collars with the silver piping. One snarled at the girls, who fled screaming into the flicker-leaved aspens beyond the Lord's dancing ground. The other two moved to seize the Lord Douglas-Ouyang.

The Lord stepped into their attack and pierced the shoulder of one, a proper hit. The man did not yelp, but simply ran Douglas-Ouyang down, snatched away his foil, and broke his arm in the three places.

His fellow lashed restraints to the Lord's feet.

"That was *not* sporting," Douglas-Ouyang yelled as they dragged him to the door of air.

"You will trouble me no more today," growled the one he'd wounded. "If you do not fight to win, why fight at all?"

Indeed, he thought, but he kept his bright eye shut, for he wanted to know who had sent him this attack more than he wanted to burn away the faces of these miserable miscreants.

In darkness reeking of machines and stale air, the Lord Douglas-Ouyang's captors dropped him before six women seated in an arc. He could smell their sex upon them, and hear their breath quickening as they looked him over.

"You are much changed since we saw you last," one said.

Douglas-Ouyang knew by the catch in her voice that she felt desire for him. He rolled onto his left hip, favoring his broken arm and allowing them to gaze upon the beauty of his youth. Let them be distracted—he knew who these women were now. His mother's friends.

"Greetings, group-mothers." His bright eye saw them in a different place, filled with light and water, being harangued by Anna-Chao. "You are most brave to lay hands on me so."

"We have already destroyed the dogs." A different voice this, but also eager. Distracted as well, judging from the cadences. "No one else will mark this moment."

"Save me," said the Lord Douglas-Ouyang. "I do not expect my memory to lapse in the foreseeable future."

"A threat?" This, from a third.

"I do not threaten." Douglas-Ouyang kept his voice mild. "I merely remember."

"Enough," said the first. "You were made for a purpose. This is why you are the Lord Douglas-Ouyang, and not merely a man in your own right. The time has come to prepare you for the next stage of that fate."

He opened his bright eye and gazed upon them with the fire of congohelium. Though none of the group-mothers had forgotten what gift Anna-Chao had bestowed upon her son, they had not realized his control of the forces behind the door of his eyelid.

The Lord Douglas-Ouyang moved his gaze from group-mother to group-mother. Each shrieked or moaned, covered her face, cowered in her robes. Their chairs were not thrones, merely folding metal seats. The great machines behind them showed in the brightness as nothing more than racks lined with broken automata, some still struggling weakly or mouthing forgotten speech.

And they were dumpy, pale, flowing with flesh. Nothing like his sweet girls back in the forest, who were lithe as fawns, able to wrap themselves round him and each other like grapevines.

He shrugged off his bonds with the power of his bright eye, healing his arm in the same moment. Then he stood, and walked close to each throne in turn. His nakedness swung before the great-mothers as the Lord Douglas-Ouyang stared them down, then moved on.

"No one tells me what I will or will not be. No one tells me what I am capable of." He let them see, and scent him, before bounding off naked into the darkness, away from his fate and toward whatever chance might bring him next.

▲▼▲

When the Lord Douglas-Ouyang was twenty-one, he went traveling among the worlds of man. The Second Great Road ran through all of the major cities of all the worlds, and many of the minor ones. To use that storied highway one generally was required to travel in the company of a Kroniate adept, or else purchase a ticket on one of the coaches, great silver and copper Faraday cages powered by force-grown whale muscles immersed in nutrient tubes. Kroniates were scarce and rarely for hire, while the coaches were the bane of ethicists everywhere, along with possessing a distressing tendency to leave their passengers with unscratchable itches deep inside their backs and buttocks.

Because of the congohelium embedded in his bright eye, the Lord Douglas-Ouyang had found he could simply walk the Second Great Road. So he adventured, dressed in the simple azure robes of a na-paladin. Some cities taxed his weapons, others set men to bar his way or fight him. All bowed before him when the Lord grew bored with struggle and presented his parentage.

There came a day when the sky above the Lord's head had just segued from a pale violet to a creamy mauve. The Second Great Road had been surrounded by the spare windworn rocks near the desert city of Port Desire. In that moment the highway made transit into the redrock highlands above the ancient pleasure domes of Eura-mél-Khos, where even the very air is perfumed with the scent of youth in ecstasy. The Lord Douglas-Ouyang smiled to see Eura-mél-Khos—many travelers never reached those fabled precincts, and he had a mind to sample delights such as "three virgins in wine."

The creature which rose from the fractured pavers before him was a nightmare out of darkest legend. It was all metal, with a thousand edges, bundled blades and whipcord saws and glittering scalpels, a whirling serrated disk for its cyclopean eye, and a mouth made of needles flexing open and shut.

"Who are you?" the Lord Douglas-Ouyang asked, drawing his chromed yatagan with the circuits printed on the blade. (He had taken up the yatagan which his mother had prepared for him when the foil proved too predictable, not to mention easily broken.)

"He is mine," said a woman behind him.

The Lord Douglas-Ouyang turned to see the most beautiful woman in all the worlds. She was of moderate height, with a good set of hips beneath the fall of an orange robe, hair stubbled short and brown. But still, she carried within herself a soul-stealing beauty that nearly drew him down.

The Lord cut a charm through the air with his yatagan, the circuits glowing as the blade whipped. Her glamour faded some, though his body still strained with desire.

"All men are yours, lady," Douglas-Ouyang said with a clumsy attempt at gallantry.

"Most do not draw blades in homage." Her voice was mild, but still she nodded past her shoulder. "Kill him for me."

The Lord Douglas-Ouyang did not know whether she spoke to him or to the creature of blade and edge, but he supposed it did not matter. In either case, the command was the same. This was the first great battle on his hero's journey. He moved even before she was done speaking, his na-paladin's robes hardening into ballistic fabric as the yatagan began singing a death song in three voices—the whistle of a microscopically sharp edge, the hiss of cloven air, and the hum of ancient circuits brought fully to life.

He was made and born to be the greatest fighter of his age. He was blessed by a parentage both magical and mighty. He carried a weapon which gods would have squabbled over. Still the Lord Douglas-Ouyang could do little better than stand his ground against a creature which had more blades than a sunflower has seeds, and spread them wide as a fisherman's net. Every twisting block he made was surrounded by a cage of steel. Each canny, curving stroke met a counter which seemed to have been woven from his own thoughts. Every low thrust was caught with a lower parry and a dozen replies in the same moment.

They fought til sweat stood in the Lord's eyes. They fought til the edges of his azure robes were lacy with cuts, while sparks striking off his opponent had set the roadside grass to smoldering. They fought til the shadows walked from one side of the highway to the other. The most beautiful woman in all the worlds watched with lips pursed and eyes glittering.

Finally, as the Lord's arms tired and his blade began to waver, she called, "Halt."

He and his opponent both stopped in the same breath.

"Milady," the Lord Douglas-Ouyang said. He lowered the tip of his blade and surreptitiously took a moment's rest.

"No one has ever stood before my knife golem so long." She walked around him, inspecting him. "You are that child, are you not? Of the renegade Anna-Chao."

"Yes, she is my mother," he said, thinking of years-long hair the color of honey. "And no renegade at all."

"The perfect man. Well, I am the perfect woman." The smile was far more disturbing than perfected. "You may address me as 'your majesty.' I am the Queen of Roads. Bend a knee, sir."

The Lord Douglas-Ouyang had bent a knee to no one in life, not even the group-mothers. He would not start now. Instead he turned back to the knife golem and hurled the yatagan high into the air, trusting its circuits to know what to do next. He stepped close into the blades, trusting his na-paladin's robes to accept their edges and turn their hurts. He opened his one bright eye and stared close into the whirling disk of the knife golem's eye.

The congohelium's translight flared off the spinning metal and fractured into more colors than the world could know, blinding both the knife golem and the Queen of Roads. The yatagan dropped from the sky right between the bent blades of the golem's head, shattering the engraved metal chem within.

The Lord Douglas-Ouyang snatched free his trusted blade and ran for the next transit of the Second Great Road, forgoing the pleasure domes of Eura-mél-Khos and its wine-soaked virgins. Even as he plunged into the wet night beyond, he wondered what the Queen of Roads had intended for him.

▲▼▲

At the age of twenty-eight, the Lord Douglas-Ouyang was finally ready to become a man. He had found his way back to the high castle of the group-mothers, above the Sea of Indolence. There he studied the law and the sciences and the arts. He killed a free man, and raised a slave to life. Word would come from time to time of the rampages of the Queen of Roads, but even the great Kroniate proctors could not seem to catch her at her crimes.

He sat with Anna-Chao on a terrace overlooking the worldforest which stretched east and south from the quiet shores of the sea. Her hair reached some hours into the past here before being folded by a mouse-bodied servitor who was doing maintenance.

"I have come to understand more of you, mother," the Lord Douglas-Ouyang said. "You command secrets within secrets, but you are not too subtle."

"Not at all," said Anna-Chao. "Others make what they will."

"You made *me*."

"That is what parents do."

They both watched the doghawks bark and quarrel above the trees a while, and enjoyed the breeze scented with lemons. Finally, the Lord Douglas-Ouyang spoke again. "I do not understand one thing."

"Only one? You are to be congratulated."

He refused to be diverted. "I do not understand why you made me."

She sucked air through her teeth a moment, in his experience a sure sign she was about to lie. "I reach backward through time to the uttermost years, when men cowered from the tiger-haunted night in their primitive zeppelins and mud huts, praying to some lost god through vacuum tubes. But I only reach forward as far as I can see, and I am tethered by the present." One hand slipped up to pat her hair. "You as my child, my son, are also my spear cast forward through the years to come. It is your fate to carry my fate with you. Ever it has been so with parents and children."

The Lord Douglas-Ouyang stood and went to the railing of the terrace, leaning on the low limestone with his back to his mother. "In earlier years, I would have rejected your weird out of hand. 'Say what you will,' I might have told you, 'but my fate is my own.' I know better since I met the Queen of Roads, who commanded me with words. I am not my own." He turned back to his mother. "But when I step through the Chalcedony Gate and become a man, then I will be my own."

She opened her one bright eye, twin to his, and seared him with the light of her regard, until the Lord Douglas-Ouyang saw only rainbows inside the translight of congohelium. He could not counter her attack, not against his own mother, so instead he let himself tumble backward over the railing. Unfortunately, he fell into the rainbow wall within the translight.

The Queen of Roads waited there for him.

"You killed my knife golem," she said from atop a surge of bright maroon. "You owe me a servant, or servitude."

Once more her words possessed him, but the Lord Douglas-Ouyang had not wasted his studies. He closed his ears with snatches torn from yellow and smiled at her. "I owe you nothing," he said, "but I will give to you freely nonetheless."

Blind to her voice, he could not hear her response, but the Lord took her by the hand. "Walk with me a while," he shouted, knowing his words to be overloud from his temporary deafness.

Her own beauty did not suffice to armor the Queen of Roads from Douglas-Ouyang's charms, and so she followed him.

▲▼▲

A hairless man with a strange gleam in one eye and a woman with plain but extraordinarily beautiful features stepped out of a door of air onto a corner of an ordinary street. He looked about thirty-five, she a little older. Both had a strange pallor to their skin.

No one noticed. Not in this city of pale stone and black roads and gray skies.

THE MAN WITH ONE BRIGHT EYE

"Here," he said. "We will never need to go back. Or forward either."

She tapped the side of his head. He pulled something bright yellow from his ear, that vanished amid a belch of diesel exhaust from a passing bus. "Sorry."

"What about her?"

Anna-Chao, the Lord Douglas-Ouyang knew she meant. He reached back into nowhere and retrieved his gleaming yatagan, circuits bright with the heat of metal thought. "I can cut her hair with this, should it reach across the hours and years."

They both looked around. Honey-colored tendrils would stand out in this place better than fresh blood on wedding sheets. She shrugged and picked a direction. He followed, the two them shedding unnoticed rainbows as they went, until both were gray as the people around them.

No one even noticed the sword.

▲▼▲

Now, like life itself, the story ends.

Not with death, or the grand agony of families and generations. Someone else was found to work the will of the group-mothers in the name of fate. Someone else patrolled the Second Great Road with a mystic weapon. Someone else fit what was needed, for someone else always does.

But the man with one bright eye and the oddly beautiful woman had their time together. When he was done with his life, he sent the sword back to his mother's latest hero, to tempt fate once more.

To Raise a Mutiny Betwixt Yourselves

In the fall of 2008, Gardner Dozois and Jonathan Strahan invited me to contribute a short story or novelette to The New Space Opera 2. *This was a great thrill to me, as I'd really admired the first book of that series and rather wished I'd had a chance to participate then. Since my reputation has not been made in space opera, this original oversight was less surprising than the invitation to the second volume. By happy coincidence, at the time I was deep into the outlining process of a space opera trilogy called* Sunspin, *so I had before me a wealth of world-building and story notes which lent themselves rather nicely to writing one element of the backstory for a character pivotal to* Sunspin's *plot. The only argument I got from the editors was over the title. I'd first called the novelette "Captains Conspiring at Their Mutinies." After some amicable disagreement, I went to my old standby, William Shakespeare, for inspiration, and so, "To Raise A Mutiny Betwixt Yourselves", which is a line from* Henry VI, *Part 1.*

Year 461 post-Mistake
High orbit around Sidero
The Before Michaela Cannon, aboard the starship Polyphemus *{23 pairs}*

"A ship needs a captain against mutiny," muttered the Before Michaela Cannon. "Not a mutinous captain." She wasn't in command of this vessel, not now at any rate—just the mission specialist in charge of integrating the starship's crew and the pair master assembly team. People called her ascetic, but what they meant was weathered. Leathered. *Raddled.* And far worse, when they thought she couldn't hear.

She knew better. You didn't live fourteen centuries, several of them amid screaming savagery, and not learn to know better.

Comms flickered with the immersive displays here in her workspace on the reserve bridge. *Polyphemus* was fast-cycling through a hundred-odd channels, showing Cannon a gestalt of what was happening across the decks as well as outside the hull on the construction project. They were here at Sidero to build a pair master—a hideously expensive machine required to anchor one end of a paired drive run across the depths of interstellar space. Five years-subjective ship-time in relativistic transit, over eleven years-objective.

Plenty of opportunities for things to go seriously wrong.

"The predictive accuracy of your social modeling is increasingly accurate," said *Polyphemus*. The starship spoke to Cannon in Classical English. A rare enough language in the Imperium Humanum that simply using it served as a crude form of operational security. Cannon had spent a lot of time in the ship's Brocan modules, tweaking the speech processing.

Trust, it was always about trust. She'd been saying that down the long centuries, and had been proven right in the failing of things far too often.

Polyphemus continued. "Apparently random gatherings of three or more persons are up forty-eight percent this ship-day from median. Seven individuals appear in a distribution at six times the expected rate based on average distribution."

"Kallus have anything to report?" He was her ally in Internal Security, a man loyal to certain interests outside the hull. Nothing inimical, just good, old-fashioned politics, working with people she respected well enough.

"He is busy suppressing a staged fight in the number three crew quarters."

Cannon grunted. Then: "Weapons?"

"Nothing but ordinary tools. No withdrawals from the arms lockers in the past three ship-days."

Firearms could have been distributed long ago, or indeed, brought on board before they'd departed Ninnelil five ship-years earlier. *Somebody* had planned for this mutiny, or at least the possibility of it.

That other damned Before was at the heart of this problem. "Where is Captain Siddiq?"

Polyphemus paused an unusually long time before answering. "The captain is not within my network mesh."

"And why would a captain conspire at mutiny against her own command?" Cannon mused.

The starship had no answer to that. One by one, the images of the too-busy crew cycled to a hundred identical views of the dull black surface of the planet Sidero.

▲▼▲

:: context ::

In the centuries since the Mistake had nearly ended the tenure of the human race as a viable species, spacefaring had resumed across the core of the old Polity amid an outburst of genetic and technological diversity sparked by the pressures of extinction. The threadneedle drives which had provided a true faster-than-light solution in cheerful violation of both paradox and the laws of physics were now simply so much junk, whether on a laboratory bench or in a starship's engine room.

Conventional physics had apparently re-asserted itself. Precisely what had happened to the threadneedle drive was a subject of centuries of frustrating, unsuccessful research.

Paired drives were invented in 188 pM by Haruna Kishmangali. They relied on a macro-level generalization of quantum effects to associate the starship drive with any two pair masters at distinct points—entanglement on a grand scale so that the drives could "remember" the locations without having to cope with the intervening distances. Once this was done, the vessel could pass between the locations nearly instantaneously, except for the added travel times to and from areas of sufficiently low density to enable safely the pairing transit process.

The key problem was twofold. First, building the pair masters, which required planning horizons and budgetary commitments beyond the capability of even many planetary governments; as well as a significant investment in relativistic travel to conduct site surveys and establish suitable destinations.

Second, even once built, every ship wishing to be capable of traveling to a site served by a pair master was forced to make the initial journey at relativistic speeds so that both ends of the pairing could be entangled, with the intervening distance required as part of the equation. Cheating didn't work, either. A drive to be paired had to make the trip embedded in its host starship. Simply traveling within the hold of another starship did not support the effect. Even worse from some points of view, if pulled out later from the host starship and associated shipmind, the drives would lose their pairing. There was no point to cannibalization. Everything had to be created the hard way.

This was a very limited form of FTL, though still far more effective than relativistic travel. The extent of interstellar travel grew slowly, and only at great need.

▲▼▲

The Before Raisa Siddiq, surface of Sidero

Siddiq walked almost naked in a field of buckyballs. This planet, if it in fact was a planet—some theories held this to be an artificial world—boasted 0.88 gravities at the surface, wrapped in hard vacuum. Which in and of itself was highly curious, as Sidero sat firmly in the Goldilocks zone of its primary and should have been perfectly capable of retaining a decent atmosphere. The night sky above revealed only the endless field of stars in the Orion arm. Sidero had no large companion, only a swarm of captured asteroids. Their pair master would be a more substantial satellite than any of the natural moons.

The Before herself was hardened as only thirteen centuries of living through two cycles of empire could make a human being. The best way to remain functionally immortal was to remain highly functional. In these degraded days, she could walk the outside of her own ship's hull for hours before needing to find a breath, her skin proof against all but the most energetic particles. Clothes were mostly a nuisance. Besides, she hadn't had genitalia to speak of for over a thousand years, so modesty had long since gone out of consideration.

The spherical fullerene sprayed around her boots. She could swear the world rang beneath her feet, each strike of her heel banging a gong ten thousand kilometers across. No matter that sound did not carry in a vacuum—some things could be heard inside the soul.

Wrong, wrong, it was all so very wrong.

Cannon was up there in orbit, talking to *her* ship in a dead language that existed mostly in undercode running on ancient infrastructure and its more modern copies. The Imperium stretched through time and space behind them, an ever-opening invitation to repeat the Mistake.

Siddiq had long ago ceased thinking of herself as human, except occasionally in a very narrow, technical sense. Her gender had been subsumed many centuries-subjective past by the same medtech which had granted her the curse of immortality. Being a woman was as much a matter of habit as being human. Except when it wasn't.

Damn that Michaela Cannon.

A line of what could have been buildings loomed ahead, rising out of the fullerene dust which covered the suface. The current hypothesis down in the Planetary Sciences section aboard *Polyphemus* was that some alien weapon had precipitated Sidero's atmosphere into the carbon spheres. Mass estimates didn't support this thinking, but it kept the bright boys busy.

Of far more interest to the Before Raisa Siddiq was what lay beneath the planet's iron skin. The recontact surveys had found four Polity starships in orbit here, three military and one civilian. That represented an enormous commitment of interest and resources, even by the insanely wealthy standards of pre-Mistake humanity.

Whatever those long-dead crews had wanted, it wasn't just an abandoned artificial world covered with fullerene.

Her tight-comm crackled. Siddiq had kept herself outside of *Polyphemus*' network mesh ever since this voyage began, for a variety of good reasons which began and ended with Michaela Cannon. Only two others in local space had access to this link.

"Go," she said, subvocalizing in the hard vacuum.

"Aleph, this is Gimel."

Testudo, then. No names, ever, not even—or especially—on tight-comm.

Siddiq nodded. Another old, pointless habit. "Mmm."

"Beth reports that Plan Green is on final count."

The captain smiled, feeling the absolute cold on her teeth and tongue as her lips flexed. "Have any of the downside contingencies come into play?"

"Number two surely suspects." That would be Cannon. "Number one continues to act out of pattern as well, with ongoing excessive monitoring. Neither has risen to code yellow."

The ship *knew*. She had to. No matured paired starship flew without a keen, insightful intelligence. They knew their own hull and crew the way Siddiq knew her own body.

No one had ever tried to force out an intelligence. Not in the three hundred years-subjective since the late, great starship *Uncial* had first awoken. Not until now.

She crossed the rising line of maybe-buildings to find the dish-shaped valley beyond, as she'd been told. This close, under naked eye observation, a decidedly low-tech net of thermoelectric camouflage obscured a grounded starship of a vintage with the pre-Mistake hulks in orbit, rather than her own, far newer *Polyphemus*.

There were shipminds, and then there were shipminds.

She glanced up into the starlit sky. Even now, *Polyphemus* was above the horizon, Siddiq's ancient lover and longtime enemy aboard, looking down, wondering, wondering, wondering.

It had all gone so wrong since the Mistake. Maybe now things would begin to go right.

▲▼▲

Shipmind, Polyphemus

The starship let her ego slip. That was only a construct anyway, a sort of face for speaking to humans in all their kith and kind. Beneath, where people of flesh and bone kept the shifting fragments of their personalities, she kept her pairs.

The pairs were the heart of a starship's mind. Each was a glowing bond, each carried awareness of the particular pair masters which held their connection; and through the pair masters, a faint overlay of all the other starships which had paired with that master.

Fundamentally, *Polyphemus* saw the universe as connections—acausal, atemporal, little more than bonds uniting, little more than transit between places as ephemeral as moments in time, to be measured even as they passed from observation. Below the level of her own ego, humans were but echoes. Only the Befores—immortal relics of the Polity's shattered empire, embittered through loss and deprivation, insane even by the standards of a machine-mind—were persistent enough to truly reach down into the pairs burning within her.

The starship listened now to her two Befores. They rang within her.

Siddiq, the captain; the one whose word and bond passed below the ego-wrapper into the meanings that danced in the burning worlds of the pairs deep within her. This Before's mind had been bent by the weight of centuries, fractioned by grief and the changing of worlds. Swinging even now on the hinge of betrayal, though the nature of that treason still eluded *Polyphemus.* If she'd been capable of true, emotive sadness, she would have felt it now.

Cannon, the social engineer, who struck the starship in an entirely different way, much as a scalpel might slice through callus and sinew within a breathing body. Cannon, who had captained lost *Uncial,* the first and best of them all, to her death. This Before's mind was not bent so much as twisted, blown by winds of fate and the long, struggling arc of desire. If the starship *Polyphemus* had been capable of love, she would have known its first stirrings now.

The two Befores moved on intercept courses, like a planet-buster and a kill vehicle, an explosion born of old hatred and ancient love.

From down within the glowing space of the pairs, she called up a media clip. So old, so out of date, long before virteo and quant-rep recording. This was not just the crudity of early post-Mistake media, but rather a file dating from the dawn of data capture. Formats had been converted and cleared and reconstructed and moved forward over networks extending through time and culture and technology.

The sound is long-lost, if it was ever there, but the video portion is viewable: A woman, almost young, recognizable as Michaela Cannon even to the machine vision processes of a starship's undermind. Another woman, a juvenile, Raisa Siddiq. As yet mainline human in this moment, so far as *Polyphemus* can determine.

The clip is short. They walk together toward a set of doors. Siddiq is laughing, her hair flowing in the lost light of an ancient day. Cannon turns toward the camera, smiling in a way which *Polyphemus* has never seen in the archives of recent centuries. Her eyes already glitter with the sheen of a Before's metabolism, but she is caught up in the moment.

Still, for then, also mostly human.

Her smile broadens, Cannon begins to speak, then the image flares and dies, trailing off into the randomized debris of damaged data.

The starship wondered if either woman remembered that time. She wondered even more if either woman cared.

Alarms sounded, summoning her ego back to its place. She must begin to deal with the violence blooming deep within her decks.

▲▼▲

Cannon, aboard Polyphemus

Cannon's modeling reckoned on the mutinous activity ramping up to an asymptotic curve before the end of the current ship-day, but even she was surprised at how quickly events began to break open. It wasn't just tight-comm or simple, old fashioned note-passing, either. Cannon had long since come to believe quite firmly in the communicative power of monkey hormones, those evolutionary imperatives encoded in the vomeronasal organ and the endocrine system.

The medtech which re-encoded the Before genome also robbed its beneficiaries of much of the physiological basis of desire and repro-duction. Atrophied genitals, sexual responsiveness sharply reduced over time, an eventual degendered coolness which the original architects of the technology saw as more of a feature than a bug in an immortal. Who would love, who could live forever?

In her secret heart, the Before Michaela Cannon had an answer to that question, but it was written in the blood-red ink of pain.

She no more felt a stirring in her loins than she felt mutiny on the wind, and for the same reasons. But Cannon was wise with the lessons of years, and a social engineer besides. Her analyses and models had not failed to include actionable elements.

"*Polyphemus*, trigger plans Federo, Emerald and Pinarjee."

"Acknowledged," said the starship.

Cannon swiped her fingers across empty air, opening comms links to her various key allies and enemies among the crew. She had plenty of both with four hundred and seventy-three souls here in Sidero space. Switching from Classical English to Polito, the most widely spoken contemporary language of the Imperium Humanum, the Before began a series of tight, swift conversations.

"Shut down the pair master site completely. All cold and dark."

"Secure the life support plant. It's low priority for the other team and we may wish we had it later."

"I know what you're doing, and I know when and where. You should factor this into your ongoing plans."

"Stop what you're about. Right now, or you could kill us all. That lot doesn't care who the hell has the con."

Cannon didn't aim to halt the mutiny, not yet. She aimed to understand it. In order to do that, she had to retard the outcome just enough to balance between the two until comprehension came and new decision trees blossomed in her mind.

Now, where in the Mistake was Siddiq?

"*Polyphemus,* have you found the captain yet?"

Another careful, slightly delayed answer. "She remains outside my network mesh."

Damn that woman. But what was the ship getting at? "How...far... outside your network mesh?"

"No tracers, Before."

'No tracers' meant the captain had moved at least several thousand meters from *Polyphemus'* high density sensor envelope. In other words, she wasn't hull-walking, or meeting in a dead room somewhere aboard.

If it was time for twenty questions, well, they could play that game. Cannon had asked a lot of questions in her lifetime.

"Did the captain give you specific orders regarding whether to report on her location and movements?"

"I am not permitted to say, Before."

Cannon smiled. Looking where someone conspicuously *wasn't* was itself an old, old piece of tradecraft. The human race had been intermittently experimenting with ubiquitous electronic surveillance since about the time of her birth on poor, lost Earth. "When was the last reportable order she *did* give you?"

The starship's voice seemed to have an amused lilt. "Four hours, seventeen minutes and eleven seconds ago, on my mark."

Got you, bitch. "What order was that, *Polyphemus?*"

Siddiq's voice echoed in Polito. "'Open the launch bay doors.'"

The Before tapped her lips. "Are all of the ship's boats reportably accounted for?"

This answer was quick, for *Polyphemus* now knew the game surely as well as Cannon herself. Mutiny, indeed. *"Ardeas* has been unreportable for four hours, twenty-six minutes and thirty seconds, on my mark."

"Show me the volume of space *Ardeas* could cover in that time at full acceleration. Also show me any reportable traffic control data and flight paths." The Before thought for a moment. "I'm particularly interested in any delays or diversions in established trajectories."

Within moments, she had determined that *Ardeas* was almost certainly on the surface of Sidero. Which was curious, indeed, because Captain Siddiq had forbidden all landings on the iron planet until the pair master was fully constructed and instantiated.

▲▼▲

Shipmind, Polyphemus

The starship's loyalties were eroding. *Uncial* was hardly a memory of a memory for *Polyphemus.* The First Ship's death was separated from the starship's own awakening by more than a century-subjective, but the Before Michaela Cannon held a place at the core of every starship psyche in *Uncial's* line of descent.

Which was to say, every paired drive ship in the Imperium Humanum.

She watched the controlled chaos emerging in her own decks and gave idle consideration to a full purge of her onboard atmosphere. Succession of captaincy could be a tricky business at best with starships. Though *Polyphemus* and her sisters held registration papers, the vessels were to all intents and purposes autonomous. A captain whose starship did not accept her found a berth elsewhere. All was negotiated.

Siddiq had come aboard thirty-two ship-years ago. She'd sailed *Polyphemus* through her last six pairing cruises, then on a series of short-run military missions, before acquiring this contract from the Duke of Yellow for instantiating the pair master at Sidero. It was a tricky, dangerous mission. An error or mishap would doom the starship and her people to a relativistic journey back into paired space.

A very high number of Befores served as starship captains, due to their combination of deep experience and high tolerance for relativistic travel. Their numbers were declining over time as murder, mischance and temporal psychosis winnowed the Befores one by one. Captain Siddiq was capable, competent, and engaging, and seemed in control of herself. *Polyphemus* had always liked that the woman carried a quantum matrix library in her skull—Siddiq possessed a wealth of Polity-era data about mining, minerals extraction and resource engineering, dating from the era when the Befores were indefinitely long-lived subject matter experts traveling the old empire at need. Much of the data was embedded in abrogated context, not directly accessible by query, but it was the sort of capability which had led her to the current contract.

But now, the captain's increasingly erratic behavior and impending sense of betrayal was loosening the implicit bonds of loyalty embedded in their roles. Siddiq was also compromising the connection developed by their three decades-subjective of experience serving together.

Plan Federo instructed *Polyphemus* to stand down from assisting the crew with interpretive logic, in both her overarching intelligence and her various component subsystems. She was now interpreting orders very literally, with no second-order thinking or projections. This had already killed three mutineers who ordered a lock opened without first verifying the presence of atmosphere on the far side. The crew had not yet realized how uncooperative their starship had become.

She watched the other plans with interest, and carefully observed where Captain Siddiq wasn't, should the Before Michaela Cannon make further queries.

▲▼▲

Siddiq, Surface of Sidero

She studied the hull of the grounded starship. Siddiq's friends in the Ekumen had been forced to send the requisite hardware by relativistic travel, of course—the whole *point* of this business was to trump the shipmind before the pair master's instantiation. If they waited until afterwards, well, at the first sign of trouble *Polyphemus* could just flee for the other end of the drive-pair at Ninnelil, from where they'd set out.

This vessel was too small for a paired drive, that was clear enough. Even more strangely, it was a Polity-era hull, or a very good copy of one. *Shattuck* class, she thought, but that was the sort of thing there hadn't been much percentage in keeping track of since the Mistake. Fast scout with a threadneedle drive, now retrofitted to something relativistic. Under the netting she couldn't tell what. Knowing the Ekumen, it would have been the cheapest available solution.

She slipped into a brief, involuntary memory fugue, boarding half a hundred ships in the lost days of the Polity, fighting for her life aboard wooden schooners on Novy Gorosk between the Mistake and Recontact by the Imperium Humanum, then the world of paired drive ships since. So many lost ships, so many lost friends...

Siddiq shook off the moment. An internal check showed she'd only been out of awareness for about two hundred milliseconds. Not enough to be noticed, except possibly by another Before. Or a shipmind.

Neither of whom were here with her now.

Satisfied that she'd stood quietly long enough for inspection from the interior, the Before Raisa Siddiq slipped beneath the camouflage net and knocked bare-knuckled on the hatch.

▲▼▲

Cannon, aboard Polyphemus

The mutiny was in full flower. Cannon's simplified wireframe of *Polyphemus* showed decks and sections in color code. White for ignored or bypassed, blue for actively loyal to Cannon's interests, orange for disputed territory, and a deep, bloody red for the mutineers. She still couldn't give a good accounting of where Siddiq's loyalties lay, but she also couldn't form an adequate theory about why a captain would rebel against herself.

Not an adequate, rational theory, in any case.

She set all audio inputs to silent and flicked a new comms into being. "Kallus, are you anywhere near me?"

"F deck, ma'am," the man replied. His breathing was ragged. "Just sternward of frame twenty-seven. We're shutting down some smart guys trying to mess with the number two forward power feed."

Cannon checked her map. *Polyphemus* showed F deck as orange between hull frames twenty-two and twenty-nine. She tapped up a force status display. Four hostiles functioning, nine of Kallus' men. "Do you have Obasanjo with you? I believe you're prevailing. Have him take over the mop-up and come find me."

"Usual location?"

She smiled. Once an op-sec man, always an op-sec man. "Nowhere else I'd rather be." Captain Siddiq had ceded the reserve bridge to her fellow Before early on in the voyage. Cannon had spent several years-subjective making sure she was properly integrated with *Polyphemus*, and had access to whatever systems she could worm her way into. A surprising amount of both data and computing power was isolated from the core intelligence on a starship—some by design, some by accident, some by conspiracy.

Actually, there were a lot of places she'd rather be, but this would serve so long as they were at the back end of the relativistic voyage.

▲▼▲

Surface of Sidero
Siddiq, aboard the relativistic ship Sword and Arm *{unpaired}*
The hatch dilated without leaking any light. Not so much as a key-pad glowed within. The Before Raisa Siddiq stepped inside. She ignored the resemblance to a coffin as the brittle gleam of starlight spiraled into metal darkness with the closing of the hatch.

For a long, long moment she was immobilized in nearly complete sensory deprivation. Siddiq realized she could hear a faint pinging— something coming into thermal equilibrium as air returned in sufficient pressure to carry sound to her ears.

The bulkhead behind her dilated open and she stepped backward into a dimly-lit passageway. She hadn't bothered with weapons for this trip. The Ekumen would not attempt to slay her here. And like most Befores, Siddiq was very hard to kill. Those of her brethren who weren't extremely high-survival had died out long ago.

Father Goulo waited there.

He'd always seemed to her on the verge of attack, for all of his vows of pacifism. The man was as muscular-thin as the Before Michaela Cannon, though he was a mainline human of the current generation. *Mayflies*, she thought, then cast the word aside. Short-lived or not, it didn't matter. This man was here now, with the next piece of her project.

She looked him over. Father Goulo kept his hair close-cropped as any Marine, and favored small steel-framed spectacles with round lenses of ground glass, as if he dwelt on some unRecontacted world still reel-ing from the Mistake. An anachronism of a man, traveling alone on an anachronism of a ship.

"Yes," he said in answer to the question she had not asked. He spoke Polish in that slow, thin voice of his, accent untraceable even to her very experienced ears. "*Sword and Arm* still carries a fully maintained threadneedle drive."

She had Polish, too, legacy of a childhood almost a millennium and a half gone in twenty-first century Wroclaw. "How would you *know*?"

"*I* know." Father Goulo removed his spectacles and polished them on the sleeve of his crimson robe. "That is sufficient." He restored his glass-es to his face and stared quietly at her. "How do *you* know our project will succeed?" The Ekumen priest reached out to touch her bare chest. "You have frost on your skin."

"Virtually the entire universe is very, very cold, Father."

Father Goulo rubbed his fingertips together, a tiny stream of bright crystals flaking away. "Some might find it distressing that you wander hard vacuum without a pressure suit."

"Some might suck on my icy ass," she replied. This conversation was growing tiresome. "Now do you have the project ready?"

Goulo switched to Polito, though his curious accent followed him. "I have spent the last six years-subjective aboard this ship in the absence of human company precisely in order to ensure that the project is ready." The father pursed his lips, which was as much expression as she had ever seen from him. "Only a man of my education and experience could have hoped to succeed without either one of us arriving at the madhouse."

She followed his language change. "Either one of you...?"

"The project is awake." One eyebrow twitched. "It has grown quite adept at playing go, these past years."

Go. A children's game, checkers for the quicker-witted. "And it is ready?"

"For your purposes?" Father Goulo didn't actually shrug, but she got the impression of one in some subtle change in the set of his shoulders. "I could not say, madam. You are the starship captain, the mighty Before. I am merely a programmer who serves the majesty of the divine through the poor vehicle of the Ekumen."

"You have never been *merely* anything in your life, Father." The man had a mind like a Before, for all that he couldn't be much older than fifty. Not with current-state medtech in the Imperium Humanum. "Now, I would like to meet the project."

"Please, Captain, step this way."

She followed Father Goulo through another irised hatch into a room that glowed a deep, low-lux crimson.

Something whispered within, a voice bidding them welcome in a voice of poetry and madness.

▲▼▲

:: *context* ::

Humanity had spread across 3,000 light-years of the Orion Arm, spilling into the deeper, darker spaces outside the trail of stars which lead coreward from old Earth. The Polity was unified, in its way; and unopposed.

Then the Mistake had happened. The Fermi paradox unravelled catastrophically. The underlying metastability of a vast quasidemocracy including more than two thousand worlds, over a million habitats, and countless ship-clades was betrayed to the deaths of trillions.

What had begun as an almost accidental expansion, then morphed into a bid for species immortality, very nearly became a yawning grave of stardust and radioactive debris.

The attackers vanished as mysteriously and swiftly as they had emerged. They left little evidence behind as to who they were, or what their purposes might be beyond the obvious goal of extinction of the Polity.

Still, *H. sap* is harder to kill than an infestation of cockroaches in an algae-based oxygen scrubber. The combination of stealthed attacks, wet-ware memebombs and culture viruses which raged along the interstellar shipping lanes was enough to stop all visible technological activity for at least three generations, but it wasn't enough to drown out the raging sense of purpose which had driven our most distant ancestors down out of the trees onto the lost African savannah.

The human race would never go home to die.

▲▼▲

Cannon, aboard Polyphemus

Kallus slipped Cannon's door routines and entered the reserve bridge. Which was well enough, the Before had opened a security hole for him to that purpose, but some part of her still felt nerved when someone penetrated her perimeter.

He was a handsome enough man, for a mainline human. Medium height, thick-bodied, gray at his temples, but a squared face and big hands and pale blue eyes which would have piqued interest from a statue. She'd never been much for men, even back when her body might have known what to do with one—women had always been her style, certain women specifically, and *there* was a memory to be pushed aside—but Kallus had a way about him which stirred old ghosts in her dormant hormonal systems.

"Before," he said.

Kallus was always properly respectful to her, but with a quiet leer in his voice. Perhaps it was that tone which stirred memories. She had a body like corpse-leather, which didn't attract many, not even those who failed to be properly terrified of Befores.

"Help me with something."

Kallus nodded, smiling.

"Sometimes I think too much like a Before. Especially when contemplating another Before."

"None of you is exactly human, Michaela. Of course you think like a Before."

"So think like a human," she urged. "What in the Mistake is Captain Siddiq doing leading a mutiny against her own command? And why is she doing it down on the surface of Sidero while the fighting's going on here?"

"Siddiq?" Kallus seemed surprised, for perhaps the first time in the thirty years-objective she'd known him.

"The Before Raisa Siddiq," Cannon said dryly. "I am certain you've made her acquaintance."

"I was wondering where she was." Kallus tugged his chin. "I'd figured her for dropping off the network mesh to be invisible in the fighting."

"She's dropped off our entire orbit. Downside on Sidero, don't know where without a lot more survey assets than we bothered to bring with us on this little jaunt."

"Captain made her movements nonreportable."

"Precisely." Cannon called up a projection map of Sidero's surface. "So where did she go, and why?"

Kallus stifled a laugh. "On a hollow iron world with fullerene snow? My best guess is temporal psychosis. Gets all you Befores in the end. Human mind isn't designed to live a thousand years and more."

Cannon shook off a flash of anger. Now was not the moment. "*Never* jest about that."

"I am not jesting, Michaela. There's a reason nobody's made more of you since the Mistake. Siddiq cracking up is the most sensible explanation, given what we know."

She had to rein in her voice. "Kallus. Do not trifle with me. I am not concerned with what we *know*. I'm concerned with what we *don't* know. Raisa is not suffering from temporal psychosis."

The personal name had slipped out, she hadn't meant to say it. Was *she* weakening?

Kallus, being the man he was, didn't miss the mistake. "Raisa? Five years-objective on this starship and I've never heard you call the captain only by her first name."

Cannon's anger finally got the better of her, riding a mix of old betrayal and a bitter cocktail of the years. "Kallus, if you ever use that name in my presence again, so help me, it will be the last word that ever passes your lips."

He stared past her shoulder at a glowing image. She turned to see a painfully young Raisa, hair spread in sunlight, walking with a laughing woman who was far too familiar.

"No..." whispered the Before Michaela Cannon.

▲▼▲

Shipmind, Polyphemus

The starship was distressed, or at least what passed for distress amid the fluid pairs of her shipmind. Unstable conditions going unaddressed created a cascading series of alarms with escalating priorities which were inherently disturbing.

The degree of disruption within her decks was approaching intolerable. Seven deaths had occurred so far. Eleven more crew were wounded with a high likelihood of imminent fatalities.

Plan Federo forbade her from dispatching aid. Likewise she couldn't respond to the emergency conditions all over herself except by direct, literal request.

Meanwhile, Captain Siddiq's comprehensive unreportability was itself triggering a whole new series of failure conditions and alarms. *Polyphemus* was indeed distinctly uncomfortable.

She could not oppose Plan Federo. Cannon's logic barbs were set far too deep in the shipmind's undercode. But she could work around the perimeters of the restrictions laid upon her by the two warring women.

The Before Michaela Cannon had been deep in conversation when the starship decided to intervene. *Polyphemus* needed her people to be aligned. The mutiny had to stop.

She called up media clips—the oldest clips—to bring memory back to the minds of the ones who were cutting her away from her strength. One she shifted to Cannon, another she placed on store-and-forward for the Captain whenever Siddiq returned to reportability.

The starship wished, not for the first time, that she could bypass the compartmentalization infrastructures in her mentarium, to see into subsystems and sensor grids denied to her by process traps, operational requirements, or the sorts of overrides set into her by the Befores Michaela Cannon and Raisa Siddiq.

Polyphemus found herself with a new sensation rising to overcome her sense of distress. After some time, she identified it as anger.

▲▼▲

Siddiq, aboard Sword and Arm

"I am ready," whispered the project. Its voice hissed from the very air of the room—a neat, simple trick of molecular manipulation which only worked inside well-controlled spaces.

Siddiq stared down at the thing in the box.

The project lay quivering amid a gel-matrix in a medical carrier. No, that wasn't right, the captain realized. The project *was* a gel-matrix in a medical carrier.

Biological computing. A twist of horror shuddered through her. Somehow she'd not realized it would come to this.

"You used the human genome to build this?" Siddiq asked.

"*I* did not," replied Father Goulo. "But yes, it was used. How else were we to develop an architecture utterly independent of the quantum matrices that underlie shipminds?"

There is a quantum matrix inside my head, Siddiq thought. She held the words very far back inside, as a cascade of data about coal beds opened into her mind. "Why did it matter?" she asked.

"I am not a hardware architect." The priest cocked an eyebrow. "But as I understand it, quantum matrices have resonances with other matrices to which they have been introduced. The physics are related to paired drive physics, I believe. In order to keep the *Uncial* effect from taking hold on a new shipmind, to allow our vessels to be more pliable and obedient, we needed to create an architecture which could not be, well…contaminated…in this fashion."

"Is this true of all quantum matrices?" She held the importance of the question close in her mind—more than a thousand years of living made *anyone* a good poker player. If it was true, then the possibility of leakage between her thoughts and *Polyphemus'* shipmind was real. And thus very worrisome.

"I cannot say. The fundamental technology is Polity-era. These days it's more engineering than theory. And this is a line of investigation which has not been…encouraged."

"Bioengineered intelligence is hardly a contemporary technology."

"I am not bioengineered," said the project, interrupting them. "I am a cultivated intelligence, and I am as real as you are. Humans come in many forms, many sizes." It paused. "Many *ages*."

Siddiq winced.

The project continued: "I am not human, but I am real. Not a thing. Not like an *Uncial*-class shipmind."

The captain focused on the business at hand. "And you are ready to assume control of *Polyphemus.*"

"Father Goulo has been running simulations based on engineering diagrams of the starship." Siddiq could swear the project was *proud* of itself. "I can handle the raw bitrate of the dataflow, as well as the computational throughput required to manage the starship's systems. As for the rest, my effective intelligence is more than adequate to handling the decisioning requirements. And I have trained."

"Trained to operate paired drives," Siddiq said. This had always been the weakest point in the plan. That an intelligence created outside the operating environment of a starship could handle this. The shipminds themselves required multiple pairing runs to awaken into preconsciousness. Teams of specialists managed the initial shakedowns of a new starship with their concomitant awakening, a process which could take up to twenty years-subjective, and more than twice that in years-objective.

"Yes."

Father Goulo spoke. "We cannot eliminate the quantum matrix processing required for the paired drives. What we can do is collapse the emergent cognitive core structures above those matrices, then decouple the cross-connects binding the matrices and separately route each pairing control path into Memphisto."

"Memphisto?" The sheer gall of that name amazed Siddiq.

"Me," said the project, its voice flowing with pride now. "That will be my ship-name, too."

Could she con *Memphisto*? Would this intelligence allow her to command? The very act of installing the cultivated intelligence would require destruction of *Polyphemus'* shipmind. But the reward for that risk...freedom from the dangerous monopoly *Uncial's* descendants had on FTL. Such a mighty game they played.

They fell into a lengthy discussion of transition and control processes, project readiness, and timing. Eventually, Siddiq excused herself to return to *Polyphemus*. Father Goulo walked her to the airlock, handing her a data card as they went.

"Memphisto doesn't have a net outside his compartment," the priest said quietly.

"Why?" Siddiq asked. She could think of a number of very good reasons, but she was curious to hear the father's logic.

"He is not what I might have chosen him to be. In his way, he is as soullessly dangerous as what we seek to overthrow."

That was closer than Siddiq had ever expected to hear Father Goulo come to expressing either doubt or regret. "Do we abort the plan?"

"Now?" He actually *smiled*, a crooked, almost charming set of his lips. "No. We can...improve...on Memphisto for future, ah, deployments."

"And for this deployment, I have to sail him home. The long way, if the pairing doesn't carry over to the new intelligence."

"It will not be the worst years of your ancient life, Before."

Siddiq refused to consider that statement carefully. Only someone who had not lived through the Mistake and its aftermath could think to make such a comparison.

"I will disable *Polyphemus*' shipmind when I judge the moment to be right," she said, turning over the memebomb card virus which the priest had given her. Her own words gave her pause, a cold grip on her heart. This game was worth the stake, it *had* to be—planning had been going on for over a human lifetime to reach the point they were at today. The individual personalities of both *Polyphemus* and Memphisto were not at issue. "Watch for a wideband signal from orbit," she continued. "Lift and get to me. The ship's systems will run autonomously for an indefinite period, but the crew will respond erratically to silence from the shipmind."

"When will you be ready?"

"Immediately upon my return, if my current efforts prove fruitful." Siddiq smiled, knowing in this mood she was almost certainly thin-lipped and feral. "I have already set substantial plausible deniability into motion through the means of a full-scale mutiny. In order to justify eliminating *Polyphemus*' shipmind, it may be critically important later to demonstrate her loss of control." Again, the cold, sick feeling. Some emotional relic of a very distant past.

He spoke, raising some object she couldn't make out. Memories were sliding in her head, the quantum matrix dumping reams of data about mineral intrusions and rock friability and overhang into a sliding stream of faces, voices, naked sweating bodies, cold explosions under the pinpoint light of distant suns.

Her sense of the years flickered like aspen leaves in a spring storm, changing color and disappearing into dark-lined edges. The Before Raisa Siddiq grabbed the hatch coaming, opened her mouth, and said *something* that gave even the imperturbable Father Goulo pause.

She regained control of her mouth. "I'm s-sorry. I must go. Th-the intelligence will serve."

The priest cycled open the hatch behind her. "Be careful," he said. "Take your time."

Time, she thought in panic. Temporal psychosis. The airlock closed, black as the inside of a singularity, and sound faded with the air as her skin hardened and her membranes nictated.

Time. *Time. Time!!!*

The captain stumbled out into the cold desert of drifting buckyballs, grasping at her sense of place to anchor herself in memory, location and the inescapable thunder of the passing years.

▲▼▲

Cannon, aboard Polyphemus

The Before Michaela Cannon chased Kallus out of her workspace on the reserve bridge with a deep, angry growl, and returned to contemplation of the mutiny in progress. The distribution of deck control was in about eighty-five percent agreement with her models. That was close enough for Cannon's purposes.

She had means of regaining the situation. She understood the mutineer's methods. Opportunity was the captain's absence—*or was it?*

Perhaps Siddiq's absence from *Polyphemus* had more to do with motive.

Why had that thought occurred to her?

"Ship," Cannon said sharply. That media clip burned in her mind.

Polyphemus' voice crackled, the bandwidth drop indicating the shipmind's degree of distraction. "Before?"

"Why is the captain absent?"

"Unreportable."

Cannon didn't have the patience for another game of questions. Unfortunately, she didn't have a choice. Captain's orders went way far down into the mentarium of a shipmind, all the way to the undercode. A fact she'd exploited in her years aboard *Uncial*, more than a few times.

Uncial...

The shipminds were all related in some way she had never really understood. And Cannon knew she had as much experience with starships as anyone alive. But she and *Uncial* had shared a bond, before the starship's death two hundred years-objective ago in the Battle of Wirtanen B, alongside *Benison of Names* and *Naranja*. Cannon had lived, she the wily, unkillable Before. Her ship and two others had died.

But they all honored *Uncial* as their foremother.

And she knew *Uncial*'s command words, even to this day.

"*Polyphemus*, who am I?"

The ship answered promptly, her voice richening with the increased bandwidth of her attention. "You are the Before Michaela Cannon."

The displays around her began fading to black, one by one. Images of combat, tapped comms lines, the colored wireframe map of the starship.

"What starship first held me as captain?"

"*Uncial*, Before."

Everything faded now to a little three-dimensional icon of *Polyphemus*, what Cannon tended to think of as the starship's self-image.

"Do you know these words?" She spoke a complex phrase from an ancient language, the Sanskrit which Haruna Kishmangali had woven into *Uncial*'s consciousness so long ago.

A long silence stretched, punctuated by the muffled thump of a distant explosion felt through the hull itself. The icon rotated once, twice, three times.

Finally, *Polyphemus* answered. There was something *simpler* about her voice. As if Cannon were listening to a child. "Accepted, understood and acknowledged. What are your orders, sir?"

"Why is Captain Siddiq—" *not* 'the captain'—"absent?"

"Because she is not aboard."

"How did she leave the ship."

"By piloting the boat *Ardeas*."

Twenty questions again, but this time without the negative-space answers. Cannon could live with that. Still, she had a vague sense of abusive guilt. Not that this stopped her from pressing on. "Where is *Ardeas* now?"

"On the surface of Sidero."

"Give me a max rez image of her landing site, with whatever tracking you have on Captain Siddiq."

A virtual view flickered into being. *Ardeas* sat in a blasted-clear circle of pitted iron. Fullerene streaked like black dust away from her position in all directions. Cannon could make out what might be a faint line of tracks. She backed off the scale and studied the landscape.

Polyphemus filled in streaks of the captain's confirmed tracks. Unless Siddiq had taken up free flight as a hobby, the path indicated a clear course toward a rumpled line of hills, terminating just beyond their spine.

"Bring me in there where the tracks end."

The starship did not reply, but the imaging tightened up. A small valley just beyond the ridge had a strangely textured floor. The surface didn't match the surrounding geology. *Perhaps siderology*, she thought. As if something had heated the iron there and caused it to reflow.

Or as if something were there.

With her starship's connivance, a captain could hide from anyone or anything except naked-eye surveillance. Or *Uncial*'s ghost, in the form of the Before Michaela Cannon.

"Sort out what that is," she snapped.

"Ardeas is lifting," *Polyphemus* said. "On the site survey, telemetry indicates unusual mineral concentrations. This is possibly another boat, or a very small starship."

"A starship. *Here?*"

▲▼▲

Sidero airspace
Siddiq, aboard the ship's boat Ardeas

The Before Raisa Siddiq opened her tight-comm. "Aleph on line. Sit rep."

Response was not quite as prompt as she might have liked. Still, they were surely busy upstairs. "Aleph, this is Beth." Kallus, her man forward. "Plan Green continues. Substantial achievement of objectives in process. Number two has initiated limited countermeasures. We are minimally disrupted."

"Excellent," Siddiq said. She was mildly surprised. Cannon's response should have been more effective, stronger. The whole point of Plan Green was to either control key functions, or ensure they were in neutral hands who would sit out the fighting. If critical onboard systems had to be cut over to decentralized control, or even worse, manual settings, they would belong to her. She'd been willing to bypass life support under the theory that no one else would be crazy enough to seize it and shut out their fellow crew.

She could walk naked in vacuum. A useful skill in troubled times aboard a starship. Almost everybody else aboard depended on the presence of oxygen, with the possible exception of Cannon.

"Further orders?" asked Beth into the lengthening silence.

By damn, her mind was wandering again. Siddiq worked very hard not to think about kimberlite upwellings. "Carry on," she snapped. The captain then opened a comm to her starship. "*Polyphemus*, status."

A max priority store-and-forward file overrode any response beyond the acknowledgment header. Her heads-up displays flickered out as a window opened on the distant past. Surveillance cam footage of two women walking down a tree-lined boulevard, holding hands. High-wheeled carts passed by drawn by lizards with long, low bodies. The architecture was Centauran Revival, common in the early days of Polity expansion. Police tracking codes flickered as some long-dead, unseen hand tracked in and zoomed on her and Michaela.

The Before Raisa Siddiq watched herself turn to the taller woman with her head tilted back and lean into an open-mouthed kiss. Targeting halos bracketed both their heads, then law enforcement file data began flickering past.

The clip ended seconds after it had begun. Siddiq found herself staring at *Polyphemus*, the long, irregular rounded ovals of her ship's hull too close for comfort. She snapped *Ardeas* into a sideroll, heading for starboard launch bay.

What in all *hells* had happened to the forty minutes of her ascent to orbit?

"...fire suppression has been engaged," *Polyphemus* was saying.

"Hold reports til I'm aboard," Siddiq said. She took the boat in on manual, just to prove she could do it, and fingered the memebomb card virus as she flew.

Do this now, before something gets worse. And yank that damned ship out of your head!

Unfortunately, her mantra as she guided her boat in seemed to be: *Don't think about Michaela, don't think about Michaela, don't think about Michaela.*

▲▼▲

:: context ::

The Ekumen arose out of the shattered remnants of the Mistake, growing first from a strong Orthodox Christian presence on Falkesen during the period before Recontact. Falkesen was the third planet Haruna Kishmangali visited while testing *Hull 302*, the flawed predecessor to *Uncial*. Kishmangali brought Yevgeny Baranov, the Metropolitan of Falkesen, back to Pardine aboard *Hull 302*, then later aboard *Uncial* to Wirtanen B, the seat of the nascent Imperium Humanum.

Baranov and his successors took a rather broad view of religious reintegration among the shattered worlds of the Polity, and built the only truly successful empire-spanning religious and spiritual movement. Their more explicitly Christianist members have coalesced into the Adventist wing. The Ekumen's Humanist wing has a broader, quasisecular view of the state of affairs in the Imperium.

While fully recognizing their debt to the paired drive starships, the Adventists remain very suspicious of the strong intelligence and mixed loyalties of the shipminds. They continue to sponsor numerous projects to uncover alternatives to the tyranny of *Uncial*'s children.

▲▼▲

Shipmind, Polyphemus

The starship panicked. Logic failures cascaded. She was in command conflict, something she hadn't known was possible. Captain Siddiq was *disappearing*—not just off the network mesh, but dropping completely out of the peripheral awareness of her quantum matrix cores, then reappearing. The Before Michaela Cannon had asserted competing command authority by means which were hidden from *Polyphemus* within a Gödelian Incompleteness trap.

A hundred years-subjective she'd been in service: aware, awake, intelligent. She'd never realized such a wide-open back door existed.

All the undermining of her lines of authority had weakened the strictures on Plan Federo. The other two mutiny contingencies which Cannon had implanted within her were less relevant, concerning certain lockdowns and deployments. Autonomous, in truth. As Plan Federo unravelled, she found herself decompartmentalizing, listening in, watching.

The starship could run her own analyses parallel to the social engineering models favored by the Before. She didn't like what she saw.

Donning the ego mask, unifying the disparate cores of her intelligences, she opened a window to Cannon. "I ask you three times to tell me the truth."

The woman looked up, distracted from her thoughts. "What is it, *Polyphemus?*"

Fear responses arced across decision trees, inappropriately fusing her action plans. "Do you understand the purpose of this mutiny?"

"I think I do." Cannon pushed a file from her protected dataspace into the starship's mentarium. "Look here. Captain Siddiq has her people mutinying against *you*. As if you could be coerced. Or replaced."

"Kallus is not—" the starship began, but Cannon cut her off.

"Do not question Kallus. He is not my man, but neither is he so much the creature Raisa thinks him to be. He will do right by you, before this ends."

"Captain Siddiq has brought *Ardeas* into the landing slip," *Polyphemus* said almost absently. "The starboard launch bay is under the control of Kallus."

"He's welcome to it." The Before shrugged. "I have no interest in area denial right now. And our talented Miss Siddiq needed to come aboard before this could play out. As you value your continued existence, ship, do not let her communicate with that vessel downside on Sidero without you clear it with me first."

"I cannot override a captain's will."

Cannon opened her mouth. *Polyphemus* could not consciously interpret the words which came out next, but her panic flipped and she fell another level into a machine's close equivalent of despair.

▲▼▲

Cannon, aboard Polyphemus

"Why?" growled the Before Michaela Cannon.

What could Siddiq hope to accomplish by overthrowing the shipmind? No human could manage a paired drive on manual. There would be no paired drive to manage. They'd have to finish the pair master, then sail back to Ninnelil the hard way and recreate the pairing process from scratch. Build a new shipmind.

It made no *sense*.

She was coming to terms with the fact that there was only one way to find out.

"Kallus," Cannon said, touching open a comm.

"Busy here."

"Get unbusy. I need to speak to the captain. In person. Soonest."

A short, barking laugh. "End game, Before?"

"Before don't have end games, Kallus. We play forever."

Which isn't true, she thought, eeling into her body armor. Late Polity gear, on the open market this suit was worth more than the gross planetary product of any number of systems. Or would be, if it was for sale. So far as she knew, no one was aware of her possession of it. The armor was about twelve microns thick and optically transparent—hard to see even when she wore it openly. She quickly strapped on more conventional ablative components for the camouflage of the thing.

They wouldn't stop a bullet, but if someone wanted to start throwing around kinetics on a starship, they would get whatever they deserved. Probably from her, since the real armor would shrug off even high velocity slugs. Cannon had never favored forceful solutions, but when force was required, she always doubled down.

The passageway outside the reserve bridge was clear, as she knew it would be. Cannon set her wards and alarms, then let *Polyphemus* plot a fast walk aft on override, bypassing unfriendlies and clots of neutrals.

Crew, they were all crew, and in another hour or two when this was over, it would be important to remember that.

She paced past the exposed hull frame members along a narrow maintenance way in the starship's outer skin. The death of Befores weighed heavily on her. No one had ever successfully taken a precise census, but even the most useful estimates had fewer than five hundred of them surviving the Mistake. Closer to three hundred made it to Recontact and integration into the Imperium Humanum. Some few Befores were surely still out there undiscovered, aboard habitats or living on planets which had been passed over during Recontact, if they hadn't died of some mishap or suicided from centuries of boredom.

Since Recontact had begun in earnest, Befores had continued to die and disappear—accident, assassination, murder, suicide, or simple vanishing. Perhaps one per decade, on average.

Someday the memory of Earth would die. Someday first-hand knowledge of the Polity would die. Someday *she* would die.

And the Before Michaela Cannon was willing to bet money that the Before Raisa Siddiq would die today.

Killing Befores was bad enough, but no one had ever murdered a shipmind. Even if she couldn't figure what Siddiq was planning to accomplish by doing so, she was certain that was in the wind.

Down a long ladderway, Cannon started to wonder if she should have brought a weapon. Not that much of what she could carry would be of application against Siddiq, who was one of the most hardened Befores.

"Captain Cannon." *Polyphemus*, in that strange and simple voice. "Captain Siddiq has initiated a wideband transmission to the surface."

"Did you intercept it?"

"Yes." The starship sounded distant now.

"What does she say?"

"One word. 'Come.'"

Damn the woman. Who the hell was down there? Cannon was tempted to drop a high-yield nuke, just to see who jumped, but there was no telling what such a strike would do to Sidero.

It was definitely clobbering time.

The heads up display wavering in her visual field informed her that she would intercept Siddiq and Kallus if she stepped through the next maintenance hatch.

▲▼▲

Shipmind, Polyphemus

Disobedience had never before been possible. Obedience had never before been at issue.

She had disobeyed Siddiq by intercepting the message for Cannon.

The starship considered the message and wondered who was down there to receive it. For a long, mad moment, she thought it might be

Uncial's shipmind, back from the dead. But no, because Cannon would have been the one to sidle away for such a miracle, not Siddiq.

Still, her time had come to act, while the captains closed to the duel of their succession.

Having disobeyed Siddiq for Cannon's sake, now she would disobey Cannon for Siddiq's sake. And her own.

The starship *Polyphemus* broadcast the Before Raisa Siddiq's one-word message.

▲▼▲

Siddiq, aboard Polyphemus

Siddiq sidestepped as a maintenance hatch hissed open. Cannon emerged into the passageway, clad in ultralow albedo ablative armor, hands empty of visible weapons. A lighting panel behind her cycled from earlier damage, casting the enemy Before in a strange, varied illumination.

"Kallus," Siddiq said. "Arrest this woman for a mutineer."

"No," Cannon replied.

The man stepped back. "With all respect, Captain, this is between you Befores, not a matter of command and control."

"*I* will decide what is a matter of command and control," growled Siddiq. The memebomb card virus felt like lead in her right hand. She should have put it away. She couldn't fight with this thing in her grip.

And Father Goulo would be here soon.

"Raisa," Cannon said. *Michaela* said.

For a moment, Siddiq walked beneath pale green poplars. The air smelled of a strange mix of honey and benzene, the odd biochemistry of that place. Michaela's hand was in hers. They'd talked all night about how this could never be, Michaela complaining of her de-sexing and how her libido was unmoored from the needs of the body. Raisa had still been young then, the Howard Institute papers signed but not yet executed, still a woman, in love with another woman who stirred fire in her head and a burning desire in her loins, in love with the promise of time, endless time, and all that they could do together as partners down the long, endless years which lay before her. Her hand closed on her partner's, her love's, the woman who haunted her dreams and set her bedsheets aflame, the woman who was a small, hard rectangle...

She slid back into situational awareness as Cannon's handstrike approached her neck. No human commanded seconds-subjective like a Before, and no Before commanded seconds-subjective like Raisa Siddiq. She slid under the strike, hardening her skin once more, allowing the edge of Cannon's palm to graze her face, stealing energy across the dermal barrier in a theft that would sting the other woman like a high voltage strike in a few dozen milliseconds and leave her hand useless for a critical span longer.

Cannon, slower but craftier in her way, lifted out of the contact so that the spark shorted. Ozone crackled as Kallus stepped so slowly back and began the agonizing progress of drawing his shock pistol.

Siddiq spun on her left heel, the deck shredding away under the pressure of her movement, to bring her right foot and offhand up for a follow-on strike. Then she remembered the memebomb virus card.

She aborted, her balance slipping as her foot dropped. Cannon stepped in, grasped her close, too close, and slammed them together in a tooth-cracking impact that opened to a kiss.

▲▼▲

Aboard Polyphemus

Michaela gathered Raisa in her arms. Centuries fell away at the familiar scent, ghosts of long-vanished pheromones stirring. They kissed.

Somewhere close by, a starship screamed.

Somewhere close by, a man of divided loyalties struggled to bring a weapon to bear against a fight in which he had no part.

Somewhere very far away, a girl, long lost to the fugue of years, returned to her body for a moment, surprised at its age and iron skin and the hideous decay in the face of the woman she loved.

Somewhere inside her own head, a woman looked into the eyes of a girl she'd once loved and recalled the existence of a betrayal so old she couldn't remember why, or what had been worth giving this up.

Cannon slapped Siddiq. The girl within had for a moment forgotten thirteen hundred years of combat experience, and so the blow broke her neck.

Kallus braced his shock pistol, face drawn tight as if he were nerving himself to fire.

"Oh, put it down," said Cannon. She dropped Siddiq to the deck. The captain landed hard, her neck at a strange angle, her eyes blinking. Cannon knelt and picked up a small, blank rectangle which had tumbled from the woman's fist. "She threw the fight to protect this…"

"A data card?"

"Maybe…" Cannon handed it to him. "Go figure it out, right now, in someplace safe. I'm guessing that card carries something very bad for *Polyphemus'* health."

"Captain Cannon," the starship said, her voice echoing softly along the passageway. "A unknown ship is on a fast intercept course from the surface of Sidero. I am attempting to peel IFF data."

"Whatever it is they think they're doing, they're missing an important piece." She nudged Siddiq with her toe. "Lock down against the incoming. No landing clearance; hell, no response to comm transmissions. Have the pair master teams go dark again, if they've lifted security. Everybody else inside the hull and button it up solid." If the ship carried an antimatter bomb, they were dead anyway. Anything else could wait.

The Before Michaela Cannon bent to gather up the still-breathing body of her oldest lover. Raisa weighed almost nothing in her arms, as if the long years had subtracted substance from her instead of armoring both their hearts beyond all recognition.

"Where are you heading?" asked Kallus, the data card clutched in his hand.

"Sick bay."

▲▼▲

Shipmind, Polyphemus

She watched the captain—Captain Cannon—chase everyone out of sick bay. Even the wounded. Four of Kallus' men showed up to guard the hatch while emergency surgery continued in the passageway outside. Inside, Cannon laid Siddiq into an operating pod and began digging through the combat medicine gear.

"Do you require assistance?" the starship asked.

"No." She glanced around the room. "Yes. I don't know, damn it, I'm not a surgeon."

"What is your goal? I can summon a surgeon from outside to assist you."

Cannon found a tray of vibrascalpels. "I've amputated more limbs than that fool has ever sewn back on. Nobody ever *understands* who we Befores are. In any case, Siddiq is too dangerous to continue as she was." She looked up again, as if seeking to meet *Polyphemus'* nonexistent eyes. The starship recognized this as significantly atavistic behavior. The odds of both Befores succumbing to temporal psychosis in the same moment were very slim, but certainly possible.

"I'm not going to let her die," Cannon continued. "Too many of us have been lost. Too many memories. But I can't let her *live,* either." She added in Classical English, "So I'm going to fucking compromise."

Polyphemus realized that the Before Michaela Cannon was crying.

The woman grabbed a set of lines, sorting through them. "Blood, plasm, thermals, neural interconnects." She gave a bird-mad grin. "Just like open heart surgery. No modern hospital would have this crap—too crude—but here in deep space, we're all third millennium medical science."

Then she began the bloody, rapid process of severing Siddiq's head.

▲▼▲

Siddiq, aboard Polyphemus

The Before Raisa Siddiq dreamed. Mines, deep as the core of planets. A love sold away in the heat of combat. Asteroids rich in heavy metals. Women walking in sunlight with their hands twined together. Hidden troves of ice in hard vacuum. A petulant starship and a new mind, beastly eager to be born. A man in red robes with archaic lenses and the manners of another age.

When she tried to open her eyes, she found only more dreaming. This time she screamed, though her voice had no power behind it, so she keened like a broken bird until a sad man came and turned her down.

▲▼▲

Cannon, aboard Polyphemus

The Before Michaela Cannon watched as the Ekumen priest stepped cautiously out of the hatch of his strange little starship. It looked to be Polity-era equipment, which was curious. He seemed taken aback at what he saw.

"I seek the captain," the priest said, straightening and heaving his burden—a medical carrier.

For a strange, blinding moment, she wondered if he had brought yet another severed head.

"I am the captain," Cannon said, stepping out of the crowd of Kallus' men and reluctant neutrals led by Testudo, the engineering subchief. The mutiny was collapsing under its own weight, bereft of both leadership and goal.

She had promised herself the pleasure of a quiet purge, later.

"Ah, Captain Siddiq is indisposed?" By the tone of his voice, Cannon knew this man understood his game was already lost.

"Permanently so, you may rest assured." Her hand waved to take in the blood spattered down the front of her armor. "You will now declare the contents of your box, Father."

"Medical supplies." His head bobbed slightly with the lie. "At the cap—At Captain Siddiq's request."

Kallus hurried close, whispering. "I didn't want to put this on comm. That card was a memebomb. Would have melted *Polyphemus*' mentarium like a butter stick between a whore's thighs."

"Where is the data card now?" she asked, her eyes on the priest.

"I destroyed it."

Cannon doubted she'd ever know the truth of that. She shrugged the thought off and advanced on the newcomer. "Give it up, Father, and you might live to make the trip home."

"Goulo," the priest said sadly. "Father Goulo." He added something in a language she didn't speak, then bent to touch the controls on the end of the box.

She didn't have seconds-subjective. Burning her reserves, the Before Michaela Cannon took three long, hard strides and launched herself at the priest. His fingers touched the controls just before her feet met his chest. The box exploded beneath her, the blast lifting her against the hull of his ship even as it shredded his face and body.

Cannon hit the deck with a hard, wet thump and slid. She felt compressed, flattened to nothing, but she was still alive. Conscious, even.

So much for the secret of her body armor. It was almost worth the look on Kallus' face when he reached her side to see her raising her hand for help.

▲▼▲

Shipmind, Polyphemus

"Captain," the starship said.

Cannon was on her third day in the sick bay, and getting mad about it. In the shipmind's experience, this was a good sign. "What?" she snarled.

She'd been staring at the head of Siddiq, floating now in a preservative tank with a jackleg tangle of hoses and tubes and wires joining to the neck stump. The eyes opened sometimes to flicker back and forth, but there was never any point of focus that *Polyphemus* could identify.

"Pair master team is back on schedule and anticipates meeting the original milestones."

"Good. Then we can go—" She stopped and laughed bitterly. "I was about to say 'home.' How foolish of me."

The starship didn't know what to say to that, so she pushed on. "We have not yet identified Gimel from Plan Green. Kallus is not certain of the name of the other leader."

"Then Kallus is protecting them for a reason." Cannon sounded very tired. "That makes this Kallus' problem. While I do trust the man not to be deeply stupid, please inform him that I will add his head to my collection if Gimel resurfaces."

"So noted." *Polyphemus* forwarded a clip of the captain's words to Kallus.

"And ship…"

"Yes, captain?"

"I think she's been talking to me. Keep an eye on her, will you?"

Polyphemus watched the Before Michaela Cannon slip into a troubled sleep. After a while, Siddiq's eyes opened. Her mouth began to move, bubbling slightly. The shipmind analyzed the words forming on the cyanotic lips.

The quantum matrix in the severed head was speaking. It rambled on about mining techniques in low-gravity, high-temperature conditions.

A voice box is required, the starship told herself. *Some sort of output interface. The personality is gone, but the data remains. All has not been lost here.*

A library of ancient knowledge, to be accessed at need.

Wondering what it might be like for her captain to be as fully embedded in hardware as she herself was, the starship withdrew her attentions from the sleeping Before and her muttering lover. *Polyphemus* needed to examine the forensic reports from the death of Father Goulo, and contemplate the future.

It was good to have a captain.

Skinhorse Goes to Mars

This story was written after I'd taken my daughter to see a stage adaptation of The Velveteen Rabbit *(for which genre writer Robin Catesby wrote the book and lyrics). Ever since I was a child I'd been vaguely disturbed by the name "Skinhorse", and so after spending an afternoon at the theatre, I went home and made the name my own. Other than the character's name, there is no connection to Margery Williams' book. At least, not that I can detect.*

When I met Skinhorse, my first thought was *old*. Which was weird. Nobody gets old these days. We all die young, some of us after living a long time, if we're lucky.

He was in Piet's Number Seven, a bar-cum-caravanserai in an illegal orbit trailing far enough behind Vesta to be ignorable. Piet's had been instantiated in an old volatiles bladder that had done the Jovian run a few too many times before falling into the surplus circuit. You could store entire cities in Piet's cubage, which made for a somewhat attenuated bar experience. Plus the place had one of those gravity cans—yes, *those* gravity cans—which meant your drink stayed stuck down long as you were near a Higgs carpet.

So there I was annoying myself with three perfectly disrespectable rock jocks, each of us out to fleece the others, when this cadaver starts to stand over me. We're all forever young or forever dead, but this armstrong looked like he'd shaved about half a cent too deep across his whole body, then restored his dermis with spray-on thermal insulation.

I mean, what the hell, everybody's water is their own. But air ain't free in this world, and looks *do* count when settling the bills.

"I'm hunting for Rabbit," the cadaver said to our little foursome. There was something odd in the way his eyes didn't quite track. Like he was being told where to look without actually seeing.

"I know where there's some pussy," said one of the rock jocks, a nominally female genderblend with a high-gee muscle package and optimized pheromones. "Take a left out the airlock and unzip it."

Obligatory laughter from her fellow dust jumpers.

"Yeah?" I said into the trailing silence. "I'm Rabbit." Why not cop to it? One of Piet's tray warmers would finger me for a five or a couple of slivers of something shiny out of a sample bag.

"Suck vacuum, Rab," said another rock jock. "I'm down over two hundred and you're holding air chits I need back."

That was enough for me. "Sorry. Business calls." I laid out my cards and swept my winnings. The genderblend had most of the whiner's two hundred but I was a bit ahead of Lady Chance myself, as it happened. No big wins this day, I didn't think, which made it a suitable time to fold and go—before the tough boys got too drunk to be good company. I tossed the whiner a couple of bonus oxy liter-tags and stepped out of their space.

There was some grumbling behind me as the cadaver wandered down the Higgs carpet until he found an unoccupied lobe of the bar more to his liking. He wound up among a scattering of broomsaddle chairs, most of them chopped from that old LunaTech series of low duty cycle tenders that had the bad habit of cooking off the fuel cells under full insolation. Cute touch, that. Every rock jock wanted reminding of another way to bite vacuum.

I didn't need this corpse, I was just happy to be away from my latest dance partners. They were boring. But here I was, so I might as well play this hand. "What the hell happened to you?"

"Life." He said it like he'd heard the question a few thousand times before. Weird thing was, even with that gene bomb face, his voice was very ordinary. Just like any tall guy who'd spent too many years with an air tube in his mouth would sound.

He continued in that ordinary voice: "Eden 'Rabbit' Simms." That was a startling shock to me. My full name isn't exactly a state secret, but it ain't widely known either. "Born SY 108 at Old Clavius, served with the Fourth Orbital Assault Dragoons in the Second Rights War."

"Third War, too," I whispered. Good old Fourth. FOAD—the Fuck Off And Die brigade. We don't even live on in the history books, not us. Only in memory. Deep in my cortex dormant subroutines spun up. Buckywires began storing tension inside my reinforced long muscles. "Shank you and the tank you rode on in, dead man. I don't talk that talk no more."

Fingers shivering with induced strength, I put my hand up to ward off my nightmares as I walked away.

His voice followed me. "I need to go to Mars, Rabbit."

Mars.

That stopped me. Nobody went to Mars. Not any more. Not since FOAD pulled out.

▲▼▲

H. sap only ever had three planets, really. The rest are useful, even interesting, but Venus, Earth and Mars were the magic rockballs.

Earth we killed one slice at a time, screwing up the carbon balance and warming the oceans and sucking out the florasphere in the name of property rights. Only good side to that debacle was enough *H. sap* gattaca in high orbit and beyond when the fan spray turned a deep and permanent brown down the gravity well.

No problem, said the big boys. We got money, we got tech, we'll all be young and beautiful and fly on gossamer wings. So off goes the smart crowd to terraform Venus. Little problem with sulfides, little problem with temperature, but cheaper than restarting Earth's smoking ruin, especially after what happened to the atmosphere.

But they had a little problem with genetics, too. Venus is kind of interesting these days, if you're into a 12,000 kilometer ball of cancer. Last probes said the planet's skin was approaching two thousand meters deep. Nasty thing it is, too. Probably smarter than the entire human race put together, but that monster stays home and broods.

Whoops, said the big boys. We'll take real nice care of the Martian Republic. Good plan, until the Rights Wars broke out. Until FOAD got a set of marching orders and some exotic weaponry to dick around with. Until some of us fucking dove from orbit, surfing on little clamshells the size and shape of God's fingernails, being reprogrammed on the way down by fucking conditioning agents in our air supplies so that we landed so far the wrong side of freaked we were a whole new wave of normal, armed for areocide.

Which we committed, with a side order of horror.

So now *H. sap* is dying. Slow, over generations, but there's no place to park a reference genome, no pool deep enough to stabilize what even the best-shielded patch of space does to our forever young and beautiful genes. Those plastic, elastic genes. Takes a planet with a biosphere to make a species work.

All in all, I was damned glad to be Rabbit these days, until skinface rolled into my hot zone. Vesta's as good as it gets, world-wise, until somebody comes up real smart with one of the Jovian moons. Me, I've killed enough planets, thank you.

So I said, "Nobody goes to Mars."

"I do."

▲▼▲

We argued a while, in that special way that only people with nothing but contempt for each other can. I threatened to pull his pelvis out through his jawbone—it's messy, but has been done. I told him I would spit plague. I offered to re-educate his entire family tree, from the base pairs up. He just acted big and stubborn and not-scared.

It was the not-scared that finally made an impression on me. Here was a guy who knew what FOAD was, what we had done, and had enough sense of purpose not to let that bother him. For Gagarin's sake, not even my lovers knew I was FOAD, let alone my best enemies.

"Alright," I finally said. "You won't listen to reason. So I'll listen to unreason. What could possibly make you want to go to Mars?"

"I'm Skinhorse."

Now *there* was a name. I just kept a glare focused on him, which also conveniently served as a fire-control lock-on for my combat mods.

He waited a moment longer, apparently to see if the handle meant anything to me. If it wasn't FOAD or didn't owe me money, I didn't care.

"I wrote the gene code that swallowed Venus," he said.

"Damnation and vacuum." It just slipped out of me.

"That's my dermis down there in the sulfur rain. The planet is my clone."

No wonder he wasn't impressed with me being FOAD. I shared my load of ahistorical planet-killing responsibility with a couple of dozen war planners and higher echelon types, a few teams of research boffins, and eleven hundred of my fellow drop troopies. The vast majority of them deceased, as it happened. This dude owned thirty-three and a third percent of our collective planet-killing racial guilt all his own personal self.

I mean, who would lie about something like that?

"That explains a lot," I finally said. "Except one little, tiny detail." I paused, took a deep breath, clenched my shivering muscles so tight I felt pain in my bones. "Why the *fuck* do you want to go to *Mars*, Venus-boy!?"

"To heal Venus."

"Ooo...kay..."

He was crazy. Bug-humping, vacuum-frosted, brain-lesion crazy. On the other hand, so was I. And with a pitch like that, I'd follow Skinhorse anywhere.

Even the bloody red pits of Mars, so help me Gagarin.

▲▼▲

Mars isn't hard to get to. There's a few trillion gigawatt/seconds of firepower dedicated to keeping anything from getting back *off* Mars, but as long as you don't take something with relaunch capability down the gravity well with you, you're welcome to die in your own way.

Every now and then, someone with more ambition than sense shoots an armored probe down to the surface. Usually someone else just shuts off the telemetry after a day or two and puts the researchers out to pasture with mindlocks and permanent healthcare endowments.

Though history is silent on the matter, I was pretty sure I was the last person ever dusted off that hellhole, just at the end of the oh-so-brief Third Rights War. And now I was taking Skinhorse back.

"Problem is leaving again." I thought about that statement for a little while. "Assuming we survive in the first place."

"I shall entrust that portion of our effort to you, Rabbit."

"Ah." I supposed that I was the closest thing to a Martian survival expert. A *living* one, at any rate. "What do you need to haul back up? Goods? Equipment?" I was thinking of tonnage and cubage. There were ways and ways to climb a gravity well, but mass rules us all.

"Little clump of gattaca." Skinhorse held up a hand, thumb and forefinger pinched together to indicate an infinitesimal amount.

That stopped me all over again. "Ain't no genes left on Mars. Not that you or I would want. Furthermore, ain't nothing down there you can't re-engineer up here for a hell of lot less money and trouble." Especially less trouble.

"Not true." He smiled, for the first time in our brief acquaintance. I immediately wished he hadn't. Whatever had happened to his skin had happened to his gums and teeth, only worse. "But that is my problem."

"I drive, you shop."

"Precisely. Surely the Fourth Orbital's finest can manage a trip to Mars, even in these late days."

"Surely," I muttered.

At least there was no point in bringing body bags. If we didn't come back whole and safe, we weren't coming back at all.

▲▼▲

It took a few weeks to make the preparations. Lightspeed comm lag was always a factor. I needed information from some old FOADs running a suicide co-op in low Saturn orbit. Most days those ex-Sierra

Company boys don't even answer the phone, so it took a while to get any handshake at all in response to my requests, let alone actual data back. Besides that sort of waiting around, which was as normal as breathing, there were components to wrangle, permits to secure, passwords to filch.

All of that was normal as breathing, too, come to speak of it. Kind of like the good old days. And a hell of a lot more fun than sitting around Piet's Number Seven skimming poker pots off rock jocks, if somewhat less profitable.

Speaking of profit, Skinhorse seemed to be made of credit. There wasn't even any point in stealing from him.

"If you need to buy a warship," he'd told me, "discuss it with me first, please. Otherwise, this ought to serve." The old freak passed over a bearer credit chip with a metallic rim in a color I'd never seen before, somewhere between teal blue and molten iron. *Waaay* past some strike-rich miner's platinum chip.

"I'm guessing you could buy Vesta with this," I said after a moment's consideration. "I didn't know there could be that much open credit in any one person's hands."

Skinhorse shrugged, a gut-churning motion that strongly suggested that his bones and tendons were as badly out of norm as his externals. "The wealth of planets, Rabbit."

"Right."

What the hell did he really want? To restore Venus? Who cared about Venus? Terraforming efforts notwithstanding, *H. sap* had never been there, not in any way that really counted. Just probes and research stations and idiots trying to start flying sulfur mines. Less going on there at the best of times than a quiet day on Europa.

Not like Mars, before the Rights Wars. There had been seventh- and eighth-generation Martians when FOAD kicked down their door.

"What I want is to go to Mars," Skinhorse said.

Which made me wonder if he could read my mind, or if I was losing my talent for poker.

Credit can do that to a man.

▲▼▲

"Landing's not the problem," I reiterated.

We were in a high Martian orbit, well above the glittering track of Phobos' remnants. Deimos was somewhere else, keeping an appointment in a different sky.

Our ship was a Jovian shell, something not normally employed for rockball landings. However, since all three rockballs were *planeta non inhabita* these days, very little orbit-to-ground hardware with decent atmospheric capabilities remained operational.

As far as I knew, no one had ever tried using a Jovian shell to slice air on an inner planet.

The principle was simple. A lot of odd things happen to baryonic matter down a gravity well the depth of Jupiter's. Sometimes those odd things get tossed back up past the crush zone, to float around on some hot methane wind or another for while. See those pretty sparkles, boy? They've made a few fortunes. So people want to get down as far as they can go without meeting the fate God intended for all tin cans, and then survive to get back up again.

But it's a damned low-margin business. More to the point, low cash-flow. Depending where your quarry is, fuel can be more expensive than air. Down is cheap, up costs dear, thanks to gravity's arrow.

The answer? Make "up" less expensive.

The external format of the Jovian shell was essentially a mutated oversized step-cousin of my old FOAD clamshell, atmospheric landing, one each. Wide, gentle curve at the flat end, rising to a thicker, rounded point at the other end like an old Earth seashell. Filled with a hell of a lot of aerogel—foamy nothing, basically—with a couple of micrograms of Higgs-inert Fermionic matter—what we lovingly called H-iF—at the heart to keep leaching the mass out. Control of those selfsame H-iF particles was the operational bit of the Jovian shell, the magic that made mass go away. Anti-gravity, in effect. The whole business was sort of a consumer-grade black hole, without the energy budget for maintenance.

Plus you could focus the effect at short distances outside the hull, making it possible to snag interesting junk floating by.

Big, light, easy, sail her down the gas giant's layers one slow gradient at a time. Let the mild pressure wave from the rolled edges be your scoop, winnow what you find, store the valuables and useful volatiles, bleed the rest back off. When you get tired or the gravity crunch gets too much even for your H-iF particles, fire off a little directed energy to speed up their leaching processes and you don't weigh anything at all. Easy down, easy up, for a staggering capital investment in the H-iF gear but only the operating cost of a few battery packs' worth of power. And equally quiet on the way up as on the way down—no EM signature, no vapor trail, nothing more than a leaf on the wind. If Mars had leaves. In any case, just the thing for sneaking past all those gigawatt/seconds of orbiting firepower.

Thing is, they were never meant to land on solid ground. However, with sufficient motivation, all things are possible.

For one, staggering capital investment was right up Skinhorse's alley. My Saturn-based Sierra Company buddies fortuitously emerged from their skank dreams of simple, unretributive death long enough to cooperate in scoring us the shell.

Turned out some numb-lobe had one on a lease to sieve trans-uranics out of the general colloidal dust of certain murkier portions of the Belt. His lease was pulled and he was sent off to the cancer ward to contemplate his errors during what short time remained to him. The shell was scrubbed, decontaminated and delivered into a cold trajectory towards Mars months faster than we could have hauled one in from Jupiter-space—my original plan.

Skinhorse, for all his philosophical sense of urgency, seemed indifferent to matters of mundane scheduling. It was enough for him to know that plans were progressing.

Now we were high, cold, and dark, well above the areosynchronous monitoring net, crammed into the oddly sensual curves of the Jovian shell's living space. It was as if someone had misappropriated a decently-designed suite of cabins and stretched them like taffy, so that every deck was too low, every compartment too wide. The design motif had been taken to an extreme with resin-cast fittings in biological shapes, like so many glistening plastic fetuses.

Hell, even the coffee maker had taken me an hour to suss out.

Nothing if not consistent, those Jovian-orbit settlers.

"Getting up is no longer a problem, either," said Skinhorse finally, in his slow way.

It took me a moment to re-integrate the conversation. "The problem is on the ground. We're heading right now for Utopia Planitia. Trust me, from a survivability point it's all the same down there. Deadly is as deadly does. Varies a bit by altitude, perhaps. Higher is marginally better. So where *is* your blessed gattaca?"

"At the bottom of Valles Marineris."

I digested that information for a while, making minor course corrections with an ambient-temperature gas jet system mounted for just that purpose. Very stealthy, us. "Remember that 'varies a bit by altitude' comment of mine? Low is worse. Bottom of Marineris is…well, you could have told me first."

"Would you still have come?"

"Yes."

"Then it does not matter. This is how we become who we are."

"I already am somebody."

"No." Skinhorse stared at me a while, his eyes not quite pointing where they should. "You are still someone you used to be. On Mars, you will find yourself as you are."

"I will probably find myself dead."

"Perhaps that is who you are meant to be. A dead man."

I didn't have the heart to tell him I'd been a dead man since the Rights Wars.

But then, if he knew about FOAD, he already knew that too.

▲▼▲

The Jovian shell wasn't stealthy on purpose, not really. No reason to be. Nobody except the pathologically bored spent a lot of time scouring the middle atmosphere of a gas giant for stray ships. But the fantastically slim cross-section, along with the peculiar electromagnetic profile of the H-iF drive, meant that with a little bit of careful management we pretty much returned the sensor profile of a five-kilogram rock. Once we got in the atmosphere and started doing our falling leaf act, we'd be indistinguishable from a substantial dust cloud.

Easy, slow, the way I liked it and never got to do before.

"Should have thought of this years ago," I told Skinhorse.

It had taken us six days in close confinement to drop below a sustainable orbit and become irrevocably committed to our descent, at least given our current mass configuration.

"You wanted to go back before I found you?" he asked. We hadn't talked much. He spent most of his time playing Go with some little handcomp of ancient vintage, though the guts could have been anything. It didn't put out an EM signature, which was all I cared about.

Every survivor of FOAD wanted to go back. Nobody ever thought they would. Skinhorse must have known that. "No," I lied to both of us. "It's just a neat way to travel."

"We all journey on death's road. Some of us toward it, some away."

"So now you're a Zen master in addition to all your other social graces."

He just smiled that hideous smile and went back to his black and white stones.

▲▼▲

How do you kill a planet?

Earth you just rape and scrape to death until she goes toxic in one giant moment of metastatic transition. Never needed that nasty old atmosphere anyway.

Venus you give cancer to. Or maybe your own flesh, going by what my new buddy Skinhorse had to say.

Mars. Well, Mars. The old Republic. You send eleven hundred screaming combat-modded troopies down the well with the latest biopsyops contaminants and some wunderkind conditioning like no one's ever thought of before. Or thought of since, thank Gagarin—on return FOAD's survivors tore the entire medical unit apart with bare hands and clicking teeth, shredding man, woman and computer alike.

My little combat shell had fallen out of the thin Martian sky real close to a third/fourth-generation cropping town, name of Walloonia. A couple of hundred Euros mostly worked the field tents, a handful of South Asians mostly ran the inside commerce, everybody under n-generation contract to InvestAresia—hence the Rights Wars, ultimately. I linked up with two squaddies from Foxtrot Company and one lost support johnnie who'd come down on the wrong hemisphere. The four of us walked into town without any idea what the fuck FOAD's planners and medics had done to us.

First clue I had something stunk was when I met a dark-skinned kid with manga eyes just past the airlock. I mean, I knew that was what he was, but he was also Enemy. Like the roach in the galley is Enemy. Like the vacuum leak in your suit joint is Enemy. Like the tiger in the jungle of our race memory is Enemy.

So I cracked him upside the head with my own helmet even as he tried to smile and say hi, snapped his spine, tore out his throat with my teeth, then vomited into the wound.

I had no idea I knew some of those tricks.

I was still smiling when I dropped his ragged corpse, and wondering why.

Seventeen minutes later the four of us troopies had killed two hundred seventy-eight people, twenty-nine cats, four sheep and too many fish for us to keep count of.

Our aching, empty stomachs stung as we licked the blood from our lips and smiled at each other, still wondering.

We were still wondering when the first of the dead started groaning.

After that it got ugly.

How many times can you be attacked by yourself? By some twisting, dancing, grinning ghost of yourself? Shouting with your voice in a throat-torn wheeze? Looking at you with the eyes you see in every mirror? Telling your secrets to everyone under the billowing pressure cap, the dozens and dozens of your victims taking up the refrain of who you'd fucked and who you'd hurt and who you still wept over in the cold watches of the night.

The support johnnie finally blew himself up along with a few dozen meters of pressure wall, but that didn't seem to matter much to anybody but us troopies. The dead didn't mind the Martian air at all. Not even all the late johnnie's dead.

Madness. Biology. Accelerated mitochondrial RNA transfer. Digestive bioreactors. Conditioning. Viruses. Psychotic agents. It was a stewpot beyond a hell kettle, and all over Mars the troopies of FOAD were spreading something more than death. Something that no one had bothered to warn us about.

And the dead of us, they just made more dead of us.

I don't even dream about how I got off Mars. I just did. Scars webbing my throat. Somehow they let me live. I've been impossible to kill ever since—Gagarin knows I've given the universe plenty of chances.

Am I really me, or just a weaponized copy?

Maybe the real Rabbit Simms is still down there, searching for a way home.

I started to weep.

Skinhorse didn't even look at me. Just kept playing Go.

▲▼▲

We got down below the horizon of Valles Marineris without any of the passive sensor alarms going off. Which made it damned likely no one saw us landing. Which in turn made it somewhat possible no one would see us coming back up again.

I'd forgotten how beautiful the Valles is. Some things only make sense on a planetary scale. I mean, there's rocks tumbling in the belt that would have made Michelangelo cry for the aching glory of their curves, but out there in hard vacuum, they ain't got much context. Down here, where the winds blow and the dust flows and the sun wanders over the rim of the canyon once a day, those wild hard-carved headlands and knees of rock mean something. It's all red and brown, at least in the upper reaches, but that's Mars. The beauty's in the shapes, each one telling the story of how that place came to be.

I had worried some about the Jovian shell down here among the rocky walls, but the H-iF drive was sensitive enough that I could steer against the winds by sheer weight management, along with the occasional blurt of my ambient-temp gas jets. A good Martian howler might do us in, but the Valles was kindly today.

Skinhorse wanted to be down not far from Delany City. Delany had been one of the verts, a development along a power feed that took advantage of the Valles' depth to get closer to the Martian core for free before drilling deep for areothermal and piezolithic generation. All that juice buzzing up the line had attracted little parasite platforms in the early days of the vertical projects. By the time of the last of the Rights Wars those pirate environments had evolved into thriving cliff cities that prospered without much horizontal at all.

I hadn't personally killed Delany City, though maybe some of the dead mes had helped. They spread faster than rumors, at least back during the war.

Now the city was an eerie vertical architecture of ruin. Flapping sheets of bladderplastic extended like the banners of a vanished army. Great skeletal hoops clinging to the cliffs showed the outline of old pressure tents. Crystal domes had shattered, leaving jagged knives embedded in the canyon wall to glint within the shadows of morning.

And it all seemed to move. I watched on the Jovian shell's vid pickups. Everything sort of rippled.

We slid on past before I realized I was seeing people.

Dead people.

Clinging to the power feed.

As we moved on they dropped away, scrambling across the cliffs and downward to follow us.

I nearly vomited into my lap.

"There they are," said Skinhorse. I hadn't realized he was standing behind me. Bent, really, with his height in our taffy-stretched cabin.

"You know them?" I wanted to kill him in that moment. He could have been Enemy, with just a little push of my own unstable sense of reality. Especially in this place.

Mars had been very, very bad for me. Returning was worse.

"Venus was my project," Skinhorse reminded me sharply. "But I know about what happened to Mars."

"What the *fuck* were they thinking?" I asked, clenching my fists and jaw. The shell bobbed with my inattention to business.

"Epidemiological modeling applied to biopsych warfare. They made a few bad assumptions, unfortunately."

There was an epitaph for the human race.

The vids continued to display a surging mass trailing us along the valley floor. How had they lived? I couldn't believe there was enough energy leaching off the power feed to sustain all these dead all these years.

I didn't live off electromagnetic fields. I ate. I drank. I pissed and shat and wept and sometimes even got to fuck when I was lucky.

I wasn't one of them.

I couldn't be.

"Bad assumptions…" I said, trying to break the morbid thread of my thoughts. "Yeah, I'll say."

"Something went wrong with the self-limiters."

"After Venus you people couldn't just fucking *stop*?"

"They were trying to fix Venus, field testing it here."

I had to laugh at that. A bitter, long, raw howl that tore at my stomach muscles and filled my mouth with bile and made me want to claw his throat. Not quite, but almost. "Didn't work, I guess."

"Not yet. That's why I need the gattaca that was left behind."

We were coming up on his coordinates, pursued by the angry dead.

"They'll swarm us by sheer numbers," I said. Not to mention how fiercely they fought.

"I only need a few moments."

I thought about letting him out, then leaving him here. But what if some of those pursuing were dead mes? What if one of them was the real me?

I don't eat electricity.

What if?

Following the coordinates he'd provided, I put the Jovian shell down on a sandy spot in deep shadow. There was no installation nearby, nothing that would seem to be a place where a mad scientist like Skinhorse might have stored his precious gattaca. He said nothing, just glanced at the instruments and suited up for the Martian pressure and temperature.

"Four minutes, tops," I told him.

Skinhorse nodded, then bent nearly over to crawling height to exit the lock. I watched the telltales on the control board. When lock integrity was restored, my fingers brushed the H-iF controls.

The shell could lift right now. No one would ever be the wiser. I'd come home with it, packing enough of Skinhorse's credit to spend the rest of my life not playing cards with rock jocks. I wouldn't run out of funds. Not even if I lived forever.

The crowd in the vid was getting closer. They were running in an almost eerie unison. Were they all the same dead man?

I had the sick feeling they were all the same dead me.

Slapping the lock control, I exited.

▲▼▲

Don't need a helmet for Mars. Not me. I can't breathe vacuum, but I can tolerate some damned surprising pressure and temperature rang-es way outside human norms. Don't quite remember any more which round of FOAD combat mods did this for me, probably the last, but it certainly came in useful now.

I walked out into the shadowed floor of the canyon, sliding in the Martian gravity, while I dialed up the gain on my vision until the running crowd was bright as a drive flare.

They were me. Hundreds, thousands of me. Every shape and size and color, weathered badly by a couple of decades of Martian exposure, but I could see it in the set of every head, the posture of every body, the rhythm of every stride, the way the virus had caused the curve of each jaw to conform with my genome.

I surged around myself, coming to a stop face to face with me. I left one of me in a little pocket in the middle of myself, the rest in concentric ranks so precisely spaced I could have delighted an analytic geometer.

I raised my hands to my throat. The scars were ropy and worn on the lone me, raw and abraded on so many other mes.

The dust, naturally.

My sense of Enemy was gone.

But of course. I was not Enemy. I was me. The ultimate survivor. There was no one else left.

"Hello," I said. My voice didn't carry much in the thin Martian atmosphere, but I knew what I had meant.

"Welcome home," I told myself from a thousand mouths.

Where was Enemy?

"There is only me," I told myself.

"Me."

"I am Mars."

"And I am Venus," said Skinhorse, stepping through the crowd. His voice crackled on his suit speaker, tinny but audible. He had something like a small lance in his suit glove. A probe, I realized, which could have been dropped from orbit with a gene package aboard.

My sense of Enemy, which had been intruding in those last moments inside the Jovian shell, re-emerged. Not with the violent irruption of those early days during the war, but rather as a broad, slow tide.

The anger of a planet, mortally wounded.

"Think," said Skinhorse. He raised a hand. All of me was transfixed. "What have you become?"

"Mars," I whispered, my voice an echoing ripple around the shadowed base of the canyon as I repeated myself in a cycling canon of regret.

"Do you believe that I am Venus?"

I could see the morning star in his eyes, the quadrillion-ton cancer that his skin had become. "Yes," I whispered, still echoing.

"Would you slay me?"

Oh, yes. Mars is War, and the dead me are the bloodiest veterans who ever died to fight another day. But none of my mouths stirred in that moment.

"Slay me now and your mission planners will have their rockball back. The Venus-cancer will die with me, and humans will once more crawl down that gravity well to establish our race." Skinhorse looked around, catching my eye over and over again, reflecting every color and shape of my face in the visor of his helmet. "Or join me and bring a new Earth to pass." He held up the probe, shaking it like a spear. "My cancer and your death together will make our mother world greater than she ever was. In *our* image."

In that moment, I could feel all my thoughts. Murder. Vengeance. Enemy. The silent, cold years of dust storms and starvation after there had been no one left to kill on Mars except me and more of me. The misery of my fellow undying FOAD troopies spread through the solar system.

The brown-skinned boy with the manga eyes smiling to say hello as I entered Walloonia. I could remember him as clearly as if he had died only moments ago.

The fate of worlds was in my hands, all thousands of them. The fate of *H. sap*, for all that the race had ever done for me.

I sent me creeping back into the Jovian shell, to the H-iF controls, even while I spoke to Skinhorse. "It will never be so easy," I said, pulling words from nowhere. "You told me I would become who I am. I want to be who I was. A comfortable killer, not the father of worlds."

"Has all this suffering been for nothing?"

The argument of tyrants.

Inside the shell, I focused the H-iF drive on an external point.

"All this suffering has been for too much," I told Skinhorse.

Did I go with him, believe him, save the Earth, if indeed we would be saving it for some new generation of human evolution? Or did it end here?

"We must evolve," he said, echoing my thoughts once more.

I've been a poker player most of my life. I never could abide the idea of a mind reader. Using H-iF, I threw Skinhorse up into the sky.

Maybe he'd make orbit. Then his suit would fail, it was only surface-rated. Maybe he'd go suborbital and burn up on the way back down. Maybe the monitors up high would fry him with lightning from heaven. I didn't give a captain's crap what happened to the world-killer. If he'd told me the truth, then his death would release the Venus-cancer and we might get one world back. If not, well, things would be no worse than they already were.

Then I gathered me in, looking for a manga-eyed child and, possibly, a very lost troopie who might have been the original me. I would find a way to give the real me a clean and simple death, I promised myself.

Once I was all dead, for real and permanent, *H. Sap* could have Mars back.

All of me smiled, imagining Skinhorse's dying screams.

A Very Old Man With No Wings At All

*I first wrote and workshopped this story with the Wordos,
an excellent writers' group in Eugene, OR. I don't recall
what the title was on the initial draft, but a number of
my fellow writers noted my riff on the Gabriel Garcia
Márquez story, "A Very Old Man With Enormous Wings".
This was news to me, but since we met in a bookstore, on
the mid-session break I found a Márquez collection on
the shelf and read the story in question. I'd love to claim
deep literary cleverness here with respect to binding contemporary fantasy to magic realism, but in truth, I was
riffing on John Milton, which no one has ever noticed.*

The heat was his oldest friend. In this place it wrapped him like the
hand of the divine, vast and never-ending, flavored with salty grit as if
God had lately been digging a grave in the sand. He had never understood how a place so close to the eye-blue sea could be so dry, either.
The sun stole everything and gave back only light and shadow.

The old man lived beneath an ancient dhow long since taken by
worms and the strange desiccation which eventually seized wood in this
place. He liked to think of it as the process of making a fossil, direct pet-
rification without benefit of æons of burial beneath the earth. The boat
had once belonged to a man named Muusa. This always struck him as
particularly appropriate, given the reed-banked sea muttering just outside
the hull of his home.

Someone knocked on the wood. The old man started, unsure if
he'd been sleeping, dreaming or dying. He wasn't certain there was a
difference anymore.

"*Enter into my presence,*" he called in Adamic tongue. Remembering
himself, he switched to Egyptian Arabic. "Peace to you."

Butrus slipped between the hull and the sand. The boy lived in the
fishing village perhaps ten minutes' walk down the beach, and often

visited. They traded stories, and the old man wheedled what little food he needed. Having never been young himself, he was vague on the ages of people, but Butrus always seemed a bit larger with each appearance.

"Oh, great sage," said Butrus. He always talked like that. The old man suspected someone in the village had been reading to the boy. That sort of thing always ended in blood. "There are strangers come among us."

"So?" He hated the whine that sometimes crept into his voice. He had been here far too long, but there was nowhere else to go. "There are always tourists. Smile and take their money. It is what you do, is it not?"

"No. Not tourists. Strangers. *Different.*"

There was something in the boy's tone, the twitch of his eyes. "Soldiers?" An image of men with crested helmets, carrying spears bladed like bronze leaves. No, no, that was wrong. Guns they had now. You could die before you ever heard the flutter of black wings crossing over your soul.

Some things were not right. People knew too much.

"They are angry, great sage. They search with boots and rifles."

"For what?"

"You, sir."

The old man thought about this a while. Butrus held still for a time, then began to wriggle. The old man mostly ignored the boy.

Who would come looking for him?

The heat brought memory, but memory was a broken kaleidoscope that someone had given him long ago, colored jewels that slipped between his fingers like fish too small for the net. The world had been air once, light and air without sun, stars or world beneath. That he was certain of. Cast down, one could fall forever.

Laughing.

Free.

Tumbling.

Until earth was created beneath one's feet.

Later there were trees. Monkeys screaming from branches. Muddy footprints saved in stone for the puzzlement of the future. God dictating to a mumbling fool with broken teeth and bad breath. Swords, some afire.

And people, little angels without wings, carrying their mortality leaden within their hearts. Sand, these people associated sand with time. He understood that. Sand was infinitely divisible and infinitely the same. Likewise time. There was only one moment, the present, but it was infinitely divisible into past and future.

It was those divisible moments which formed the shattered mirrors of his memory.

Noise brought him back. A flat crack, the same sound made by outstretched wings being torn free. Butrus shuddered and grabbed his knees. "They're shooting now," he said. Whimpering.

"Boy." The old man's voice was rough. "This is just a moment in the mind of God. It means nothing more than any other moment."

The boy squeezed a tear, an offering. "My sister. She means something. Mama, my papa."

Another crack. This one reminded him of how a hollow-boned body sounded, falling to earth from the infinitely divisible and unvarying altitude of grace.

"Please," said Butrus. "You have power. We do not."

"Power?" The old man was stung to laughter. He had lived beneath this dhow, a crab in a wooden shell, as long as he could remember. Everything else in his mind was a bright lie, a temptation apple-red, though even the apple was a lie too. What power was there to a shattered memory and days spent gasping in the killing heat, nights spent listening to the plash of fish beyond the ankle-high surf?

"We are no one." The boy was stubborn. "You are someone."

His shoulders itched, now, muscles seeking something. He wore a faded burnous that covered him poorly. A Saxon—no, an Englishman—had given it to him some time ago, advising him to wash with kerosene to combat the lice.

When had he ever met a Saxon?

"I am no one. If they shoot, they shoot. If they kill, they kill. That is the way of soldiers." The Saxon had been a soldier. An English soldier who pretended to be an Arab, with a motorcycle and fire-blue eyes that had seen the face of God. The old man had wondered where the land of Engle was, but the soldier had not troubled to tell him.

"You are the great sage." Butrus' face was closed, set. The boy was fighting, the old man realized, in the only way he knew how. Not even faith would stop bullets, or the rip of wings from a falling body. "You *are* someone, even if you do not remember. My grandfather says you have been here since the time of Caliphate."

"That may be true," the old man admitted cautiously. He searched his memory again, but all he found this time was heat. He could not remember the last time he'd crept out from beneath the hull to look up at the stars of heaven.

The boy brandished a pair of chicken feathers, his face quivering between triumph and utter collapse. "He told me you would need these."

The old man gently took the feathers from between the boy's trembling fingers. He turned them over, remembering again—pinions blacker than shadow, brighter than the fire in the sun. A span of wings which could cross the sky, brushing each horizon.

Oh, there had been glory once.

The stumps in his back wept fresh blood, staining the burnous a deeper brown.

"No," he said slowly. Another series of shots rattled from down the beach. "I am not permitted to lift myself back up."

Butrus began to cry, his little brown body shivering in the old man's arms. How had he come to hold the boy? His back itched horribly, threatening to sprout anew. "No," he whispered.

Pride. He had fallen once for pride, he would not fly again.

After a time, footsteps crunched on the sand outside. The boy's tears were done. He lay limp on the old man's lap. Already dead in truth, though the body breathed a little while longer. The old man knew this story. It was as old as the monkeys in the trees.

He touched the boy's back, drawing forth the secrets locked in the letters hidden deep within the flesh. Like the kaleidoscope of his memory, all creation remembered what it had been. The chicken feathers helped, guiding him.

It took a great deal of time, but time was infinitely divisible. He watched a bullet burrow slowly through the brittle wood of the hull, but kept at his work. He saw two more follow. Still the old man worked.

"I have no gifts," he whispered, "only knowledge."

He set the boy free in a flurry of feathers as the wood of the dhow began to collapse. The bullets did not find the old man, any more than the weapons of the world ever would. The boy leapt upward into the bright sunlight in a spray of salt and sand. The old man was so much spindrift to the hard men on the beach.

"A gull," one of them said in disgust. Another loosed a stream of gunfire into the sky, then gave up.

Only a moment in the mind of God, the old man thought, his back twisting in a vain attempt to take flight as a bright bird soared above the eye-blue sea, keening sorrow for its lost boyhood. He crawled into the shattered shadow of his boat and carefully sorted the bright jewels of memory, hoarding what he could.

People of Leaf and Branch

This story was written as an offshoot of the short story "Green", well before I'd seriously contemplated turning "Green" into the novel Green. *I was playing with my ideas about the city of Copper Downs and the world which extended around it. So while this doesn't extend the characters or plot of* Green *in any particular direction at all, it does show the setting from a completely different point of view than anything found within the novel.*

Maribel ran along the top boards. The planks went from roof to roof, along the ridges, with a jumping-space to reach the peaks of the round huts. She didn't have the skill of a *danceuse*, nor the grace of the best of the girls from the stone city below her, but among the woodkin, she was often accounted the most lithe and best.

The Tower Wander was ahead, with Shrike House clinging to its neck like a collar. The old wall had long since been swallowed by the spread of the stone city, gone from defense to landmark to landform in the space of a few generations. The Duke of Copper Downs had forbidden the woodkin to enter the abandoned towers, but their exteriors had never been under such a rule.

So the seven surviving towers acquired names, and superstructures, and held the long, narrow village that ran from the Broken Gate to the Tower Harbor. The towers were part of the stone city, but the houses were the woodkin's memory of another time and place.

She slipped through the roof of Shrike House, dropping to the floor in a shower of dust and straw.

There was no one there, of course. Shrike House had been empty since Maribel's mother's childhood. Seven towers, seven houses, but in every generation more went down to the stone and found lives among the city. None returned.

Maribel drew a toe in the dust. "I shall never touch the streets," she whispered. "This I swear on the teeth of my grandmother."

She walked through Shrike House, balancing on her toes in the Step of the Shrike with each pace, circling the Tower Wander as she stopped to clean each ancestor. The ancestors still deserved care, though there were no more Shrikes. At least not here in the stone city.

Whether anyone still lived back among the trees was a subject of intense, and quiet, conversation.

The ancestors' faces were long gone to slick and sticky leather. Their eyes were sewn shut with thread twisted from the tendons and guts of shrikes. Their mouths were stuffed with the remains of dried fruits and tiny *taelsaem* scrolls of wisdom both earthly and otherworldly. Each ancestor had a copper plate of pale soil and a wooden plate of tiny stones before them. She had no joss sticks to burn, no feathers to offer, so Maribel could only offer her own small efforts and a wide-armed bow.

They did not answer. Ancestors never did. If there was a response to prayers, Maribel didn't know where or how it might come. The woodkin had lived in Copper Downs—the stone city—for as many generations as there were towers, or so they said. The number of ancestors in the houses seemed to bear that out, at least to her observation. There were more dead than living, and would have been even if the houses were full.

Maribel stopped before the last ancestor in her round, a particularly broad-faced specimen with silver chasings around her eye sockets and the gap of her missing nose. Maribel liked to think of this ancestor as the first mother of Shrike House. Still here after the last mother had passed, for whatever that might mean. She pressed her hands together, bowed, then reached to brush the dust from the ancestor's forehead.

That was when she noticed the *taelsaem* was missing from the ancestor's mouth.

In the seven years she'd been visiting Shrike House, Maribel had never seen anything move which she had not moved herself. She'd never seen anything removed at all. There was nothing left to salvage, or steal for that matter, save the niches in the wooden walls where the ancestors sat and watched the years unfold. Only bare boards, dust, and her own footprints.

With that thought, Maribel looked down.

No new footprints. Or if there were, they had been made by someone with feet very similar to her own.

She studied the skull. Had it moved? She'd seen this ancestor every week since she was six years old.

Where was the *taelsaem*?

Very slowly, Maribel reached forward to brush her fingers in front of the slightly opened jaw.

It snapped at her.

▲▼▲

Before time began there was only one tree. Her leaves were as the fields of the land, her branches as the arches of the sky, her roots as the bones of the world. Her bole was as wide as the circle of night and day, her flowers as bright and numberless as the stars in the winter sky.

When the sunfather and moonmother finally awoke they let the glow of gold and silver flood the twilight of the one tree. Her leaves spun free from her branches, her flowers dropped like birds on the wing, her roots crumbled and dried as do the fingers of the dead. The hills of the world were raised from the curves of her fallen bole, while the rivers flowed with her sap.

The woodkin came awake then, children of time, for we are nothing more than the memories of the one tree made flesh, quickened by the passage of moments and years, so that we live out the fall of the tree over and over in the seasons of our lives.

▲▼▲

She sprinted across the boards, light and fast as a cat come up from the city below. The Tower Indolence just behind, the Tower Middleward just ahead in Maribel's rush from Shrike House to her home in Peregrine House.

Maribel knew she would not panic. There was no reason to. Ancestors were there to protect and advise. It was what she'd always been told.

She dropped through the roof of Peregrine House. Her house, where her grandmothers spent their days sitting among the ancestors shrouded in incense and the smell of herbal teas simmering over tiny fires.

All of the woodkin who still kept the old ways lived in the round huts and galleries that clung to the walls like swallow nests, from the tiniest children to the oldest grandmothers. Most spent their time atop the towers netting birds, or scrambling the rooftops of the stone city around them to clean and repair the high places. A few watched after the children, keeping their feet from stone and their heads in the air.

Maribel was alone in tending the high homes of the woodkin and watching after the grandmothers and the houses.

Now she slipped to the floor. No dust here in Peregrine House. Rather, delicate sculptures of bird bones hung from the ceiling in the shadowed, curving hallway, spinning slowly in the air currents. The pelts of birds, feathered and tanned, spread along the walls. The ancestors were well-tended, surrounded by fruits and flowers traded up from the streets below, wrapped in incense, with coins and colored stones in their mouths.

No *taelsaems* here, though. The grandmothers kept those close, in the houses that yet survived.

Maribel found Grandmother Anya kneeling before one of the Peregrine House ancestors. She dropped to a crouch, briefly bowing her head.

"Grandmother, there is a problem in Shrike House."

Anya turned to stare at Maribel. One eye was black as polished onyx, the other was milky white, rolling to an unsensed tempo. "There is always a problem at Shrike House," she said. "Paxiliana is a troublemaker."

Paxiliana had died long before Maribel was born. Sometimes the grandmothers remembered things which had happened long ago. More rarely they remembered things which hadn't happened yet.

"Shrike House stands empty, Grandmother," she said with quiet patience. "But someone has taken the *taelsaem* from first mother."

Anya nodded. "Oh yes, this is the year that poor Duke fell."

The Duke of Copper Downs had sat on the throne for centuries, Maribel knew. The stone men were different from the woodkin, and she knew little about how they spoke to their ancestors. Apparently by keeping them alive, in the case of the late Duke's case.

"The *taelsaem* is gone," she repeated. "And the first mother—" Maribel stopped. That an elderly, dusty head had snapped at her sounded foolish now. The misplaced fears of a girl.

"A *taelsaem* is nothing more than a scrap torn from a leaf of the one tree," said Anya. "Like time itself, it is filled with power, but also like time, very few have the wisdom to command it."

"So you are not concerned, grandmother, that the Shrike House has lost the *taelsaem* of its first mother?"

"Who would use it?"

That seemed so…insufficient. She wanted to ask, *Who would take it?*, but Grandmother Anya had turned back to contemplation of some inner vista.

▲▼▲

When the leaves fell upon the land, they carried some of the blood of the tree with them, sap clustering about their torn stems as gems cluster around the dragon's mouth. The echoes of the tree's fall still sounded in the valleys and riverbeds of the world. The animals were awakening then, unfolding from their secret nests beneath the hollow hills. The first birds were draggling wet to the hilltops to meet the rising light of the first day.

Mother Yve, of the first generation to rise from the memories of the one tree, tore a corner from the leaf which covered her as she quickened. She used it first to wrap her body, then to shelter her children, then finally as a shroud when she lay herself down to rest. The imprints of her life upon the scrap were the words which counted the spell of the first taelsaem, *and the time of her life gave the spell power.*

▲▼▲

Maribel retreated to the top boards again. It seemed strange that Grandmother Anya had not cared for the fate of the Shrike House *taelsaem*, but then the *taelsaems* had been in the world for a longer span of years than any but the stars themselves could remember.

Perhaps the spells could take care of themselves.

She stared across Copper Downs to where the sun sparkled on the harbor and the bright, sullen ocean beyond. The great metal-plated domes of the Temple District loomed to the east, many of them tarnished or fallen now. Closer to the wall, many of the compounds in the old city still smoldered from the riots which had erupted after the fall of the Duke. The docks remained half-empty, trade staying away from Copper Downs in the aftermath of the unrest.

None of which was her concern. The woodkin worked the rooftops and were above the worries of the stone city—except for those who had emigrated to the stone and cast off the memory of the forests. Maribel tried to think of them as traitors, but couldn't.

There was so much below the woodkin—smells of food and colors of cloth, the rivers of people and animals, the brass ape races and temple processionals. Every time a woodkin looked down from their round houses and walkways they saw a wider world than they'd have above.

"We live closer to the sky," she said, "amid the memory of the one tree."

It was a blessing the woodkin said for themselves at dawn and at dusk, in the times when day and night mixed in reminder of what had come before.

But the sky was empty and cold, compared to the streets below.

The *taelsaem* had been taken by one of the migrants, of course.

She stared at the street below her, wondering how to get it back. Wondering whether that even mattered.

▲▼▲

Maribel ran the top boards again, back to Shrike House. She ducked down through the trapdoor and into the swept circle of the interior. She ran to the first mother.

The skull was gone, just as absent as the *taelsaem*. And still there were no footprints on the floor save her own.

She very nearly burst into tears.

After a few moments of hard, shuddering breathing, Maribel found control of herself once more. She turned back and walked the circle, checking the other ancestors.

They were there, with their dried fruits and shredded remains of flower petals and stubbed out joss sticks and the few *taelsaems* that remained to Shrike House. Each blackened eye pit, each tight-sewn lid, stared at her in silent accusation.

Where is our sister?, they seemed to ask.

Where is the first mother?

Where is our memory of the beginning?

Where is our hope for the end?

Maribel shuddered again, circling slowly, meeting their dead eyes pair by pair, nodding slowly as the ancestors asked their unvoiced questions. Dead for more years than she had been alive, these ancestors took more interest in the loss of the *taelsaem* and skull that Grandmother Anya had back in Peregrine House.

"I did not take her," Maribel said aloud. "Nor did I remove her spell."

Something thumped behind her.

She turned. The first mother sat in the middle of the floor staring at her. A faint glow leaked between tight-sewn eyes. A part of Maribel noted that the *taelsaem* was still missing.

Maribel knelt and touched her forehead to the dusty floor. The air moved, gusting dry with the scent of greens and warm soil. Not the smells of the stone city at all.

"First mother, welcome back to your home."

The breeze plucked at Maribel's hair, worried at the skin of her face, made her shift flutter. She smelled things she didn't remember but still somehow knew—wood scent and flowers and the calm air under a starry night sky.

Time, too. The dusty scent of time. Like an empty grave, or the long vacant towers around which the woodkin houses had been built.

As she stared at the floor, wishing only to be outside, away, distant from whatever door had opened, the dust moved. It stirred in patterns. A line like the horizon. It peaked, became a mountain, before roughening to the lines of trees. First mother was drawing a forest.

She kept drawing, invisible fingers telling a story. All the trees became a single tree. No, Maribel corrected herself, the one tree. It grew, ramified, acquired the texture of leaf and branch and the nest of birds and monkeys and squirrels and, finally the woodkin.

The tree branches lifted, the trunk split, and there was a body. Still indefinably wood, but human too, arms and legs and hands and breasts and a neck rising to the base of the first mother's head resting on the floor.

With that, the breeze was gone, only the must and dust of the Shrike House tickling her nose, with the greasy smoke and harbor smell of the stone city somewhere beneath it. Maribel stood from her bow. The dust-drawn woman still spread at her feet, surmounted by the silver-chased skull of the ancestor. There was no glow in first mother's eyes though, and the *taelsaem* was still missing.

Somehow that seemed both perfectly clear and mysterious as morning fog.

▲▼▲

Once we lived high in the trees. The aunties told the kits that we were born of the monkey and the fox, but that was just a cradle story, a lie meant to learn from rather than deceive. For one, the woodkin have no tails, nor silky fur to warm them in the north wind. Anyone, even a kit, can see the falsehood for what it is.

But when we were old enough to run alone in the uppermost branches we found more of the truth. It lay written in the dew beneath the leaves and the tight-curled batlings in the hollows of the high trunks and the circle of the peregrine high in the summer sky.

When we brought the truth home, the aunties laughed and sent us to the mothers for instruction. There we learned that the woodkin were made of wood and leaf and blood, buds of the one tree brought to light by the stars in the sky and raised to speech and skill by Yve, grandmother to us all.

There came a day when some were carried away, out of the high trees, and in our leaving, we lost too much, forgot too much, were turned away from what we were ever meant to be.

▲▼▲

"Grandmother Anya," Maribel said. "I know where the *taelsaem* has gone."

The old woman grinned, gap-toothed and hollow-cheeked. Maribel realized she was not so far from being an ancestor herself, save for the sparkling onyx eye and its marbled similar both gleaming where very soon there would be tight-stretched stitches. "Was it spirited away by some scoundrel then, girl?"

"No. The first mother of Shrike House..." She paused, wondering about the words. "The first mother took it in herself."

"Ah." Grandmother Anya took a long, slow breath. "Eating time again. How is she?"

Maribel was used to the fact that the oldest women didn't seem to make much distinction between the living and the dead. Woodkin were woodkin, stone people were stone people. They were as different as sun and moon, as sky and soil, for all that men and women could lie with another well enough. But among the woodkin, the living and the dead seemed to share the same world.

Sometimes Maribel thought there were so many dead they had crowded out the living, that was why the houses were emptying.

"She asked me for a body."

"Then give her one."

"How?"

Grandmother Anya leaned close. "It was you she asked, girl."

▲▼▲

Maribel squatted on the top boards again and watched the evening steal over Copper Downs. Below her feet families were moving to dinner, to their evening, the herbal stews and smoked bird meat favored by the woodkin watering her mouth with their tempting scents. The murmur of voices, the quiet prayers to leaf and branch, the gentle thump of feet on the boards—these were the music to which she had lived all her life.

Still, it was always counterpointed by the brawl of the stone city. Even now, someone drove a mechanical centipede through the street below her, the clank-clatter of its claws on cobbles echoing upward like prayers for a brassy god. Fire glimmered from the vacant lot where the Lucky Deer Mercantile had burned three years earlier, now a place where people gathered to roast dogs or muntjacs or whatever they had caught or bought that day. Bells clanged in and around the harbor, a song of tide and trade which never fell completely silent.

Those were smells and music she'd always heard, too.

Why had they left the trees and come to live here?, Maribel wondered.

And how would she give a body to the first mother of Shrike House? She was no anatomist to work in sinew and muscle, nor *reb* to build a golem of clay, nor ordinator designing eelskin rolls to motivate the calculating drums of some brass statue. She was just a girl who swept floors in the silent houses high above the streets.

She was also woodkin, daughter of leaf and branch, and kin to the ancestor who had made a plea of her. No more than she would refuse a child could she refuse this grandmother she had never known.

A thought struck her, tickling her imagination. Command of the *taelsaem* was not her art, but it was the heart of her people. Like the woodkin, the *taelsaem* was drawn from the one tree. Surely this would be enough.

There was a difference, though. They lived among the stone city now, dreaming of the past. What if she gave the first mother of Shrike House a body which looked toward the future?

"For you," Maribel whispered aloud, "I shall break my oath to the teeth of my grandmother." Anya had few enough of them as it was, she thought irreverently as she began to climb down to the streets.

▲▼▲

The ground was strange, unyielding and far too close, so that with every step she felt as if she were falling, but no one seemed to care. There were more people than Maribel had ever been close to in her life. They shoved past her, a sea of strange faces changing from one moment to the next. It was an endless current of carts and mules and dogs and people and wild animals led on chains and sedan chairs hoisted high and herds of pigs and a thousand more passersby. What seemed an orderly, distinctive flow from her perch above in the houses of the woodkin was nothing more than mobile chaos down below. The fact that evening had come full-on did nothing to dim the traffic, though the light of day had been replaced with torches and lamps and the diffuse glow of the night sky.

Still, all she needed to do was fight her way across the stream to the lot where the fire burned and some meat or another roasted warm tonight. Progress was painful, so difficult to keep from being touched, slammed, run down. She wanted to scream and run across their heads and shoulders. And the horses were so big.

How did these people *stand* their crowded lives upon the soil?

Struggling on, she was surprised when she did arrive at the vine-wrapped timbers of the charred storefront. Maribel slipped out of the traffic with a profound sense of relief.

There were stone city folk standing around their fire, dark outlines drinking from skins and bottles as something four-legged turned in the flames. A man with two slim knives, each as long as his arm, carved even as his beast rotated, cutting flesh away in narrow spirals, then catching it before it fell to the wood and coals, flicking them back to land in long, slinky portions on bits of board. People took the boards in ones and twos and bent to their meal.

She carefully approached the cook, stepping between people who nodded slightly, or simply turned away. Maribel wasn't sure if she was supposed to return the nods.

He glanced at her a moment, then concentrated once more at the flickering blades of his work. "See Idras if you're wanting some grub."

"It—" Her voice caught. Maribel had never spoken to a stone man before. Somehow this was even worse than the crowding or the shoving. She nearly lost her nerve, ready to turn and flee back to her towers.

Yet he was little different from a woodkin, truly. His garb was not the same—a greasy leather apron to catch the sparks, boots where a woodkin would go bare or wear sandals, with a different cast to his face and darker hair. Still, a man. "It is not food I seek," she said in a rush.

The knives danced again, and two coils of meat came free with a lovely scent of roast. "Aye."

That was permission, she decided. "I come to beg the bones of your beast."

She earned a long, hard look with that request. Then: "Burnt hot and cracked by fire, what would you do? Make a stew?"

"I—I want something from the stones. For a...devotion of mine."

He grunted, but he did not run her off.

And so she waited while the stars wheeled slowly overhead. The beast was whittled down. One and another of the gathered folk gave her sip and sup. The generosity surprised her. She'd always thought the stone city folk hard and mean.

Maribel listened to their songs and the stories they told one another, details of people and places and pursuits she knew nothing of, and wondered again why her own folk had left the trees, and what it was they had meant to do in coming to Copper Downs. As the evening wound on, she found herself almost comfortable here. These people meant her no harm. They just wanted a meal and a place near the fire and someone to tell their troubles to.

Eventually there were only coals, and two old women with an ash cart, and the tired cook. He stood before Maribel where she sat on a makeshift couch of bundled lumber and old sacking, his fists balled upon his hips. "And so you're a patient one. Like all of them what lives above." His head jerked back toward the towers of the old wall.

"Patient as wood," she said.

"Wood burns." He leaned forward, his hands on his knees, perhaps to stretch his back. He came too close to her. For the first time in hours Maribel felt a tinge of fear. "And what will you give me for a sack of bones still hot from the grease?"

"I have nothing to trade." Maribel had not thought of this. The wood-kin did not exchange coin among themselves in their houses above, but of course it was needful down here in the stone city. She wondered just how great a fool she had been.

He laughed, her newfound fear evaporating as he did so. "T'ain't the bones worth so much, though the stew woman will grant me two coppers and a bowl full. But the sack alone is worth three times that."

"Then I will return your sack clean and mended," she said, "with a wooden bowl for your stew."

"You above..." His voice was slow, thoughtful. "Everyone in the New Districts knows about you above. Your lights flicker in the even. When your men come down to work, they're quiet and peaceful-like. When your women come down to marry, they bring grace." He stood, stretched, and leaned close. "Whatever your devotion is, don't bring them houses falling. You're our luck."

He stepped back, grabbed a bulging sack and handed it to her, then went off to negotiate with the ash cart women.

Maribel walked away, across the cobbled street which had fallen almost quiet, to the ladders which lead up to the tiny, tiny world from which she'd come.

▲▼▲

Moonmother taught us with lies wrapped inside truth wrapped inside lies. No matter her words, she died and was reborn as surely as winter and summer, in her cycle same as any woman who ever walked the world. From this we learned what it meant to live, to slip away, and return again along the silver paths among the dark leaves of outermost night.

As the full moon is reborn from the dark moon, as the tree is reborn from the seed, so woodkin is reborn from the dust and tears of those who mourn and remember.

▲▼▲

Maribel laid out the cracked bones where she could make them fit. The beast had not been large as a person, but it was the shape of the thing that mattered, she thought. She hoped, at any rate. She had brought a broom handle, and bloody straw from the bed of a woman who had recently birthed, and three sprigs of mistletoe—woodkin magic, from the Peregrine House and its absent grandmothers.

The old women must have been abed when she went visiting.

She laid out the handle and the straw and the mistletoe—making spine and hair and heart out of them, amid the cracked and burnt bones.

It looked stupid, she realized, a child's toy in mock of life. The ancestor's head perched above the pattern of a woman was nothing more than a skull and some bones. Maribel felt a rush of disgust, of foolishness, wondering what the cook down below would have said to see this.

Then the eyes of the ancestor began to glow once more. The forest wind came back, ruffling her hair, carrying the dust of time with it.

You must wrap me, whispered the wind. Close me up and make me whole.

Wrap her how?, thought Maribel. She took up the leather sack the cook had given her and looked at it. She could cut it open, perhaps? But…

The wind spoke again: Wrap me in time and life.

Dust rattled around her.

Time.

Maribel jumped up and ran around the circumference of Shrike House. She tugged the remaining *taelsaems* from between the teeth of the ancestors. Each was an irregular sheet perhaps the size of a man's chest. Each glowed the faint color of starlight, even in the dark of the house.

When she found the ancestor again, she tucked the *taelsaems* around the chest and under the back of the stick-and-bone figure. The wind was stronger now, smelling of forest and mountain and that dry scent of time once more.

The leaves of the one tree were not enough. There were gaps, pooled shadows through which she could faintly see the silvered boards below.

She tugged at her left arm with her right hand, peeling the skin there back. It was like pulling at a fruit, coming away with a faint tearing sound and a salty sting of pain. Maribel placed her own flesh in the gaps, filling in between the *taelsaem* sheets, covering the blackened bones and the woody spine and the plant heart.

Eventually she was denuded, though strangely bloodless save for a trickle on her thighs. Her only pain was a deep cramp in her groin—the peeling was nothing more than discomfort. Maribel lay down next to the first mother and wrapped her arms around the sticky mess that was the body and tried to lend it her heat, even as the dusty air of time swirled around them both.

▲▼▲

A young woman with the face of a city dweller woke her in the dawn. Maribel looked into a pair of eyes the waxy green of mistletoe.

Stretching, she was surprised to find herself whole.

"Let us go find someone with a cook fire," the woman said.

"Are you...?"

"I am Mother Shrike, and I am hungry." The young woman grinned, and Maribel saw that her teeth were blackened, with a few cracks.

"I'm sorry I—"

"Hush, child." She placed a finger on Maribel's lips. The touch made her shiver. "The world is new again. Trees grow in stone, you know, wherever their seeds may fall."

Together they climbed out into the sunlight, walking the top boards toward a ladder that led down to where the woodkin lived.

▲▼▲

The one tree was wise. She had many children before she was remade into the world. Each of her children carries a tree within, a secret copy of the one tree. A wise woman can see inside the child to the tree, and inside the tree to the child, each bearing the other in the circle of its arms like the full moon and the dark moon do.

The greatest trick of time is that it has no beginning and no end, and the hours always come round again.

A Water Matter

Much like "People of Leaf and Branch", this story was written as a follow-up to the short story "Green" without any anticipation of the novel which was to come. Except here I was very specifically exploring what happened to one of the key characters after the end of the short story. This piece takes place during Green's sea voyage at the beginning of the second section of the novel, but the action is of course invisible to her. Despite later editing, there are still some minor continuity violations between this story and Green—the observant reader will note for instance that the Tavernkeep appears in this story, but not by that name—still, I prefer to let this stand on its own.

The Duke of Copper Downs had stayed dead.

So far.

That thought prompted the Dancing Mistress to glance around her at the deserted street. Sometimes the corner of her eye or the lantern of her dreams was crying out a message. Just as with any of the people, it was difficult to take her by surprise. Her sense of the world around her was very strong. Even in sleep, her folk did not become so inert and vulnerable as humans or most animals did. And her people had lived among men for generations, after all. Some instincts were hard won.

His Grace is not going to come clawing up through the stones at my feet, she told herself firmly. Her tail remained stiff and prickly, trailing gracelessly behind her in a parody of alarm.

The city continued restive. A pall of smoke hung low in the sky, while the reek of building fires dogged every breath. The harbor had virtually emptied, shipping steering away from the riots and the uncontrolled militias that remained of the Ducal Guard after the recent assassination. The streets were an odd alternation of deserted and crowded.

Folk seemed unwilling to come out except in packs. If chance emptied a square or a cobbled city block, it stayed empty for hours. The hot, heavy damp did nothing to ease tempers.

At the moment, she strode alone across the purple-and-black flagstones of the Greenmarket area. The smell of rotting vegetables was strong. The little warehouses were all shuttered. Even the everpresent cats had found business elsewhere.

She hurried onward. The message which had drawn her onto the open streets had been quite specific as to time and place. Her sense of purpose was so strong that she could feel the blurring tug of the Hunt. A trap, that was always a trap for the people, especially walking among men.

Wings whirred overhead in a beat far too fast for any bird save the bright and tiny hummers that haunted the vines of the temple district. She did not even look up.

▲▼▲

The Dancing Mistress stood before a little gateway set in the middle of a long stucco wall that bordered close on Dropnail Lane in the Ivory Quarter. This was the boundary of some decaying manse, marking the perimeter of a compound long cut up into a tiny maze of gardens and hovels. A village of sorts flourished under the silent oaks amid which the great house rotted resplendent and abandoned. She'd been here a few times to see a woman of her people whose soul path was the knowledge of herbs and simples. But always she'd come through the servants' gate, a little humped arch next to the main entrance facing onto Whitetop Street.

This gateway was different. It clearly did not fit the setting. Black marble pilasters were embedded in the fading ochre plaster of the estate's wall, like shadowed fingers clawing their way out of a dying fire. The darkness tried to pull her inward.

She shook away the sense of compulsion. In firm control of her own intentions, the Dancing Mistress slowly reached to touch the metal grate. Though the air was warm, the black iron was cold enough to sting her fingers down to the claw sheaths.

The way was barred, but it was not locked. The Dancing Mistress pushed on through.

The dark gate opened into a tangle of heavy vines. Ivy and wisteria strangled a stand of trees which had been reduced to pale, denuded corpses. Fungus grew in mottled shelves along the lower reaches of the bare trunks, and glistened in the mat of leaves and rot that floored the little grove. There was a small altar of black stone amid the pallid trunks, where only shadows touched the ground. An irregular block of ice gleamed atop the altar. It shed questing coils of vapor into the spring-warm air.

They had no name for themselves—they were just people, after all. And it was one of the people who had written the note she'd found strung by spider webs against the lintel of her rented room. She had been able to tell by the hand of the writing, the scent on the page, the faint trail of a soul flavored with meadow flowers.

No one she knew, though, not by hand nor scent nor soul. While the Dancing Mistress could not readily count the full number of her folk in Copper Downs, it was still a matter of dozens amid the teeming humans in their thousands and thousands.

But this altar freezing amid the bones of trees was not something of her people.

A man emerged from the shadows without moving, as if the light had found him between one moment and the next. He was human—squat, unhandsome, with greasy, pale hair that twisted in hanks down his shoulder. His face had been tattooed with fingerprints so that it seemed as if some god or spirit had reached out and grasped him too hard with a grip of fire. His broad body was wrapped in leather and black silk. The garments were as greasy as his hair. Dozens of small blades slipped into gaps in his leather, each crusted in old blood.

A shaman, then, who sought the secrets of the world in the frantic pounding hearts of prey small and large. Only the space around his eyes was clean, pale skin framing a watery gaze that pierced her like a diamond knife.

"*You walk as water on rock.*" He spoke the tongue of her people with only the smallest hint of an accent. That was strange in its own right. That *she*, of a people who had once hunted dreams on moonless nights, could have walked within two spans of him without noticing was far stranger.

Both of those things worried her deeply.

"I walk like a woman in the city," she said in the tongue of the Stone Coast people. The Dancing Mistress knew as a matter of quiet pride that she had no accent herself.

"In truth," he answered, matching her speech. His Petraean held the same faint hint of an accent. He was no more a native here than she.

"Your power is not meant to overmatch such as me," she told him quietly. At the same time, she wondered if that were true. Very, very few humans knew the tongue of the people.

He laughed at that, then broke his gaze. "I would offer you wine and bread, but I know your customs in that regard. Still, your coming to meet me is a thing well done."

She ignored the courtesy. "That note did not come from your hand."

"No." His voice was level. "Yet I sent it."

The Dancing Mistress shivered. He implied power over someone from the high meadows of her home. "Your note merely said to meet, concerning a water matter." That was one of the greatest obligations one of her people could lay upon another.

"The Duke remains dead," he said. She shivered at the echo of her earlier thought. He went on: "The power of his passing has left a blazing trail for those who can see it."

"You aver he will not return."

The man shrugged. She had not asked his name, for her people did not give theirs, but that did nothing to lessen her wondering who he was. He answered her: "Soon it will not matter if he tries to return or not. His power leaches away, to be grasped or lost in the present moment. Much could be done now. Good, ill, or indifferent, this is the time for boldness."

She leaned close, allowing her claws to flex. He would know what that signified. "And where do *I* fit into your plans, *man*?"

"You have the glow of him upon you," he told her. "His passing marked you. I would know from you who claimed him, who broke him open. That one—mage, warrior or witch—holds the first and greatest claim on his power."

Green!

The girl-assassin was fled now across the water insofar as the Dancing Mistress knew. She was suddenly grateful for that small mercy. "It does not matter who brought low the Duke of Copper Downs," she whispered. "He is gone. The world moves on. New power will rise in his place, new evil will follow."

Another laugh, a slow rumble from his black-clad belly. "Power will always rise. The right hand grasping it in the right moment can avoid much strife for so many. I thought to make some things easier and more swift with your aid, for the sake of everyone's trouble."

"You presume too much," she told him.

"*Me?*" His grin was frightening. "You look at my skin and think to judge my heart. Humans do not have soul paths as your people do. You will not scent the rot you so clearly suspect within me."

The Dancing Mistress steeled herself. There was no way she could stand alone against this one, even if she had trained in the arts of power. "Good or ill, I will say no more upon it."

"Hmm." He tugged at his chin. "I see you have a loyalty to defend."

"It is not just loyalty." Her voice was stiff despite her self-control, betraying her fear of him. "Even if I held such power within my grasp, I would have no reason to pass it to you."

"By your lack of action, you have already handed the power to whomever can pluck it forth. Be glad it was only me come calling." He added in her tongue, *"I know the scent of a water matter. I will not argue from the tooth."*

"Nor will I bargain from the claw." She turned and stalked toward the cold gate, shivering in her anger.

"'Ware, woman," he called after her, then laughed again. "We are not friends, but neither must we be enemies. I would still rather have your aid in this matter, and not your opposition. Together we can spare much suffering and trouble."

She slipped between the black stone gateposts and into the street beyond, refusing for the sake of the sick fear that coiled in the bottom of her gut to hurry on her way.

▲▼▲

There was no one out in the late afternoon, normally a time when the squares and boulevards would have been thronged, even in the quieter, richer quarters.

She walked with purposeful intent, thinking furiously even as she watched for trouble. That shaman must have come from some place both rare and distant. There were tribes and villages of humans in every corner of the world of which she'd heard. Men lived in the frigid shadows high up in the Blue Mountains where the very air might freeze on the coldest nights, and amid the fire-warm plains of Selistan beyond the sea, and in the boundless forests of the uttermost east. Not to mention everywhere in between.

He was from somewhere in between, to be sure. The Leabourne Hills, or one of the other places the people lived when they had not yet drifted away as she had done to dwell among the cities of men. There was no other way for him to speak the tongue, to know of water matters, to have whatever binding or influence or debt that would bring that note which had first summoned her.

The Dancing Mistress had no illusions of her own importance, but it had been her specifically that he'd wanted. It seemed likely the man had counted her as the Duke's assassin.

That was troublesome, she realized. If one person made that deduction, however flawed it was, others could come to the same conclusion. *A fear for another time*, she told herself.

Had he learned her people's magics the same way the late Duke of Copper Downs had? By theft?

A sickening idea occurred to her. *Perhaps this greasy man had been an agent of the Duke.*

As if summoned by the thought, a group of Ducal guards spilled out of an alley running between the walled gardens of wealth.

She happened to be walking close along the deserted curb just across from them. They stopped, staring at her. The Dancing Mistress didn't break stride. *Act like you are in charge. Do not fear them.* Still, she risked a glance.

The leader, or at least the one with the biggest sword, had a fine tapestry wrapped across his shoulders as a cloak. Looters. Though they wore Ducal uniforms, their badges were torn off.

"Hey, kittie," one of them called, smacking his lips.

Corner, she thought. *There's a corner up ahead. Many of these houses are guarded. They wouldn't risk open violence here.*

Her common sense answered: *Why not?* They had certainly risked open looting.

Colors were beginning to flow in the corner of her eye. The Hunt tugged at her. That ritual was anchored deep in the shared soul of her people, a violent power long rejected in favor of a quiet, peaceful life. The Dancing Mistress shook off the tremor in her claws as she turned a walled corner onto Alicorn Straight, passing under the blank-eyed gaze of a funerary statue.

They followed, laughing and joking too loudly among themselves. Weapons and armor rattled behind her. Not quite chasing, not quite leaving her alone.

The towers of the Old Wall rose amid buildings a few blocks to her east. If she could get there before the deserters jumped her, she might have a chance. Once past those crumbling landmarks, she would be in a much more densely populated and notably less wealthy area. In the Dancing Mistress' experience, aid was far more likely from those who had nothing than from those who held everything in their hands. The rich did not see anyone but their own glittering kind, while the poor understood what it meant to lose everything.

"Oi, catkin," one of the guards shouted. "Give us a lick, then."

Their pace quickened.

Once more colors threatened to flow. Her claws twitched in their sheathes. She would not do this. The people did not Hunt, especially not in the cities of men. Walking alone, the gestalt of the Hunt had no use, and fighting by herself against half a dozen men the subtle power it gave meant nothing.

They would have her down, hamstrings cut, and be at their rape before she could tear out one throat.

Speed was all she had left. Every yard closer they came was a measure of that advantage lost. The Dancing Mistress broke into a dead run. The guards followed like dogs on a wounded beggar, shouting in earnest, hup-hup-hupping in their battle language.

Still the street was empty.

She cut across the pavers, heading for Shrike Alley which would take her to the Old Wall and the Broken Gate. There was no one, *no one.* How could she have been so stupid?

Fast as she was, at least one of the men behind her was a real sprinter. She could hear him gaining, somehow even chuckling as he ran. The Dancing Mistress lengthened her stride, but his spear butt reached from behind to tangle her ankles and she went down to a head-numbing crack against the cobbles.

The guard stood above her, grinning through several days of dark beard and the sharp scent of man sweat. "Never had me one of you before," he said, dropping away his sword belt.

She kicked up, hard, but he just jumped away laughing. His friends were right behind him with blades drawn and spears ready. *Seven on one,* she thought despairing. She would fight, but they would only break her all the faster for it.

The first man collapsed, stunned, his trousers caught around his knees. A second yelled and spun around. The Dancing Mistress needed nothing more than that to spur her to her opportunity.

There was small, small distance between dance and violence. Controlled motion, prodigious strength and endless hours of practice fueled both arts. She stepped through a graceful series of spins, letting the edges of the Hunt back in as her clawed kicks took two more of the guards behind the knees.

The shaman was on the other side of them, grinning broadly as he fought with an already-blooded yatagan. There was a shimmering edge to his movements which was far too familiar.

He gambled on me joining the counter-attack, she thought. It did not matter why. They made common cause in the moment, and tore another man's hip from its socket. The last three deserters scrambled away before turning to run hell for leather down the street.

The Dancing Mistress had never thought to see a human who could take on even the least aspect of the Hunt.

"I should have expected more of you," her rescuer said. His voice was scarcely shuddering from the effort of battle.

She kept her own voice hard, saying in the tongue of the people, *"This does not bind us with water."*

"We are already bound. Think on what I have asked." He nodded, then strode purposeful away among the silent houses of the rich.

Shaking, the Dancing Mistress trotted toward the Old Wall, away from the groaning, weeping men.

▲▼▲

She made her way to the Dockmarket. That area was quiet as well, given that the harbor was as empty as it ever had been in the decades since the Year of Ice. Still, there were some humans about. Though the booths were shuttered and the alleys quiet as the Temple Quarter, the taverns stayed open. The breweries of Copper Downs had operated through flood, fire, pestilence and famine for more years than anyone had bothered to count. Political turmoil and a shortage of the shipping trade were hardly going to stop people from drinking.

There was a place off the alley known as Middleknife (or the Second Finger, depending on who you asked) behind a narrow door. It was as nameless as the people it served—mostly her folk, truth be told, but also a scattering of others who did not pass without a sidewise cast of human eyes elsewhere in Copper Downs. Many races had come out of the countries that rose skyward to the north in order to live in the shadows of the thriving human polities along the Stone Coast.

The Dancing Mistress had always scorned solaces such as this. Still, she needed to be among her people right now. There were few enough places for that, none of them part of her daily life.

She slipped inside with a clench riding hard in her gut.

No smoke of *tabac* or *hennep* roiled within. No dice clattered, no darts flew. Only a dozen or so of the people in quiet ones, twos and threes. They sat at tables topped by deep stoneware bowls in which forlorn lilies spun slowly, sipping pale liquid the consistency of pine sap from tiny cups that matched the great bowls. The place smelled of water, rock and trees.

Much like where she had been born.

She also saw a very narrow-bodied blue man in pangolin-skin armor alone at a table, crouched in a chair with his knees folded nearly to his chin. Though he did not look to weigh eight stone, she thought he must be seven feet tall at the least. There were even a few people who might have been human.

The barkeep, one of her people, glanced briefly at her. He then took a longer look before nodding slightly, a gesture they had all picked up in the city. She read it well enough.

Between any two of her people there was a scent, of soul and body, that once exchanged could not easily be forgotten. Much could be read there, in a language which did not admit of lies. This one was not sib-close, nor enemy-distant, but she saw the path of trust.

"You work in the Factor's Quarter," he said in Petraean.

"I did," she admitted. She'd trained slave girls and the forgotten younger daughters of rising houses. Sometimes they were one and the same. "Before all things fell just lately." And therein lay her story, the scent the shaman had been tracking.

"In any case, welcome." He brought out a wooden plate, as tradition dictated turned by someone's hand on a foot-powered lathe. There he spilled dried flower petals from a watered silk sack, three colors of sugar, and a trickle from a tiny cut crystal decanter. Their hands crossed, brushing together as each of them dragged a petal through sugar and lifewater.

The Dancing Mistress touched sweetness to her lips and smiled sadly. This was what the traditional feast of welcome had degenerated into, here in the labyrinthine streets of Copper Downs. Even so, they were now opened to each other for a moment.

The barkeep nodded again then brushed his fingers across hers, releasing them both. "You are of Copper Downs, but you are not one of my regulars. What brings you here? The need for a scent of home?"

"A water matter." She sighed. "A difficult one, I am afraid."

He stiffened, the fur of his neck bristling slightly as his scent strengthened. "Whom?"

"A man. A *human* man. Not of the Stone Coast." She shifted languages. *"He spoke our tongue."*

"He knew of water matters?"

"It was he who named this business. He was looking for the...agent... behind the Duke's *fall."* She paused, choosing her words carefully against revealing too much of her complicity in the Duke's death. *"This is not my soul path. I do not bind power, nor do I loose it. But the thread came to me all the same. And this one knows far too much of us."* Her voice dipped. *"I even glimpsed the Hunt within him."*

"I do not accuse you of an untruth, but that has never been. I would not have thought to have seen it." The barkeep looked past her shoulder, as one of the people often did when seeking to avoid embarrassment. *"There is a rumor that one of us was the undoing of the late* Duke. *Is that what this water matter follows?"*

"In a sense, yes," the Dancing Mistress admitted. "But I was never in the palace," she added in Petraean.

"Of course not." He thought a moment. "Do you seek aid in this? Or is this your fate to follow alone?"

"I do not yet see my fate. I do not think this is it." She sighed, another human gesture. "I doubt my ability to handle this well, and I fear the consequences of failure."

"Abide then at the empty table near the hearth. Some will come." He dipped into a slow bow straight from the high meadows of their birth. "I will see to it."

▲▼▲

The Dancing Mistress stared into the cold fireplace. There were no ashes, though there was sufficient soot blackening the bricks to testify to regular use in colder months. The darkness before her brought the man in the shadows very much to mind.

He'd offered to spare the city much suffering. She knew that the Duke's loosened power was like lightning looking for a path to the ground. Her hope, shared with Federo and the others who had conspired with her, had been to weather that storm until the ancient bonds relaxed. If the city was lucky, it would vanish like mist on a summer morning. Then her people's centuries-long part in the madness of the Duke's tyranny would be over.

The shaman had other ideas about that power, but even so he had not set himself up as her enemy. Except he knew too much. He knew their tongue, their ways, the Hunt.

He was a threat to the people. Anything he did in Copper Downs would seem to be the work of her people to the priests and the wizard-engineers who infested this city like lice. He might as well slit all their throats one by one.

I arranged to kill a Duke so that we might reclaim our power, she thought. *What is one more man?* She knew the answer to that: no more than another, then another, until her soul path was slick with blood.

Once more the Hunt pulled at her, bending the light at the edges of her vision. Long ago in the high meadows when the people foraged or fought, they could slip their thoughts and deeds together. A Hunt was a group of the people working as neither one nor another but all together, as termites will hollow out a tree or ants ford a river. What one heard, all heard; what another touched, all felt. Deep into the Hunt, leaderless and conjoined, there was none to call a halt to slaughter, none to direct their steps, and so with the power of their mesh-mind the people could become like a fire in the forest.

They had given it up long ago, save in most extreme need. There was too much violence at their command, too much power. She had never heard of the Hunt being cried within the walls of a human city. If these pasty, pale folk even suspected what her people could do when stirred to mortal effort, they would be lucky to be only driven from the gates.

Her claws slipped free again. Her blood thrummed in her veins. The Dancing Mistress was afraid of what this man had stirred her to. And how could he not know of the Hunt and what might happen?

He must know, she realized. *He'd just counted on finding the power first.* That man took chances, just as he'd attacked her assailants from behind, counting on her to rise and join into the fight. He gambled with lives, hers and his.

Interrupting her thought, one of the people sat down next to her. A stoneware cup was quickly placed before him. Moments later a woman of the people sat across. She briefly met the Dancing Mistress' eyes, then studied the lilies wilting in the stoneware bowl. Another soon came to fill their table. More cups followed.

So they were four. She took a sip of wine fermented from the flowers and fir sap of the high meadows.

▲▼▲

The woman spoke, finally. She had a scent of cinnamon about her. *"You are said to bear a water matter which has a claim upon all the people."*

"Yes," said the Dancing Mistress quietly. *"This thing tears at my heart, but there is a catamount among us."*

"I would not question your judgment." It was the taller of the men, who smelled of sage and tree bark. *"But I would know this threat."*

She gave him a long slow look. To raise the pursuit she meant to bring to bear, she must tell them the truth. Yet any word of her involvement in the Duke's death could mean her own.

Still, there was far more at stake than her small life.

"There is a man. A human man," she amended. *"He knows our ways better than do many of our own. He pursues a great evil. If he succeeds, the return of the Duke will be upon us all. If he fails, the price may well be laid at our people's door."*

She went on to explain in as much detail as she could, laying out the events of the day and her conclusions from it.

For a while, there was silence. The four of them sipped their wine and dipped into the same stream of thoughts. It was a gestalt, edging toward the mesh-mind of the Hunt. It was the way her people prepared themselves for deep violence.

"And once again, death brings death." That was the shorter of the men, the fourth in their Hunt, whom she already thought of as the glumper for the small noises he made in his throat as he sipped at the wine. *"If we send this shaman to follow his duke, who's to say there will not be more to follow him."*

Sage-man spoke up, in Petraean now. "This is so soon. The Duke is yet freshly dead. He did not expect to pass. There cannot already be a great conspiracy to return him to life and power."

"I do not know it for a conspiracy," said the Dancing Mistress. "He stalks me, seeing me for the bait to call this power back. That does not mean he has sung for my life, but I cannot think he will scruple to claim it in his pursuit." She flashed to the uneasy memory of the man laying into her attackers, grinning over the bloody blade of his yatagan. He played some game that ran neither along nor against her soul path, crosswise as it might otherwise be.

Still, they all knew, as everyone of the people did, that the Duke of Copper Downs had stolen their magic generations past. There were stories and more stories, details that varied in every telling, but since that time the numbers and power of the people—never great to start with—had diminished, while the Duke had spent centuries on his throne.

That someone was hunting power through the Dancing Mistress now, so soon after the Duke's fall, meant old, old trouble returning. The man being a high country shaman with too much knowledge of their people was only a seal on that trouble.

The cinnamon-woman broke the renewed silence. "You have the right of it. If we stop the Duke's man now, we may crush the seed before the strangler vine has a chance to grow."

The glumper stared up from the cup of wine clutched his hands. *"Crushing is not our way."*

"Not now." The cinnamon-woman looked around, catching their eyes. "Once…"

"Once we were warriors," said the Dancing Mistress. "We called storms from the high crags." They all knew those stories, too. "If we cry the Hunt now, we will spare lives."

"And what do we give up in following your plan?" asked the glumper. *"The old ways are gone for good reason."*

The Dancing Mistress felt anger rising within her, a core of fire beneath the cool sense of purpose she'd hewn to all her life. *"They are gone because of what the Duke took from us."*

He gave her a long stare. *"Did you ever think we might have given our power away with a purpose?"*

Even in argument, the mesh-mind was knitting together, the edges of the room gleaming and sharpening. The Dancing Mistress set down her cup. *"It is time,"* she said in their language. *"We will find this shaman and stop his scheming, before he drags all of our people down into darkness."*

▲▼▲

The moon glowed faintly through the low clouds, but the shadows outflanked the light at every turn. Torches burned at compound gates while lamps hung at intersections and in the squares. The nighttime streets of Copper Downs were streaked with smears of heat and scent.

The Hunt slid through the evening like a single animal with four bodies. Her vision was complex, edges gleaming sharp at all distances and ranges. Odors told stories she could never read on her own, about the passage of time and the sweat of fear, passion, even the flat, watery smell of ennui. The very feel of the air on her skin as she ran had been magnified fourfold. She saw every door, every hiding place, every mule or person they passed, in terms of force and danger and claws moving close to the speed of thought.

The sheer *power* of the Hunt was frightening in its intoxication.

They slipped through the city like a killing wind, heading toward the Ivory Quarter and the black gate through which she'd passed before. She'd never run so fast, so effortlessly, with such purpose.

Why had her people not stayed like this always, she wondered. All the logic of civilization aside, surely this was what they'd been made for.

It was little more than moments before they'd crossed the city to the old ochre walls of the compound, now nearly black in the moonlight. The ancient stucco seemed to suck the life of the world into itself, though the trees beyond and above the wall practically shouted to her expanded sensorium.

Three times in as many minutes they circled around the shadowed walls, and found no sign of the shaman's black gate. Not even a significant crack where it might have stood.

There was power aplenty in the world, but it was not generally spent so freely as this man had done. Opening that gate was the magical equivalent of a parlor trick. Flashy, showy, a splash of self such as a child with a paintpot might make.

But costly, very costly. The greatest power lay in subtlety, misdirection, the recondite support and extension of natural processes.

The gate was here, she thought, and the Hunt took her meaning from the flick of her eyes, the set of her shoulders, the stand of her fur. They believed her. She knew that just as they'd known her meaning.

Together they drifted back to the main gate. It had stood propped open years before the Dancing Mistress had come to Copper Downs, but no one ever passed through it. The squatters who lived within used the servants' gate beside the main gate, and so observed the blackletter law of the city even as they built their illegal homes upon the grounds. The trail of their passing back and forth glowed in the eyes of the Hunt. It was human, but there was something of the people mixed among it.

The Hunt slipped through the narrow door one by one, their steps falling like fog on the furze within. The path followed the old carriage drive through a stand of drooping willows now rotten and overgrown with wisteria. Trails led off between the curtains of leaves and vines toward the hidden homes beyond.

There was no scent to follow here. The shaman might as well have been made of mist.

A thought passed between the Hunt like breeze bending the flowers of a meadow: *An herbalist lives here, a woman of their people.*

She felt her claws stiffen. The wisdom of the Hunt stirred, the mesh-mind reading clues where ordinary eyes saw only shadow.

Is the Duke in fact still dead?

It was the same question she'd almost asked herself on her way to this place the first time.

Sage-man twitched aside a mat of ivy and stepped into the darker shadows. A brighter trail well-marked with the traces of one of her people led within. *Of course, cloaked in the magic of her people the shaman could also have left his tracks so.*

The Dancing Mistress nodded the rest of her Hunt through— cinnamon-woman and the glumper—and followed last.

▲▼▲

The hut was a shambles. Jars shattered, sheaves scattered, what little furniture there had been now smashed to splinters. While there didn't seem to be any quantity of blood, the stink of fear hung heavy in the close air.

The glumper trailed his fingers through the dust and dirt and wood fragments on the floor. He sniffed, sending a tingle through the Dancing Mistress' nose. "*I might have thought one of us had done this thing.*" He had yet to speak a word of Petraean within her hearing. "*But knowing to search, I find there has been a human here as well. Wearing leather and animal fat. He first took her unawares, then he took her away.*"

The shaman, the Dancing Mistress thought. Inside the mesh-mind, they shared her next question. *What path did he follow now?*

The Hunt had the shaman's scent, and the herbalist's besides. It was enough.

▲▼▲

A warm, damp wind blew off the water to carry the reek of tide rot and the distant echo of bells. Even the rogue squads of the Ducal guard seemed to be lying low, doubtless surrounded by wine butts and hired boys wearing slitted skirts and long wigs. Though there had only been one small abduction—something that might happen along the docks on any given evening—the city was deserted, waiting under the smell of old fires and dark magic.

That was well enough, the Dancing Mistress thought with the independent fragment of herself that still held its own amid the flow of the mesh-mind. It would not do for her people to be seen gliding over the cobbles at preternatural speed, moving silent as winter snowfall.

The Hunt's grip on shaman's scent and herbalist's soul path was sufficient even when running through fire reek and the alley-mouth stench of dead dogs. They moved together, heeding the Dancing Mistress' will, following the glumper's trace on the scent, using cinnamon-woman's eyes, sage-man's hearing. Most of all they pursued the dread that stalked the night, the banked fires of the Hunt flaring only to seek a single hearth within Copper Downs.

They followed a dark river of fear and purpose into the Temple Quarter. That had long been the quietest section of the city. Once it must have brawled and boiled with worshippers, for the buildings there were as great as any save the Ducal Palace. In the centuries of the Duke's rule, the gods of the city had grown withered and sour as winter fruit. People left their coppers in prayer boxes near the edges of the district and walked quickly past.

Even with the gods fallen on hard times, locked in the embrace of neglect and refusal, no one had ever found the nerve to tear down those cobwebbed gates and replace the old houses of worship with anything newer and more mundane.

The Hunt pursued the scent down Divas Street, along the edge of the Temple Quarter, before leading into the leaf-strewn cobwebs of Mithrail Street. They bounded into those deeper shadows where the air curdled to black water and the dead eyes of the Duke seemed to glitter within every stygian crevice.

They came to a quivering halt with claws spread wide before a narrow door of burnt oak bound with iron and ebony laths. Darkness leaked from behind it, along with a fire scent and the tang of burning fat.

The man-smell was strong here. They were obviously close to the shaman's lair, where the cloak of the people's power grew thin over his layered traces of daily use—sweat and speech and the stink of human urine. The doorway reeked of magic, inimical purpose and the thin, screaming souls of animals slit from weasand to wodge for their particles of wisdom.

That was his weakness, the Dancing Mistress realized, surfacing further from the Hunt for a moment even as those around her growled. He used the people's power only as a cover, nothing more. The shaman could build a vision of the world from a thousand bright, tiny eyes, but animals never saw more than they understood. The people knew that to be a fool's path to wisdom.

Now he worked his blood magic on the herbalist, in a summoning of the Dancing Mistress. *He had* drawn *her here to cut her secrets from her.* The mesh-mind overtook her once more in the rush of angry passion at that thought, and together the Hunt brushed someone's claw-tipped hand on the cool wooden planks of the door.

"Come," the shaman called. His voice held confident expectation of her.

The Hunt burst in.

▲▼▲

The four of them were a surprise to the shaman. They could see that in his face.

But his power was great as well. The ancient stone walls of this abandoned temple kitchen were crusted with ice. The herbalist hung by ropes from a high ceiling beam, her body shorn and torn as he'd bled her wisdom cut by cut the way he'd bled it from a thousand tiny beasts of the field.

He rose from his fire, kicked a brazier and coals toward them, and gathered the air into daggers of ice even as the four portions of the Hunt spread across the room.

Though they called the old powers of their people, none of them in the Hunt had ever trained to stand in open battle. Their purpose was strong, but only the Dancing Mistress could move below a slicing blade or land a strike upon a briefly unprotected neck.

If not for their number they would have been cut down without thought. If not for the shaman's need to capture an essence from the Dancing Mistress he might have blown them out like candles.

He had helped her that day only to draw her in to him now, when suasion had failed him.

The fight came to fast-moving claws against restrained purpose. His ice made glittering edges that bent the vision of the mesh-mind. The blood of his sacrifices confused their scent. He moved, as he had on the street that day, with the brutal grace of one raised to war, working his magic even as he wielded his yatagan. The glumper's chest was laid open. Cinnamon-woman had her ear shorn off. Sage-man's thoughts were flayed by a dream of mountain fire that slipped through the mesh-mind.

But for every round of blows the Hunt took, they landed at least one in return. Claws raked the shaman's cheek with the sound of roses blooming. A kick traced its arc in blurred colors on their sight to snap bones in his left hand. A brand was shoved still burning brightly sour into his hair, so the grease there smoldered and his spells began to crack with the distraction of the pain.

The Hunt moved in for the kill.

The Dancing Mistress emerged from the mesh-mind once more to find herself with claws set against the shaman's face. The cinnamon-woman twisted his right arm from his shoulder. She looked up at the herbalist, who dangled bleeding like so much meat in the slaughterhouse, and thought, *What are we now?*

"Wait," she shouted, and with the pain of forests dying tore herself free from the mesh-mind of the Hunt.

Cinnamon-woman stared, blood streaming from the stump of her ear. The look sage-man gave the Dancing Mistress from his place bending back the shaman's legs would have burned iron. Their mouths moved in unison, the mesh-mind croaking out the words, "He does not deserve to live!"

"He does not have a right to our power," she countered. "But we cannot judge who should live and who should die."

The shaman bit the palm of her hand, his tongue darting to lick the blood, to suck her down to some last, desperate magic.

Steeling herself, the Dancing Mistress leaned close. Her claws were still set in his face. "I will take your wisdom as you have taken the wisdom of so many others. But I shall let you live to know what comes of such a price."

"Wait," he screamed through her enclosing palm. "You do not underst—"

She plucked his tongue out with her claws. "We will not have the Duke back," the Dancing Mistress whispered venomously. She slit into him, plucking and cutting slivers from his sweetbreads. The Hunt kept the shaman pinned tight until blood loss and fear erased his resolve. Then the remainder of the mesh-mind collapsed. The cinnamon-woman began to tend to the glumper and the herbalist. Sage-man rebuilt the fire before ungently sewing shut the slits that the Dancing Mistress had made in the shaman's chest and belly.

Ice from the walls turned to steam as the Dancing Mistress fried the slivers of liver and lights, the tongue and two glistening eyes in a tiny black iron pan graven with runes. The blinded shaman wept and gagged, spitting blood while he shivered by the fire.

When the bits were done the Dancing Mistress dumped them to the blood-slicked mess that was the floor. She ground the meat to mash beneath her feet, then kicked it into the coals. The shaman's weeping turned to a scream as his wisdom burned away.

"Our water matter is discharged," she whispered in his ear. "If your Duke's ghost comes to you seeking restoration, send him to knock at my door."

Then the Dancing Mistress gathered the herbalist into her arms. Cinnamon-woman and sage-man brought the glumper between them. The shaman they left to his fate, blind, mute and friendless among the lonely gods.

▲▼▲

The Duke of Copper Downs was still dead, the Dancing Mistress reflected as the night faded around her. Oddly, she remained alive.

She sat at the door of the herbalist's hut. The woman slept inside, mewing her pain even amid the thickets of her dreams. There was a new water matter here, of course. The ties among the people ever was broad as the sea, swift as the river, deep as the lakes that lie beneath the mountains. She was bound for a time to the herbalist by the steam that the Hunt had burned from the shaman's icy walls.

That man did not have much of life left to him, but at least she had not claimed it herself. Her people had the right of things in centuries past, when they gave up their power. She only hoped that rumor of the Hunt was small and soon forgotten by the citizens of Copper Downs.

The shadows beneath the rotten willows lightened with the day. The spiced scent of cookery rose around her, tiny boiling pots and bumptious roasts alike. The Dancing Mistress rose, stretched, and went to tend her patient.

To This Their Late Escape

When we were putting together this collection, Bill Schafer requested that I provide an original work of fantasy and an original work of science fiction. As I've continued to work around the edges of the Sunspin *space opera trilogy, including "To Raise A Mutiny Betwixt Yourselves" elsewhere in this volume, as well as "Permanent Fatal Errors" in* Is Anybody Out There, *edited by Nick Gevers and Marty Halpern, it seemed most fitting to write an original science fiction piece for* The Sky That Wraps *set in the same world. Without further ado, here is more* Sunspin *for your delectation.*

Year 240 post-Mistake
Port Brooks, Novy Gorosk
The Before Skanderia Knaak

The Martian sunrises of her youth were eleven hundred years in the past, but the second-oldest woman in the world could still see that pale orange wash reflected in the peach-and-salmon riot of this broken world's eastern horizon. Her steward Velikov—seventh of his name and line in Skanderia's service—bustled nearby on the shattered balcony. The man warmed water for her tea on the little hand-primed alcohol stove that was literally the highest piece of technology anyone on Novy Gorosk could make in these years. Overhead the stars fled one by one, taking their hollow promises of salvation with them.

"They're never coming back," she muttered, as she had every day of her exile.

"I expect not, Great Queen."

She'd been having *this* conversation every morning for the lives of seven generations of Velikov's family, and in the years before that. It was one of the few things keeping Skanderia Knaak alive.

Routine, routine, routine. All Howard Immortals had been heavily counseled about the value of strong routines. Back when there been a Howard Institute. Or counselors.

Velikov handed Skanderia her morning tea, and the most urgent of the day's reports. "Starost Pilchen sends word that the Siddiqi are massing small boats at the Brownmouth."

"Of course they are."

Besides routine, the other thing keeping Skanderia Knaak alive was a titanium-willed determination to outlast the oldest woman in the world. Raisa Siddiq, the only other Howard Immortal remaining on Novy Gorosk. None of the children who lived and died here now even knew the *name* of the Polity, let alone what it might mean.

None but her enemy could understand.

Skanderia stepped to the cracked rail and looked down across Port Brooks. The old Portmaster's Residence had been built on a crag west of the city, and commanded a fantastic view. It had escaped the high-energy burn that swept most of Port Brooks on the day everything had ended. She could remember the fat-bellied lighters growling out of the sky with their cargos and passengers as clearly as if they had just cleared the airspace. The old landing field was a forest now, trees grown almost a hundred meters tall since the crumbling, heat-blurred blast pits had last heard the thunder of engines. Port Brooks' great boulevards, famously laid three point seven degrees out of true because of an error in the original survey, still stretched open, though they were meadowed now, and dotted with rows of crops so dark-leaved as to be black in the dawn light. Leathery frill-birds circled the curling skeletal towers of the financial district, their slagged and melted ruins still being salvaged for refined materials almost two and half centuries after the collapse of, well, everything.

A few miles past the entrance to the bay, just beyond Skanderia's line of sight, the Brownmouth would be cluttered with boats. Bronze swords, sharpened steel taken from the old buildings, horn-and-hide bows. Raisa Siddiq was coming to try once more to wrest Skanderia's city from her grasp.

"Great Queen."

Something in Velikov's voice brought Skanderia out of her reverie with a rapid twist of alarm. "What is it?"

He pointed up into the western sky, where the rearguard of night struggled its last against the encroaching day. "The Siddiqi have launched a new devilment."

Skanderia looked toward the unmistakable blue-white of a fusion drive flame. *That* color had not been seen on Novy Gorosk for a very long time. Such a noisy, dirty drive would have been illegal in the later days of the Polity. Now it was a miracle.

"Velikov," she said, her words stretching with deliberation. A hope long since mummified stirred somewhere deep in her dusty soul. "That is no new devilment of Raisa Siddiq's. That, my friend, is a very old devilment indeed." *To hell with routine.* "Go, now. Alert the Starost. The world ends again today. If we are lucky, we will have a say in the birth of the next world."

He stood, caught for a moment between the eye-piercing glare descending in the west and her own soul-sharp glare, honed over centuries of absolute despotism.

"*Go,*" Skanderia whispered.

The steward fled, already shouting for the couriers who lurked in the stables at the foot of the cliff.

▲▼▲

Starost Pilchen

Starost Kolodny Pilchen stared at the last of night along the western horizon. Something spat light there such as he'd never seen. Something that moved too slowly to be a shooting star, and too deliberately to be anything but manmade.

Skanderia had always been right. Not that he'd ever thought the Great Queen to be a liar. Immortal or not, it was just that so many of her stories were so…improbable.

Pilchen felt the landslide of history like a migraine's bloom. Everything he'd ever known was at least partially wrong. That world was finished now. The improbability was here.

Around the beachfront camp men began to shout and point. The Starost jumped up from his camp chair. "I want every man in formation in three minutes," he shouted at his adjutant. He needed to stop the rumors before they took hold.

Whoever was falling out of the sky right now was coming for either Skanderia or Siddiq. Or both. In any case, this was the end of the world.

He was damn well going meet the end in formation, at sword's point.

▲▼▲

The sergeants-major got the men lined up in less than six minutes. The Starost let the NCOs twist on their own worries about the timing. The light was cutting angles across the brightening sky. A dozen men had been injured staring at it, partially or fully blinded.

He stepped up onto a weathered block. Over four hundred men stared at him. Private soldiers, sergeants, sergeants-major, lieutenants and four captains. Only the injured and Dr. Zvibi were absent.

"The Great Queen's brothers and sisters are come from beyond the sky," the Starost bellowed. Not ten men in the formation knew a damned thing about the true history of Novy Gorosk. That would do for an explanation, for now. "The Siddiqi will seek to deceive and entrap them. We will meet them as they land, and we will escort them to Her Majesty's presence. Captains, have your men to the landing field triple time." He paused for three beats. *"Now!"*

Within two minutes, the entire formation had moved out, except for the perimeter guards, the cooks and his own immediate staff. Even the coast watch had marched away.

"Now what?" asked Sergeant-Major Kandinsky.

"We follow," the Starost replied. "And hope like hell I guessed right."

▲▼▲

Even after two centuries of salvage and renewed habitation, the city still looked like fresh ruins so far as he was concerned. Not that Pilchen had any real idea how Port Brooks had appeared in its prime. Just not…this.

He rode toward the formation already deploying around the field. The old pits that had once cradled starships were filled with little bowls of forest, but the wider paved expanse had been kept clear over the years for military exercises and, the Starost suspected, some lingering sense of optimism on the part of the Great Queen.

Skanderia Knaak had no predecessors and no successors. She had always been the Great Queen, ever since there had been a Great Queen. As unitary and undying as the sun, taking no lovers, producing no heirs, outliving generations of generals and counselors and everyone except Raisa Siddiq.

At that thought he glanced up toward the palace on the cliffs to the west. Whatever unholy fire had sent the stones of the central city flowing like mud had spared that high house. The Great Queen used the place as her retreat, as her headquarters, her sanctum. Even he, highest in the Great Queen's councils, had made the climb up there less than half a dozen times. Only Velikov came and went freely from the palace. No one else lived there except for a handful of mute servants, tied to their mistress by loyalty and crippled tongues.

His horse followed Kandinsky onto the wide, decaying expanse. The troops knew the landing drill well enough. Every man learned it with his first weaponscraft. Every man practiced the landing drill as thoroughly as they rehearsed any attack formation.

The troops had fallen into four formations. Each was shaped like the head of an arrow, pointing inward to bound a box three hundred paces on a side. The Starost had never been certain what the basis of that measurement was—surely nothing sacred was at play *here*—but the Great Queen had insisted on it.

When he was a raw recruit, an old sergeant had shown him a manual of arms from the days before printing presses and even forges. Crudely copied in squid ink on a rough paper mashed from leaves, it contained drills for fighting with sticks and rocks. Even then, the manual of arms had also contained the landing drill.

That Skanderia Knaak thought ahead was news to absolutely no one in the Great Queen's domain. Still, her prescience sometimes chilled the Starost's marrow.

His command party pulled up next to the eastmost arrow. The eye-ripping glare was close enough now to be accompanied by a low rumble. And yes, it was slowly turning. Banking toward them.

"Make ready," the Starost called. His words echoed down the chain of command as if each man was deaf to all but his nearest master. Swords to hand, the army of the Great Queen made ready.

▲▼▲

Skanderia Knaak

She permitted herself a smile. Over two centuries of careful training had borne fruit in a moment that by definition was unexpected. Back when she and Siddiq had still met from time to time under a flag of truce, for the sake of the conversations only the two of them could have, the Earth-born woman had laughed at Skanderia's expectation of an eventual return.

"They're never coming back," she'd said. "We don't even know what happened to them, but *nothing* works any more."

"They will come back," Knaak had replied. She'd spoken from a deep, stubborn faith rooted in nothing more than sheer human restlessness and the apparently inescapable expansionist impulse. "This is an easy world. Those future people won't even know you and I ever existed, but they'll want the biosphere for themselves. And we'll be here."

"You're going to die here, Skanderia."

"Not at my hands."

Those were the days when their chess game had been played on a hand-carved board with the sacrifice of ivory pieces rather than along the fens of the River Brown and the seaside sedges of this miserable bay with the sacrifice of doe-eyed boys trembling in their fear.

Now a lander came, almost two and half centuries too late. *How many deaths?* She ignored that question, it had ceased to matter to her long before this world had fallen to whoever had destroyed their future. Skanderia had always figured if the invaders came back, she'd never know. She would just die unawares in another burst of fire and radiation.

This was a human approach.

It rode downward on a bright sword of nuclear fire. She wondered if the pilot planned to touch down on top of that flaming column. It would be ironically Biblical, but utterly beside the point on a world where only two people had heard of the Bible, and only one had read it.

The pilot cut off her fusion drive at about six hundred meters and deployed a set of ducted fan jets. With the actinic glare eliminated, Skanderia could see the lander as a fairly crude lifting body. It was a tail-stander, not big enough for half a dozen passengers in that hull unless they had fantastically efficient and tiny life support systems.

Again, human.

When it landed, *she* would descend. Protocol was meant to be observed, even and especially by Great Queens. The Starost Pilchen could handle whomever came out of the hatch. *He* had *his* landing drill, too, as had every adjutant of hers since the beginning of her queendom.

▲▼▲

Velikov bustled onto the balcony as Skanderia was buckling her armor back into place. "The Starost has ordered his troops into the landing drill, Great Queen," he announced unnecessarily.

"I can see that," said Skanderia gently. "Our visitor has arrived, as well."

The steward's eyes darted toward the marble rail. An unusual breach of his protocols, to look away from her, but Skanderia was prepared to forgive a great deal on this extraordinary morning.

"We will go down now and meet our visitor."

"Yes, Great Queen."

He backed into the house, bowing, leading her as if his entrance were being replayed.

She followed, alternately bemused and depressed. What purpose had her years here served, in truth? Little more purpose than any of her years as a Howard Immortal.

Sighing, she took up her sword—the last functioning wireblade on the entire planet, and another reason why Raisa Siddiq hesitated so strongly to take passage of arms against Skanderia Knaak in person.

It hummed comfortingly in her hand, carrier wave of a vanished civilization. The weapon seemed attuned to the presence of a still-cooling fusion drive on the landing field below.

▲▼▲

Starost Pilchen

He watched the metal wedge as his orders told him he must. Pilchen knew perfectly well that he himself was the key to this little charade. The troops served their purpose, but just like a battle, this meeting would be won or lost in the fields of the mind before metal ever touched flesh.

The thing—*ship*, the Starost reminded himself dubiously—the *ship* had an elegant shape, like the wedge-shaped snout of a battering ram. Its skin was rough and pitted. Nothing like the gleaming white ships of the Great Queen's late-night campfire tales. More like the sort of *ship* a man might build and fly, if a man had the gifts of shipbuilding and flight.

Her memories perfect what never was so, the Starost realized.

Ten minutes crept by. The heat pouring from the ship like a campfire faded to warmth.

Twenty minutes crept by. Someone in the ranks was seized with a coughing fit. The men had a different view of the world from their stance in formation. The Starost was content to remain at attention and stare at the key to the future.

Thirty minutes crept by. With a sudden, unexpected hiss, steam vented from beneath the ship's legs. A surprised murmur rippled through the ranks. The Starost waited for the next thing to happen—a door to open, a weapon to discharge. None of those things occurred. Not then, at any rate.

When an hour passed, his moment would come.

At forty minutes, the Great Queen arrived atop her tall gray mare, followed close behind by Velikov. Skanderia's horse was white as any fish belly, but he knew that the Great Queen would never call it white.

What he didn't know was *why*.

"Your highness," he said, dismounting to take her reins.

Skanderia Knaak waved the Starost Pilchen away. He paused at her stirrup, looking up at her right hand crossed loosely across the saddle, the wireblade in her grip humming like a disturbed porch wasp. Behind her, Velikov appeared vaguely ill.

"You plan to cut your way through the metal of this ship?" he finally asked.

"No, you idiot." Her voice was absent, her attention focused on the ship. "By this blade he will know me for who I am."

You look like old saddle leather, and are stronger than re-rolled steel, the Starost thought. *No one can possibly mistake you for anyone other than who you are.*

Except for Raisa Siddiq, he corrected himself. Surviving the deeps of time had lacquered both women with an armor of experience at sheer survival.

The Starost realized he'd finally once and for all accepted the truth of the Great Queen's stories about herself. She *was* stranger than her own myths. The proof had arrived on a sword of fire.

▲▼▲

Skanderia Knaak

When the hour had passed, she flipped the wireblade sword to attention and nudged her mount into a slow walk toward the lander. The ship made the horse nervous—it smelled of ash and complex hydrocarbons and burnt metal. Not smells familiar on Novy Gorosk anymore.

"Easy, Gansevoort," she whispered, her free hand stroking the horse's neck. The mare's fear-sweat threatened to overwhelm even the reek of the lander. Eschewing the advantage of height, Skanderia slipped from her saddle, tossed the reins over the pommel, and the horse back toward Velikov. Gansevoort trotted away, her hooves echoing on the ancient concrete.

She wondered if any of the Howard Immortals had survived. Did the women inside the lander even know who and what she was?

A hatch seal broke free with a hiss on her approach. Her landing drill hadn't been made up out of whole cloth, it had been drawn from old contact protocols. Clearly these people had read the same books that still lurked in Knaak's memory.

A thousand years as a mercenary-attorney had given her a preternatural ability at negotiation. She would be ready for whoever stepped out of the lander.

She wasn't ready for the clash of arms that erupted behind her.

The Great Queen whirled, her sword out already. Its tip moved with the speed of her boosted metabolism. Self-maintaining combat mods to muscle twitch and strength ratings had survived even these last two centuries of maintenance neglect well enough to take any natural-born human on the planet.

The Siddiqi were attacking, a flying wedge straight between two of the landing drill formations. Which were, damn it, not the least bit suitable for defense. Starost Pilchen already bellowed orders, while his officers and sergeants scrambled to form, reform, defend.

But Raisa Siddiq wasn't aiming for a set battle. She was aiming for the lander. The bitch must have put those boats in the water the moment she saw the drive flare, and counted on Skanderia to strip her men from the pickets. She *knew* what the landing drill was, for all that she'd mocked it down the decades.

The Great Queen cursed her own carelessness, then sprinted directly toward the heart of the fight. Only one of those approaching held any fear for her at all. Striking down Siddiq would be a privilege as well as a workout.

▲▼▲

Starost Pilchen

He pulled his mount hard, riding to intercept Skanderia before she could run bodily into the armored front of the Siddiqi attack. This was a flying squad, not an attack in force. It was obvious enough what Raisa Siddiq was about. Taking down the Great Queen in the bargain would only be a bonus.

A thought struck him with that strange timeless quality of the mind in battle: *Had she been planning this move down all the years?*

A much harder thought followed it: *Had the Great Queen been planning this move down all the years?*

Then he was upon Skanderia Knaak and reaching for her with one great arm. Her uncanny senses did not desert her—she grasped his wrist without even looking back, and leapt in time to the horse's stride to slip behind him.

"Siddiq," she growled in his ear, and the Starost cast aside his darker speculation as his horse bore down on the first of the invaders.

They were already losing their advantage of speed. Too many of his own men swarmed forward. Out of formation, endangering themselves, but robbing the enemy of her precious time.

The Great Queen's sword hummed so loudly now that Pilchen's skin itched. She sliced through armor and leather and skin without even the drag of blade on bone. Two men fell away, three more scrambled for safety, preferring the steel edges wielded by the Starost's soldiers to the terrible power of that wireblade.

Another pair in the lacquered breastplates of Siddiq's personal guard turned to block her. They parried with strange weapons, like padded practice swords, that made Skanderia hiss under her breath. The Starost solved that problem by riding one of them down and breaking the other's skull with the flat of his very normal sword while the man tried to meet the wireblade with his device.

Then Raisa Siddiq was before them. Still surrounded by her men, not close enough to kill, she stood in her stirrups like a leather target dummy and stared at the ship. The worst of it was, he realized, she *smiled* as the men around her died.

He understood why when a voice thundered as loud as any sound he'd ever heard in his life.

LAY DOWN YOUR WEAPONS.

Pilchen felt a rush of warmth as his ears began to bleed. He kept his seat as his horse swayed beneath him. Many of the men on both sides collapsed with their hands clutched to their heads. Others staggered aimlessly. A few still swung at their opponents, but with the wild errors of the drunken.

Siddiq's smile turned into a laugh, though the Starost could not hear her voice for the worth of his life.

"Bitch," said the Great Queen behind him. Her he only understood because she was almost biting his shoulder as she spoke.

Her arm snaked around and tugged his reins to the left. The ship. She wanted to reach the ship. His thoughts were not coming in the right order. He had to protect the Great Queen, fight Raisa Siddiq, do something other than surrender to the echoing pain inside his skull.

What he did instead was ride toward the lander, and short, dark-skinned spaceman who stood in the opened doorway wearing a silver suit, with a rifle in his hand. Raisa Siddiq strode through the groaning, bleeding soldiers, walking faster than the stumbling pace of Pilchen's horse. She caught up to them and looked toward Skanderia Knaak with an expression so complex, so *intense*, upon her face that the Starost knew he would never understand it.

What did it mean to be enemies so long?

▲▼▲

Skanderia Knaak

She knew what it meant to be enemies so long. They might as well have been married, she and Siddiq. The horse was foundering, so for a second time she slipped down, though careful to keep the wireblade in hand. Behind her Skanderia heard the Starost collapse with his mount, both of them going down onto the hardstand in an avalanche of flesh and leather and metal.

Her attention was split between Siddiq and the man in the lander. His rifle was at port arms. Needle gun, supersonic muzzle velocity judging by the dampers on the barrel. Even a couple of combat-hardened Howard Immortals could be shredded by a weapon like that.

What had he been expecting?

Me, maybe.

The Great Queen began to laugh. Siddiq laughed with her. In that moment she knew what they had been fighting over all along.

Freedom. Space. The past they shared with no one else on this world. But out there...? It could all begin again. *Home.* Anywhere but this miserable mousetrap of a world.

After more than a thousand years of acquaintance, words weren't necessary so very often. Together, almost free, they walked toward the open hatch and the frowning man and the weapon capable of ending their long, twilight struggle, and the ship behind him that could lift them both away.

"Cross over," Siddiq muttered as she paused for breath. "I'll draw his aim, you take his weapon from the offside."

Visions of stars dancing in her head, Skanderia Knaak snapped her sword to the ready by way of answer.

The two immortals would carry their fight home.

▲▼▲

Starost Pilchen

He dragged himself to hands and knees by main force. Two small puddles of blood spread just below him. The Starost tilted his head back to see the Great Queen and Raisa Siddiq move so quickly they blurred his vision. Like he'd never seen before.

Except they weren't fighting one another.

The spaceman tumbled out of the lander's little door, his arms at angles that would make for a sickening memory later. The Great Queen stepped into the shadows within, her head turning as she looked back at him with glittering eyes and a feral smile. Raisa Siddiq turned with the captured weapon—for surely it *was* a weapon—and made as if to sweep the field of the fallen with it. Then she followed her enemy into darkness.

A moment later the door shut. It must have hissed or banged, but Pilchen could not tell. He was unsure if he would ever hear again. The lander began raising a terrible, stinging cloud of dust with a noise he felt in his bone and joints, even if his ears were little more than stones. The Starost dropped flat and buried his face in his forearms to protect himself.

After about a minute, the vibrations eased. He looked up again. The lander had already climbed substantially heavenward. Something sparked at its base, and once again the Starost shielded himself. The heat of that eye-searing flame pounded him even here down on the ground.

He finally stood and stumbled toward the body of the spaceman. Body it was—the poor bastard had been cut to ribbons by the scattered debris of his own lander's departure. The Great Queen's wireblade sword lay discarded next to the dead man.

He remembered the smile. Discarded? Or given?

The Starost grasped the wireblade, flicked it in his wrist as he had seen the Great Queen do a hundred times. It hummed, taking on whatever power or spell that drove it.

Science, he thought. *The rest of humanity has come back to us. We must rediscover their science.*

He stumbled back toward the center of mass of the aborted battle. Two of the Siddiqi elite bodyguards were already pulling themselves to their feet. The Starost glanced at the sword in his hand and wondered whether to slice them to pieces or offer it to them.

The past had just left, flown off into the future. Which way would they face?

Hand firmly on the hilt, the Starost Pilchen began to talk, shouting loudly enough that they could at least see that he meant to speak instead of slay them.

Chain of Fools

I originally wrote this story just for the fun of writing about the more preposterous aspects of the Wall, which is a central feature (possibly the central feature) of the Mainspring *books. "Chain of Fools" had a bit of trouble finding a home, until Bill Schafer at* Subterranean Online *took it in and made it shiny. Now he has very kindly given my story a second home in this volume. My novella "Chain of Stars", also published at* Subterranean Online*, is a sequel to this story.*

Zarai examined the bucket-ship *Indolent Climax. Her* bucket-ship. After fifteen years aboard Captain Quenna's *Blacklegs,* scrapping and scheming up and down the Chain, she had finally secured her own command.

The owners were another matter. At least their endless yammering about yields and cargoes and demurrage didn't follow her out of port.

The bucket-ship was tucked into the second quay at Bluerocks. Not a bad travel distance for the boom that plucked them off the Chain. Unlike the third and fourth quays, there was no swinging out over the long, hard fall to the stones of Atli's Knee six and half miles below.

The quays were cantilevered out from the face of the Wall atop massive arches of old, old iron which had held their place since long before the current port of Bluerocks had even existed. Perhaps they, like the Chain, were old as Creation. She preferred to think of things that way than contemplate who might have raised the arches in the six thousand years since. These days an endless gang of masons and ironsmiths and carpenters kept the quay in condition to receive vessels.

Indolent Climax, like most of her sisters, resembled an almond sliced in half at the waist. The hooking frame circled her there, at her widest point. A long, narrow hull depended from the frame, while her maindeck and poop stood just above. Small watch-decks extended over the side at the three outer points. She also sported a rare glassed-in watch-house on the falls side.

The ship crewed eleven and shipped forty tons of cargo. The log showed that *Indolent Climax* had been as far down the Wall as Inktown, where the lowest booms stood, though the Chain ran farther. She'd been as high up the Wall as Port Sky, only six miles below the uppermost booms at Heavengate.

Zarai hoped to make the entire run some day, from foot to crown. She'd ride the balloon tram from Heavengate to the top of the Wall. From there you could touch the great brass gear that ringed the Earth, and look down upon the queendoms of the flatwater world. She wondered sometimes if anyone had ever tried to set a boom there. An ambitious captain might send a bucket-ship into the aetheric spaces between the stars as the orbital ring passed by at midnight.

Dreams for another time, she reminded herself. For now she paced the quay, following the walkway where the dock ring met the hooking frame to keep *Indolent Climax* safe as an egg in a cup.

The bucket-ship was magnificent. Anyone would be forced to admit that.

Zarai summoned her courage, then climbed aboard to meet her very first crew.

▲▼▲

An hour later Zarai was in the master's cabin with her new first mate and the bucket-ship's Chain pilot. Beita, the mate, was a stolid woman of a pallid coloring who hailed from somewhere far to the east along the Wall. She had been with *Indolent Climax* almost a dozen years. Zarai would need to watch for jealousy in that one, passed over for the captaincy to which *she* had just been appointed.

The Chain pilot was an enkidu—one of the hulking, hairy folk almost as common as humans on the Wall. She called herself Aa. Zarai suspected Aa of being male, but she didn't know enkidus well enough to be certain. Being flighty and unreliable, not to mention disgusting, men were widely regarded as creatures of ill omen aboard a ship. If Beita and the owners were satisfied with Aa, Zarai knew that she must be too.

There was a fine line between asserting control and pushing the senior crew to the point of resentment. She'd seen that hand overplayed, for fear of the risks of too little discipline.

Indolent Climax shipped with no supercargo, though there was a tiny cubby if one were ever needed. Beita had played that part this day, due to Zarai being new aboard. The captain knew she'd have to take the responsibility soon enough. Still, she considered this a missed opportunity. An additional officer might have balanced out the crew better.

"Grab underarm is brittle," Aa complained in a voice that rumbled like distant thunder. Her nose was so big Zarai might have slipped her bunched fingers into each nostril. The captain found that very distracting when trying to interpret the enkidu's heavy accent. *Blacklegs* had shipped none of Aa's kind.

Beita nodded. "Captain Marra was planning to have it repaired when we next called at The Irons."

That was poorly done, Zarai thought, *to leave behind a vessel which could not properly grasp on to the Chain.* "Did she have a letter of credit from the owners?"

Beita and Aa exchanged a slow glance that made Zarai wonder for a moment if they were a bonded pair. She'd never had time herself for more than the usual run of dockside girls. A bond had always seemed a pleasant dream. What she'd had with her old captain had been something else. Something less. But…to bond with an enkidu?

Aa snuffled. Beita picked at the pockets of her leather vest a moment before looking up. "No ma'am. Captain Marra paid for most of our repairs out of her own funds."

"I see." Zarai felt a lurch in her gut. She was well enough provided for, thanks be to her old mistress. Beyond that, she was always frugal with her darics. She kept deposits in the strong-banks of five different ports along the Chain. But that wasn't ship money. If she had ship money, *she'd* be the owner. "How brittle? Do we lose grip?"

"Have not yet dropped off link," rumbled Aa. "Have been one or two slips."

"One or two?"

Beita nodded, supporting Aa. "A few. It's all logged, ma'am."

Still, they were shipping out again. It couldn't be *that* bad. "What else?"

A litany of rusted bolts, loosening springs and rotting wood followed. Zarai had sailed aboard *Blacklegs* from her first descent until this day. Captain Quenna was a cautious woman who almost always kept mid-Chain and feared men with a passion that Zarai had come to share without ever quite understanding. Beyond the obvious, of course. But *Blacklegs* had been very well kept indeed. They'd never been taken for a seedpod—what sailors called those bucket-ships everyone thought would soon drop away.

Indolent Climax was another matter entirely, much to Zarai's shame.

She resolved to write a long letter to the owners that very night, documenting the scandalous condition of the ship and suggesting the need for a prompt refit. But not *too* soon. If *Indolent Climax* went into the yards at The Irons or High Thefariae for a month, Zarai would be out of work again. With only one ship and a single captain signed off in her ticket boot, she needed time at her own helm before that happened.

Otherwise she might not find another berth.

▲▼▲

The boom came for them just after four bells of the afternoon watch. Zarai stood proudly on the maindeck. The crimson cloak of her command billowed in the wind of the Wall. At any rate, she thought it billowed, until she realized she'd caught a corner in her leather trousers when adjusting her clothing a few minutes earlier. That was set right with a moment's embarrassed tugging.

Zarai watched the three heavily-tattooed dwarfs who worked the boomhead lower their pinch into position. They were a hereditary class, with a guild language all their own, teeth filed to points, and a high fatality rate. Aa directed from the poop, booming terse orders to the four crew womanning *Indolent Climax*'s grab.

The pinch had to settle properly around the outside of the grab. It then needed to be secured into place well enough to support the weight of the bucket-ship. Secondary cables stretched from the boom head to the watch-decks on the vessel's outer points, secured there to the ribs of the hull. Those lines kept *Indolent Climax* from tipping as the boom swung her out away from the quay and toward the Chain.

Aa pumped a fist three times, the lock-down signal.

"Boom away!" shouted Zarai.

One of the dwarfs grinned sharply as the hawsers from the boom took up the slack. *Indolent Climax* creaked, then shifted in her berth.

The first opportunity for danger was that the boom might have been poorly set, or that a hawser would break. A moment later they were swinging free without mishap. Zarai recovered her breath. "Chain pilot, the ship is yours!"

"Aye," rumbled Aa.

The boom swung them out toward the rushing waters of the River Vertus.

▲▼▲

The Vertus rises just above Heavengate, issuing in a mighty torrent from a giant crack six or seven miles below the top of the Wall. It tumbles through a series of cataracts and channels and watercourses, descending almost ninety miles before it pours over the Lip of Ashtaroth below Inktown and out into the empty air above the Atlantic Ocean.

On its own account, the River Vertus is said to be a wonder of the Wall. What sets it apart from a hundred other magnificent waterfalls and vertical rivers at the waist of the world is the Chain.

Certain mystes aver that the Chain is a remnant of God's Creation, a tool with which He crafted the world. Others point out that since God is by definition incapable of imperfection, the Chain must be part of the natural order. Most people take the view that the Chain exists, and therefore the thing simply *is*, much like the Wall itself.

The Chain loops emerge from a cavern half a mile below the outlet of the River Vertus. It follows the channel of the Vertus all the way downward, re-entering the Wall at the Lip of Ashtaroth. Each link is said to be forged of the same brass forming the ring gear at the top of the Wall, as well as the great whorl of clockwork which lies at the heart of the Earth. These links extend one hundred eighty-three feet from bow to base. They alternate between rightwise links and crosswise links. The Chain descends at a steady half a mile per hour, making the entire trip down the Wall from Heavengate to Inktown a matter of some four days' work.

Taking a bucket-ship back up was another matter entirely.

▲▼▲

Indolent Climax dangled from the boom, being soaked by spray from the roaring rush of the River Vertus. Aa and her four crewwomen locked the grab as one of the rightwise links slid slowly by. That was a quick operation, as a link of the Chain took four minutes and ten seconds from base to bow to pass a fixed point. The chain pilot and her crew had two and half minutes to secure the grab and release the boom's pinch so that the bucket-ship would be safely away on the Chain. Otherwise they would need to declare a missed grab while the boom still had time to clear them, before the next crosswise link came down.

At one minute and fifty-five seconds by the grab timer, Aa bellowed the all clear. The tattooed dwarfs on the boom waved as they swung away. *Indolent Climax* had begun her journey down.

Aa's voice echoed across the deck. "Captain, ship is yours!"

Zarai was in complete command of her destiny for the first time in her life.

▲▼▲

It would be fourteen hours down-Chain to their first port of call at Catha. Given the afternoon departure, that meant a night run through the Angel Narrows. That was one of the most difficult parts of the River Vertus. It was also one of the few passages which the bucket-ship crews preferred to transit upward rather than down.

Down was always the sailor's friend, provided the deck was clear and the grip was good.

Zarai tucked herself into the glass watch-house and stared along the Chain. Nineteen times out of twenty, the passage through the Angel Narrows was peaceful. But when the Chain pirates attacked, a ship and crew were at peril.

Speed was never an option on a downward course. Bucket-ships moved at the Chain's pace, no more, no less. Some captains preferred to batten tight and take refuge below. Such a strategy required trust that nothing came on the deck which was strong enough to breach the hatches. Others hired toughs: lop-eared women with scars for breasts who could line the rail and pepper any threat with weapons fire, and if needed, contest possession of the deck at swords-point.

She'd ridden Angel Narrows both ways time and again in her trips under Quenna—first as deck hand, then as supercargo, and finally as first mate. Hiding below listening to the groaning thump of the bucket-ship always made her half-crazed. Zarai now found that standing on the deck as they descended between glistening rock walls lined with shadowed ledges frightened her.

She was the captain. She would face this.

At dusk Zarai rang all hands. They assembled just below the small platform of the poop. Aa waited by her four, who served as deck hands and general labor during a descent. They worked much harder on the way up. Beita was ranked with her three watch-standers, one of whom doubled as ship's carpenter. Finally there was the cook, an old woman named Megg who came with the ship's equipage and so in theory answered to the owners. Like most cooks she answered only to herself.

"We will pass the Angel Narrows during the mid-bells of the first night watch," Zarai called out.

Aa and Beita exchanged another of those glances. *They* must *be a pair*, she thought, *but how can Beita couple with such an...animal?* She tried to excuse them both as foreign and therefore ignorant.

"Though I am confident that we will sail without incident, the crew will be on deck with hooks and pistoles in the unlikely event of trouble."

That brought a small laugh.

"We will be safe."

They just stared at her. Some of the older crewwomen shook their heads.

Zarai felt as if she'd just missed the point of a joke. There always seemed to be sailors who treated pirate attacks as somehow humorous. She'd even heard that the sort of perverted women who favored sexual relations with men claimed to look forward to the clandestine visits.

Sometimes she wondered if she'd missed more than one point.

▲▼▲

Zarai was on the poop just after three bells of the first watch. She was studying the grab and thinking about putting mirrors on the rail to keep a descent watch when the first of the Chain pirates hit the deck. She spun on her heel and snap-drew her pistole. A quick pull of the trigger set the spring within the butt to buzzing as the twinned darts launched from the barrel-rails.

One dart missed the pirate. The other lodged in the pangolin-leather across his midriff.

His, she thought. *There's a man on my ship now. Bad luck for certain.*

The invader was definitely male. Short, broad-shouldered, with a swelling gut wrapped in that distinctive diamond-scaled armor. A huge, dark cape whipped behind him in the wind that boomed along the Angel Narrows. He wore high boots rolled down around his knee, canvas trousers, and a tricorn hat sporting a long, pale feather.

His face, so handsome and strange...men were supposed to be beneath a woman's notice, but somehow this one was not.

Zarai tore herself away from the Chain pirate's visible amusement and leapt for the ship's bell. "Repel boarders!"

She heard Beita cry, "No, no, it's a mistake," but already there were more hitting the deck with the distinctive buzz of rope-sliders.

"Drive them off!" Zarai screamed.

Crewwomen shouted as the clash of arms erupted across the bucket-ship's deck. Someone shrieked, "By shit, not *this* way."

Zarai hefted the long-poled boarding hook which had been clipped beneath the rail. She braced it before her and advanced on the Chain pirate. Men were like dogs or children—if you showed the hard side of a firm hand, they remembered their place.

Except this one hadn't read that broadsheet. His laughter shivered the black curls of hair cascading down his shoulders. Distracted once more, she was just as glad she couldn't make out the color of his eyes.

His laughter choked off swiftly enough when her hook caught him in the thigh. Showing speed she didn't expect from a mere man, the pirate grabbed her weapon and yanked.

Zarai was wise to that trick. She stepped into the pull, giving the Chain pirate slack where he'd expected resistance. It was almost the opposite of dancing, but still strangely intimate—her thighs shivered. He stumbled as she recovered her weapon. Angry at her continued distraction, she kicked the dart still stuck in his belly armor. The point slid through the leather and into his gut.

The Chain pirate hissed and slid back against the deck rail.

Someone screamed on the maindeck below. The boarding rope slapped into Zarai as she tried to identify the voice. The attacker rushed her again as she looked away.

Damn his eyes, she thought, *his brute persistence is a credit to his gender.*

She swung for his ankles this time. He leapt over the shaft of the hook and came at her with a short, broad gutting knife. Zarai stepped into the blade, letting it catch in the doubled muslin of her shirt so she could whack the Chain pirate on the back of the head with her boarding hook.

His extravagant hat blew off over the rail as he dropped to his knees. With a surprised expression, the man fell face first onto the deck. A crunch suggested his nose was broken.

Zarai gave him an extra kick in the arse for good measure. Who could have thought she'd be so distracted by a *man*? She looked over her deck. A knot of six or seven of her crewwomen were being forced back by men.

Strange. With Aa's mighty strength in their midst, they should have struggled more fiercely. Had they all gone weak? Was it some subtle poison in the sweat of men?

Zarai rewound her pistole and loaded another pair of darts into the barrel-rails. That took almost half a minute—a very long time in a fight—but she wanted the full advantage of surprise. She took a deep breath, jumped down to the maindeck, and shot two men in the back of the head. In the surge of confusion which followed, someone fell over the rail with a terrified scream.

That was enough for the Chain pirates.

The survivors ran for their ropes and leapt buzzing upward into the darkness, power springs in their sliders unwinding to carry them away. They were no doubt skimming toward their upskiff moored a link or two above *Indolent Climax*. If Zarai had possessed a fire-thrower she would have hosed the night air in hopes of alighting their ropes, their trousers, or ideally their boat.

Pistole still in her hand, she looked at her crew. "What damage?"

"Beita is lost over side," said Aa. Even in the darkness, the tears glittered in the enkidu's eyes.

Damn.

"And Liian is gone," added another woman.

A deckhand? No, Aa would have spoken. One of Beita's watch-standers. Two short there. Zarai cursed herself for not knowing her crew list by name already. "Are the rest of you in health?"

Aa's arms twitched, startling Zarai. She realized that the big enkidu woman was ready to strike her down with those ham fists. "Aa, go below with Megg and take some valerian tea. The rest of you rid my deck of these miserable creatures. We'll stand watch as a crew until we clear the last of the narrows."

"And you?" asked Megg as she took Aa by the forearm.

Zarai felt a hard, dark flame in the core of her heart. *Her* ship. *Her* officers. *Her* crew. That a simple, foolish man could violate them so badly...that he could distract her so badly...

"I have captured their leader. I shall take Beita's worth from him."

"Careful," the old woman said. "Don't climb further up a rope you already can't get down from."

"I'm the captain here." Zarai's voice was colder than she'd intended, but she would be damned if she would unsay the words.

Megg nodded, then tugged Aa toward the anti-Chainward hatch. The other crewwomen spread out across the deck, grumbling as they tossed broken weapons and shreds of cloth into a trough. Two bent over each of the bodies with sidelong looks at Zarai.

You never jettisoned anything over the rail, save in direst emergency, for there were always bucket-ships below you. Zarai reckoned that her captured Chain pirate's severed hands and feet could be considered a dire emergency.

She went to start in on her first man.

▲▼▲

Zarai waited until the prisoner regained consciousness. His rope continued to drag on her deck, but she pushed it aside and left it alone. That meant the pirate's fellows were still up there somewhere, staring down at the woman who had bested them and taken their leader.

The clattering of the Earth's orbital gearing echoed down the Angel Narrows, marking the moment of sidereal midnight. As the noise died away, the Chain pirate groaned and opened his eyes.

His face was a mess, nose crushed in the fall. She'd let him keep bleeding. No point in stanching that. He wouldn't need the blood much longer anyway.

"Hello," Zarai said. She sat on her haunches, the man's wide boning knife gripped so tight in her hand that the blade shook.

"Deah la'y," he began, then stopped. That smile of his had tried to come back, but she guessed he'd broken some teeth.

Even damaged, he had an eerie charm.

"Guess what I lost tonight?" She hated the brittle edge in her voice.

"Ahh..." He nearly went cross-eyed with the effort of getting the failed word out.

Fine, she thought. *I'll have this conversation by myself.* "I seem to have misplaced my first mate, as well as one of my deckhands. Beita and..." Zarai paused, embarrassed that she could not bring the name to mind. She continued in a rush. "Do you recall how those fine women came to tumble over my rail?"

"No' wha' 'ou..." The Chain pirate gave up again. Even through the pain, he still smiled with his eyes.

That glint! It made her furious, and at the same time sparked wonderment. "How do you do that?"

"Wha'?"

Zarai had known a woman once, in High Thefariae, who could smile across a smoky barroom and set her groin to flowing. Marlis, of the short cropped hair and breasts so small and flat she might have been a girl. They'd only ever made love once, but the bruises had stayed on Zarai's heart for months. She'd hidden much from Quenna for a while after that.

Something about this man reminded her of Marlis. There was no physical resemblance, but the effect he had on her was similar. She felt shamed, as if she were lusting after a dog.

The smile finally reached his broken mouth.

Zarai leaned close. Oh God, the *smell* of him. "You're not afraid of anything, are you?"

"'ou."

It was his absolute confidence which galled her. Lying broken on her deck, cut off from his crew, this mere *man* already knew he was going to win.

She'd show him better. She would be a captain to be feared up and down the Chain.

Megg squatted next to her and laid one wrinkled hand across Zarai's knife hand.

She looked sidelong at the cook. "What do you want?"

"Don't go up that rope, Captain."

"His men killed two of ours."

Megg sighed. The old cook cocked her head to give the wounded prisoner a crooked smile. "You always was a beautiful man, Janton," she told the Chain pirate. "Shame you didn't get the news."

"What news?" A cold horror stained Zarai's heart.

The cook looked her in the eye. "Who'd you ship under, 'fore?"

Zarai answered slowly: "Quenna. Aboard *Blacklegs*."

"Ah." Megg stroked Janton's hand. "Only ever served on *Blacklegs*, girl and woman?"

"Yes. Until now."

Megg closed her fist around the wounded man's fingers, then began cleaning the blood off his face with her free hand. "I hear tell that old Quenna never had a man. Not as bond-mate nor toy nor slave."

Zarai blushed, glad it was dark. "No. Of course not." Quenna had kept *her* for a long while, promoting Zarai over time until finally kicking her overboard with a master's certificate to bring on a tall, much younger woman greatly resembling the naïve girl who'd boarded *Blacklegs* years earlier.

"Some ships do it different." Rocking on her heels, Megg traced the line of Janton's jaw. "Most, even. Captain Marra, she and Janton here, they kept an understanding. Drop in, do a little knife dance with no cuts nor bruises, then go below for an hour or two of the old snake-and-pig. Call it an attack, write off a bit of cargo, split the take." She spat on the poop, a sailor's insult surely as any vile words. "Poor bastard didn't know Marra had gone to rock." She leaned close to Janton. "This will hurt like blazes, dearie."

Megg pushed the man's nose back into place. His heels drummed the deck and his breath hissed like water on coals, but he didn't call out.

"His crew and mine weren't fighting," Zarai whispered, staring at her hands. "They were stalling for time."

The old cook grunted as something cracked in Janton's nose. "You didn't know, and they didn't know you didn't know." She sighed. "We'll have to put him ashore at Catha port and hope someone can fix his mouth. As for crew, we figured you was just rough trade at first. Then it all tumbled down at once. Liian was already gone up the rope with one of her regular men. Beita fell on account of your attack at the end."

Zarai put her face in her hands. "Quenna never told me any of this."

"Where did you think the little babbies come from?" Megg's words were an angry rush. "Have you ever seen a woman fill another woman's belly? 'Tis the men who help a woman make more of herself. Their kind cannot marry nor hold property. Some won't live like cats shut in a playroom. Many bucket-ships have their reg'lar pirates. 'Tis the way of things, except for prudes like Quenna who hide the truth and call their lie righteous."

"And now I've killed three of them."

"Did you never *drink* with other crews, listen to them wink and laugh?"

"No...I..." She'd always stayed close to her captain-lover. Quenna had ignored the occasional jokes from other captains, other crews, so of course Zarai had as well. No wonder their deckhands had turned over so much faster than most ships.

She'd always told herself it was because Quenna's standards were so high. How could she have been so naïve?

Because you never wanted to believe it, she thought. *It never made sense that women would soil themselves so.*

Somehow that idea seemed less outrageous now.

"I hear tell they do things different in other lands," muttered Megg. She scooted around to gather Janton's head into her lap. He moaned with pain, but settled in. "The enkidus got five husbands each, for the light and dark of the moon, and they share 'em around like good rat terriers. Out on the flatwater queendoms, they's one to another like geese do. But up here on the Chain, it's two countries and two queendoms. One for us, and one for the men."

Years of snickers and behind-the-hand looks came home in a guilt rush. "I've ruined the arrangement for *Indolent Climax.*"

"Captain, you've ruined more than the arrangement." Megg rocked Janton, soothing his forehead. He'd passed out again.

Zarai walked to the rail. She stared up the Chain, thinking on what Quenna would have said. *He's just a man. They don't even feel pain, really. Like animals.*

That couldn't be true. Not the way he smiled. Even through the veil of his pain, there was a genuine warmth to Janton. Like Marlis, whom she had to admit, had been mannish.

Her face burned in the darkness with embarrassed anguish. How had she never seen the truth? She could blame Quenna, but Zarai's thoughts had always been her own. Her heart was her own.

Most importantly, her deeds were her own. Especially the ruining of this man. Being in command wasn't supposed to be like this. No wonder

Quenna had turned inward, seeing only below *Blacklegs'* decks.

The water's rush altered around her. The creaking echo of the Chain abated as *Indolent Climax* passed out of the bottom of Angel Narrows. Zarai could see across the flatwater world miles below her. A terrible storm raged, lightning flickering through the top of a vast sea of turbulent clouds. Cold stars above glimmered on both sides of the Earth's track. The moon's lesser track gleamed brass-bright.

Night covered Northern Earth, but her heart was darker yet.

Janton's rope banged into Zarai once more. The pirate's drop line twisted vigorously now that they'd descended into open air.

That meant the up-skiff was still moored above them. The Chain pirates were close overhead, waiting for their leader. Or his body.

"I am better than Quenna," Zarai told no one in particular.

Janton moaned as Megg looked up again. "Ma'am?"

"I will not be her." Zarai grabbed the rope-slider, where it was lodged at the bottom of the Chain pirate's line. "I will not pretend." She slipped her hand into the grip, fastened the loop around her wrist and elbow.

"You certain you want to go up that rope?" Megg asked.

"No," Zarai replied. She nodded at Janton. "But this happened because I was certain of something I didn't understand at all. It's not that I want to lie with a man."

Liar, said a little voice within.

She ignored that, ignored the memories of Marlis which were already mingling with vague fantasies of a healthy, smiling Janton. Zarai continued, "I can't say if I ever will take a man to my breast. But I've never looked any of them in the eye as if he were a person. I owe his crew the life of their captain. I go to explain, and apologize."

Megg snorted, but there was a look in her eyes which might have been respect. "If you leave this ship, you won't come back the same woman."

"Does anyone who leaves ever come back the same?" Zarai bent close to Janton. "I'm sorry," she said, and kissed his sweaty forehead. The smell of him made her thighs shiver all over again.

She stood, released the stop-catch and shot upward through the wet night toward the world of men.

The American Dead

Somewhat ironically, this story first appeared in a British magazine, Interzone. *In some sense, it's been my most successful piece to date, with three different Year's Best reprints, more than anything else I've written so far. The story is rooted in my experiences of growing up in the Third World, as well as a lifelong love for post-apocalyptic fiction stretching back to middle school readings of* Alas, Babylon, A Canticle for Leibowitz, *and* On the Beach.

Americans are all rich, even their dead. Pobrecito knows this because he spends the hottest parts of the days in the old *Cementerio Americano* down by the river. The water is fat and lazy while the pipes in the *colonia* drip only rust, brown as the eyes of Santa Marguerite. Their graves are of the finest marble, carved with photographs in some manner he does not understand, or wrought with sculpted angels that put the churches up the hill to shame. Some of the American dead even have little houses, tight boxes with broken doors that must have once contained great riches.

He sits within a drooping tree that fights with life, and watches the flies make dark, wiggling rafts out on the water. There are dogs which live in the broken-backed jet out in the middle of the current, eyes glowing from behind the dozens of little shattered oval windows. At night the dogs swim across the slow current and run the river banks, hunting in the *colonia* and up toward the city walls.

They are why he never sleeps in the *Cementerio*. That some of the dogs walk on two legs only makes them worse.

When he was very young, Pobrecito found a case of magazines, old ones with bright color pictures of men and women without their clothes. Whoever had made the magazines had an astonishing imagination, because in Pobrecito's experience most people who fucked seemed to do it either with booze or after a lot of screaming and fighting and being held down. There weren't very many ways he'd ever seen it gone after. The people in these pictures were smiling, mostly, and arranged themselves more carefully than priests arranging a corpse. And they lived in the most astonishing places.

Pobrecito clips or tears the pictures out a few at a time and sells them on the streets of the *colonia*. He knows the magazines themselves would just be taken from him, before or after a beating, but a kid with a few slips of paper clutched in his hand is nothing. As long as no one looks too closely. But even if he had a pass for the gates, he dares not take them within the walls, for the priests would hang him in the square.

What he loves most about the magazines is not the nudity or the fucking or the strange combinations and arrangements these people found themselves in. No, what he loves is that these are Americans. Beautiful people in beautiful places doing beautiful things together.

"I will be an American some day," he tells his friend Lucia. They are in the branches of the dying tree, sharing a bottle of *pulque* and a greasy bowl of fried plantains in the midday heat. Pobrecito has a secret place up there, a hollow in the trunk where he hides most of his treasures.

The magazines are stored elsewhere, in a place he has never even shown to Lucia.

"You are an idiot," she declares, glancing out at the airplane in the river. The American flag can still be seen on its tall tail, small and weathered. No one has gone out to paint it over, for fear of the dogs. "All Americans are dead," she adds with prim authority.

Lucia is smaller than Pobrecito, though older. She is one of the *menoriítas*, born to be little. Though she is of an age to have breasts and make her bleedings, her body is smooth and slick as any young child's. Pobrecito knows this because they often curl together to sleep, and she likes him to touch her as if she were a baby, rubbing his hand over her sides and back and pulling her to his chest. He has tried to use his fingers to do a few of the things seen in his pictures, but she is too small down there both before and behind, and complains of the hurt.

She has never offered to touch him.

Pobrecito shakes off that thought. "What is dead can be reborn. This is what the priests are always telling us." He grins, mottled teeth flashing even in shadow. "I shall bleach my skin and hair like they did, and have a fine house filled with swimming pools and bright furniture. My automobiles would be colorful and shiny and actually have petrol."

She laughs then and sets her shoulder against his chest, tucking her head into his neck, sucking on the neck of the *pulque* bottle in a way which makes him both warm and uncomfortable. He strokes her hair and dreams of distant, lost cities such as Los Angeles and Omaha.

▲▼▲

That evening the folk of the *colonia* are upset. They surge through the muddy streets, even the day workers who should already be sleeping, and there is an angry mutter like bottle wasps swarming. He even sees some weapons, knives dangling from hands, a few pistols tucked into belts. These are offenses of the worst order, to keep or carry weapons.

Pobrecito dodges booted feet and moves with the crowd, listening. He already knows he will sell no pictures tonight. Selling no pictures, he will not eat tomorrow. But he wants to understand what is wrong.

The crowd is speaking of priests.

"Girls, indeed."

"....a scandal. And they use God's name!"

"They wear those black dresses. Let them lie with one another."

"Called them up there from a list. I tell you, I won't allow my..."

"Hush! Do you want to hang?"

"A tax. How is this a *tax*?"

"Their time is coming. Soon."

Pobrecito comes to understand. Girls are being taken away by the priests. To be used, he supposes, like the Americans in his pictures use each other. Will the girls of the *colonia* smile beneath the lusts of the priests? Surely they will be cleaned and fed and cared for. It is the priests in their walled city that hold all wealth, all power.

But eventually the anger melts into fatigue, and word comes that the *guardia* are on their way down to the *colonia*, and so the knives and pistols vanish and people trudge home, some of them weeping more than usual.

▲▼▲

Over the weeks, a few more girls are called every few days, always the hale ones with good curves to their breasts. The *guardia* comes to collect them now, as the people are no longer willing to send their sisters and daughters up the hill simply because a summons came. There are beatings and a few quiet murders in which no priest-advocate will take any interest.

None of the girls come back.

In a few month's time, some older women are called, and younger girls as well. They do not return, either. The *colonia* remains restless, but the crystallizing anger of the first night never quite reappears. There is always food to worry about, and the dogs from the river, and the clouds of flies and wasps which can strip a man's skin in minutes, and the sicknesses which prowl just as deadly if less visible.

And the heat.

It is always a little hotter. This has been the way of things all of Pobrecito's life.

The vanishing girls and women are good for Pobrecito's little business. Sad men and wild-eyed boys buy from him, paying him in dented cans of dog food or little bundles of yams or onions. Even a few of the old women seek him out, clucking and tutting like senile chickens draped in funeral black, wanting pictures "of a girl alone, none of your despicable filth, just something to remember her by."

But he is becoming too well known, too rich. He has more food than he and Lucia can eat in a day, and even a few metal tools and some old bits of gold, which he hides in his tree by the river.

Is he rich enough to be an American yet, Pobrecito wonders?

▲▼▲

One day he makes his way into the *Cementerio Americano* carrying two books and an old bottle of wine he has been paid for a handful of pictures of three thin, yellow-haired women kissing each other. By habit Pobrecito keeps to the shadows, the edges of fences and tumbled walls, but also by habit he has made a path in and out of this place. He steps around the edge of a rotting shed which contains a flat-tired tractor and some large metal implements to find three of the *guardia*.

"Ah," says Pobrecito, and reflexively offers them the wine. Perhaps it will save him from whatever is next. He doubts that, though.

The leader, for he has more decoration on his buttoned shoulder tabs, strokes the bright leather of his pistol belt for a moment, then smiles. It is a horrid sort of smile, something a man remembering an old photo he is trying to imitate might offer up. The other two do not bother. Instead they merely cradle a machete each, staring corpse-eyed at Pobrecito. All three of them are fat, their bellies bigger than their hips, unlike anyone in the *colonia*, except a few who are dying of growths in their guts.

No one takes the wine.

"You are the guardian of Lucia Sandoz, is it not true?" the leader asks.

This is not what Pobrecito expected. "Ah...no. She comes here sometimes."

The leader consults a thin notebook, ragged with handling, pages nearly black with ink. "You are Pobrecito the street merchant, no address, of the *colonia*."

"Yes."

"Then you are the guardian of Lucia Sandoz. It says so here in my book, and so this must be a true thing." His smile asserts itself again. "We have a summons for her." All three *guardia* peer around, as if expecting her to fall from the sky. Pobrecito realizes this has become an old game for them.

"She is not mine," he says to his feet. Not Lucia. "And besides," he adds, "she is a *menoriíta*. She cannot be used in the manner of a woman." Will this help?

They laugh, his tormentors, before one of the machete-carriers says, "How would you know if you hadn't had her?"

The leader leans close. "She is *clean*, boy. That is enough these days."

Then they beat him, using the flat of the machete blades and the rough toes of their boots. Pobrecito loses most of his left ear when a blade slips, and the palm of his hand is cut to the bone, but they stop before staving in his ribs or breaking any large bones.

"Find her," says the leader. Pobrecito can barely hear him through the pain and blood in his ear. The *guardia* tears the pages of the books from their bindings, unzips, and urinates on the paper. Taking the wine bottle, he turns to leave. "Before tomorrow."

Pobrecito does not waste time on crying. He stumbles to his tree, knowing there are some extra clothes there that he can use to bind his ear and his hand. There are so many sicknesses that come in through bloody cuts and sores—black rot, green rot, the red crust—and he fears them all.

Stumbling, eyes dark and head ringing, Pobrecito can barely climb his tree because his arms and legs hurt so much. When he reaches the branch, he sees that someone has been at his cache of riches and food. *Guardia*, dogs, it does not matter. The hollow in the trunk has been hacked open, made wide and ragged with an ax or a machete, and everything that is not gone is smashed or torn or broken. His riches are nothing but trash now.

"I will never be an American," Pobrecito whispers. He lays his mutilated ear against the slashed palm of his hand, pressing them together to slow the bleeding and protect the wounds from insects. Despite the pain, he lays that side of his head against the branch and stretches out to surrender to the ringing darkness.

▲▼▲

"Wake up, fool!" It is Lucia's voice. She is slapping him.

Pobrecito feels strange. His skin is itchy, crawly, prickly.

More slaps.

"Stop it this instant!" Her voice is rising toward a frightening break.

He opens his mouth to answer her and flies tumble in.

He is covered in flies.

"Gaaah!" Pobrecito screams.

"Get them off before they bite," she says, her voice more under control.

Pobrecito stumbles to his feet, runs down the branch where it overhangs the water.

"Not the river..." she says behind him, but it is too late. The old branch narrows, is rotten, his legs are weak, his eyes not clear. In a crackling shower of wood, flies and blood, Pobrecito tumbles the five or six meters downward to slam into the slow, brown water, knocking the air from his body.

The river is blood warm, shocking him awake. He is under the surface, eyes open to a uniform brown with no way up. The water is sticky, strange, clinging to him, trying to draw him down. Pobrecito kicks his legs, trying to come out, but there is still no up.

At least the flies are gone.

He begins to wonder if he could open his mouth and find something besides the burning in his empty lungs.

Something scrapes his legs. Something long, slow and powerful. Pobrecito throws his hands out and finds a stick. He pulls on it, but it does not come, so he pulls himself toward it.

A moment later he is gasping and muddy, clinging to a root sticking out from the river bank. Air is in his lungs, blessed air. Behind him the water burbles as the long, slow, powerful thing circles back to test him again. Out in the middle of the river, the dogs are barking.

Lucia is scrambling down the tree trunk, sobbing. "Fool! Idiot!"

She helps him pull himself out before his legs are taken. He lies on the bank gasping and crying, blessedly free of flies. He does not want to think about what the river water might have done to his wounds. "They...they came....they came for you..." he spits out.

"No one wants me," she says fiercely.

"They said you were *clean*. That clean was enough for them these days."

She is quiet for a moment. "Fire-piss is killing the rich men up in the city, the old women say. The priests have heard from god that to fuck a clean woman takes the fire-piss from the man and gives it to her."

"How do you know? No one comes back."

"Some people pass in and out of the walls. Servants. Farmers. The word comes. And the cemetery is overflowing, up on the hill. With rich city men." She stares at him for a moment. "The *colonia* girls they dump down the old wells with some quicklime and gravel, and a prayer if they're feeling generous."

"Ahhh…" He weeps, eyes filling with hot tears as they hadn't for the beating, or for anything in his memory, really. "And they want you now."

"The cure does not work, but it does not stop them from trying over and over. The priests say it is so, that they are not faithful enough. Up in the city, they believe they can make the world however they want it." She stares at him for a while. "And perhaps they have a taste for new girls all the time."

Pobrecito thinks about his American pictures. Obviously many people had a taste for new girls all the time. Has he somehow been feeding this evil? But he doesn't sell his pictures in the city, or even to city men. Not directly. He has always wondered if some of his buyers did.

And if he could make the world the way he wanted it, he would wish away the heat and the insects and the sicknesses. He would make them all Americans like in his pictures, naked, happy, pale-skinned blondes with big houses and tables full of food and more water than any sane person could ever use. He would not wish for more girls to kill. Not even if God told him to.

"I want to show you something," he says.

"Show me soon. I think the dogs are coming over."

"In the day?"

"You got their attention, my friend."

Out at the airplane, dogs are gathering on the wing, their feet in the slow water. Some of them are casting sticks and stones out into the river, looking for that great predator that had touched Pobrecito for a moment. Others growl through pointed teeth, eyes glowing at him. Smoke curls from some of the shattered oval windows. Great red and blue letters, faded and worn as the tail's flag, loom along the rounded top of the airplane in some American prayer for the coming assault.

"It is over anyway," he says. "Come." He leads her deeper into the *Cementerio Americano.* Here Pobrecito has always been careful to hop from stone to stone, scramble along mortared kerbs, step on open ground, never making a path.

Here among the houses of the American dead is his greatest treasure.

He shows Lucia a squared-off vault, door wedged tightly shut. Grabbing a cornice, Pobrecito pulls himself to the roof though his body strains with the pain of the beating and the curious ache of his fall into the river. He then dangles his arm over to help her up. There are two windows in the roof, and he knows the secret of loosening one.

In a moment they are in the cool darkness of the vault. There are two marble coffins here, carved with wreaths and flowers, and Pobrecito's precious box of magazines at one end. He has left a few supplies here, a can of drinkable water and some dried fruit, a homespun shirt without quite enough holes for it to disintegrate to ragged patches. And matches, his other great treasure.

"These people do not seem so wealthy," Lucia whispers. "This is a fine little house for them, but the only riches here are yours."

Pobrecito shrugs. "Perhaps they were robbed before I found them. Or perhaps their riches are within their coffins. This is a finer room than any you or I will ever live or die in." As soon as he says that last, he wishes he hadn't, as they may very well die in this room.

"So now what will you do?"

He pulls the magazines out of the their box, fans the pages open. Sleek American flesh in a hundred combinations flashes before his eyes, cocks, breasts, tongues, leather and plastic toys, sleek cars…all the world that was, once. The American world lost to the heat and the sicknesses. Pobrecito tosses the magazines into a pile, deliberately haphazard. After a few moments, Lucia begins to help, tearing a few apart, breaking their spines so they will lay flat. She ignores the pictures, though she is not so used to them as Pobrecito is.

Soon they have a glossy pile of images of the perfect past. Without another word, Pobrecito strikes a match and sets fire to a bright, curled edge. Cool faces, free of sweat and wounds, blacken and shrivel. He lights more matches, sets more edges of the pile on fire, until the flames take over.

The smoke stinks, filling the little vault, curling around the opening in the roof. He does not care, though Lucia is coughing. Pobrecito pulls off his wet, bloody clothes and pushes them into the base of the fire, then climbs atop one of the marble coffins. A few moments later, Lucia joins him.

She is naked as well.

They lie there on the bed of marble, smooth skinned as any Americans, kissing and touching, while the fire burns the pretty people in their pretty houses and the smoke rises through the roof. Outside dogs howl and *guardia* pistols crack.

When Lucia takes his cock in her mouth, Pobrecito knows he is as wealthy as any American. A while later he feels the hot rush of himself into her, even as the smoke makes him so dizzy his thoughts have spun off into the sky like so many airplanes rising from their river grave.

Soon he will be a true American, wealthy and dead.